'Saki'

TOBEMORY
and other stories

Selected by Martin Stephen

PHŒNIX

A PHOENIX PAPERBACK
First published in 1998 by Phoenix, a division of Orion Books Ltd,
Orion House, 5 Upper St Martin's Lane, London, WC2H 9EA
Selection © Phoenix Paperbacks 1998

Typeset by Deltatype Ltd, Birkenhead, Merseyside
Printed in Great Britain by
The Guernsey Press Co. Ltd, Guernsey, C. I.

British Library Cataloguing-in-Publication
Data is available upon request.

ISBN 0 75380 449 2

Contents

Note on the Author and Editor

HECTOR HUGH MUNRO ('Saki') was born at Akyab, Burma on 18 December 1870. After his mother's death he was brought up in Pilton, Devon by two aunts. He was educated in Exmouth and at Bedford Grammar School, then travelled with his father in France, Germany and Switzerland. In 1893 he joined the military police in Burma, but resigned after a year because of ill-health and went to London to earn his living as a writer. He wrote political satire ('The Westminster Alice') for the *Westminster Gazette*, and from 1902 to 1908 was a foreign correspondent for the *Morning Post* in the Balkans and Paris. Almost all his early stories appeared in the *Westminster Gazette*, and they were published in book form as *Reginald* (1904). Other collections of humorous short stories are *Reginald in Russia* (1910), *The Chronicles of Clovis* (1911) and *Beasts and Super-Beasts* (1914). *The Toys of Peace* appeared posthumously in 1919 and *The Square Egg* in 1924. In addition, Saki published *The Unbearable Bassington*, a novel, in 1912 and *When William Came*, a novel fantasizing about a German occupation of England, in 1914. He also wrote three plays, *The Death-Trap*, *Karl-Ludwig's Widow* and *The Watched Pot*. In the First World War he enlisted with the Royal Fusiliers. He was killed at Beaumont-Hamel on 14 November 1916.

MARTIN STEPHEN was educated at Uppingham School, and took a combined degree in English and History from the University of Leeds. In the past ten years he has written twelve books, ranging from *British Warship Design Since 1906* to *English Literature*. He is a regular contributor to various journals on literature, education and military history. Formerly Second Master of Sedbergh School, he is now High Master of Manchester Grammar School. Recent work includes *Poems of the First World War* and *The Great War and Modern Myth: Death by Orthodoxy*.

Introduction

The most important thing of all to realize about the work of Saki is that it is not the preserve of a dry, academic readership, but something which over a period of years has appealed to the widest range of readers. Time has its own way of dealing with authors. Who now remembers the work of John Oxenham, a popular poet who sold quite literally millions of copies of his work in the period leading up to and including the First World War? In contrast, the world of Saki grows in popularity year by year. Saki is a member of an elite club, those writers who died in the First World War and whose reputation has been kept alive through popular demand. It is popular demand that has prompted this reissue of some of Saki's greatest stories, and popular demand that will ensure his popularity well into the next century, the advantages, extravagances and excesses of which he would undoubtedly have been able to typify and satirize as well as he did those of his own age.

This selection of stories was chosen by a poll of the readers of Britain's best-selling serious daily newspaper, who wrote in their hundreds when asked to nominate the best short stories of Saki. The response to that request shows the huge following that Saki commands. The unanimity of the choice made the selection the easiest job an editor could wish to have. This edition is therefore the general reader's Saki – those same readers who have ensured that Saki's reputation has remained as strong as it ever was, and established Saki as one of the great short story writers of all time.

It is tempting to see Saki as an alternative version of Oscar Wilde, a savagely witty satirist tortured by his homosexuality. The truth is that Saki's blend of the macabre, the comic and the satiric is unique. His use of animals as 'agents of revenge upon mankind' and the dry savagery of his humour make him not only one of the best short story writers in history, but also one of the most quintessentially British.

Whilst Saki is remembered as a short story writer, he also

wrote journalistic pieces, political satire and two novels – *The Unbearable Bassington* (1912) and *When William Came* (1913). His short stories were first published in *Reginald* (1904), *Reginald in Russia* (1910) (partly based on his work as a correspondent for the *Morning Post* in Poland and Russia), *The Chronicles of Clovis* (1911) and *Beasts and Super-Beasts* (1914). There was also the posthumous publication of *The Toys of Peace* (1919) and *The Square Egg* (1924).

In Saki's stories, a cat suddenly learns to speak, thereby reducing to terror the members of a country house party whose every action has been observed by an animal that has never had explained to him that 'discretion' about sexual misdoings which not only typifies but holds together the English upper class. It is typical of Saki that after the cat has run its verbal claws across the hearts, minds and reputation of some outwardly respectable humans, the threat is removed not by any action of their own, but by a fight with another cat. Saki is never less than fair. Unfortunately that inherent fairness reveals all too often that human pretension is all that we have. In the face of a human boy who turns by night into a wolf-like creature we are both defenceless and unbelieving. Saki makes it impossible not to laugh at the posturing of humankind. At the same time he makes it quite terrifying.

Saki was never quite the English gentleman – he spent only a short time at Bedford School – but in his best stories his satire of country house and gentlemanly conduct was unequalled. His decision to enlist as an ordinary soldier in 1914 bears comparison with the similar desire to enlist in the ranks of another famous Englishman, T. E. Lawrence. It is tempting to see in Saki's narrators – Clovis and Reginald – a picture of Saki himself. They are, of course, a part and a projection of Saki himself, but only a part. In his narrators there is a cruelty and lack of any moral base that, one suspects, was never present in Hector Hugh Munro to anywhere near the same extent.

Perhaps for many of us Saki's short stories are most admirable and deserving through their capacity to allow the child to wreak vengeance on the adult world. Saki commences his look on childhood with an alarming sense of grievance. His children are allowed the power their adult supervisors are unwilling to afford them, and the result is that the adult world – typified by 'aunties'

– is subjected to the same type of discipline they are so willing to impose on those younger than themselves. We welcome it just as they revile and suffer through it.

Unusually for a novelist, Saki had the knack of creating immensely memorable one or two-liners. Perhaps the most famous is:

The cook was a good cook, as cooks go; and as cooks go she went.

Perhaps more terrifying for a modern audience is:

Children are given us to discourage our better emotions.

Saki never encourages the reader: he amuses and he flays alive, he entertains just as he destroys. As such he is one of the most wayward, amusing and entertaining of all British writers.

MARTIN STEPHEN

Acknowledgements

The publishers and the editor would like to acknowledge the assistance of the following in compiling this selection, and all those who wrote in with anonymous suggestions: A. J. Alexander; F. Allfrey; N. A. Alton; J. R. Anderson; M. Ambell; J. Angus; D. Apter; R. Baxter; A. B. Blythe; W. Braddy; H. Brown; W. S. Brown; R. Boggis; D. Bousfield; M. Bryant; N. Busk; S. Byfield; J. Clarke; B. Clovis; A. S. Complin; P. J. Connyngham; M. L. Conquer; B. O. Cooper; M. B. Cowal; E. Cust; B. Davis; J. Davies; L. Dee; M. W. Dewar; F. R. Donald; D. V. Durell; E. J. Dyer; P. L. Farmer; K. H. Farrow; M. J. Fletcher; C. Fraser; C. French; P. K. Furness; J. Grigson; A. H. Gordon Clark; P. J. Gorman; H. C. Gough; J. J. Grist; C. Groom; S. Gueney; S. D. Harley; J. Hazel Hill; W. P. Hazlitt; D. Heald; L. Henry; N. Herriot; P. Hine; J. Honey; W. Hopkins; J. M. G. Hughes; J. E. Hyne; M. R. Inglis; J. Inman; L. James; M. James; T. H. Keyes; I. J. Korff; M. B. Kowal; H. Laurie; Q. Letts; N. Linton; J. S. Lipscombe; L. Lloyd; M. A. Lloyd; H. A. Macpherson; P. Madden; N. T. Malden; R. M. Morris; J. Morse; W. R. Mosley; E. L. Mundy; M. Murson; A. R. Pargeter; F. G. Pennington; W. N. Pye; J. A. Robens; H. Royds; P. G. Rubinstein; T. Russell; H. Ryde; L. Saunders; P. Spear; A. Spiers; K. S. Steward; I. Stirling; R. H. Stockbridge; D. Stokes; G. M. Streatfield; Q. Stummer; H. Sumnall; D. Symonds; K. Thorp; P. F. Wade; K. Washill; C. Waring; G. A. Wearing; J. Williams; S. Williams; J. S. H. Woodhouse; K. Young; S. J. Young.

The publishers and editor are also grateful to the Regiment of the Royal Fusiliers and, in particular, are indebted to L. F. Stewart, Archivist of the regiment's Museum.

TOBERMORY
and other stories

The Woman who Told the Truth

There was once (said Reginald) a woman who told the truth. Not all at once, of course, but the habit grew upon her gradually, like lichen on an apparently healthy tree. She had no children – otherwise it might have been different. It began with little things, for no particular reason except that her life was a rather empty one, and it is so easy to slip into the habit of telling the truth in little matters. And then it became difficult to draw the line at more important things, until at last she took to telling the truth about her age; she said she was forty-two and five months – by that time, you see, she was veracious even to months. It may have been pleasing to the angels, but her elder sister was not gratified. On the Woman's birthday, instead of the opera-tickets which she had hoped for, her sister gave her a view of Jerusalem from the Mount of Olives, which is not quite the same thing. The revenge of an elder sister may be long in coming, but, like a South-Eastern express, it arrives in its own good time.

The friends of the Woman tried to dissuade her from over-indulgence in the practice, but she said she was wedded to the truth; whereupon it was remarked that it was scarcely logical to be so much together in public. (No really provident woman lunches regularly with her husband if she wishes to burst upon him as a revelation at dinner. He must have time to forget; an afternoon is not enough.) And after a while her friends began to thin out in patches. Her passion for the truth was not compatible with a large visiting-list. For instance, she told Miriam Klopstock *exactly* how she looked at the Ilexes' ball. Certainly Miriam had asked for her candid opinion, but the Woman prayed in church every Sunday for peace in our time, and it was not consistent.

It was unfortunate, everyone agreed, that she had no family; with a child or two in the house, there is an unconscious check upon too free an indulgence in the truth. Children are given us to discourage our better emotions. That is why the stage, with all its efforts, can never be as artificial as life; even in an Ibsen drama one must reveal to the audience things that one would suppress before the children or servants.

Fate may have ordained the truth-telling from the commencement and should justly bear some of the blame; but in having no children the Woman was guilty, at least, of contributory negligence.

Little by little she felt she was becoming a slave to what had once been merely an idle propensity; and one day she knew. Every woman tells ninety per cent of the truth to her dressmaker; the other ten per cent is the irreducible minimum of deception beyond which no self-respecting client trespasses. Madame Draga's establishment was a meeting-ground for naked truths and overdressed fictions, and it was here, the Woman felt, that she might make a final effort to recall the artless mendacity of past days. Madame herself was in an inspiring mood, with the air of a sphinx who knew all things and preferred to forget most of them. As a War Minister she might have been celebrated, but she was content to be merely rich.

'If I take it in here, and – Miss Howard, one moment, if you please – and there, and round like this – so – I really think you will find it quite easy.'

The Woman hesitated; it seemed to require such a small effort to simply acquiesce in Madame's views. But habit had become too strong. 'I'm afraid,' she faltered, 'it's just the least little bit in the world too –'

And by that least little bit she measured the deeps and eternities of her thraldom to fact. Madame was not best pleased at being contradicted on a professional matter, and when Madame lost her temper you usually found it afterwards in the bill.

And at last the dreadful thing came, as the Woman had foreseen all along that it must; it was one of those paltry little truths with which she harried her waking hours. On a raw Wednesday morning, in a few ill-chosen words, she told the cook that she drank. She remembered the scene afterwards as vividly as though it had been painted in her mind by Abbey. The cook was a good cook, as cooks go; and as cooks go she went.

Miriam Klopstock came to lunch the next day. Women and elephants never forget an injury.

The Bag

'The Major is coming in to tea,' said Mrs Hoopington to her niece. 'He's just gone round to the stables with his horse. Be as bright and lively as you can; the poor man's got a fit of the glooms.'

Major Pallaby was a victim of circumstances, over which he had no control, and of his temper, over which he had very little. He had taken on the Mastership of the Pexdale Hounds in succession to a highly popular man who had fallen foul of his committee, and the Major found himself confronted with the overt hostility of at least half the hunt, while his lack of tact and amiability had done much to alienate the remainder. Hence subscriptions were beginning to fall off, foxes grew provokingly scarcer, and wire obtruded itself with increasing frequency. The Major could plead reasonable excuse for his fit of the glooms.

In ranging herself as a partisan on the side of Major Pallaby Mrs Hoopington had been largely influenced by the fact that she had made up her mind to marry him at an early date. Against his notorious bad temper she set his three thousand a year, and his prospective succession to a baronetcy gave a casting vote in his favour. The Major's plans on the subject of matrimony were not at present in such an advanced stage as Mrs Hoopington's, but he was beginning to find his way over to Hoopington Hall with a frequency that was already being commented on.

'He had a wretchedly thin field out again yesterday,' said Mrs Hoopington. 'Why you didn't bring one or two hunting men down with you, instead of that stupid Russian boy, I can't think.'

'Vladimir isn't stupid,' protested her niece; 'he's one of the most amusing boys I ever met. Just compare him for a moment with some of your heavy hunting men –'

'Anyhow, my dear Norah, he can't ride.'

'Russians never can; but he shoots.'

'Yes; and what does he shoot? Yesterday he brought home a woodpecker in his game-bag.'

'But he'd shot three pheasants and some rabbits as well.'

'That's no excuse for including a woodpecker in his game-bag.'

'Foreigners go in for mixed bags more than we do. A Grand Duke pots a vulture just as seriously as we should stalk a bustard. Anyhow, I've explained to Vladimir that certain birds are beneath his dignity as a sportsman. And as he's only nineteen, of course, his dignity is a sure thing to appeal to.'

Mrs Hoopington sniffed. Most people with whom Vladimir came in contact found his high spirits infectious, but his present hostess was guaranteed immune against infection of that sort.

'I hear him coming in now,' she observed. 'I shall go and get ready for tea. We're going to have it here in the hall. Entertain the Major if he comes in before I'm down, and, above all, be bright.'

Norah was dependent on her aunt's good graces for many little things that made life worth living, and she was conscious of a feeling of discomfiture because the Russian youth whom she had brought down as a welcome element of change in the country-house routine was not making a good impression. That young gentleman, however, was supremely unconscious of any short-comings, and burst into the hall, tired, and less sprucely groomed than usual, but distinctly radiant. His game-bag looked comfortably full.

'Guess what I have shot,' he demanded.

'Pheasants, wood-pigeons, rabbits,' hazarded Norah.

'No; a large beast; I don't know what you call it in English. Brown, with a darkish tail.' Norah changed colour.

'Does it live in a tree and eat nuts?' she asked, hoping that the use of the adjective 'large' might be an exaggeration.

Vladimir laughed.

'Oh, no; not a *biyelka*.'

'Does it swim and eat fish?' asked Norah, with a fervent prayer in her heart that it might turn out to be an otter.

'No,' said Vladimir, busy with the straps of his game-bag; 'it lives in the woods, and eats rabbits and chickens.'

Norah sat down suddenly, and hid her face in her hands.

'Merciful Heaven!' she wailed; 'he's shot a fox!'

Vladimir looked up at her in consternation. In a torrent of agitated words she tried to explain the horror of the situation. The boy understood nothing, but was thoroughly alarmed.

'Hide it, hide it!' said Norah frantically, pointing to the still unopened bag. 'My aunt and the Major will be here in a moment. Throw it on the top of that chest; they won't see it there.'

Vladimir swung the bag with fair aim; but the strap caught in its flight on the outstanding point of an antler fixed in the wall, and the bag, with its terrible burden, remained suspended just above the alcove where tea would presently be laid. At that moment Mrs Hoopington and the Major entered the hall.

'The Major is going to draw our covers tomorrow,' announced the lady, with a certain heavy satisfaction. 'Smithers is confident that we'll be able to show him some sport; he swears he's seen a fox in the nut copse three times this week.'

'I'm sure I hope so; I hope so,' said the Major moodily. 'I must break this sequence of blank days. One hears so often that a fox has settled down as a tenant for life in certain covers, and then when you go to turn him out there isn't a trace of him. I'm certain a fox was shot or trapped in Lady Widden's woods the very day before we drew them.'

'Major, if anyone tried that game on in my woods they'd get short shrift,' said Mrs Hoopington.

Norah found her way mechanically to the tea-table and made her fingers frantically busy in rearranging the parsley round the sandwich dish. On one side of her loomed the morose countenance of the Major, on the other she was conscious of the scared, miserable eyes of Vladimir. And above it all hung *that*. She dared not raise her eyes above the level of the tea-table, and she almost expected to see a spot of accusing vulpine blood drip down and stain the whiteness of the cloth. Her aunt's manner signalled to her the repeated message to 'be bright'; for the present she was fully occupied in keeping her teeth from chattering.

'What did you shoot today?' asked Mrs Hoopington suddenly of the unusually silent Vladimir.

'Nothing – nothing worth speaking of,' said the boy.

Norah's heart, which had stood still for a space, made up for lost time with a most disturbing bound.

'I wish you'd find something that was worth speaking about,' said the hostess; 'everyone seems to have lost their tongues.'

'When did Smithers last see that fox?' said the Major.

'Yesterday morning; a fine dog-fox, with a dark brush,' confided Mrs Hoopington.

'Aha, we'll have a good gallop after that brush tomorrow,' said the Major, with a transient gleam of good humour. And then gloomy silence settled again round the tea-table, a silence broken only by despondent munchings and the occasional feverish rattle of a teaspoon in its saucer. A diversion was at last afforded by

Mrs Hoopington's fox-terrier, which had jumped on to a vacant chair, the better to survey the delicacies of the table, and was now sniffing in an upward direction at something apparently more interesting than cold tea-cake.

'What is exciting him?' asked his mistress, as the dog suddenly broke into short, angry barks, with a running accompaniment of tremulous whines.

'Why,' she continued, 'it's your game-bag, Vladimir! What *have* you got in it?'

'By Gad,' said the Major, who was now standing up; 'there's a pretty warm scent!'

And then a simultaneous idea flashed on himself and Mrs Hoopington. Their faces flushed to distinct but harmonious tones of purple, and with one accusing voice they screamed, 'You've shot the fox!'

Norah tried hastily to palliate Vladimir's misdeed in their eyes, but it is doubtful whether they heard her. The Major's fury clothed and reclothed itself in words as frantically as a woman up in town for one day's shopping tries on a succession of garments. He reviled and railed at fate and the general scheme of things, he pitied himself with a strong, deep pity too poignant for tears, he condemned everyone with whom he had ever come in contact to endless and abnormal punishments. In fact, he conveyed the impression that if a destroying angel had been lent to him for a week it would have had very little time for private study. In the lulls of his outcry could be heard the querulous monotone of Mrs Hoopington and the sharp staccato barking of the fox-terrier. Vladimir, who did not understand a tithe of what was being said, sat fondling a cigarette and repeating under his breath from time to time a vigorous English adjective which he had long ago taken affectionately into his vocabulary. His mind strayed back to the youth in the old Russian folk-tale who shot an enchanted bird with dramatic results. Meanwhile, the Major, roaming round the hall like an imprisoned cyclone, had caught sight of and joyfully pounced on the telephone apparatus, and lost no time in ringing up the hunt secretary and announcing his resignation of the Mastership. A servant had by this time brought his horse round to the door, and in a few seconds Mrs Hoopington's shrill monotone had the field to itself. But after the Major's display her best efforts at vocal violence missed their full effect; it was as though one had come straight out from a Wagner opera into a rather tame thunderstorm. Realizing, perhaps, that her tirades were something of an anticlimax, Mrs Hoopington broke suddenly into some rather necessary tears and marched out of the room, leaving behind her a silence almost as terrible as the turmoil which had preceded it.

'What shall I do with – *that?*' asked Vladimir at last.

'Bury it,' said Norah.

'Just plain burial?' said Vladimir, rather relieved. He had almost expected that some of the local clergy would have insisted on being present, or that a salute might have to be fired over the grave.

And thus it came to pass that in the dusk of a November evening the Russian boy, murmuring a few of the prayers of his Church for luck, gave hasty but decent burial to a large polecat under the lilac trees at Hoopington.

Gabriel-Ernest

'There is a wild beast in your woods,' said the artist Cunningham, as he was being driven to the station. It was the only remark he had made during the drive, but as Van Cheele had talked incessantly his companion's silence had not been noticeable.

'A stray fox or two and some resident weasels. Nothing more formidable,' said Van Cheele. The artist said nothing.

'What did you mean about a wild beast?' said Van Cheele later, when they were on the platform.

'Nothing. My imagination. Here is the train,' said Cunningham.

That afternoon Van Cheele went for one of his frequent rambles through his woodland property. He had a stuffed bittern in his study, and knew the names of quite a number of wild flowers, so his aunt had possibly some justification in describing him as a great naturalist. At any rate, he was a great walker. It was his custom to take mental notes of everything he saw during his walks, not so much for the purpose of assisting contemporary science as to provide topics for conversation afterwards. When the bluebells began to show themselves in flower he made a point of informing everyone of the fact; the season of the year might have warned his hearers of the likelihood of such an occurrence, but at least they felt that he was being absolutely frank with them.

What Van Cheele saw on this particular afternoon was, however, something far removed from his ordinary range of experience. On a shelf of smooth stone overhanging a deep pool in the hollow of an oak coppice a boy of about sixteen lay asprawl, drying his wet brown limbs luxuriously in the sun. His wet hair, parted by a recent dive, lay close to his head, and his light-brown eyes, so light that there was an almost tigerish gleam in them, were turned towards Van Cheele with a certain lazy watchfulness. It was an unexpected apparition, and Van Cheele found himself engaged in the novel process of thinking before he spoke. Where on earth could this wild-looking boy hail from? The miller's wife had lost a child some two months ago, supposed to have been swept away by the mill-race, but that had been a mere baby, not a half-grown lad.

'What are you doing there?' he demanded.

'Obviously, sunning myself,' replied the boy.

'Where do you live?'

'Here, in these woods.'

'You can't live in the woods,' said Van Cheele.

'They are very nice woods,' said the boy, with a touch of patronage in his voice.

'But where do you sleep at night?'

'I don't sleep at night; that's my busiest time.'

Van Cheele began to have an irritated feeling that he was grappling with a problem that was eluding him.

'What do you feed on?' he asked.

'Flesh,' said the boy, and he pronounced the word with slow relish, as though he were tasting it.

'Flesh! What flesh?'

'Since it interests you, rabbits, wild-fowl, hares, poultry, lambs in their season, children when I can get any; they're usually too well locked in at night, when I do most of my hunting. It's quite two months since I tasted child-flesh.'

Ignoring the chaffing nature of the last remark, Van Cheele tried to draw the boy on the subject of possible poaching operations.

'You're talking rather through your hat when you speak of

feeding on hares.' (Considering the nature of the boy's toilet, the simile was hardly an apt one.) 'Our hillside hares aren't easily caught.'

'At night I hunt on four feet,' was the somewhat cryptic response.

'I suppose you mean that you hunt with a dog?' hazarded Van Cheele.

The boy rolled slowly over on to his back, and laughed a weird low laugh, that was pleasantly like a chuckle, and disagreeably like a snarl.

'I don't fancy any dog would be very anxious for my company, especially at night.'

Van Cheele began to feel that there was something positively uncanny about the strange-eyed, strange-tongued youngster.

'I can't have you staying in these woods,' he declared authoritatively.

'I fancy you'd rather have me here than in your house,' said the boy.

The prospect of this wild, nude animal in Van Cheele's primly ordered house was certainly an alarming one.

'If you don't go I shall have to make you,' said Van Cheele.

The boy turned like a flash, plunged into the pool, and in a moment had flung his wet and glistening body half-way up the bank where Van Cheele was standing. In an otter the movement would not have been remarkable; in a boy Van Cheele found it sufficiently startling. His foot slipped as he made an involuntary backward movement, and he found himself almost prostrate on the slippery weed-grown bank, with those tigerish yellow eyes not very far from his own. Almost instinctively he half-raised his hand to his throat. The boy laughed again, a laugh in which the snarl had nearly driven out the chuckle, and then, with another of his astonishing lightning movements, plunged out of view into a yielding tangle of weed and fern.

'What an extraordinary wild animal!' said Van Cheele as he picked himself up. And then he recalled Cunningham's remark, 'There is a wild beast in your woods.'

Walking slowly homeward, Van Cheele began to turn over in his mind various local occurrences which might be traceable to the existence of this astonishing young savage.

Something had been thinning the game in the woods lately,

poultry had been missing from the farms, hares were growing unaccountably scarcer, and complaints had reached him of lambs being carried off bodily from the hills. Was it possible that this wild boy was really hunting the countryside in company with some clever poacher dog? He had spoken of hunting 'four-footed' by night, but then, again, he had hinted strangely at no dog caring to come near him, 'especially at night'. It was certainly puzzling. And then, as Van Cheele ran his mind over the various depredations that had been committed during the last month or two, he came suddenly to a dead stop, alike in his walk and his speculations. The child missing from the mill two months ago – the accepted theory was that it had tumbled into the mill-race and been swept away; but the mother had always declared she had heard a shriek on the hill side of the house, in the opposite direction from the water. It was unthinkable, of course, but he wished that the boy had not made that uncanny remark about child-flesh eaten two months ago. Such dreadful things should not be said even in fun.

Van Cheele, contrary to his usual wont, did not feel disposed to be communicative about his discovery in the wood. His position as a parish councillor and justice of the peace seemed somehow compromised by the fact that he was harbouring a personality of such doubtful repute on his property; there was even a possibility that a heavy bill for damages for raided lambs and poultry might be laid at his door. At dinner that night he was quite unusually silent.

'Where's your voice gone to?' said his aunt. 'One would think you had seen a wolf.'

Van Cheele, who was not familiar with the old saying, thought the remark rather foolish; if he *had* seen a wolf on his property his tongue would have been extraordinarily busy with the subject.

At breakfast next morning Van Cheele was conscious that his feeling of uneasiness regarding yesterday's episode had not wholly disappeared, and he resolved to go by train to the neighbouring cathedral town, hunt up Cunningham, and learn from him what he had really seen that had prompted the remark about a wild beast in the woods. With this resolution taken, his usual cheerfulness partially returned, and he hummed a bright little melody as he sauntered to the morning-room for his customary cigarette. As he entered the room the melody made way abruptly for a pious invocation. Gracefully asprawl on the ottoman, in an attitude of almost exaggerated repose, was the boy of the woods. He was drier than when Van Cheele had last seen him, but no other alteration was noticeable in his toilet.

'How dare you come here?' asked Van Cheele furiously.

'You told me I was not to stay in the woods,' said the boy calmly.

'But not to come here. Supposing my aunt should see you!'

And with a view to minimizing that catastrophe Van Cheele hastily obscured as much of his unwelcome guest as possible under the folds of a *Morning Post*. At that moment his aunt entered the room.

'This is a poor boy who has lost his way – and lost his memory. He doesn't know who he is or where he comes from,' explained Van Cheele desperately, glancing apprehensively at the waif's face to see whether he was going to add inconvenient candour to his other savage propensities.

Miss Van Cheele was enormously interested.

'Perhaps his underlinen is marked,' she suggested.

'He seems to have lost most of that, too,' said Van Cheele, making frantic little grabs at the *Morning Post* to keep it in its place.

A naked homeless child appealed to Miss Van Cheele as warmly as a stray kitten or derelict puppy would have done.

'We must do all we can for him,' she decided, and in a very short time a messenger, dispatched to the rectory, where a page-boy was kept, had returned with a suit of pantry clothes, and the necessary accessories of shirt, shoes, collar, etc. Clothed, clean and groomed, the boy lost none of his uncanniness in Van Cheele's eyes, but his aunt found him sweet.

'We must call him something till we know who he really is,' she said. 'Gabriel-Ernest, I think; those are nice suitable names.'

Van Cheele agreed, but he privately doubted whether they were being grafted on to a nice suitable child. His misgivings were not diminished by the fact that his staid and elderly spaniel had bolted out of the house at the first incoming of the boy, and now obstinately remained shivering and yapping at the farther end of the orchard, while the canary, usually as vocally industrious as Van Cheele himself, had put itself on an allowance of frightened cheeps. More than ever he was resolved to consult Cunningham without loss of time.

As he drove off to the station his aunt was arranging that Gabriel-Ernest should help her to entertain the infant members of her Sunday-school class at tea that afternoon.

Cunningham was not at first disposed to be communicative.

'My mother died of some brain trouble,' he explained, 'so you will understand why I am averse to dwelling on anything of an impossibly fantastic nature that I may see or think that I have seen.'

'But what did you see?' persisted Van Cheele.

'What I thought I saw was something so extraordinary that no really sane man could dignify it with the credit of having actually happened. I was standing, the last evening I was with you, half-hidden in the hedgegrowth by the orchard gate, watching the dying glow of the sunset. Suddenly I became aware of a naked boy, a bather from some neighbouring pool, I took him to be, who was standing out on the bare hillside also watching the sunset. His pose was so suggestive of some wild faun of Pagan myth that I instantly wanted to engage him as a model, and in another moment I think I should have hailed him. But just then the sun dipped out of view, and all the orange and pink slid out of the landscape, leaving it cold and grey. And at the same moment an astounding thing happened – the boy vanished too!'

'What! vanished away into nothing?' asked Van Cheele excitedly.

'No; that is the dreadful part of it,' answered the artist; 'on the open hillside where the boy had been standing a second ago, stood a large wolf, blackish in colour, with gleaming fangs and cruel, yellow eyes. You may think –'

But Van Cheele did not stop for anything as futile as thought. Already he was tearing at top speed towards the station. He dismissed the idea of a telegram. 'Gabriel-Ernest is a werewolf' was a hopelessly inadequate effort at conveying the situation, and his aunt would think it was a code message to which he had omitted to give her the key. His one hope was that he might reach home before sundown. The cab which he chartered at the other end of the railway journey bore him with what seemed exasperating slowness along the country roads, which were pink and mauve with the flush of the sinking sun. His aunt was putting away some unfinished jams and cake when he arrived.

'Where is Gabriel-Ernest?' he almost screamed.

'He is taking the little Toop child home,' said his aunt. 'It was getting so late, I thought it wasn't safe to let it go back alone. What a lovely sunset, isn't it?'

But Van Cheele, although not oblivious of the glow in the western sky, did not stay to discuss its beauties. At a speed for which he was scarcely geared he raced along the narrow lane that led to the home of the Toops. On one side ran the swift current of the mill-stream, on the other rose the stretch of bare hillside. A dwindling rim of red sun showed still on the skyline, and the next turning must bring him in view of the ill-assorted couple he was pursuing. Then the colour went suddenly out of things, and a grey light settled itself with a quick shiver over the landscape. Van Cheele heard a shrill wail of fear, and stopped running.

Nothing was ever seen again of the Toop child or Gabriel-Ernest, but the latter's discarded garments were found lying in the road, so it was assumed that the child had fallen into the water, and that the boy had stripped and jumped in, in a vain endeavour to save it. Van Cheele and some workmen who were near by at the time testified to having heard a child scream loudly just near the spot where the clothes were found. Mrs Toop, who had eleven other children, was decently resigned to her bereavement, but Miss Van Cheele sincerely mourned her lost foundling. It was on her initiative that a memorial brass was put up in the parish church to 'Gabriel-Ernest, an unknown boy, who bravely sacrificed his life for another.'

Van Cheele gave way to his aunt in most things, but he flatly refused to subscribe to the Gabriel-Ernest memorial.

The Mouse

Theodoric Voler had been brought up, from infancy to the confines of middle age, by a fond mother whose chief solicitude had been to keep him screened from what she called the coarser realities of life. When she died she left Theodoric alone in a world that was as real as ever, and a good deal coarser than he

considered it had any need to be. To a man of his temperament
and upbringing even a simple railway journey was crammed
with petty annoyances and minor discords, and as he settled
himself down in a second-class compartment one September
morning he was conscious of ruffled feelings and general mental
discomposure. He had been staying at a country vicarage, the
inmates of which had been certainly neither brutal nor baccha-
nalian, but their supervision of the domestic establishment had
been of that lax order which invites disaster. The pony carriage
that was to take him to the station had never been properly
ordered, and when the moment for his departure drew near the
handy-man who should have produced the required article was
nowhere to be found. In this emergency Theodoric, to his mute
but very intense disgust, found himself obliged to collaborate
with the vicar's daughter in the task of harnessing the pony,
which necessitated groping about in an ill-lighted outhouse
called a stable, and smelling very like one – except in patches
where it smelt of mice. Without being actually afraid of mice,
Theodoric classed them among the coarser incidents of life, and
considered that Providence, with a little exercise of moral
courage, might long ago have recognized that they were not
indispensable, and have withdrawn them from circulation. As
the train glided out of the station Theodoric's nervous imagination accused himself of exhaling a weak odour of stableyard, and
possibly of displaying a mouldy straw or two on his usually well-
brushed garments. Fortunately the only other occupant of the
compartment, a lady of about the same age as himself, seemed
inclined for slumber rather than scrutiny; the train was not due
to stop till the terminus was reached, in about an hour's time,
and the carriage was of the old-fashioned sort, that held no
communication with a corridor, therefore no further travelling
companions were likely to intrude on Theodoric's semi-privacy.
And yet the train had scarcely attained its normal speed before he
became reluctantly but vividly aware that he was not alone with
the slumbering lady; he was not even alone in his own clothes. A
warm, creeping movement over his flesh betrayed the unwelcome and highly resented presence, unseen but poignant, of a
strayed mouse, that had evidently dashed into its present retreat
during the episode of the pony harnessing. Furtive stamps and
shakes and wildly directed pinches failed to dislodge the intruder,

whose motto, indeed, seemed to be Excelsior; and the lawful occupant of the clothes lay back against the cushions and endeavoured rapidly to evolve some means of putting an end to the dual ownership. It was unthinkable that he should continue for the space of a whole hour in the horrible position of a Rowton House for vagrant mice (already his imagination had at least doubled the numbers of the alien invasion). On the other hand, nothing less drastic than partial disrobing would ease him of his tormentor, and to undress in the presence of a lady, even for so laudable a purpose, was an idea that made his eartips tingle in a blush of abject shame. He had never been able to bring himself even to the mild exposure of open-work socks in the presence of the fair sex. And yet – the lady in this case was to all appearances soundly and securely asleep; the mouse, on the other hand, seemed to be trying to crowd a Wanderjahr into a few strenuous minutes. If there is any truth in the theory of transmigration, this particular mouse must certainly have been in a former state a member of the Alpine Club. Sometimes in its eagerness it lost its footing and slipped for half an inch or so; and then, in fright, or more probably temper, it bit. Theodoric was goaded into the most audacious undertaking of his life. Crimsoning to the hue of a beetroot and keeping an agonized watch on his slumbering fellow-traveller, he swiftly and noiselessly secured the ends of his railway-rug to the racks on either side of the carriage, so that a substantial curtain hung athwart the compartment. In the narrow dressing-room that he had thus improvised he proceeded with violent haste to extricate himself partially and the mouse entirely from the surrounding casings of tweed and half-wool. As the unravelled mouse gave a wild leap to the floor, the rug, slipping its fastening at either end, also came down with a heart-curdling flop, and almost simultaneously the awakened sleeper opened her eyes. With a movement almost quicker than the mouse's, Theodoric pounced on the rug, and hauled its ample folds chin-high over his dismantled person as he collapsed into the further corner of the carriage. The blood raced and beat in the veins of his neck and forehead, while he waited dumbly for the communication-cord to be pulled. The lady, however, contented herself with a silent stare at her strangely muffled companion. How much had she seen, Theodoric queried to himself, and in any case what on earth must she think of his present posture?

'I think I have caught a chill,' he ventured desperately.

'Really, I'm sorry,' she replied. 'I was just going to ask you if you would open this window.'

'I fancy it's malaria,' he added, his teeth chattering slightly, as much from fright as from a desire to support his theory.

'I've got some brandy in my hold-all, if you'll kindly reach it down for me,' said his companion.

'Not for worlds – I mean, I never take anything for it,' he assured her earnestly.

'I suppose you caught it in the Tropics?'

Theodoric, whose acquaintance with the Tropics was limited to an annual present of a chest of tea from an uncle in Ceylon, felt that even the malaria was slipping from him. Would it be possible, he wondered, to disclose the real state of affairs to her in small instalments?

'Are you afraid of mice?' he ventured, growing, if possible, more scarlet in the face.

'Not unless they came in quantities, like those that ate up Bishop Hatto. Why do you ask?'

'I had one crawling inside my clothes just now,' said Theodoric in a voice that hardly seemed his own. 'It was a most awkward situation.'

'It must have been, if you wear your clothes at all tight,' she observed; 'but mice have strange ideas of comfort.'

'I had to get rid of it while you were asleep,' he continued; then, with a gulp, he added, 'it was getting rid of it that brought me to – to this.'

'Surely leaving off one small mouse wouldn't bring on a chill,' she exclaimed, with a levity that Theodoric accounted abominable.

Evidently she had detected something of his predicament, and was enjoying his confusion. All the blood in his body seemed to have mobilized in one concentrated blush, and an agony of abasement, worse than a myriad mice, crept up and down over his soul. And then, as reflection began to assert itself, sheer terror took the place of humiliation. With every minute that passed the train was rushing nearer to the crowded and bustling terminus where dozens of prying eyes would be exchanged for the one paralysing pair that watched him from the further corner of the carriage. There was one slender despairing chance, which the next few minutes must decide. His fellow-traveller might relapse into a blessed slumber. But as the minutes throbbed by, that chance ebbed away. The furtive glance which Theodoric stole at her from time to time disclosed only an unwinking wakefulness.

'I think we must be getting near now,' she presently observed.

Theodoric had already noted with growing terror the recurring stacks of small, ugly dwellings that heralded the journey's end. The words acted as a signal. Like a hunted beast breaking cover and dashing madly towards some other haven of momentary safety he threw aside his rug, and struggled frantically into his dishevelled garments. He was conscious of dull surburban stations racing past the window, of a choking, hammering sensation of his throat and heart, and of an icy silence in that corner towards which he dared not look. Then as he sank back in his seat, clothed and almost delirious, the train slowed down to a final crawl, and the woman spoke.

'Would you be so kind', she asked, 'as to get me a porter to put me into a cab? It's a shame to trouble you when you're feeling unwell, but being blind makes one so helpless at a railway station.'

The Reticence of Lady Anne

Egbert came into the large, dimly lit drawing-room with the air of a man who is not certain whether he is entering a dovecote or a bomb factory, and is prepared for either eventuality. The little domestic quarrel over the luncheon-table had not been fought to a definite finish, and the question was how far Lady Anne was in a mood to renew or forego hostilities. Her pose in the armchair by the tea-table was rather elaborately rigid; in the gloom of a December afternoon Egbert's pince-nez did not materially help him to discern the expression of her face.

By way of breaking whatever ice might be floating on the surface he made a remark about a dim religious light. He or Lady Anne were accustomed to make that remark between 4.30 and 6 on winter and late autumn evenings; it was a part of their married life. There was no recognized rejoinder to it, and Lady Anne made none.

Don Tarquinio lay astretch on the Persian rug, basking in the firelight with superb indifference to the possible ill-humour of Lady Anne. His pedigree was as flawlessly Persian as the rug, and his ruff was coming into the glory of its second winter. The page-boy, who had Renaissance tendencies, had christened him Don Tarquinio. Left to themselves, Egbert and Lady Anne would unfailingly have called him Fluff, but they were not obstinate.

Egbert poured himself out some tea. As the silence gave no sign of breaking on Lady Anne's initiative, he braced himself for another Yermak effort.

'My remark at lunch had a purely academic application,' he announced; 'you seem to put an unnecessarily personal signifi-cance into it.'

Lady Anne maintained her defensive barrier of silence. The bullfinch lazily filled in the interval with an air from *Iphigénie en Tauride*. Egbert recognized it immediately, because it was the only air the bullfinch whistled, and he had come to them with the reputation for whistling it. Both Egbert and Lady Anne would have preferred something from *The Yeoman of the Guard*, which was their favourite opera. In matters artistic they had a similarity of taste. They leaned towards the honest and explicit in art, a picture, for instance, that told its own story, with generous assistance from its title. A riderless warhorse with harness in obvious disarray, staggering into a courtyard full of pale swooning women, and marginally noted 'Bad News', suggested to their minds a distinct interpretation of some military catastro-phe. They could see what it was meant to convey, and explain it to friends of duller intelligence.

The silence continued. As a rule Lady Anne's displeasure became articulate and markedly voluble after four minutes of introductory muteness. Egbert seized the milk-jug and poured some of its contents into Don Tarquinio's saucer; as the saucer was already full to the brim an unsightly overflow was the result. Don Tarquinio looked on with a surprised interest that evanesced into elaborate unconsciousness when he was appealed to by Egbert to come and drink up some of the spilt matter. Don Tarquinio was prepared to play many rôles in life, but a vacuum carpet-cleaner was not one of them.

'Don't you think we're being rather foolish?' said Egbert cheerfully.

If Lady Anne thought so she didn't say so.

'I daresay the fault has been partly on my side,' continued Egbert, with evaporating cheerfulness. 'After all, I'm only human, you know. You seem to forget that I'm only human.'

He insisted on the point, as if there had been unfounded suggestions that he was built on Satyr lines, with goat continuations where the human left off.

The bullfinch recommenced its air from *Iphigénie en Tauride*. Egbert began to feel depressed. Lady Anne was not drinking her tea. Perhaps she was feeling unwell. But when Lady Anne felt unwell she was not wont to be reticent on the subject. 'No one knows what I suffer from indigestion,' was one of her favourite statements; but the lack of knowledge can only have been caused by defective listening; the amount of information available on the subject would have supplied material for a monograph.

Evidently Lady Anne was not feeling unwell.

Egbert began to think he was being unreasonably dealt with; naturally he began to make concessions.

'I daresay,' he observed, taking as central a position on the hearth-rug as Don Tarquinio could be persuaded to concede him, 'I may have been to blame. I am willing, if I can thereby restore things to a happier standpoint, to undertake to lead a better life.'

He wondered vaguely how it would be possible. Temptations came to him, in middle age, tentatively and without insistence, like a neglected butcher-boy who asks for a Christmas box in February for no more hopeful reason than that he didn't get one in December. He had no more idea of succumbing to them than he had of purchasing the fish-knives and fur boas that ladies are impelled to sacrifice through the medium of advertisement columns during twelve months of the year. Still, there was something impressive in this unasked for renunciation of possibly latent enormities.

Lady Anne showed no sign of being impressed.

Egbert looked at her nervously through his glasses. To get the worst of an argument with her was no new experience. To get the worst of a monologue was a humiliating novelty.

'I shall go and dress for dinner,' he announced in a voice into which he intended some shade of sternness to creep.

At the door a final access of weakness impelled him to make a further appeal.

'Aren't we being very silly?'

'A fool,' was Don Tarquinio's mental comment as the door closed on Egbert's retreat. Then he lifted his velvet forepaws in the air and leapt lightly on to a bookshelf immediately under the bullfinch's cage. It was the first time he had seemed to notice the bird's existence, but he was carrying out a long-formed theory of action with the precision of mature deliberation. The bullfinch, who had fancied himself something of a despot, depressed himself of a sudden into a third of his normal displacement; then he fell to a helpless wing-beating and shrill cheeping. He had cost twenty-seven shillings without the cage, but Lady Anne made no sign of interfering. She had been dead for two hours.

The Easter Egg

It was distinctly hard lines for Lady Barbara, who came of good fighting stock, and was one of the bravest women of her generation, that her son should be so undisguisedly a coward. Whatever good qualities Lester Slaggby may have possessed, and he was in some respects charming, courage could certainly never be imputed to him. As a child he had suffered from childish timidity, as a boy from unboyish funk, and as a youth he had exchanged unreasoning fears for others which were more formidable from the fact of having a carefully thought-out basis. He was frankly afraid of animals, nervous with firearms, and never crossed the Channel without mentally comparing the numerical proportion of lifebelts to passengers. On horseback he seemed to require as many hands as a Hindu god, at least four for clutching the reins, and two more for patting the horse soothingly on the neck. Lady Barbara no longer pretended not to see her son's prevailing weakness; with her usual courage she faced the knowledge of it squarely, and, motherlike, loved him none the less.

Continental travel, anywhere away from the great tourist tracks, was a favoured hobby with Lady Barbara, and Lester joined her as often as possible. Eastertide usually found her at

Knobaltheim, an upland township in one of those small prince-doms that make freckles on the map of Central Europe.

A long-standing acquaintanceship with the reigning family made her a personage of due importance in the eyes of her old friend the Burgomaster, and she was anxiously consulted by that worthy on the momentous occasion when the Prince made known his intention of coming in person to open a sanatorium outside the town. All the usual items in a programme of welcome, some of them fatuous and commonplace, others quaint and charming, had been arranged for, but the Burgomaster hoped that the resourceful English lady might have something new and tasteful to suggest in the way of loyal greeting. The Prince was known to the outside world, if at all, as an old-fashioned reactionary, combating modern progress, as it were, with a wooden sword; to his own people he was known as a kindly old gentleman with a certain endearing stateliness which had nothing of standoffishness about it. Knobaltheim was anxious to do its best. Lady Barbara discussed the matter with Lester and one or two acquaintances in her little hotel, but ideas were difficult to come by.

'Might I suggest something to the gnädige Frau?' asked a sallow high-cheek-boned lady to whom the Englishwoman had spoken once or twice, and whom she had set down in her mind as probably a Southern Slav.

'Might I suggest something for the Reception Fest?' she went on, with a certain shy eagerness. 'Our little child here, our baby, we will dress him in a little white coat, with small wings, as an Easter angel, and he will carry a large white Easter egg, and inside shall be a basket of plover eggs, of which the Prince is so fond, and he shall give it to his Highness as Easter offering. It is so pretty an idea; we have seen it done once in Styria.'

Lady Barbara looked dubiously at the proposed Easter angel, a fair, wooden-faced child of about four years old. She had noticed it the day before in the hotel, and wondered rather how such a tow-headed child could belong to such a dark-visaged couple as the woman and her husband; probably, she thought, an adopted baby, especially as the couple were not young.

'Of course gnädige Frau will escort the little child up to the Prince,' pursued the woman; 'but he will be quite good, and do as he is told.'

'We haf some pluffers' eggs shall come fresh from Wien,' said the husband.

The small child and Lady Barbara seemed equally unenthusiastic about the pretty idea; Lester was openly discouraging, but when the Burgomaster heard of it he was enchanted. The combination of sentiment and plovers' eggs appealed strongly to his Teutonic mind.

On the eventful day the Easter angel, really quite prettily and quaintly dressed, was a centre of kindly interest to the gala crowd marshalled to receive his Highness. The mother was unobtrusive and less fussy than most parents would have been under the circumstances, merely stipulating that she should place the Easter egg herself in the arms that had been carefully schooled how to hold the precious burden. Then Lady Barbara moved forward, the child marching stolidly and with grim determination at her side. It had been promised cakes and sweeties galore if it gave the egg well and truly to the kind old gentleman who was waiting to receive it. Lester had tried to convey to it privately that horrible smackings would attend any failure in its share of the proceedings, but it is doubtful if his German caused more than an immediate distress. Lady Barbara had thoughtfully provided herself with an emergency supply of chocolate sweetmeats; children may sometimes be time-servers, but they do not encourage long accounts. As they approached nearer to the princely daïs Lady Barbara stood discreetly aside, and the stolid-faced infant walked forward alone, with staggering but steadfast gait, encouraged by a murmur of elderly approval. Lester, standing in the front row of the onlookers, turned to scan the crowd for the beaming faces of the happy parents. In a side-road which led to the railway station he saw a cab; entering the cab with every appearance of furtive haste were the dark-visaged couple who had been so plausibly eager for the 'pretty idea'. The sharpened instinct of cowardice lit up the situation to him in one swift flash. The blood roared and surged to his head as though thousands of floodgates had been opened in his veins and arteries, and his brain was the common sluice in which all the torrents met. He saw nothing but a blur around him. Then the blood ebbed away in quick waves, till his very heart seemed drained and empty, and he stood nervously, helplessly, dumbly watching the child, bearing its accursed burden with slow, relentless steps nearer and nearer to the group that waited sheep-like to receive him. A fascinated curiosity compelled Lester to turn his head towards the fugitives; the cab had started at hot pace in the direction of the station.

The next moment Lester was running, running faster than any of those present had ever seen a man run, and – he was not running away. For that stray fraction of his life some unwonted impulse beset him, some hint of the stock he came from, and he ran unflinchingly towards danger. He stooped and clutched at the Easter egg as one tries to scoop up the ball in Rugby football. What he meant to do with it he had not considered, the thing was to get it. But the child had been promised cakes and sweetmeats if it safely gave the egg into the hands of the kindly old gentleman; it uttered no scream, but it held to its charge with limpet grip. Lester sank to his knees, tugging savagely at the tightly clasped burden, and angry cries rose from the scandalized onlookers. A questioning, threatening ring formed round him, then shrank back in recoil as he shrieked out one hideous word. Lady Barbara heard the word and saw the crowd race away like scattered sheep, saw the Prince forcibly hustled away by his attendants; also she saw her son lying prone in an agony of overmastering terror, his spasm of daring shattered by the child's unexpected resistance, still clutching frantically, as though for safety, at that white-satin gew-gaw, unable to crawl even from its deadly neighbourhood, able only to scream and scream and scream. In her brain she was dimly conscious of balancing, or striving to balance, the abject shame which had him now in thrall against the one compelling act of courage which had flung him grandly and madly on to the point of danger. It was only for the fraction of a minute that she stood watching the two entangled figures, the infant with its woodenly obstinate face and body tense with dogged resistance, and the boy limp and already nearly dead with a terror that almost stifled his screams; and over them the long gala streamers flapping gaily in the sunshine. She never forgot the scene; but then, it was the last she ever saw.

Lady Barbara carries her scarred face with its sightless eyes as bravely as ever in the world, but at Eastertide her friends are careful to keep from her ears any mention of the children's Easter symbol.

Esmé

'All hunting stories are the same,' said Clovis; 'just as all Turf stories are the same, and all –'

'My hunting story isn't a bit like any you've ever heard,' said the Baroness. 'It happened quite a while ago, when I was about twenty-three. I wasn't living apart from my husband then; you see, neither of us could afford to make the other a separate allowance. In spite of everything that proverbs may say, poverty keeps together more homes than it breaks up. But we always hunted with different packs. All this has nothing to do with the story.'

'We haven't arrived at the meet yet. I suppose there was a meet,' said Clovis.

'Of course there was a meet,' said the Baroness; 'all the usual crowd were there, especially Constance Broddle. Constance is one of those strapping florid girls that go so well with autumn scenery or Christmas decorations in church. "I feel a presentiment that something dreadful is going to happen," she said to me; "am I looking pale?"

'She was looking about as pale as a beetroot that has suddenly heard bad news.

'"You're looking nicer than usual," I said, "but that's so easy for you." Before she had got the right bearings of this remark we had settled down to business; hounds had found a fox lying out in some gorse-bushes.'

'I knew it,' said Clovis; 'in every fox-hunting story that I've ever heard there's been a fox and some gorse-bushes.'

'Constance and I were well mounted,' continued the Baroness serenely, 'and we had no difficulty in keeping ourselves in the first flight, though it was a fairly stiff run. Towards the finish, however, we must have held rather too independent a line, for we lost the hounds, and found ourselves plodding aimlessly along miles away from anywhere. It was fairly exasperating, and my temper was beginning to let itself go by inches, when on pushing our way through an accommodating hedge we were gladdened by the sight of hounds in full cry in a hollow just beneath us.

'"There they go," cried Constance, and then added in a gasp, "In Heaven's name, what are they hunting?"

'It was certainly no mortal fox. It stood more than twice as high, had a short, ugly head, and an enormous thick neck.

'"It's a hyena," I cried; "it must have escaped from Lord Pabham's Park."

'At that moment the hunted beast turned and faced its pursuers, and the hounds (there were only about six couple of them) stood round in a half-circle and looked foolish. Evidently they had broken away from the rest of the pack on the trail of this alien scent, and were not quite sure how to treat their quarry now they had got him.

'The hyena hailed our approach with unmistakable relief and demonstrations of friendliness. It had probably been accustomed to uniform kindness from humans, while its first experience of a pack of hounds had left a bad impression. The hounds looked more than ever embarrassed as their quarry paraded its sudden intimacy with us, and the faint toot of a horn in the distance was seized on as a welcome signal for unobtrusive departure. Constance and I and the hyena were left alone in the gathering twilight.

'"What are we to do?" asked Constance.

'"What a person you are for questions," I said.

'"Well, we can't stay here all night with a hyena," she retorted.

'"I don't know what your ideas of comfort are," I said; "but I shouldn't think of staying here all night even without a hyena. My home may be an unhappy one, but at least it has hot and cold water laid on, and domestic service, and other conveniences which we shouldn't find here. We had better make for that ridge of trees to the right; I imagine the Crowley road is just beyond."'

'We trotted off slowly along a faintly marked cart-track, with the beast following cheerfully at our heels.

'"What on earth are we to do with the hyena?" came the inevitable question.

'"What does one generally do with hyenas?" I asked crossly.

'"I've never had anything to do with one before," said Constance.

'"Well, neither have I. If we even knew its sex we might give it a name. Perhaps we might call it Esmé. That would do in either case."

'There was still sufficient daylight for us to distinguish wayside objects, and our listless spirits gave an upward perk as we came upon a small half-naked gipsy brat picking blackberries from a low-growing bush. The sudden apparition of two horsewomen and a hyena set it off crying, and in any case we should scarcely have gleaned any useful geographical information from that source; but there was a probability that we might strike a gipsy encampment somewhere along our route. We rode on hopefully but uneventfully for another mile or so.

'"I wonder what that child was doing there," said Constance presently.

'"Picking blackberries. Obviously."

'"I don't like the way it cried," pursued Constance; "somehow its wail keeps ringing in my ears."

'I did not chide Constance for her morbid fancies; as a matter of fact the same sensation, of being pursued by a persistent fretful wail, had been forcing itself on my rather over-tired nerves. For company's sake I hulloed to Esmé, who had lagged somewhat behind. With a few springy bounds he drew up level, and then shot past us.

'The wailing accompaniment was explained. The gipsy child was firmly, and I expect painfully, held in his jaws.

'"Merciful Heaven!" screamed Constance, "what on earth shall we do? What are we to do?"

'I am perfectly certain that at the Last Judgement Constance will ask more questions than any of the examining Seraphs.

'"Can't we do something?" she persisted tearfully, as Esmé cantered easily along in front of our tired horses.

'Personally I was doing everything that occurred to me at the moment. I stormed and scolded and coaxed in English and French and gamekeeper language; I made absurd, ineffectual cuts in the air with my thongless hunting-crop; I hurled my sandwich case at the brute; in fact, I really don't know what more I could have done. And still we lumbered on through the deepening dusk, with that dark uncouth shape lumbering ahead of us, and a drone of lugubrious music floating in our ears. Suddenly Esmé bounded aside into some thick bushes, where we could not follow; the wail rose to a shriek and then stopped altogether. This part of the story I always hurry over, because it is really rather horrible. When the beast joined us again, after an absence of a few minutes, there was an air of patient understanding about him, as though he knew that he had done something of which we disapproved, but which he felt to be thoroughly justifiable.

'"How can you let that ravening beast trot by your side?" asked Constance. She was looking more than ever like an albino beetroot.

'"In the first place, I can't prevent it," I said; "and in the second place, whatever else he may be, I doubt if he's ravening at the present moment."

'Constance shuddered. "Do you think the poor little thing suffered much?" came another of her futile questions.

'"The indications were all that way," I said; "on the other hand, of course, it may have been crying from sheer temper. Children sometimes do."

'It was nearly pitch-dark when we emerged suddenly into the high road. A flash of lights and the whir of a motor went past us at the same moment at uncomfortably close quarters. A thud and a sharp screeching yell followed a second later. The car drew up, and when I had ridden back to the spot I found a young man bending over a dark motionless mass lying by the roadside.

'"You have killed my Esmé," I exclaimed bitterly.

'"I'm so awfully sorry," said the young man; "I keep dogs myself, so I know what you must feel about it. I'll do anything I can in reparation."

'"Please bury him at once," I said; "that much I think I may ask of you."

'"Bring the spade, William," he called to the chauffeur. Evidently hasty roadside interments were contingencies that had been provided against.

'The digging of a sufficiently large grave took some little time. "I say, what a magnificent fellow," said the motorist as the corpse was rolled over into the trench. "I'm afraid he must have been rather a valuable animal."

'"He took second in the puppy class at Birmingham last year," I said resolutely.

'Constance snorted loudly.

'"Don't cry, dear," I said brokenly; "it was all over in a moment. He couldn't have suffered much."

"Look here," said the young fellow desperately, "you simply must let me do something by way of reparation."

'I refused sweetly, but as he persisted I let him have my address.

'Of course, we kept our own counsel as to the earlier episodes of the evening. Lord Pabham never advertised the loss of his hyena; when a strictly fruit-eating animal strayed from his park a year or two previously he was called upon to give compensation in eleven cases of sheep-worrying and practically to re-stock his neighbours' poultry-yards, and an escaped hyena would have mounted up to something on the scale of a Government grant. The gipsies were equally unobtrusive over their missing offspring; I don't suppose in large encampments they really know to a child or two how many they've got.'

The Baroness paused reflectively, and then continued:

'There was a sequel to the adventure, though. I got through the post a charming little diamond brooch, with the name Esmé set in a sprig of rosemary. Incidentally, too, I lost the friendship of Constance Broddle. You see, when I sold the brooch I quite properly refused to give her any share of the proceeds. I pointed out that the Esmé part of the affair was my own invention, and the hyena part of it belonged to Lord Pabham, if it really was his hyena, of which, of course, I've no proof.

Filboid Studge, the Story of a Mouse that Helped

'I want to marry your daughter,' said Mark Spayley with faltering eagerness. 'I am only an artist with an income of two hundred a year, and she is the daughter of an enormously wealthy man, so I suppose you will think my offer a piece of presumption.'

Duncan Dullamy, the great company inflator, showed no outward sign of displeasure. As a matter of fact, he was secretly relieved at the prospect of finding even a two-hundred-a-year husband for his daughter Leonore. A crisis was rapidly rushing upon him, from which he knew he would emerge with neither money nor credit; all his recent ventures had fallen flat, and flattest of all had gone the wonderful new breakfast food, Pipenta, on the advertisement of which he had sunk such huge sums. It could scarcely be called a drug in the market; people bought drugs, but no one bought Pipenta.

'Would you marry Leonore if she were a poor man's daughter?' asked the man of phantom wealth.

'Yes,' said Mark, wisely avoiding the error of over-protestation. And to his astonishment Leonore's father not only gave his consent, but suggested a fairly early date for the wedding.

'I wish I could show my gratitude in some way,' said Mark with genuine emotion. 'I'm afraid it's rather like the mouse proposing to help the lion.'

'Get people to buy that beastly muck,' said Dullamy, nodding savagely at a poster of the despised Pipenta, 'and you'll have done more than any of my agents have been able to accomplish.'

'It wants a better name,' said Mark reflectively, 'and something distinctive in the poster line. Anyway, I'll have a shot at it.'

Three weeks later the world was advised of the coming of a new breakfast food, heralded under the resounding name of 'Filboid Studge'. Spayley put forth no pictures of massive babies springing up with fungus-like rapidity under its forcing influence, or of representatives of the leading nations of the world scrambling with fatuous eagerness for its possession. One huge sombre poster depicted the Damned in Hell suffering a new torment from their inability to get at the Filboid Studge which elegant young fiends held in transparent bowls just beyond their reach. The scene was rendered even more gruesome by a subtle suggestion of the features of leading men and women of the day in the portrayal of the Lost Souls; prominent individuals of both political parties, Society hostesses, well-known dramatic authors and novelists, and distinguished aeroplanists were dimly recognizable in that doomed throng; noted lights of the musical-comedy stage flickered wanly in the shades of the Inferno, smiling still from force of habit, but with the fearsome smiling rage of baffled effort. The poster bore no fulsome allusions to the merits of the new breakfast food, but a single grim statement ran in bold letters along its base: 'They cannot buy it now.'

Spayley had grasped the fact that people will do things from a sense of duty which they would never attempt as a pleasure. There are thousands of respectable middle-class men who, if you

found them unexpectedly in a Turkish bath, would explain in all
sincerity that a doctor had ordered them to take Turkish baths; if
you told them in return that you went there because you liked it,
they would stare in pained wonder at the frivolity of your motive.
In the same way, whenever a massacre of Armenians is reported
from Asia Minor, everyone assumes that it has been carried out
'under orders' from somewhere or another; no one seems to think
that there are people who might *like* to kill their neighbours now
and then.

And so it was with the new breakfast food. No one would have
eaten Filboid Studge as a pleasure, but the grim austerity of its
advertisement drove housewives in shoals to the grocers' shops to
clamour for an immediate supply. In small kitchens solemn
pig-tailed daughters helped depressed mothers to perform the
primitive ritual of its preparation. On the breakfast-tables of
cheerless parlours it was partaken of in silence. Once the
womenfolk discovered that it was thoroughly unpalatable, their
zeal in forcing it on their households knew no bounds. 'You
haven't eaten your Filboid Studge!' would be screamed at the
appetiteless clerk as he hurried wearily from the breakfast-
table, and his evening meal would be prefaced by a warmed-up
mess which would be explained as 'your Filboid Studge that you
didn't eat this morning'. Those strange fanatics who ostentatiously mortify themselves, inwardly and outwardly, with health
biscuits and health garments, battened aggressively on the new
food. Earnest spectacled young men devoured it on the steps of
the National Liberal Club. A bishop who did not believe in a
future state preached against the poster, and a peer's daughter
died from eating too much of the compound. A further advertisement was obtained when an infantry regiment mutinied and shot
its officers rather than eat the nauseous mess; fortunately, Lord
Birrell of Blatherstone, who was War Minister at the moment,
saved the situation by his happy epigram, that 'Discipline to be
effective must be optional'.

Filboid Studge had become a household word, but Dullamy
wisely realized that it was not necessarily the last word in
breakfast dietary; its supremacy would be challenged as soon as
some yet more unpalatable food should be put on the market.
There might even be a reaction in favour of something tasty and
appetizing, and the Puritan austerity of the moment might be

banished from domestic cookery. At an opportune moment, therefore, he sold out his interests in the article which had brought him in colossal wealth at a critical juncture, and placed his financial reputation beyond the reach of cavil. As for Leonore, who was now an heiress on a far greater scale than ever before, he naturally found her something a vast deal higher in the husband market than a two-hundred-a-year poster designer. Mark Spayley, the brainmouse who had helped the financial lion with such untoward effect, was left to curse the day he produced the wonder-working poster.

'Ministers of Grace'

Although he was scarcely yet out of his teens, the Duke of Scaw was already marked out as a personality widely differing from others of his caste and period. Not in externals; therein he conformed correctly to type. His hair was faintly reminiscent of Houbigant, and at the other end of him his shoes exhaled the right *soupçon* of harness-room; his socks compelled one's attention without losing one's respect; and his attitude in repose had just that suggestion of Whistler's mother, so becoming in the really young. It was within that the trouble lay, if trouble it could be accounted, which marked him apart from his fellows. The Duke was religious. Not in any of the ordinary senses of the word; he took small heed of High Church or Evangelical standpoints, he stood outside of all the movements and missions and cults and crusades of the day, uncaring and uninterested. Yet in a mystical-practical way of his own, which had served him unscathed and unshaken through the fickle years of boyhood, he was intensely and intensively religious. His family were naturally, though unobtrusively, distressed about it. 'I am so afraid it may affect his bridge,' said his mother.

The Duke sat in a pennyworth of chair in St James's Park, listening to the pessimisms of Belturbet, who reviewed the existing political situation from the gloomiest of standpoints.

'Where I think you political spade-workers are so silly,' said the Duke, 'is in the misdirection of your efforts. You spend thousands of pounds of money, and Heaven knows how much dynamic force of brain power and personal energy, in trying to elect or displace this or that man, whereas you could gain your ends so much more simply by making use of the men as you find them. If they don't suit your purpose as they are, transform them into something more satisfactory.'

'Do you refer to hypnotic suggestion?' asked Belturbet, with the air of one who is being trifled with.

'Nothing of the sort. Do you understand what I mean by the verb to koepenick? That is to say, to replace an authority by a spurious imitation that would carry just as much weight for the moment as the displaced original; the advantage, of course, being that the koepenick replica would do what you wanted, whereas the original does what seems best in its own eyes.'

'I suppose every public man has a double, if not two or three,' said Belturbet; 'but it would be a pretty hard task to koepenick a whole bunch of them and keep the originals out of the way.'

'There have been instances in European history of highly successful koepenickery,' said the Duke dreamily.

'Oh of course, there have been False Dimitris and Perkin Warbecks, who imposed on the world for a time,' assented Belturbet, 'but they personated people who were dead or safely out of the way. That was a comparatively simple matter. It would be far easier to pass oneself off as dead Hannibal than as living Haldane, for instance.'

'I was thinking,' said the Duke, 'of the most famous case of all, the angel who koepenicked King Robert of Sicily with such brilliant results. Just imagine what an advantage it would be to have angels deputizing, to use a horrible but convenient word, for Quinston and Lord Hugo Sizzle, for example. How much smoother the Parliamentary machine would work than at present!'

'Now you're talking nonsense,' said Belturbet; 'angels don't exist nowadays, at least, not in that way, so what is the use of dragging them into a serious discussion? It's merely silly.'

'If you talk to me like that I shall just *do* it,' said the Duke.

'Do what?' asked Belturbet. There were times when his young friend's uncanny remarks rather frightened him.

'I shall summon angelic forces to take over some of the more troublesome personalities of our public life, and I shall send the ousted originals into temporary retirement in suitable animal organisms. It's not everyone who would have the knowledge or the power necessary to bring such a thing off –'

'Oh, stop that inane rubbish,' said Belturbet angrily; 'it's getting wearisome. Here's Quinston coming,' he added, as there approached along the almost deserted path the well-known figure of a young Cabinet Minister, whose personality evoked a curious mixture of public interest and unpopularity.

'Hurry along, my dear man,' said the young Duke to the Minister, who had given him a condescending nod; 'your time is running short,' he continued in a provocative strain; 'the whole inner crowd of you will shortly be swept away into the world's waste-paper basket.'

'You poor little strawberry-leafed nonentity,' said the Minister, checking himself for a moment in his stride and rolling out his words spasmodically; 'who is going to sweep us away, I should like to know? The voting masses are on our side, and all the ability and administrative talent is on our side too. No power of earth or Heaven is going to move us from our place till we choose to quit it. No power of earth or –'

Belturbet saw, with bulging eyes, a sudden void where a moment earlier had been a Cabinet Minister; a void emphasized rather than relieved by the presence of a puffed-out bewildered-looking sparrow, which hopped about for a moment in a dazed fashion and then fell to a violent cheeping and scolding.

'If we could understand sparrow-language,' said the Duke serenely, 'I fancy we should hear something infinitely worse than "strawberry-leafed nonentity".'

'But good Heavens, Eugène,' said Belturbet hoarsely, 'what has become of – Why, there he is! How on earth did he get there?' And he pointed with a shaking finger towards a semblance of the vanished Minister, which approached once more along the unfrequented path.

The Duke laughed.

'It is Quinston to all outward appearance,' he said composedly, 'but I fancy you will find, on closer investigation, that it is an angel understudy of the real article.'

The Angel-Quinston greeted them with a friendly smile.

'How beastly happy you two look sitting there!' he said wistfully.

'I don't suppose you'd care to change places with poor little us,' replied the Duke chaffingly.

'How about poor little me?' said the Angel modestly. 'I've got to run about behind the wheels of popularity, like a spotted dog behind a carriage, getting all the dust and trying to look as if I was an important part of the machine. I must seem a perfect fool to you onlookers sometimes.'

'I think you are a perfect angel,' said the Duke.

The Angel-that-had-been-Quinston smiled and passed on his way, pursued across the breadth of the Horse Guards' Parade by a tiresome little sparrow that cheeped incessantly and furiously at him.

'That's only the beginning,' said the Duke complacently; 'I've made it operative with all of them, irrespective of parties.'

Belturbet made no coherent reply; he was engaged in feeling his pulse. The Duke fixed his attention with some interest on a black swan that was swimming with haughty, stiff-necked aloofness amid the crowd of lesser water-fowl that dotted the ornamental water. For all its pride of bearing, something was evidently ruffling and enraging it; in its way it seemed as angry and amazed as the sparrow had been.

At the same moment a human figure came along the pathway. Belturbet looked up apprehensively.

'Kedzon,' he whispered briefly.

'An Angel-Kedzon, if I am not mistaken,' said the Duke. 'Look, he is talking affably to a human being. That settles it.'

A shabbily-dressed lounger had accosted the man who had been Viceroy in the splendid East, and who still reflected in his mien some of the cold dignity of the Himalayan snowpeaks.

'Could you tell me, sir, if them white birds is storks or halbatrosses? I had an argyment –'

The cold dignity thawed at once into genial friendliness.

'Those are pelicans, my dear sir. Are you interested in birds? If you would join me in a bun and a glass of milk at the stall yonder, I could tell you some interesting things about Indian birds. Right oh! Now the hill-mynah, for instance –'

The two men disappeared in the direction of the bun-stall, chatting volubly as they went, and shadowed from the other side of the railed enclosure by a black swan, whose temper seemed to have reached the limit of inarticulate rage.

Belturbet gazed in an open-mouthed wonder after the retreating couple, then transferred his attention to the infuriated swan, and finally turned with a look of scared comprehension at his young friend lolling unconcernedly in his chair. There was no longer any room to doubt what was happening. The 'silly talk' had been translated into terrifying action.

'I think a prairie oyster on the top of a stiffish brandy-and-soda might save my reason,' said Belturbet weakly as he limped towards his club.

It was late in the day before he could steady his nerves sufficiently to glance at the evening papers. The Parliamentary report proved significant reading, and confirmed the fears that he had been trying to shake off. Mr Ap Dave, the Chancellor, whose lively controversial style endeared him to his supporters and embittered him, politically speaking, to his opponents, had risen in his place to make an unprovoked apology for having alluded in a recent speech to certain protesting taxpayers as 'skulkers'. He had realized on reflection that they were in all probability perfectly honest in their inability to understand certain legal technicalities of the new finance laws. The House had scarcely recovered from this sensation when Lord Hugo Sizzle caused a further flutter of astonishment by going out of his way to indulge in an outspoken appreciation of the fairness, loyalty, and straightforwardness not only of the Chancellor, but of all the members of the Cabinet. A wit had gravely suggested moving the adjournment of the House in view of the unexpected circumstances that had arisen.

Belturbet anxiously skimmed over a further item of news printed immediately below the Parliamentary report: 'Wild cat found in an exhausted condition in Palace Yard.'

'Now I wonder which of them —' he mused, and then an appalling idea came to him. 'Supposing he's put them both into the same beast!' He hurriedly ordered another prairie oyster.

Belturbet was known in his club as a strictly moderate drinker; his consumption of alcoholic stimulants that day gave rise to considerable comment.

The events of the next few days were piquantly bewildering to the world at large; to Belturbet, who knew dimly what was happening, the situation was fraught with recurring alarms. The old saying that in politics it's the unexpected that always happens received a justification that it had hitherto somewhat lacked, and the epidemic of startling personal changes of front was not wholly confined to the realm of actual politics. The eminent chocolate magnate, Sadbury, whose antipathy to the Turf and everything connected with it was a matter of general knowledge, had evidently been replaced by an Angel-Sadbury, who proceeded to electrify the public by blossoming forth as an owner of race-horses, giving as a reason his matured conviction that the sport was, after all, one which gave healthy open-air recreation to large numbers of people drawn from all classes of the community, and incidentally stimulated the important industry of horse-breeding. His colours, chocolate and cream hoops spangled with pink stars, promised to become as popular as any on the Turf. At the same time, in order to give effect to his condemnation of the evils resulting from the spread of the gambling habit among wage-earning classes, who lived for the most part from hand to mouth, he suppressed all betting news and tipsters' forecasts in the popular evening paper that was under his control. His action received instant recognition and support from the Angel-proprietor of the *Evening Views*, the principal rival evening halfpenny paper, who forthwith issued an ukase decreeing a similar ban on betting news, and in a short while the regular evening press was purged of all mention of starting prices and probable winners. A considerable drop in the circulation of all these papers was the immediate result, accompanied, of course, by a falling-off in advertisement value, while a crop of special betting broadsheets sprang up to supply the newly-created want. Under their influence the betting habit became if anything rather more widely diffused than before. The Duke had possibly overlooked the futility of koepenicking the leaders of the nation with excellently intentioned angel understudies, while leaving the mass of the people in its original condition.

Further sensation and dislocation was caused in the press world by the sudden and dramatic *rapprochement* which took place between the Angel-Editor of the *Scrutator* and the Angel-Editor of the *Anglian Review*, who not only ceased to criticize and disparage the tone and tendencies of each others' publication, but agreed to exchange editorships for alternating periods. Here again public support was not on the side of the angels; constant readers of the *Scrutator* complained bitterly of the strong meat which was thrust upon them at fitful intervals in place of the almost vegetarian diet to which they had become confidently accustomed; even those who were not mentally averse to strong meat as a separate course were pardonably annoyed at being supplied with it in the pages of the *Scrutator*. To be suddenly confronted with a pungent herring salad when one had attuned oneself to tea and toast, or to discover a richly truffled segment of *paté-de-foie* dissembled in a bowl of bread and milk would be an experience that might upset the equanimity of the most placidly disposed mortal. An equally vehement outcry arose from the regular subscribers of the *Anglian Review*, who protested against being served from time to time with literary fare which no young person of sixteen could possibly want to devour in secret. To take infinite precautions, they complained, against the juvenile perusal of such eminently innocuous literature was like reading the Riot Act on an uninhabited island. Both reviews suffered a serious falling-off in circulation and influence. Peace hath its devastations as well as war.

The wives of noted public men formed another element of discomfiture which the young Duke had almost entirely left out of his calculations. It is sufficiently embarrassing to keep abreast of the possible wobblings and veerings-round of a human husband, who, from the strength or weakness of his personal character, may leap over or slip through the barriers which divide the parties; for this reason a merciful politician usually marries late in life, when he has definitely made up his mind on which side he wishes his wife to be socially valuable. But these trials were as nothing compared to the bewilderment caused by the angel-husbands, who seemed in some cases to have revolutionized their outlook on life in the interval between breakfast and dinner, without premonition or preparation of any kind, and apparently without realizing the least need for subsequent explanation. The temporary peace which brooded over the Parliamentary situation was by no means reproduced in the home circles of the leading statesmen and politicians. It had been frequently and extensively remarked of Mrs Exe that she would try the patience of an angel; now the tables were reversed, and she unwittingly had an opportunity for discovering that the capacity for exasperating behaviour was not all on one side.

And then, with the introduction of the Navy Estimates,

Parliamentary peace suddenly dissolved. It was the old quarrel between Ministers and the Opposition as to the adequacy or the reverse of the Government's naval programme. The Angel Quinston and the Angel Hugo Sizzle contrived to keep the debates free from personalities and pin-pricks, but an enormous sensation was created when the elegant lackadaisical Halfan Halfour threatened to bring up fifty thousand stalwarts to wreck the House if the Estimates were not forthwith revised on a Two-Power basis. It was a memorable scene when he rose in his place, in response to the scandalized shouts of his opponents, and thundered forth, 'Gentlemen, I glory in the name of Apache.'

Belturbet, who had made several fruitless attempts to ring up his young friend since the fateful morning in St James's Park, ran him to earth one afternoon at his club, smooth and spruce and unruffled as ever.

'Tell me, what on earth have you turned Cocksley Coxon into?' Belturbet asked anxiously, mentioning the name of one of the pillars of unorthodoxy in the Anglican Church. 'I don't fancy he *believes* in angels, and if he finds an angel preaching orthodox sermons from his pulpit while he's been turned into a fox-terrier, he'll develop rabies in less than no time.'

'I rather think it was a fox-terrier,' said the Duke lazily.

Belturbet groaned heavily and sank into a chair.

'Look here, Eugène,' he whispered hoarsely, having first looked well round to see that no one was within hearing range, 'you've got to stop it. Consols are jumping up and down like bronchos, and that speech of Halfour's in the House last night has simply startled everybody out of their wits. And then on the top of it, Thistlebery –'

'What has he been saying?' asked the Duke quickly.

'Nothing. That's just what's so disturbing. Everyone thought it was simply inevitable that he should come out with a great epoch-making speech at this juncture, and I've just seen on the tape that he has refused to address any meetings at present, giving as a reason his opinion that something more than mere speechmaking was wanted.'

The young Duke said nothing, but his eyes shone with quiet exultation.

'It's so unlike Thistlebery,' continued Belturbet; 'at least,' he said suspiciously, 'it's unlike the *real* Thistlebery –'

'The real Thistlebery is flying about somewhere as a vocally-industrious lapwing,' said the Duke calmly; 'I expect great things of the Angel-Thistlebery,' he added.

At this moment there was a magnetic stampede of members towards the lobby, where the tape-machines were ticking out some news of more than ordinary import.

'*Coup d'état* in the North. Thistlebery seizes Edinburgh Castle. Threatens civil war unless Government expands naval programme.'

In the babel which ensued Belturbet lost sight of his young friend. For the best part of the afternoon he searched one likely haunt after another, spurred on by the sensational posters which the evening papers were displaying broadcast over the West End. 'General Baden-Baden mobilizes Boy-Scouts. Another *coup d'état* feared. Is Windsor Castle safe?' This was one of the earlier posters, and was followed by one of even more sinister purport: 'Will the Test-match have to be postponed?' It was this disquietening question which brought home the real seriousness of the situation to the London public, and made people wonder whether one might not pay too high a price for the advantages of party government. Belturbet, questing round in the hope of finding the originator of the trouble, with a vague idea of being able to induce him to restore matters to their normal human footing, came across an elderly club acquaintance who dabbled extensively in some of the more sensitive market securities. He was pale with indignation, and his pallor deepened as a breathless newsboy dashed past with a poster inscribed: 'Premier's constituency harried by moss-troopers. Halfour sends encouraging telegram to rioters. Letchworth Garden City threatens reprisals. Foreigners taking refuge in Embassies and National Liberal Club.'

'This is devils' work!' he said angrily.

Belturbet knew otherwise.

At the bottom of St James's Street a newspaper motor-cart, which had just come rapidly along Pall Mall, was surrounded by a knot of eagerly talking people, and for the first time that afternoon Belturbet heard expressions of relief and congratulation.

It displayed a placard with the welcome announcement: 'Crisis ended. Government gives way. Important expansion of naval programme.'

There seemed to be no immediate necessity for pursuing the quest of the errant Duke, and Belturbet turned to make his way homeward through St James's Park. His mind, attuned to the alarums and excursions of the afternoon, became dimly aware that some excitement of a detached nature was going on around him. In spite of the political ferment which reigned in the streets, quite a large crowd had gathered to watch the unfolding of a tragedy that had taken place on the shore of the ornamental water. A large black swan, which had recently shown signs of a savage and dangerous disposition, had suddenly attacked a young gentleman who was walking by the water's edge, dragged him down under the surface, and drowned him before anyone could come to his assistance. At the moment when Belturbet arrived on the spot several park-keepers were engaged in lifting the corpse into a punt. Belturbet stooped to pick up a hat that lay near the scene of the struggle. It was a smart soft felt hat, faintly reminiscent of Houbigant.

More than a month elapsed before Belturbet had sufficiently recovered from his attack of nervous prostration to take an interest once more in what was going on in the world of politics. The Parliamentary Session was still in full swing, and a General Election was looming in the near future. He called for a batch of morning papers and skimmed rapidly through the speeches of the Chancellor, Quinston, and other Ministerial leaders, as well as those of the principal Opposition champions, and then sank back in his chair with a sigh of relief. Evidently the spell had ceased to act after the tragedy which had overtaken its invoker. There was no trace of angel anywhere.

Mrs Packletide's Tiger

It was Mrs Packletide's pleasure and intention that she should shoot a tiger. Not that the lust to kill had suddenly descended on her, or that she felt that she would leave India safer and more wholesome than she had found it, with one fraction less of wild beast per million inhabitants. The compelling motive for her sudden deviation towards the footsteps of Nimrod was the fact that Loona Bimberton had recently been carried eleven miles in an aeroplane by an Algerian aviator, and talked of nothing else;

only a personally procured tiger-skin and a heavy harvest of Press photographs could successfully counter that sort of thing. Mrs Packletide had already arranged in her mind the lunch she would give at her house in Curzon Street, ostensibly in Loona Bimberton's honour, with a tiger-skin rug occupying most of the foreground and all of the conversation. She had also already designed in her mind the tiger-claw brooch that she was going to give Loona Bimberton on her next birthday. In a world that is supposed to be chiefly swayed by hunger and by love, Mrs Packletide was an exception; her movements and motives were largely governed by dislike of Loona Bimberton.

Circumstances proved propitious. Mrs Packletide had offered a thousand rupees for the opportunity of shooting a tiger without overmuch risk or exertion, and it so happened that a neighbouring village could boast of being the favoured rendezvous of an animal of respectable antecedents, which had been driven by the increasing infirmities of age to abandon game-killing and confine its appetite to the smaller domestic animals. The prospect of earning the thousand rupees had stimulated the sporting and commercial instinct of the villagers; children were posted night and day on the outskirts of the local jungle to head the tiger back in the unlikely event of his attempting to roam away to fresh hunting-grounds, and the cheaper kinds of goats were left about with elaborate carelessness to keep him satisfied with his present quarters. The one great anxiety was lest he should die of old age before the date appointed for the memsahib's shoot. Mothers carrying their babies home through the jungle after the day's work in the fields hushed their singing lest they might curtail the restful sleep of the venerable herd-robber.

The great night duly arrived, moonlit and cloudless. A platform had been constructed in a comfortable and conveniently placed tree, and thereon crouched Mrs Packletide and her paid companion, Miss Mebbin. A goat, gifted with a particularly persistent bleat, such as even a partially deaf tiger might be reasonably expected to hear on a still night, was tethered at the correct distance. With an accurately sighted rifle and a thumb-nail pack of patience cards the sportswoman awaited the coming of the quarry.

'I suppose we are in some danger?' said Miss Mebbin.

She was not actually nervous about the wild beast, but she had a morbid dread of performing an atom more service than she had been paid for.

'Nonsense,' said Mrs Packletide; 'it's a very old tiger. It couldn't spring up here even if it wanted to.'

'If it's an old tiger I think you ought to get it cheaper. A thousand rupees is a lot of money.'

Louisa Mebbin adopted a protective elder-sister attitude towards money in general, irrespective of nationality or denomination. Her energetic intervention had saved many a rouble from dissipating itself in tips in some Moscow hotel, and francs and centimes clung to her instinctively under circumstances which would have driven them headlong from less sympathetic hands. Her speculations as to the market depreciation of tiger remnants were cut short by the appearance on the scene of the animal itself. As soon as it caught sight of the tethered goat it lay flat on the earth, seemingly less from a desire to take advantage of all available cover than for the purpose of snatching a short rest before commencing the grand attack.

'I believe it's ill,' said Louisa Mebbin, loudly in Hindustani, for the benefit of the village headman, who was in ambush in a neighbouring tree.

'Hush!' said Mrs Packletide, and at that moment the tiger commenced ambling towards his victim.

'Now, now!' urged Miss Mebbin with some excitement; 'if he doesn't touch the goat we needn't pay for it.' (The bait was an extra.)

The rifle flashed out with a loud report, and the great tawny beast sprang to one side and then rolled over in the stillness of death. In a moment a crowd of excited natives had swarmed on to the scene, and their shouting speedily carried the glad news to the village, where a thumping of tom-toms took up the chorus of triumph. And their triumph and rejoicing found a ready echo in the heart of Mrs Packletide; already that luncheon-party in Curzon Street seemed immeasurably nearer.

It was Louisa Mebbin who drew attention to the fact that the goat was in death-throes from a mortal bullet-wound, while no trace of the rifle's deadly work could be found on the tiger. Evidently the wrong animal had been hit, and the beast of prey had succumbed to heart-failure, caused by the sudden report of the rifle, accelerated by senile decay. Mrs Packletide was pardonably annoyed at the discovery; but at any rate, she was the possessor of a dead tiger, and the villagers, anxious for their thousand rupees, gladly connived at the fiction that she had shot the beast. And Miss Mebbin was a paid companion. Therefore did Mrs Packletide face the cameras with a light heart, and her pictured fame reached from the pages of the *Texas Weekly Snapshot* to the illustrated Monday supplement of the *Novoe Vremya*. As for Loona Bimberton, she refused to look at an illustrated paper for weeks, and her letter of thanks for the gift of a tiger-claw brooch was a model of repressed emotions. The luncheon-party she declined; there are limits beyond which repressed emotions become dangerous.

From Curzon Street the tiger-skin rug travelled down to the Manor House, and was duly inspected and admired by the county, and it seemed a fitting and appropriate thing when Mrs Packletide went to the County Costume Ball in the character of Diana. She refused to fall in, however, with Clovis's tempting suggestion of a primeval dance party, at which every one should wear the skins of beasts they had recently slain. 'I should be in rather a Baby Bunting condition,' confessed Clovis, 'with a miserable rabbit-skin or two to wrap up in, but then,' he added, with a rather malicious glance at Diana's proportions, 'my figure is quite as good as that Russian dancing boy's.'

'How amused everyone would be if they knew what really happened,' said Louisa Mebbin a few days after the ball.

'What do you mean?' asked Mrs Packletide quickly.

'How you shot the goat and frightened the tiger to death,' said Miss Mebbin, with her disagreeably pleasant laugh.

'No one would believe it,' said Mrs Packletide, her face changing colour as rapidly as though it were going through a book of patterns before post-time.

'Loona Bimberton would,' said Miss Mebbin. Mrs Packletide's face settled on an unbecoming shade of greenish white.

'You surely wouldn't give me away?' she asked.

'I've seen a week-end cottage near Dorking that I should rather like to buy,' said Miss Mebbin with seeming irrelevance. 'Six hundred and eighty, freehold. Quite a bargain, only I don't happen to have the money.'

Louisa Mebbin's pretty week-end cottage, christened by her 'Les

Fauves', and gay in summer-time with its garden borders of tigerlilies, is the wonder and admiration of her friends.

'It is a marvel how Louisa manages to do it,' is the general verdict.

Mrs Packletide indulges in no more big-game shooting.

'The incidental expenses are so heavy,' she confides to inquiring friends.

Sredni Vashtar

Conradin was ten years old, and the doctor had pronounced his professional opinion that the boy would not live another five years. The doctor was silky and effete, and counted for little, but his opinion was endorsed by Mrs De Ropp, who counted for nearly everything. Mrs De Ropp was Conradin's cousin and guardian, and in his eyes she represented those three-fifths of the world that are necessary and disagreeable and real; the other two-fifths, in perpetual antagonism to the foregoing, were summed up in himself and his imagination. One of these days Conradin supposed he would succumb to the mastering pressure of wearisome necessary things – such as illnesses and coddling restrictions and drawn-out dullness. Without his imagination, which was rampant under the spur of loneliness, he would have succumbed long ago.

Mrs De Ropp would never, in her honestest moments, have confessed to herself that she disliked Conradin, though she might have been dimly aware that thwarting him 'for his good' was a duty which she did not find particularly irksome. Conradin hated her with a desperate sincerity which he was perfectly able to mask. Such few pleasures as he could contrive for himself gained an added relish from the likelihood that they would be displeasing to his guardian, and from the realm of his imagination she was locked out – an unclean thing, which should find no entrance.

In the dull, cheerless garden, overlooked by so many windows that were ready to open with a message not to do this or that, or a reminder that medicines were due, he found little attraction. The few fruit-trees that it contained were set jealously apart from his plucking, as though they were rare specimens of their kind blooming in an arid waste; it would probably have been difficult to find a market-gardener who would have offered ten shillings for the entire yearly produce. In a forgotten corner, however, almost hidden behind a dismal shrubbery, was a disused tool-shed of respectable proportions, and within its walls Conradin found a haven, something that took on the varying aspects of a playroom and a cathedral. He had peopled it with a legion of familiar phantoms, evoked partly from fragments of history and partly from his own brain, but it also boasted two inmates of flesh and blood. In one corner lived a ragged-plumaged Houdan hen, on which the boy lavished an affection that had scarcely another outlet. Further back in the gloom stood a large hutch, divided into two compartments, one of which was fronted with close iron bars. This was the abode of a large polecat-ferret, which a friendly butcher-boy had once smuggled, cage and all, into its present quarters, in exchange for a long-secreted hoard of small silver. Conradin was dreadfully afraid of the lithe, sharp-fanged beast, but it was his most treasured possession. Its very presence in the tool-shed was a secret and fearful joy, to be kept scrupulously from the knowledge of the Woman, as he privately dubbed his cousin. And one day, out of Heaven knows what material, he spun the beast a wonderful name, and from that moment it grew into a god and a religion. The Woman indulged in religion once a week at a church near by, and took Conradin with her, but to him the church service was an alien rite in the House of Rimmon. Every Thursday, in the dim and musty silence of the tool-shed, he worshipped with mystic and elaborate ceremonial before the wood hutch where dwelt Sredni Vashtar, the great ferret. Red flowers in their season and scarlet berries in the winter-time were offered at his shrine, for he was a god who laid some special stress on the fierce impatient side of things, as opposed to the Woman's religion, which, as far as Conradin could observe, went to great lengths in the contrary direction. And on great festivals powdered nutmeg was strewn in front of his hutch, an important feature of the offering being that the nutmeg had to be stolen. These festivals were of irregular occurrence, and were chiefly appointed to celebrate some passing event. On one occasion, when Mrs De Ropp suffered from acute toothache for three days, Conradin kept up the festival during the entire three days, and almost succeeded in persuading himself that Sredni Vashtar was personally responsible for the toothache. If the malady had lasted for another day the supply of nutmeg would have given out.

The Houdan hen was never drawn into the cult of Sredni Vashtar. Conradin had long ago settled that she was an Anabaptist. He did not pretend to have the remotest knowledge as to what an Anabaptist was, but he privately hoped that it was dashing and not very respectable. Mrs De Ropp was the ground plan on which he based and detested all respectability.

After a while Conradin's absorption in the tool-shed began to attract the notice of his guardian. 'It is not good for him to be pottering down there in all weathers,' she promptly decided, and at breakfast one morning she announced that the Houdan hen had been sold and taken away overnight. With her short-sighted eyes she peered at Conradin, waiting for an outbreak of rage and sorrow, which she was ready to rebuke with a flow of excellent precepts and reasoning. But Conradin said nothing: there was nothing to be said. Something perhaps in his white set face gave her a momentary qualm, for at tea that afternoon there was toast on the table, a delicacy which she usually banned on the ground that it was bad for him; also because the making of it 'gave trouble', a deadly offence in the middle-class feminine eye.

'I thought you liked toast,' she exclaimed, with an injured air, observing that he did not touch it.

'Sometimes,' said Conradin.

In the shed that evening there was an innovation in the worship of the hutch-god. Conradin had been wont to chant his praises, tonight he asked a boon.

'Do one thing for me, Sredni Vashtar.'

The thing was not specified. As Sredni Vashtar was a god he must be supposed to know. And choking back a sob as he looked at that other empty corner, Conradin went back to the world he so hated.

And every night, in the welcome darkness of his bedroom, and every evening in the dusk of the tool-shed, Conradin's bitter litany went up: 'Do one thing for me, Sredni Vashtar.'

Mrs De Ropp noticed that the visits to the shed did not cease, and one day she made a further journey of inspection.

'What are you keeping in that locked hutch?' she asked. 'I believe it's guinea-pigs. I'll have them all cleared away.'

Conradin shut his lips tight, but the Woman ransacked his bedroom till she found the carefully hidden key, and forthwith marched down to the shed to complete her discovery. It was a cold afternoon, and Conradin had been bidden to keep to the house. From the furthest window of the dining-room the door of the shed could just be seen beyond the corner of the shrubbery, and there Conradin stationed himself. He saw the Woman enter, and then he imagined her opening the door of the sacred hutch and peering down with her short-sighed eyes into the thick straw bed where his god lay hidden. Perhaps she would prod at the straw in her clumsy impatience. And Conradin fervently breathed his prayer for the last time. But he knew as he prayed that he did not believe. He knew that the Woman would come out presently with that pursed smile he loathed so well on her face, and that in an hour or two the gardener would carry away his wonderful god, a god no longer, but a simple brown ferret in a hutch. And he knew that the Woman would triumph always as she triumphed now, and that he would grow ever more sickly under her pestering and domineering and superior wisdom, till one day nothing would matter much more with him, and the doctor would be proved right. And in the sting and misery of his defeat, he began to chant loudly and defiantly the hymn of his threatened idol:

Sredni Vashtar went forth,
His thoughts were red thoughts and his teeth were white.
His enemies called for peace, but he brought them death.
Sredni Vashtar the Beautiful.

And then of a sudden he stopped his chanting and drew closer to the window-pane. The door of the shed still stood ajar as it had been left, and the minutes were slipping by. They were long minutes, but they slipped by nevertheless. He watched the starlings running and flying in little parties across the lawn; he counted them over and over again, with one eye always on that swinging door. A sour-faced maid came in to lay the table for tea, and still Conradin stood and waited and watched. Hope had crept by inches into his heart, and now a look of triumph began to blaze in his eyes that had only known the wistful patience of defeat. Under his breath, with a furtive exultation, he began once again the paean of victory and devastation. And presently his eyes were rewarded: out through that doorway came a long, low, yellow-and-brown beast, with eyes a-blink at the waning daylight, and dark wet stains around the fur of jaw and throat. Conradin dropped on his knees. The great polecat ferret made its way down to a small brook at the foot of the garden, drank for a moment, then crossed a little plank bridge and was lost to sight in the bushes. Such was the passing of Sredni Vashtar.

'Tea is ready,' said the sour-faced maid; 'where is the mistress?' 'She went down to the shed some time ago,' said Conradin.

And while the maid went to summon her mistress to tea, Conradin fished a toasting-fork out of the sideboard drawer and proceeded to toast himself a piece of bread. And during the toasting of it and the buttering of it with much butter and the slow enjoyment of eating it, Conradin listened to the noises and silences which fell in quick spasms beyond the dining-room door. The loud foolish screaming of the maid, the answering chorus of wondering ejaculations from the kitchen region, the scuttering footsteps and hurried embassies for outside help, and then, after a lull, the scared sobbings and the shuffling tread of those who bore a heavy burden into the house.

'Whoever will break it to the poor child? I couldn't for the life of me!' exclaimed a shrill voice. And while they debated the matter among themselves, Conradin made himself another piece of toast.

The Music on the Hill

Sylvia Seltoun ate her breakfast in the morning-room at Yessney with a pleasant sense of ultimate victory, such as a fervent Ironside might have permitted himself on the morrow of Worcester fight. She was scarcely pugnacious by temperament, but belonged to that more successful class of fighters who are pugnacious by circumstance. Fate had willed that her life should be occupied with a series of small struggles, usually with the odds slightly against her, and usually she had just managed to come through winning. And now she felt she had brought her hardest and certainly her most important struggle to a successful issue. To have married Mortimer Seltoun, 'Dead Mortimer' as his more intimate enemies called him, in the teeth of the cold hostility of his family, and in spite of his unaffected indifference to women, was indeed an achievement that had needed some determination and adroitness to carry through; yesterday she had brought her victory to its concluding stage by wrenching her husband away from Town and its group of satellite watering-places and 'settling him down', in the vocabulary of her kind, in this remote wood-girt manor farm which was his country house.

'You will never get Mortimer to go,' his mother had said carpingly, 'but if he once goes he'll stay; Yessney throws almost as much a spell over him as Town does. One can understand what holds him to Town, but Yessney –' and the dowager had shrugged her shoulders.

There was a sombre almost savage wildness about Yessney that was certainly not likely to appeal to town-bred tastes, and Sylvia, notwithstanding her name, was accustomed to nothing much more sylvan than 'leafy Kensington'. She looked on the country as something excellent and wholesome in its way, which was apt to become troublesome if you encouraged it overmuch. Distrust of town-life had been a new thing with her, born of her marriage with Mortimer, and she had watched with satisfaction the gradual fading of what she called 'the Jermyn-street-look' in his eyes as the woods and heather of Yessney had closed in on them yesternight. Her will-power and strategy had prevailed; Mortimer would stay.

Outside the morning-room windows was a triangular slope of turf, which the indulgent might call a lawn, and beyond its low hedge of neglected fuchsia bushes a steeper slope of heather and bracken dropped down into cavernous combes overgrown with oak and yew. In its wild open savagery there seemed a stealthy linking of the joy of life with the terror of unseen things. Sylvia smiled complacently as she gazed with a School-of-Art appreciation at the landscape, and then of a sudden she almost shuddered.

'It is very wild,' she said to Mortimer, who had joined her; 'one could almost think that in such a place the worship of Pan had never quite died out.'

'The worship of Pan never has died out,' said Mortimer. 'Other newer gods have drawn aside his votaries from time to time, but he is the Nature-God to whom all must come back at last. He has been called the Father of all the Gods, but most of his children have been stillborn.'

Sylvia was religious in an honest vaguely devotional kind of way, and did not like to hear her beliefs spoken of as mere aftergrowths, but it was at least something new and hopeful to hear Dead Mortimer speak with such energy and conviction on any subject.

'You don't really believe in Pan?' she asked incredulously.

'I've been a fool in most things,' said Mortimer quietly, 'but I'm not such a fool as not to believe in Pan when I'm down here. And if you're wise you won't disbelieve in him too boastfully while you're in his country.'

It was not till a week later, when Sylvia had exhausted the attractions of the woodland walks round Yessney, that she ventured on a tour of inspection of the farm buildings. A farmyard suggested in her mind a scene of cheerful bustle, with churns and flails and smiling dairymaids, and teams of horses drinking knee-deep in duck-crowded ponds. As she wandered among the gaunt grey buildings of Yessney manor farm her first impression was one of crushing stillness and desolation, as though she had happened on some lone deserted homestead long given over to owls and cobwebs; then came a sense of furtive watchful hostility, the same shadow of unseen things that seemed to lurk in the wooded combes and coppices. From behind heavy doors and shuttered windows came the restless stamp of hoof or rasp of chain halter, and at times a muffled bellow from some stalled beast. From a distant corner a shaggy dog watched her with intent unfriendly eyes; as she drew near it slipped quietly into its kennel, and slipped out again as noiselessly when she had passed by. A few hens, questing for food under a rick, stole away under a gate at her approach. Sylvia felt that if she had come across any human beings in this wilderness of barn and byre they would have fled wraith-like from her gaze. At last, turning a corner quickly, she came upon a living thing that did not fly from her. Astretch in a pool of mud was an enormous sow, gigantic beyond the town-woman's wildest computation of swine-flesh, and speedily alert to resent and if necessary repel the unwonted intrusion. It was Sylvia's turn to make an unobtrusive retreat. As she threaded her way past rickyards and cowsheds and long blank walls, she started suddenly at a strange sound –

the echo of a boy's laughter, golden and equivocal. Jan, the only boy employed on the farm, a tow-headed, wizen-faced yokel, was visibly at work on a potato clearing half-way up the nearest hill-side, and Mortimer, when questioned, knew of no other probable or possible begetter of the hidden mockery that had ambushed Sylvia's retreat. The memory of that untraceable echo was added to her other impressions of a furtive sinister 'something' that hung around Yessney.

Of Mortimer she saw very little; farm and woods and trout-streams seemed to swallow him up from dawn till dusk. Once, following the direction she had seen him take in the morning, she came to an open space in a nut copse, further shut in by huge yew trees, in the centre of which stood a stone pedestal surmounted by a small bronze figure of a youthful Pan. It was a beautiful piece of workmanship, but her attention was chiefly held by the fact that a newly cut bunch of grapes had been placed as an offering at its feet. Grapes were none too plentiful at the manor house, and Sylvia snatched the bunch angrily from the pedestal. Contemptuous annoyance dominated her thoughts as she strolled slowly homeward, and then gave way to a sharp feeling of something that was very near fright; across a thick tangle of undergrowth a boy's face was scowling at her, brown and beautiful, with unutterably evil eyes. It was a lonely pathway, all pathways round Yessney were lonely for the matter of that, and she sped forward without waiting to give a closer scrutiny to this sudden apparition. It was not till she had reached the house that she discovered that she had dropped the bunch of grapes in her flight.

'I saw a youth in the wood today,' she told Mortimer that evening, 'brown-faced and rather handsome, but a scoundrel to look at. A gipsy lad, I suppose.'

'A reasonable theory,' said Mortimer, 'only there aren't any gipsies in these parts at present.'

'Then who was he?' asked Sylvia, and as Mortimer appeared to have no theory of his own, she passed on to recount her finding of the votive offering.

'I suppose it was your doing,' she observed; 'it's a harmless piece of lunacy, but people would think you dreadfully silly if they knew of it.'

'Did you meddle with it in any way?' asked Mortimer.

'I – I threw the grapes away. It seemed so silly,' said Sylvia, watching Mortimer's impassive face for a sign of annoyance.

'I don't think you were wise to do that,' he said reflectively. 'I've heard it said that the Wood Gods are rather horrible to those who molest them.'

'Horrible perhaps to those that believe in them, but you see I don't,' retorted Sylvia.

'All the same,' said Mortimer in his even, dispassionate tone, 'I should avoid the woods and orchards if I were you, and give a wide berth to the horned beasts on the farm.'

It was all nonsense, of course, but in that lonely wood-girt spot nonsense seemed able to rear a bastard brood of uneasiness.

'Mortimer,' said Sylvia suddenly, 'I think we will go back to Town some time soon.'

Her victory had not been so complete as she had supposed; it had carried her on to ground that she was already anxious to quit.

'I don't think you will ever go back to Town,' said Mortimer. He seemed to be paraphrasing his mother's prediction as to himself.

Sylvia noted with dissatisfaction and some self-contempt that the course of her next afternoon's ramble took her instinctively clear of the network of woods. As to the horned cattle, Mortimer's warning was scarcely needed, for she had always regarded them as of doubtful neutrality at the best: her imagination unsexed the most matronly dairy cows and turned them into bulls liable to 'see red' at any moment. The ram who fed in the narrow paddock below the orchards she had adjudged, after ample and cautious probation, to be of docile temper; today, however, she decided to leave his docility untested, for the usually tranquil beast was roaming with every sign of restlessness from corner to corner of his meadow. A long, fitful piping, as of some reedy flute, was coming from the depth of a neighbouring copse, and there seemed to be some subtle connection between the animal's restless pacing and the wild music from the wood. Sylvia turned her steps in an upward direction and climbed the heatherclad slopes that stretched in rolling shoulders high above Yessney. She had left the piping notes behind her, but across the wooded combes at her feet the wind brought her another kind of music, the straining bay of hounds in full chase. Yessney was just on the outskirts of the Devon-and-Somerset country, and the hunted deer sometimes came that way. Syliva could presently see a dark body, breasting hill after hill, and sinking again and again out of sight as he crossed the combes, while behind him steadily swelled the relentless chorus, and she grew tense with the excited sympathy that one feels for any hunted thing in whose capture one is not directly interested. And at last he broke through the outermost line of oak scrub and fern and stood panting in the open, a fat September stag carrying a well-furnished head. His obvious course was to drop down to the brown pools of Undercombe, and thence make his way towards the red deer's favoured sanctuary, the sea. To Sylvia's surprise, however, he turned his head to the upland slope and came lumbering resolutely onward over the heather. 'It will be dreadful,' she thought, 'the hounds will pull him down under my very eyes.' But the music of the pack seemed to have died away for a moment, and in its place she heard again that wild piping, which rose now on this side, now on that, as though urging the failing stag to a final effort. Sylvia stood well aside from his path, half hidden in a thick growth of whortle bushes, and watched him swing stiffly upward, his flanks dark with sweat, the coarse hair on his neck showing light by contrast. The pipe music shrilled suddenly around her, seeming to come from the bushes at her very feet, and at the same moment the great beast slewed round and bore directly down upon her. In an instant her pity for the hunted animal was changed to wild terror at her own danger; the thick heather roots mocked her scrambling efforts at flight, and she looked frantically downward for a glimpse of oncoming hounds. The huge antler spikes were within a few yards of her, and in a flash of numbing fear she remembered Mortimer's warning, to beware of horned beasts on the farm. And then with a quick throb of joy she saw that she was not alone; a human figure stood a few paces aside, knee-deep in the whortle bushes.

'Drive it off!' she shrieked. But the figure made no answering movement.

The antlers drove straight at her breast, the acrid smell of the hunted animal was in her nostrils, but her eyes were filled with the horror of something she saw other than her oncoming death. And in her ears rang the echo of a boy's laughter, golden and equivocal.

The Quest

An unwonted peace hung over the Villa Elsinore, broken, however, at frequent intervals, by clamorous lamentations suggestive of bewildered bereavement. The Momebys had lost their infant child; hence the peace which its absence entailed; they were looking for it in wild, undisciplined fashion, giving tongue the whole time, which accounted for the outcry which swept through house and garden whenever they returned to try the home coverts anew. Clovis, who was temporarily and unwillingly a paying guest at the villa, had been dozing in a hammock at the far end of the garden when Mrs Momeby had broken the news to him.

'We've lost Baby,' she screamed.

'Do you mean that it's dead, or stampeded, or that you staked it at cards and lost it that way?' asked Clovis lazily.

'He was toddling about quite happily on the lawn,' said Mrs Momeby tearfully, 'and Arnold had just come in, and I was asking him what sort of sauce he would like with the asparagus –'

'I hope he said hollandaise,' interrupted Clovis, with a show of quickened interest, 'because if there's anything I hate –'

'And all of a sudden I missed Baby,' continued Mrs Momeby in a shriller tone. 'We've hunted high and low, in house and garden and outside the gates, and he's nowhere to be seen.'

'Is he anywhere to be heard?' asked Clovis; 'if not, he must be at least two miles away.'

'But where? And how?' asked the distracted mother.

'Perhaps an eagle or a wild beast has carried him off,' suggested Clovis.

'There aren't eagles and wild beasts in Surrey,' said Mrs Momeby, but a note of horror had crept into her voice.

'They escape now and then from travelling shows. Sometimes I think they let them get loose for the sake of the advertisement. Think what a sensational headline it would make in the local papers: "Infant son of prominent Nonconformist devoured by spotted hyena." Your husband isn't a prominent Nonconformist, but his mother came of Wesleyan stock, and you must allow the newspapers some latitude.'

'But we should have found his remains,' sobbed Mrs Momeby.

'If the hyena was really hungry and not merely toying with his food there wouldn't be much in the way of remains. It would be like the small-boy-and-apple story – there ain't going to be no core.'

Mrs Momeby turned away hastily to seek comfort and counsel in some other direction. With the selfish absorption of young motherhood she entirely disregarded Clovis's obvious anxiety about the asparagus sauce. Before she had gone a yard, however, the click of the side-gate caused her to pull up sharp. Miss Gilpet, from the Villa Peterhof, had come over to hear details of the bereavement. Clovis was already rather bored with the story, but Mrs Momeby was equipped with that merciless faculty which finds as much joy in the ninetieth time of telling as in the first.

'Arnold had just come in; he was complaining of rheumatism –'

'There are so many things to complain of in this household that it would never have occurred to me to complain of rheumatism,' murmured Clovis.

'He was complaining of rheumatism,' continued Mrs Momeby, trying to throw a chilling inflection into a voice that was already doing a good deal of sobbing and talking at high pressure as well.

She was again interrupted.

'There is no such thing as rheumatism,' said Miss Gilpet. She said it with the conscious air of defiance that a waiter adopts in announcing that the cheapest-priced claret in the wine-list is no more. She did not proceed, however, to offer the alternative of some more expensive malady, but denied the existence of them all.

Mrs Momeby's temper began to shine out through her grief.

'I suppose you'll say next that Baby hasn't really disappeared.'

'He has disappeared,' conceded Miss Gilpet, 'but only because you haven't sufficient faith to find him. It's only lack of faith on your part that prevents him from being restored to you safe and well.'

'But if he's been eaten in the meantime by a hyena and partly digested,' said Clovis, who clung affectionately to his wild beast theory, 'surely some ill-effects would be noticeable?'

Miss Gilpet was rather staggered by this complication of the question.

'I feel sure that a hyena has not eaten him,' she said lamely.

'The hyena may be equally certain that it has. You see, it may have just as much faith as you have, and more special knowledge as to the present whereabouts of the baby.'

Mrs Momeby was in tears again. 'If you have faith,' she sobbed, struck by a happy inspiration, 'won't you find our little Erik for us? I am sure you have powers that are denied to us.'

Rose-Marie Gilpet was thoroughly sincere in her adherence to Christian Science principles; whether she understood or correctly expounded them the learned in such matters may best decide. In the present case she was undoubtedly confronted with a great opportunity, and as she started forth on her vague search she strenuously summoned to her aid every scrap of faith that she possessed. She passed out into the bare and open high road, followed by Mrs Momeby's warning, 'It's no use going there, we've searched there a dozen times.' But Rose-Marie's ears were already deaf to all things save self-congratulation; for sitting in the middle of the highway, playing contentedly with the dust and some faded buttercups, was a white-pinafored baby with a mop of tow-coloured hair tied over one temple with a pale-blue ribbon. Taking first the usual feminine precaution of looking to see that no motor-car was on the distant horizon, Rose-Marie dashed at the child and bore it, despite its vigorous opposition, in through the portals of Elsinore. The child's furious screams had already announced the fact of its discovery, and the almost hysterical parents raced down the lawn to meet their restored offspring. The aesthetic value of the scene was marred in some degree by Rose-Marie's difficulty in holding the struggling infant, which was borne wrong-end foremost towards the agitated bosom of its family. 'Our own little Erik come back to us,' cried the Momebys in unison; as the child had rammed its fists tightly into its eyesockets and nothing could be seen of its face but a widely gaping mouth, the recognition was in itself almost an act of faith.

'Is he glad to get back to Daddy and Mummy again?' crooned Mrs Momeby; the preference which the child was showing for its dust and buttercup distractions was so marked that the question struck Clovis as being unnecessarily tactless.

'Give him a ride on the roly-poly,' suggested the father brilliantly as the howls continued with no sign of early abatement. In a moment the child had been placed astride the big garden roller and a preliminary tug was given to set it in motion.

From the hollow depths of the cylinder came an earsplitting roar, drowning even the vocal efforts of the squalling baby, and immediately afterwards there crept forth a white-pinafored infant with a mop of tow-coloured hair tied over one temple with a pale blue ribbon. There was no mistaking either the features or the lung-power of the new arrival.

'Our own little Erik,' screamed Mrs Momeby, pouncing on him and nearly smothering him with kisses; 'did he hide in the rolypoly to give us all a big fright?'

This was the obvious explanation of the child's sudden disappearance and equally abrupt discovery. There remained, however, the problem of the interloping baby, which now sat whimpering on the lawn in a disfavour as chilling as its previous popularity had been unwelcome. The Momebys glared at it as though it had wormed its way into their short-lived affections by heartless and unworthy pretences. Miss Gilpet's face took on an ashen tinge as she stared helplessly at the bunched-up figure that had been such a gladsome sight to her eyes a few moments ago.

'When love is over, how little of love even the lover understands,' quoted Clovis to himself.

Rose-Marie was the first to break the silence.

'If that is Erik you have in your arms, who is – that?'

'That, I think, is for you to explain,' said Mrs Momeby stiffly.

'Obviously,' said Clovis, 'it's a duplicate Erik that your powers of faith called into being. The question is, what are you going to do with him?'

The ashen pallor deepened in Rose-Marie's cheeks. Mrs Momeby clutched the genuine Erik closer to her side as though she feared that her uncanny neighbour might out of sheer pique turn him into a bowl of gold-fish.

'I found him sitting in the middle of the road,' said Rose-Marie weakly.

'You can't take him back and leave him there,' said Clovis; 'the highway is meant for traffic, not to be used as a lumber-room for disused miracles.'

Rose-Marie wept. The proverb 'Weep, and you weep alone,' broke down as badly on application as most of its kind. Both babies were wailing lugubriously, and the parent Momebys had scarcely recovered from their earlier lachrymose condition. Clovis alone maintained an unruffled cheerfulness.

'Must I keep him always?' asked Rose-Marie dolefully.

'Not always,' said Clovis consolingly; 'he can go into the Navy when he's thirteen.' Rose-Marie wept afresh.

'Of course,' added Clovis, 'there may be no end of a bother about his birth certificate. You'll have to explain matters to the Admiralty, and they're dreadfully hidebound.'

It was rather a relief when a breathless nursemaid from the Villa Charlottenburg over the way came running across the lawn to claim little Percy, who had slipped out of the front gate and disappeared like a twinkling from the high road.

And even then Clovis found it necessary to go in person to the kitchen to make sure about the asparagus sauce.

The Secret Sin of Septimus Brope

'Who and what is Mr Brope?' demanded the aunt of Clovis suddenly.

Mrs Riversedge, who had been snipping off the heads of defunct roses, and thinking of nothing in particular, sprang hurriedly to mental attention. She was one of those old-fashioned hostesses who consider that one ought to know something about one's guests, and that the something ought to be to their credit.

'I believe he comes from Leighton Buzzard,' she observed by way of preliminary explanation.

'In these days of rapid and convenient travel,' said Clovis, who was dispersing a colony of green-fly with visitations of cigarette smoke, 'to come from Leighton Buzzard does not necessarily denote any great strength of character. It might only mean mere restlessness. Now if he had left it under a cloud, or as a "protest against the incurable and heartless frivolity of its inhabitants", that would tell us something about the man and his mission in life.'

'What does he do?' pursued Mrs Troyle magisterially.

'He edits the *Cathedral Monthly*,' said her hostess, 'and he's enormously learned about memorial brasses and transepts and the influence of Byzantine worship on modern liturgy, and all those sort of things. Perhaps he is just a little bit heavy and immersed in one range of subjects, but it takes all sorts to make a good house-party, you know. You don't find him *too* dull, do you?'

'Dullness I could overlook,' said the aunt of Clovis: 'what I cannot forgive is his making love to my maid.'

'My dear Mrs Troyle,' gasped the hostess, 'what an extraordinary idea! I assure you Mr Brope would not dream of doing such a thing.'

'His dreams are a matter of indifference to me; for all I care his slumbers may be one long indiscretion of unsuitable erotic advances, in which the entire servants' hall may be involved. But in his waking hours he shall not make love to my maid. It's no use arguing about it, I'm firm on the point.'

'But you must be mistaken,' persisted Mrs Riversedge; 'Mr Brope would be the last person to do such a thing.'

'He is the first person to do such a thing, as far as my information goes, and if I have any voice in the matter he certainly shall be the last. Of course, I am not referring to respectably-intentioned lovers.'

'I simply cannot think that a man who writes so charmingly and informingly about transepts and Byzantine influences would behave in such an unprincipled manner,' said Mrs Riversedge; 'what evidence have you that he's doing anything of the sort? I don't want to doubt your word, of course, but we mustn't be too ready to condemn him unheard, must we?'

'Whether we condemn him or not, he has certainly not been unheard. He has the room next to my dressing-room, and on two occasions, when I daresay he thought I was absent, I have plainly heard him announcing through the wall, "I love you, Florrie." Those partition walls upstairs are very thin; one can almost hear a watch ticking in the next room.'

'Is your maid called Florence?'

'Her name is Florinda.'

'What an extraordinary name to give a maid!'

'I did not give it to her; she arrived in my service already christened.'

'What I mean is,' said Mrs Riversedge, 'that when I get maids with unsuitable names I call them Jane; they soon get used to it.'

'An excellent plan,' said the aunt of Clovis coldly, 'unfortunately I have got used to being called Jane myself. It happens to be my name.'

She cut short Mrs Riversedge's flood of apologies by abruptly remarking:

'The question is not whether I'm to call my maid Florinda, but whether Mr Brope is to be permitted to call her Florrie. I am strongly of opinion that he shall not.'

'He may have been repeating the words of some song,' said Mrs Riversedge hopefully; 'there are lots of those sorts of silly refrains with girls' names,' she continued, turning to Clovis as a possible authority on the subject. "You mustn't call me Mary –"'

'I shouldn't think of doing so,' Clovis assured her; 'in the first place, I've always understood that your name was Henrietta; and then I hardly know you well enough to take such a liberty.'

'I mean there's a *song* with that refrain,' hurriedly explained Mrs Riversedge, 'and there's "Rhoda, Rhoda kept a pagoda," and "Maisie is a daisy," and heaps of others. Certainly it doesn't sound like Mr Brope to be singing such songs, but I think we ought to give him the benefit of the doubt.'

'I had already done so,' said Mrs Troyle, 'until further evidence came my way.'

She shut her lips with the resolute finality of one who enjoys the blessed certainty of being implored to open them again.

'Further evidence!' exclaimed her hostess; 'do tell me!'

'As I was coming upstairs after breakfast Mr Brope was just passing my room. In the most natural way in the world a piece of paper dropped out of a packet that he held in his hand and fluttered to the ground just at my door. I was going to call out to him "You've dropped something," and then for some reason I held back and didn't show myself till he was safely in his room. You see it occurred to me that I was very seldom in my room just at that hour, and that Florinda was almost always there tidying up things about that time. So I picked up that innocent-looking piece of paper.'

Mrs Troyle paused again, with the self-applauding air of one who has detected an asp lurking in an apple-charlotte.

Mrs Riversedge snipped vigorously at the nearest rose bush, incidentally decapitating a Viscountess Folkestone that was just coming into bloom.

'What was on the paper?' she asked.

'Just the words in pencil, "I love you, Florrie," and then

underneath, crossed out with a faint line, but perfectly plain to read, "Meet me in the garden by the yew."'

There *is* a yew tree at the bottom of the garden,' admitted Mrs Riversedge.

'At any rate he appears to be truthful,' commented Clovis.

'To think that a scandal of this sort should be going on under my roof!' said Mrs Riversedge indignantly.

'I wonder why it is that scandal seems so much worse under a roof,' observed Clovis; 'I've always regarded it as a proof of the superior delicacy of the cat tribe that it conducts most of its scandals above the slates.'

'Now I come to think of it,' resumed Mrs Riversedge, 'there are things about Mr Brope that I've never been able to account for. His income, for instance: he only gets two hundred a year as editor of the *Cathedral Monthly*, and I know that his people are quite poor, and he hasn't any private means. Yet he manages to afford a flat somewhere in Westminster, and he goes abroad to Bruges and those sorts of places every year, and always dresses well, and gives quite nice luncheon-parties in the season. You can't do all that on two hundred a year, can you?'

'Does he write for any other papers?' queried Mrs Troyle.

'No, you see he specializes so entirely on liturgy and ecclesiastical architecture that his field is rather restricted. He once tried the *Sporting and Dramatic* and an article on church edifices in famous fox-hunting centres, but it wasn't considered of sufficient general interest to be accepted. No, I don't see how he can support himself in his present style merely by what he writes.'

'Perhaps he sells spurious transepts to American enthusiasts,' suggested Clovis.

'How could you sell a transept?' said Mrs Riversedge; 'such a thing would be impossible.'

'Whatever he may do to eke out his income,' interrupted Mrs Troyle, 'he is certainly not going to fill in his leisure moments by making love to my maid.'

'Of course not,' agreed her hostess; 'that must be put a stop to at once. But I don't quite know what we ought to do.'

'You might put a barbed wire entanglement round the yew tree as a precautionary measure,' said Clovis.

'I don't think that the disagreeable situation that has arisen is improved by flippancy,' said Mrs Riversedge; 'a good maid is a treasure –'

'I am sure I don't know what I should do without Florinda,' admitted Mrs Troyle; 'she understands my hair. I've long ago given up trying to do anything with it myself. I regard one's hair as I regard husbands: as long as one is seen together in public one's private divergences don't matter. Surely that was the luncheon gong.'

Septimus Brope and Clovis had the smoking-room to themselves after lunch. The former seemed restless and preoccupied, the latter quietly observant.

'What is a lorry?' asked Septimus suddenly; 'I don't mean the thing on wheels, of course I know what that is, but isn't there a bird with a name like that, the larger form of a lorikeet?'

'I fancy it's a lorry, with one "r",' said Clovis lazily, 'in which case it's no good to you.'

Septimus Brope stared in some astonishment.

'How do you mean, no good to me?' he asked, with more than a trace of uneasiness in his voice.

'Won't rhyme with Florrie,' explained Clovis briefly.

Septimus sat upright in his chair, with unmistakable alarm on his face.

'How did you find out? I mean, how did you know I was trying to get a rhyme to Florrie?' he asked sharply.

'I didn't know,' said Clovis, 'I only guessed. When you wanted to turn the prosaic lorry of commerce into a feathered poem flitting through the verdure of a tropical forest, I knew you must be working up a sonnet, and Florrie was the only female name that suggested itself as rhyming with lorry.'

Septimus still looked uneasy.

'I believe you know more,' he said.

Clovis laughed quietly, but said nothing.

'How much do you know?' Septimus asked desperately.

'The yew tree in the garden,' said Clovis.

'There! I felt certain I'd dropped it somewhere. But you must have guessed something before. Look here, you have surprised my secret. You won't give me away, will you? It is nothing to be ashamed of, but it wouldn't do for the editor of the *Cathedral Monthly* to go in openly for that sort of thing, would it?'

'Well, I suppose not,' admitted Clovis.

'You see,' continued Septimus, 'I get quite a decent lot of money out of it. I could never live in the style I do on what I get as editor of the *Cathedral Monthly*.'

Clovis was even more startled than Septimus had been earlier in the conversation, but he was better skilled in repressing surprise.

'Do you mean to say you get money out of – Florrie?' he asked.

'Not out of Florrie, as yet,' said Septimus; 'in fact, I don't mind saying that I'm having a good deal of trouble over Florrie. But there are a lot of others.'

Clovis's cigarette went out.

'This is *very* interesting,' he said slowly. And then, with Septimus Brope's next words, illumination dawned on him.

'There are heaps of others; for instance:

> Cora with the lips of coral,
> You and I will never quarrel.

'That was one of my earliest successes, and it still brings me in royalties. And then there is – "Esmeralda, when I first beheld her," and "Fair Teresa, how I love to please her," both of those have been fairly popular. And there is one rather dreadful one,' continued Septimus, flushing deep carmine, 'which has brought me in more money than any of the others:

> Lively little Lucie
> With her naughty nez retroussé.

'Of course, I loathe the whole lot of them; in fact, I'm rapidly becoming something of a woman-hater under their influence, but I can't afford to disregard the financial aspect of the matter. And at the same time you can understand that my position as an authority on ecclesiastical architecture and liturgical subjects would be weakened, if not altogether ruined, if it once got about that I was the author of "Cora with the lips of coral" and all the rest of them.'

Clovis had recovered sufficiently to ask in a sympathetic if rather unsteady, voice what was the special trouble with 'Florrie'.

'I can't get her into lyric shape, try as I will,' said Septimus mournfully. 'You see, one has to work in a lot of sentimental, sugary compliment with a catchy rhyme, and a certain amount of personal biography or prophecy. They've all of them got to have a long string of past successes recorded about them, or else you've got to foretell blissful things about them and yourself in the future. For instance, there is:

> Dainty little girlie Mavis,
> She is such a rara avis,
> All the money I can save is
> All to be for Mavis mine.

'It goes to a sickening namby-pamby waltz tune, and for months nothing else was sung and hummed in Blackpool and other popular centres.'

This time Clovis's self-control broke down badly.

'Please excuse me,' he gurgled, 'but I can't help it when I remember the awful solemnity of that article of yours that you so kindly read us last night, on the Coptic Church in its relation to early Christian worship.'

Septimus groaned.

'You see how it would be,' he said; 'as soon as people knew me to be the author of that miserable sentimental twaddle, all respect for the serious labours of my life would be gone. I dare say I know more about memorial brasses than anyone living, in fact I hope one day to publish a monograph on the subject, but I should be pointed out everywhere as the man whose ditties were in the mouths of nigger minstrels along the entire coastline of our Island home. Can you wonder that I positively hate Florrie all the time that I'm trying to grind out sugar-coated rhapsodies about her?'

'Why not give free play to your emotions and be brutally abusive? An uncomplimentary refrain would have an instant success as a novelty if you were sufficiently outspoken.'

'I've never thought of that,' said Septimus, 'and I'm afraid I couldn't break away from the habit of fulsome adulation and suddenly change my style.'

'You needn't change your style in the least,' said Clovis; 'merely reverse the sentiment and keep to the inane phraseology of the thing. If you'll do the body of the song I'll knock off the refrain, which is the thing that principally matters, I believe. I shall charge half-shares in the royalties, and throw in my silence as to your guilty secret. In the eyes of the world you shall still be the man who has devoted his life to the study of transepts and Byzantine ritual; only sometimes, in the long winter evenings, when the wind howls drearily down the chimney and the rain beats against the windows, I shall think of you as the author of "Cora with the lips of coral". Of course, if in sheer gratitude at my silence you like to take me for a much-needed holiday to the Adriatic or somewhere equally interesting, paying all expenses, I shouldn't dream of refusing.'

Later in the afternoon Clovis found his aunt and Mrs Riversedge indulging in gentle exercise in the Jacobean garden.

'I've spoken to Mr Brope about F.,' he announced.

'How splendid of you! What did he say?' came in a quick chorus from the two ladies.

'He was quite frank and straightforward with me when he saw that I knew his secret,' said Clovis, 'and it seems that his intentions were quite serious, if slightly unsuitable. I tried to show him the impracticability of the course that he was following. He said he wanted to be understood, and he seemed to think that Florinda would excel in that requirement, but I pointed out that there were probably dozens of delicately nurtured, pure-hearted young English girls who would be capable of understanding him, while Florinda was the only person in the world who understood my aunt's hair. That rather weighed with him, for he's not really a selfish animal, if you take him in the right way, and when I appealed to the memory of his happy childish days, spent amid the daisied fields of Leighton Buzzard (I suppose daisies do grow there), he was obviously affected. Anyhow, he gave me his word that he would put Florinda absolutely out of his mind, and he has agreed to go for a short trip abroad as the best distraction for his thoughts. I am going with him as far as Ragusa. If my aunt should wish to give me a really nice scarf-pin (to be chosen by myself), as a small recognition of the very considerable service I have done her, I shouldn't dream of refusing. I'm not one of those who think that because one is abroad one can go about dressed anyhow.'

A few weeks later in Blackpool and places where they sing, the following refrain held undisputed sway:

How you bore me, Florrie,

With those eyes of vacant blue;
You'll be very sorry, Florrie,
If I marry you.
Though I'm easy-goin', Florrie,
This I swear is true,
I'll throw you down a quarry, Florrie,
If I marry you.

The Story of St Vespaluus

'Tell me a story,' said the Baroness, staring out despairingly at the rain; it was that light, apologetic sort of rain that looks as if it was going to leave off every minute and goes on for the greater part of the afternoon.

'What sort of story?' asked Clovis, giving his croquet mallet a valedictory shove into retirement.

'One just true enough to be interesting and not true enough to be tiresome,' said the Baroness.

Clovis rearranged several cushions to his personal solace and satisfaction; he knew that the Baroness liked her guests to be comfortable, and he thought it right to respect her wishes in that particular.

'Have I ever told you the story of St Vespaluus?' he asked.

'You've told me stories about grand-dukes and lion-tamers and financiers' widows and a postmaster in Herzogovina,' said the Baroness, 'and about an Italian jockey and an amateur governess who went to Warsaw, and several about your mother, but certainly never anything about a saint.'

'This story happened a long while ago,' he said, 'in those uncomfortable piebald times when a third of the people were Pagan, and a third Christian, and the biggest third of all just followed whichever religion the Court happened to profess. There was a certain king called Hkrikros, who had a fearful temper and no immediate successor in his own family; his married sister, however, had provided him with a large stock of nephews from which to select his heir. And the most eligible and royally-approved of all these nephews was the sixteen-year-old Vespaluus. He was the best looking, and the best horseman and javelin-thrower, and had that priceless princely gift of being able to walk past a supplicant with an air of not having seen him, but would certainly have given something if he had. My mother has that gift to a certain extent; she can go smilingly and financially unscathed through a charity bazaar, and meet the organizers next day with a solicitous "had I but known you were in need of funds" air that is really rather a triumph in audacity. Now Hkrikros was a Pagan of the first water, and kept the worship of the sacred serpents, who lived in a hallowed grove on a hill near the royal palace, up to a high pitch of enthusiasm. The common people were allowed to please themselves, within certain discreet limits, in the matter of private religion, but any official in the service of the Court who went over to the new cult was looked down on, literally as well as metaphorically, the looking down being done from the gallery that ran round the royal bear-pit. Consequently there was considerable scandal and consternation when the youthful Vespaluus appeared one day at a Court function with a rosary tucked into his belt, and announced in reply to angry questionings, that he had decided to adopt Christianity, or at any rate to give it a trial. If it had been any of the other nephews the king would possibly have ordered something drastic in the way of scourging and banishment, but in the case of the favoured Vespaluus he determined to look on the whole thing much as a modern father might regard the announced intention of his son to adopt the stage as a profession. He sent accordingly for the Royal Librarian. The royal library in those days was not a very extensive affair; and the keeper of the king's books had a great deal of leisure on his hands. Consequently he was in frequent demand for the settlement of other people's affairs when these strayed beyond normal limits and got temporarily unmanageable.

'"You must reason with Prince Vespaluus," said the king, "and impress on him the error of his ways. We cannot have the heir to the throne setting such a dangerous example."

'"But where shall I find the necessary arguments?" asked the Librarian.

'"I give you free leave to pick and choose your arguments in the royal woods and coppices," said the king; "if you cannot get together some cutting observations and stinging retorts suitable to the occasion you are a person of very poor resource."

'So the Librarian went into the woods and gathered a goodly

selection of highly argumentative rods and switches, and then proceeded to reason with Vespaluus on the folly and iniquity and above all the unseemliness of his conduct. His reasoning left a deep impression on the young prince, an impression which lasted for many weeks during which time nothing more was heard about the unfortunate lapse into Christianity. Then a further scandal of the same nature agitated the Court. At a time when he should have been engaged in audibly invoking the gracious protection and patronage of the holy serpents, Vespaluus was heard singing a chant in honour of St Odilo of Cluny. The king was furious at this new outbreak, and began to take a gloomy view of the situation; Vespaluus was evidently going to show a dangerous obstinacy in persisting in his heresy. And yet there was nothing in his appearance to justify such perverseness; he had not the pale eye of the fanatic or the mystic look of the dreamer. On the contrary, he was quite the best-looking boy at Court; he had an elegant well-knit figure, a healthy complexion, eyes the colour of very ripe mulberries, and dark hair, smooth and very well cared for.'

'It sounds like a description of what you imagine yourself to have been like at the age of sixteen,' said the Baroness.

'My mother has probably been showing you some of my early photographs,' said Clovis. Having turned the sarcasm into a compliment, he resumed his story.

'The king had Vespaluus shut up in a dark tower for three days, with nothing but bread and water to live on, the squealing and fluttering of bats to listen to, and drifting clouds to watch through one little window-slit. The anti-Pagan section of the community began to talk portentously of the boy-martyr. The martyrdom was mitigated, as far as the food was concerned, by the carelessness of the tower warden, who once or twice left a portion of his own supper of broiled meat and fruit and wine by mistake in the prince's cell. After the punishment was over, Vespaluus was closely watched for any further symptom of religious perversity, for the king was determined to stand no more opposition on so important a matter, even from a favourite nephew. If there was any more of this nonsense, he said, the succession to the throne would have to be altered.

'For a time all went well; the festival of summer sports was approaching, and the young Vespaluus was too engrossed in wrestling and foot-running and javelin-throwing competitions to bother himself with the strife of conflicting religious systems. Then, however, came the great culminating feature of the summer festival, the ceremonial dance round the grove of the sacred serpents, and Vespaluus, as we should say, "sat it out". The affront to the State religion was too public and ostentatious to be overlooked, even if the king had been so minded, and he was not in the least so minded. For a day and a half he sat apart and brooded, and everyone thought he was debating within himself the question of the young prince's death or pardon; as a matter of fact he was merely thinking out the manner of the boy's death. As the thing had to be done, and was bound to attract an enormous amount of public attention in any case, it was as well to make it as spectacular and impressive as possible.

'"Apart from his unfortunate taste in religions," said the king, "and his obstinacy in adhering to it, he is a sweet and pleasant youth, therefore it is meet and fitting that he should be done to death by the winged envoys of sweetness."

'"Your Majesty means –?" said the Royal Librarian.

'"I mean," said the king, "that he shall be stung to death by bees. By the royal bees, of course."

'"A most elegant death," said the Librarian.

'"Elegant and spectacular, and decidedly painful," said the king; "it fulfils all the conditions that could be wished for."

'The king himself thought out all the details of the execution ceremony. Vespaluus was to be stripped of his clothes, his hands were to be bound behind him, and he was then to be slung in a recumbent position immediately above three of the largest of the royal beehives, so that the least movement of his body would bring him in jarring contact with them. The rest could be safely left to the bees. The death throes, the king computed, might last anything from fifteen to forty minutes, though there was division of opinion and considerable wagering among the other nephews as to whether death might be almost instantaneous, or, on the other hand, whether it might not be deferred for a couple of hours. Anyway, they all agreed, it was vastly preferable to being thrown down into an evil-smelling bear-pit and being clawed and mauled to death by imperfect carnivorous animals.

'It so happened, however, that the keeper of the royal hives had leanings towards Christianity himself, and moreover, like most of the Court officials, he was very much attached to Vespaluus. On the eve of the execution, therefore, he busied himself with removing the stings from all the royal bees; it was a long and delicate operation, but he was an expert bee-master, and by working hard nearly all night he succeeded in disarming all, or almost all, of the hive inmates.'

'I didn't know you could take the sting from a live bee,' said the Baroness incredulously.

'Every profession has its secrets,' replied Clovis; 'if it hadn't it wouldn't be a profession. Well, the moment for the execution arrived; the king and Court took their places, and accommodation was found for as many of the populace as wished to witness the unusual spectacle. Fortunately the royal bee-yard was of considerable dimensions, and was commanded, moreover, by the terraces that ran round the royal gardens; with a little squeezing and the erection of a few platforms room was found for everybody. Vespaluus was carried into the open space in front of the hives, blushing and slightly embarrassed, but not at all displeased at the attention which was being centred on him.'

'He seems to have resembled you in more things than in appearance,' said the Baroness.

'Don't interrupt at a critical point in the story,' said Clovis. 'As soon as he had been carefully adjusted in the prescribed position over the hives, and almost before the gaolers had time to retire to a safe distance, Vespaluus gave a lusty and well-aimed kick, which sent all three hives toppling one over another. The next moment he was wrapped from head to foot in bees; each individual insect nursed the dreadful and humiliating knowledge that in this supreme hour of catastrophe it could not sting, but each felt that it ought to pretend to. Vespaluus squealed and wriggled with laughter, for he was being tickled nearly to death, and now and again he gave a furious kick and used a bad word as one of the few bees that had escaped disarmament got its protest home. But the spectators saw with amazement that he showed no signs of approaching death agony, and as the bees dropped wearily away in clusters from his body his flesh was seen to be as white and smooth as before the ordeal, with a shiny glaze from the honey-smear of innumerable bee-feet, and here and there a small red spot where one of the rare stings had left its mark. It was obvious that a miracle had been performed in his favour, and one loud murmur, of astonishment or exultation, rose from the onlooking crown. The king gave orders for Vespaluus to be taken down to await further orders, and stalked silently back to his midday meal, at which he was careful to eat heartily and drink copiously as though nothing unusual had happened. After dinner he sent for the Royal Librarian.

'"What is the meaning of this fiasco?" he demanded.

'"Your Majesty," said the official, "either there is something radically wrong with the bees –"

'"There is nothing wrong with the bees," said the king haughtily, "they are the best bees."

'"Or else," said the Librarian, "there is something irremediably right about Prince Vespaluus."

'"If Vespaluus is right I must be wrong," said the king.

'The Librarian was silent for a moment. Hasty speech has been the downfall of many; ill-considered silence was the undoing of the luckless Court functionary.

'Forgetting the restraint due to his dignity, and the golden rule which imposes repose of mind and body after a heavy meal, the king rushed upon the keeper of the royal books and hit him repeatedly and promiscuously over the head with an ivory chessboard, a pewter wine flagon, and a brass candlestick; he knocked him violently and often against an iron torch sconce, and kicked him thrice round the banqueting chamber with rapid, energetic kicks. Finally, he dragged him down a long passage by the hair of his head and flung him out of a window into the courtyard below.'

'Was he much hurt?' asked the Baroness.

'More hurt than surprised,' said Clovis. 'You see, the king was notorious for his violent temper. However, this was the first time he had let himself go so unrestrainedly on the top of a heavy meal. The Librarian lingered for many days – in fact, for all I know, he may have ultimately recovered, but Hkrikros died that same evening. Vespaluus had hardly finished getting the honey stains off his body before a hurried deputation came to put the coronation oil on his head. And what with the publicly witnessed miracle and the accession of a Christian sovereign, it was not surprising that there was a general scramble of converts to the new religion. A hastily consecrated bishop was overworked with a rush of baptisms in the hastily improvised Cathedral of St Odilo.

And the boy-martyr-that-might-have-been was transposed in the popular imagination into a royal boy-saint, whose fame attracted throngs of curious and devout sightseers to the capital. Vespaluus, who was busily engaged in organizing the games and athletic contests that were to mark the commencement of his reign, had no time to give heed to the religious fervour which was effervescing round his personality; the first indication he had of the existing state of affairs was when the Court Chamberlain (a recent and very ardent addition to the Christian community) brought for his approval the outlines of a projected ceremonial cutting-down of the idolatrous serpent-grove.

'"Your Majesty will be graciously pleased to cut down the first tree with a specially consecrated axe," said the obsequious official.

'"I'll cut off your head first, with any axe that comes handy," said Vespaluus indignantly; "do you suppose that I'm going to begin my reign by mortally affronting the sacred serpents? It would be most unlucky."

'"But your Majesty's Christian principles?" exclaimed the bewildered Chamberlain.

'"I never had any," said Vespaluus; "I used to pretend to be a Christian convert just to annoy Hkrikros. He used to fly into such delicious tempers. And it was rather fun being whipped and scolded and shut up in a tower all for nothing. But as to turning Christian in real earnest, like you people seem to do, I couldn't think of such a thing. And the holy and esteemed serpents have always helped me when I've prayed to them for success in my running and wrestling and hunting, and it was through their distinguished intercession that the bees were not able to hurt me with their stings. It would be black ingratitude to turn against their worship at the very outset of my reign. I hate you for suggesting it."

'The Chamberlain wrung his hands despairingly.

'"But, your Majesty," he wailed, "the people are reverencing you as a saint, and the nobles are being Christianized in batches, and neighbouring potentates of that Faith are sending special envoys to welcome you as a brother. There is some talk of making you the patron saint of beehives, and a certain shade of honey-yellow has been christened Vespaluusian gold at the Emperor's Court. You can't surely go back on all this."

'"I don't mind being reverenced and greeted and honoured," said Vespaluus; "I don't even mind being sainted in moderation, as long as I'm not expected to be saintly as well. But I wish you clearly and finally to understand that I will *not* give up the worship of the august and auspicious serpents."

'There was a world of unspoken bear-pit in the way he uttered those last words, and the mulberry-dark eyes flashed dangerously.

'"A new reign," said the Chamberlain to himself, "but the same old temper."

'Finally, as a State necessity, the matter of the religions was compromised. At stated intervals the king appeared before his subjects in the national cathedral in the character of St Vespaluus, and the idolatrous grove was gradually pruned and lopped away till nothing remained of it. But the sacred and esteemed serpents were removed to a private shrubbery in the royal gardens, where Vespaluus the Pagan and certain members of his household devoutly and decently worshipped them. That possibly is the reason why the boy-king's success in sports and hunting never deserted him to the end of his days, and that is also the reason why, in spite of the popular veneration for his sanctity, he never received official canonization.'

'It has stopped raining,' said the Baroness.

The Unrest-Cure

On the rack in the railway carriage immediately opposite Clovis was a solidly wrought travelling bag, with a carefully written label, on which was inscribed, 'J. P. Huddle, The Warren, Tilfield, near Slowborough'. Immediately below the rack sat the human embodiment of the label, a solid, sedate individual, sedately dressed, sedately conversational. Even without his conversation (which was addressed to a friend seated by his side, and touched chiefly on such topics as the backwardness of Roman hyacinths and the prevalence of measles at the Rectory), one could have gauged fairly accurately the temperament and mental outlook of the travelling bag's owner. But he seemed unwilling to leave anything to the imagination of a casual observer, and his talk grew presently personal and introspective.

'I don't know how it is,' he told his friend, 'I'm not much over forty, but I seem to have settled down into a deep groove of elderly middle-age. My sister shows the same tendency. We like everything to be exactly in its accustomed place; we like things to happen exactly at their appointed times; we like everything to be usual, orderly, punctual, methodical, to a hair's breadth, to a minute. It distresses and upsets us if it is not so. For instance, to take a very trifling matter, a thrush has built its nest year after year in the catkin-tree on the lawn; this year, for no obvious reason, it is building in the ivy on the garden wall. We have said very little about it, but I think we both feel that the change is unnecessary, and just a little irritating.'

'Perhaps,' said the friend, 'it is a different thrush.'

'We have suspected that,' said J. P. Huddle, 'and I think it gives us even more cause for annoyance. We don't feel that we want a change of thrush at our time of life! and yet, as I have said, we have scarcely reached an age when these things should make themselves seriously felt.'

'What you want,' said the friend, 'is an Unrest-cure.'

'An Unrest-Cure? I've never heard of such a thing.'

'You've heard of Rest-cures for people who've broken down under stress of too much worry and strenuous living; well, you're suffering from overmuch repose and placidity, and you need the opposite kind of treatment.'

'But where would one go for such a thing?'

'Well, you might stand as an Orange candidate for Kilkenny, or do a course of district visiting in one of the Apache quarters of Paris, or give lectures in Berlin to prove that most of Wagner's music was written by Gambetta; and there's always the interior of Morocco to travel in. But, to be really effective, the Unrest-cure ought to be tried in the home. How you would do it I haven't the faintest idea.'

It was at this point in the conversation that Clovis became galvanized into alert attention. After all, his two days' visit to an elderly relative at Slowborough did not promise much excitement. Before the train had stopped he had decorated his sinister shirt-cuff with the inscription, 'J. P Huddle, The Warren, Tilfield near Slowborough.'

Two mornings later Mr Huddle broke in on his sister's privacy as she sat reading *Country Life* in the morning room. It was her day and hour and place for reading *Country Life*, and the intrusion was absolutely irregular; but he bore in his hand a telegram, and in that household telegrams were recognized as happening by the hand of God. This particular telegram partook of the nature of a thunderbolt. 'Bishop examining confirmation class in neighbourhood unable stay rectory on account measles invokes your hospitality sending secretary arrange.'

'I scarcely know the Bishop; I've only spoken to him once,' exclaimed J. P. Huddle, with the exculpating air of one who realizes too late the indiscretion of speaking to strange Bishops. Miss Huddle was the first to rally; she disliked thunderbolts as fervently as her brother did, but the womanly instinct in her told her that thunderbolts must be fed.

'We can curry the cold duck,' she said. It was not the appointed day for curry, but the little orange envelope involved a certain departure from rule and custom. Her brother said nothing, but his eyes thanked her for being brave.

'A gentleman to see you,' announced the parlour-maid.

'The secretary!' murmured the Huddles in unison; they instantly stiffened into a demeanour which proclaimed that, though they held all strangers to be guilty, they were willing to hear anything they might have to say in their defence. The young gentleman, who came into the room with a certain elegant haughtiness, was not at all Huddle's idea of a bishop's secretary; he had not supposed that the episcopal establishment could have afforded such an expensively upholstered article when there were so many other claims on its resources. The face was fleetingly familiar; if he had bestowed more attention on the fellow-traveller sitting opposite him in the railway carriage two days before he might have recognized Clovis in his present visitor.

'You are the Bishop's secretary?' asked Huddle, becoming consciously deferential.

'His confidential secretary,' answered Clovis. 'You may call me Stanislaus; my other name doesn't matter. The Bishop and Colonel Alberti may be here to lunch. I shall be here in any case.'

It sounded rather like the programme of a Royal visit.

'The Bishop is examining a confirmation class in the neighbourhood, isn't he?' asked Miss Huddle.

'Ostensibly,' was the dark reply followed by a request for a large-scale map of the locality.

Clovis was still immersed in a seemingly profound study of the map when another telegram arrived. It was addressed to 'Prince Stanislaus, care of Huddle, The Warren, etc.' Clovis glanced at the contents and announced: 'The Bishop and Alberti won't be here till late in the afternoon.' Then he returned to his scrutiny of the map.

The luncheon was not a very festive function. The princely secretary ate and drank with fair appetite, but severely discouraged conversation. At the finish of the meal he broke suddenly into a radiant smile, thanked his hostess for a charming repast, and kissed her hand with deferential rapture. Miss Huddle was unable to decide in her mind whether the action savoured of Louis Quatorzian courtliness or the reprehensive Roman attitude towards the Sabine women. It was not her day for having a headache, but she felt that the circumstances excused her, and retired to her room to have as much headache as was possible before the Bishop's arrival. Clovis, having asked the way to the nearest telegraph office, disappeared presently down the carriage drive. Mr Huddle met him in the hall some two hours later, and asked when the Bishop would arrive.

'He is in the library with Alberti,' was the reply.

'But why wasn't I told? I never knew he had come!' exclaimed Huddle.

'No one knows he is here,' said Clovis; 'the quieter we can keep matters the better. And on no account disturb him in the library. Those are his orders.'

'But what is all this mystery about? And who is Alberti? And isn't the Bishop going to have tea?'

'The Bishop is out for blood, not tea.'

'Blood!' gasped Huddle, who did not find that the thunderbolt improved on acquaintance.

'Tonight is going to be a great night in the history of Christendom,' said Clovis. 'We are going to massacre every Jew in the neighbourhood.'

'To massacre the Jews!' said Huddle indignantly. 'Do you mean to tell me there's a general rising against them?'

'No, it's the Bishop's own idea. He's in there arranging all the details now.'

'But – the Bishop is such a tolerant, humane man.'

'This is precisely what will heighten the effect of his action. The sensation will be enormous.'

That at least Huddle could believe.

'He will be hanged!' he exclaimed with conviction.

'A motor is waiting to carry him to the coast, where a steam yacht is in readiness.'

'But there aren't thirty Jews in the whole neighbourhood,' protested Huddle, whose brain, under the repeated shocks of the day, was operating with the uncertainty of a telegraph wire during earthquake disturbances.

'We have twenty-six on our list,' said Clovis, referring to a bundle of notes. 'We shall be able to deal with them all the more thoroughly.'

'Do you mean to tell me that you are meditating violence against a man like Sir Leon Birberry,' stammered Huddle, 'he's one of the most respected men in the country.'

'He's down on our list,' said Clovis carelessly; 'after all, we've got men we can trust to do our job, so we shan't have to rely on local assistance. And we've got some Boy-scouts helping us as auxiliaries.'

'Boy-scouts!'

'Yes; when they understood there was real killing to be done they were even keener than the men.'

'This thing will be a blot on the Twentieth Century!'

'And your house will be the blotting-pad. Have you realized that half the papers of Europe and the United States will publish pictures of it? By the way, I've sent some photographs of you and your sister, that I found in the library, to the *Matin* and *Die Woche*; I hope you don't mind. Also a sketch of the staircase; most of the killing will probably be done on the staircase.'

The emotions that were surging in J. P. Huddle's brain were almost too intense to be disclosed in speech, but he managed to gasp out: 'There aren't any Jews in this house.'

'Not at present,' said Clovis.

'I shall go to the police,' shouted Huddle with sudden energy.

'In the shrubbery,' said Clovis, 'are posted ten men, who have orders to fire on any one who leaves the house without my signal of permission. Another armed picquet is in ambush near the front gate. The Boy-scouts watch the back premises.'

At this moment the cheerful hoot of a motor-horn was heard from the drive. Huddle rushed to the hall door with the feeling of a man half-awakened from a nightmare, and beheld Sir Leon Birberry, who had driven himself over in his car. 'I got your telegram,' he said; 'what's up?'

Telegram? It seemed to be a day of telegrams.

'Come here at once. Urgent. James Huddle,' was the purport of the message displayed before Huddle's bewildered eyes.

'I see it all!' he exclaimed suddenly in a voice shaken with agitation, and with a look of agony in the direction of the shrubbery he hauled the astonished Birberry into the house. Tea had just been laid in the hall, but the now thoroughly panic-stricken Huddle dragged his protesting guest upstairs, and in a few minutes' time the entire household had been summoned to that region of momentary safety. Clovis alone graced the tea-table with his presence; the fanatics in the library were evidently too immersed in their monstrous machinations to dally with the solace of teacup and hot toast. Once the youth rose, in answer to the summons of the front-door bell, and admitted Mr Paul Isaacs, shoemaker and parish councillor, who had also received a pressing invitation to The Warren. With an atrocious assumption of courtesy, which a Borgia could hardly have outdone, the secretary escorted this new captive of his net to the head of the stairway, where his involuntary host awaited him.

And then ensued a long ghastly vigil of watching and waiting. Once or twice Clovis left the house to stroll across to the shrubbery, returning always to the library, for the purpose evidently of making a brief report. Once he took in the letters from the evening postman, and brought them to the top of the stairs with punctilious politeness. After his next absence he came half-way up the stairs to make an announcement.

'The Boy-scouts mistook my signal, and have killed the postman. I've had very little practice in this sort of thing, you see. Another time I shall do better.'

The housemaid, who was engaged to be married to the evening postman, gave way to clamorous grief.

'Remember that your mistress has a headache,' said J. P. Huddle. (Miss Huddle's headache was worse.)

Clovis hastened downstairs, and after a short visit to the library returned with another message:

'The Bishop is sorry to hear that Miss Huddle has a headache. He is issuing orders that as far as possible no firearms shall be used near the house; any killing that is necessary on the premises will be done with cold steel. The Bishop does not see why a man should not be a gentleman as well as a Christian.'

That was the last they saw of Clovis; it was nearly seven o'clock, and his elderly relative liked him to dress for dinner. But, though he had left them for ever, the lurking suggestion of his presence haunted the lower regions of the house during the long hours of the wakeful night, and every creak of the stairway, every rustle of wind through the shrubbery, was fraught with horrible meaning. At about seven next morning the gardener's boy and the early postman finally convinced the watchers that the Twentieth Century was still unblotted.

'I don't suppose,' mused Clovis, as an early train bore him townwards, 'that they will be in the least grateful for the Unrest-cure.'

Tobermory

It was a chill, rain-washed afternoon of a late August day, that indefinite season when partridges are still in security or cold storage, and there is nothing to hunt – unless one is bounded on the north by the Bristol Channel, in which case one may lawfully gallop after fat red stags. Lady Blemley's house-party was not bounded on the north by the Bristol Channel, hence there was a full gathering of her guests round the tea-table on this particular afternoon. And, in spite of the blankness of the season and the triteness of the occasion, there was no trace in the company of that fatigued restlessness which means a dread of the pianola and a subdued hankering for auction bridge. The undisguised openmouthed attention of the entire party was fixed on the homely negative personality of Mr Cornelius Appin. Of all her guests, he was the one who had come to Lady Blemley with the vaguest reputation. Someone had said he was 'clever', and he had got his invitation in the moderate expectation, on the part of his hostess, that some portion at least of his cleverness would be contributed to the general entertainment. Until tea-time that day she had been unable to discover in what direction, if any, his cleverness lay. He was neither a wit nor a croquet champion, a hypnotic force nor a begetter of amateur theatricals. Neither did his exterior suggest a generous measure of mental deficiency. He had subsided into mere Mr Appin, and the Cornelius seemed a piece of transparent baptismal bluff. And now he was claiming to have launched on the world a discovery beside which the invention of gunpowder, of the printing-press, and of steam locomotion were inconsiderable trifles. Science had made bewildering strides in many directions during recent decades, but this thing seemed to belong to the domain of miracle rather than to scientific achievement.

'And do you really ask us to believe,' Sir Wilfrid was saying, 'that you have discovered a means for instructing animals in the art of human speech, and that dear old Tobermory has proved your first successful pupil?'

'It is a problem at which I have worked for the last seventeen years,' said Mr Appin, 'but only during the last eight or nine months have I been rewarded with glimmerings of success. Of course I have experimented with thousands of animals, but latterly only with cats, those wonderful creatures which have assimilated themselves so marvellously with our civilization while retaining all their highly developed feral instincts. Here and there among cats one comes across an outstanding superior intellect, just as one does among the ruck of human beings, and when I made the acquaintance of Tobermory a week ago I saw at once that I was in contact with a 'Beyond-cat' of extraordinary intelligence. I had gone far along the road to success in recent experiments; with Tobermory, as you call him, I have reached the goal.'

Mr Appin concluded his remarkable statement in a voice which he strove to divest of a triumphant inflection. No one said 'Rats', though Clovis's lips moved in a monosyllabic contortion, which probably invoked those rodents of disbelief.

'And do you mean to say,' asked Miss Resker, after a slight pause, 'that you have taught Tobermory to say and understand easy sentences of one syllable?'

'My dear Miss Resker,' said the wonder-worker patiently, 'one teaches little children and savages and backward adults in that piecemeal fashion; when one has once solved the problem of making a beginning with an animal of highly developed intelligence one has no need for those halting methods. Tobermory can speak our language with perfect correctness.'

This time Clovis very distinctly said, 'Beyond-rats!' Sir Wilfrid was more polite, but equally sceptical.

'Hadn't we better have the cat in and judge for ourselves?' suggested Lady Blemley.

Sir Wilfrid went in search of the animal, and the company settled themselves down to the languid expectation of witnessing some more or less adroit drawing-room ventriloquism.

In a minute Sir Wilfrid was back in the room, his face white beneath its tan and his eyes dilated with excitement.

'By Gad, it's true!'

His agitation was unmistakably genuine, and his hearers started forward in a thrill of awakened interest.

Collapsing into an armchair he continued breathlessly; 'I found him dozing in the smoking-room, and called to him to come for his tea. He blinked at me in his usual way, and I said, "Come on Toby; don't keep us waiting;" and, by Gad! he drawled out in a most horribly natural voice that he'd come when he dashed well pleased! I nearly jumped out of my skin!'

Appin had preached to absolutely incredulous hearers; Sir Wilfrid's statement carried instant conviction. A Babel-like chorus of startled exclamation arose, amid which the scientist sat mutely enjoying the first fruit of his stupendous discovery.

In the midst of the clamour Tobermory entered the room and made his way with velvet tread and studied unconcern across to the group seated round the tea-table.

A sudden hush of awkwardness and constraint fell on the company. Somehow there seemed an element of embarrassment in addressing on equal terms a domestic cat of acknowledged dental ability.

'Will you have some milk, Tobermory?' asked Lady Blemley in a rather strained voice.

'I don't mind if I do,' was the response, couched in a tone of even indifference. A shiver of suppressed excitement went through the listeners, and Lady Blemley might be excused for pouring out the saucerful of milk rather unsteadily.

'I'm afraid I've spilt a good deal of it,' she said apologetically.

'After all, it's not my Axminster,' was Tobermory's rejoinder.

Another silence fell on the group, and then Miss Resker, in her best district-visitor manner, asked if the human language had been difficult to learn. Tobermory looked squarely at her for a moment and then fixed his gaze serenely on the middle-distance. It was obvious that boring questions lay outside his scheme of life.

'What do you think of human intelligence?' asked Mavis Pellington lamely.

'Of whose intelligence in particular?' asked Tobermory coldly.

'Oh, well, mine for instance,' said Mavis, with a feeble laugh.

'You put me in an embarrassing position,' said Tobermory, whose tone and attitude certainly did not suggest a shred of embarrassment. 'When your inclusion in this house-party was suggested Sir Wilfrid protested that you were the most brainless woman of his acquaintance, and that there was a wide distinction between hospitality and the care of the feeble-minded. Lady Blemley replied that your lack of brain-power was the precise quality which had earned you your invitation, as you were the only person she could think of who might be idiotic enough to buy their old car. You know, the one they call "The Envy of Sisyphus", because it goes quite nicely up-hill if you push it.'

Lady Blemley's protestations would have had greater effect if she had not casually suggested to Mavis only that morning that the car in question would be just the thing for her down at her Devonshire home.

Major Barfield plunged in heavily to effect a diversion.

'How about your carrying-on with the tortoise-shell puss up at the stables, eh?'

The moment he had said it everyone realized the blunder.

'One does not usually discuss these matters in public,' said Tobermory frigidly. 'From a slight observation of your ways since you've been in this house I should imagine you'd find it inconvenient if I were to shift the conversation on to your own little affairs.'

The panic which ensued was not confined to the Major.

'Would you like to go and see if cook has got your dinner ready?' suggested Lady Blemley hurriedly, affecting to ignore the fact that it wanted at least two hours to Tobermory's dinner-time.

'Thanks,' said Tobermory, 'not quite so soon after my tea. I don't want to die of indigestion.'

'Cats have nine lives, you know,' said Sir Wilfrid heartily.

'Possibly,' answered Tobermory; 'but only one liver.'

'Adelaide!' said Mrs Cornett, 'do you mean to encourage that cat to go out and gossip about us in the servants' hall?'

The panic had indeed become general. A narrow ornamental balustrade ran in front of most of the bedroom windows at the Towers, and it was recalled with dismay that this had formed a favourite promenade for Tobermory at all hours, whence he could watch the pigeons – and heaven knew what else besides. If he intended to become reminiscent in his present outspoken strain the effect would be something more than disconcerting. Mrs Cornett, who spent much time at her toilet table, and whose complexion was reputed to be of a nomadic though punctual disposition, looked as ill at ease as the Major. Miss Scrawen, who wrote fiercely sensuous poetry and led a blameless life, merely displayed irritation; if you are methodical and virtuous in private you don't necessarily want every one to know it. Bertie van Tahn, who was so depraved at seventeen that he had long ago given up trying to be any worse, turned a dull shade of gardenia white, but he did not commit the error of dashing out of the room like Odo Finsberry, a young gentleman who was understood to be reading for the Church and who was possibly disturbed at the thought of scandals he might hear concerning other people. Clovis had the presence of mind to maintain a composed exterior; privately he was calculating how long it would take to procure a box of fancy mice through the agency of the *Exchange and Mart* as a species of hush-money.

Even in a delicate situation like the present, Agnes Resker could not endure to remain too long in the background.

'Why did I ever come down here?' she asked dramatically.

Tobermory immediately accepted the opening.

'Judging by what you said to Mrs Cornett on the croquet-lawn yesterday, you were out for food. You described the Blemleys as the dullest people to stay with that you knew, but said they were clever enough to employ a first-rate cook otherwise they'd find it difficult to get anyone to come down a second time.

'There's not a word of truth in it! I appeal to Mrs Cornett –' exclaimed the discomfited Agnes.

'Mrs Cornett repeated your remark afterwards to Bertie van Tahn,' continued Tobermory, 'and said "That woman is a regular

Hunger Marcher; she'd go anywhere for four square meals a day," and Bertie van Tahn said –'

At this point the chronicle mercifully ceased. Tobermory had caught a glimpse of the big yellow Tom from the Rectory working his way through the shrubbery towards the stable wing. In a flash he had vanished through the open French window.

With the disappearance of his too brilliant pupil Cornelius Appin found himself beset by a hurricane of bitter upbraiding, anxious inquiry, and frightened entreaty. The responsibility for the situation lay with him, and he must prevent matters from becoming worse. Could Tobermory impart his dangerous gift to other cats? was the first question he had to answer. It was possible, he replied, that he might have initiated his intimate friend the stable puss into his new accomplishment, but it was unlikely that his teaching could have taken a wider range as yet.

'Then,' said Mrs Cornett, 'Tobermory may be a valuable cat and a great pet; but I'm sure you'll agree, Adelaide, that both he and the stable cat must be done away with without delay.'

'You don't suppose I've enjoyed the last quarter of an hour, do you?' said Lady Blemley bitterly. 'My husband and I are very fond of Tobermory – at least, we were before this horrible accomplishment was infused into him but now, of course, the only thing is to have him destroyed as soon as possible.'

'We can put some strychnine in the scraps he always gets at dinner-time,' said Sir Wilfrid, 'and I will go and drown the stable cat myself. The coachman will be very sore at losing his pet, but I'll say a very catching form of mange has broken out in cats and we're afraid of it spreading to the kennels.'

'But my great discovery!' expostulated Mr Appin; 'after all my years of experiment –'

'You can go and experiment on the short-horns at the farm, who are under proper control,' said Mrs Cornett, 'or the elephants at the Zoological Gardens. They're said to be highly intelligent, and they have this recommendation, that they don't come creeping about our bedrooms and under chairs, and so forth.'

An archangel ecstatically proclaiming the Millennium, and then finding that it clashed unpardonably with Henley and would have to be indefinitely postponed, could hardly have felt more crestfallen than Cornelius Appin at the reception of his wonderful achievement. Public opinion, however, was against him – in fact, had the general voice been consulted on the subject it is probable that a strong minority vote would have been in favour of including him in the strychnine diet.

Defective train arrangements and a nervous desire to see matters brought to a finish prevented an immediate dispersal of the party, but dinner that evening was not a social success. Sir Wilfrid had had rather a trying time with the stable cat and subsequently with the coachman. Agnes Resker ostentatiously limited her repast to a morsel of dry toast, which she bit as though it were a personal enemy; while Mavis Pellington maintained a vindictive silence throughout the meal. Lady Blemley kept up a flow of what she hoped was conversation, but her attention was fixed on the doorway. A plateful of carefully dosed fish scraps was in readiness on the sideboard, but sweets and savoury and dessert went their way, and no Tobermory appeared either in the dining-room or kitchen.

The sepulchral dinner was cheerful compared with the subsequent vigil in the smoking room. Eating and drinking had at least supplied a distraction and cloak to the prevailing embarrassment. Bridge was out of the question in the general tension of nerves and tempers, and after Odo Finsberry had given a lugubrious rendering of 'Mélisande in the Wood' to a frigid audience, music was tacitly avoided. At eleven the servants went to bed, announcing that the small window in the pantry had been left open as usual for Tobermory's private use. The guests read steadily through the current batch of magazines, and fell back gradually on the 'Badminton Library' and bound volumes of *Punch*. Lady Blemley made periodic visits to the pantry, returning each time with an expression of listless depression which forestalled questioning.

At two o'clock Clovis broke the dominating silence.

'He won't turn up tonight. He's probably in the local newspaper office at the present moment, dictating the first instalment of his reminiscences. Lady What's-her-name's book won't be in it. It will be the event of the day.'

Having made his contribution to the general cheerfulness, Clovis went to bed. At long intervals the various members of the house-party followed his example.

The servants taking round the early tea made a uniform

announcement in reply to a uniform question. Tobermory had not returned.

Breakfast was, if anything, a more unpleasant function than dinner had been, but before its conclusion the situation was relieved. Tobermory's corpse was brought in from the shrubbery, where a gardener had just discovered it. From the bites on his throat and the yellow fur which coated his claws it was evident that he had fallen in unequal combat with the big Tom from the Rectory.

By midday most of the guests had quitted the Towers, and after lunch Lady Blemley had sufficiently recovered her spirits to write an extremely nasty letter to the Rectory about the loss of her valuable pet.

Tobermory had been Appin's one successful pupil, and he was destined to have no successor. A few weeks later an elephant in the Dresden Zoological Garden, which had shown no previous signs of irritability, broke loose and killed an Englishman who had apparently been teasing it. The victim's name was variously reported in the papers as Oppin and Eppelin, but his front name was faithfully rendered Cornelius.

'If he was trying German irregular verbs on the poor beast,' said Clovis, 'he deserved all he got.'

The Boar-Pig

'There is a back way on to the lawn,' said Mrs Philidore Stossen to her daughter, 'through a small grass paddock and then through a walled fruit garden full of gooseberry bushes. I went all over the place last year when the family were away. There is a door that opens from the fruit garden into a shrubbery, and once we emerge from there we can mingle with the guests as if we had come in by the ordinary way. It's much safer than going in by the front entrance and running the risk of coming bang up against the hostess; that would be so awkward when she doesn't happen to have invited us.'

'Isn't it a lot of trouble to take for getting admittance to a garden party?'

'To a garden party, yes; to *the* garden party of the season, certainly not. Everyone of any consequence in the county, with the exception of ourselves, has been asked to meet the Princess, and it would be far more troublesome to invent explanations as to why we weren't there than to get in by a roundabout way. I stopped Mrs Cuvering in the road yesterday and talked very pointedly about the Princess. If she didn't choose to take the hint and send me an invitation it's not my fault, is it? Here we are: we just cut across the grass and through that little gate into the garden.'

Mrs Stossen and her daughter, suitably arrayed for a county garden party function with an infusion of Almanack de Gotha, sailed through the narrow grass paddock and the ensuing gooseberry garden with the air of state barges making an unofficial progress along a rural trout stream. There was a certain amount of furtive haste mingled with the stateliness of their advance as though hostile searchlights might be turned on them at any moment; and, as a matter of fact, they were not unobserved. Matilda Cuvering, with the alert eyes of thirteen years old and the added advantage of an exalted position in the branches of a medlar tree, had enjoyed a good view of the Stossen flanking movement and had foreseen exactly where it would break down in execution.

'They'll find the door locked, and they'll jolly well have to go back the way they came,' she remarked to herself. 'Serves them right for not coming in by the proper entrance. What a pity Tarquin Superbus isn't loose in the paddock. After all, as everyone else is enjoying themselves, I don't see why Tarquin shouldn't have an afternoon out.'

Matilda was of an age when thought is action; she slid down from the branches of the medlar tree, and when she clambered back again, Tarquin, the huge white Yorkshire boar-pig, had exchanged the narrow limits of his sty for the wider range of the grass paddock. The discomfited Stossen expedition, returning in recriminatory but otherwise orderly retreat from the unyielding obstacle of the locked door, came to a sudden halt at the gate dividing the paddock from the gooseberry garden.

'What a villainous-looking animal,' exclaimed Mrs Stossen; 'it wasn't there when we came in.'

'It's there now, anyhow,' said her daughter. 'What on earth are we to do? I wish we had never come.'

The boar-pig had drawn nearer to the gate for a close

inspection of the human intruders, and stood champing his jaws and blinking his small red eyes in a manner that was doubtless intended to be disconcerting, and, as far as the Stossens were concerned, thoroughly achieved that result.

'Shoo! Hish! Hish! Shoo!' cried the ladies in chorus.

'If they think they're going to drive him away by reciting lists of the kings of Israel and Judah they're laying themselves out of disappointment,' observed Matilda from her seat in the medlar tree. As she made the observation aloud Mrs Stossen became for the first time aware of her presence. A moment or two earlier she would have been anything but pleased at the discovery that the garden was not as deserted as it looked, but now she hailed the fact of the child's presence on the scene with absolute relief.

'Little girl, can you find someone to drive away –' she began hopefully.

'*Comment? Comprends pas*,' was the response.

'Oh, are you French? *Étes vous française?*'

'*Pas de tous. 'Suis anglaise.*'

'Then why not talk English? I want to know if –'

'*Permettez-moi expliquer*. You see, I'm rather under a cloud,' said Matilda. 'I'm staying with my aunt, and I was told I must behave particularly well today, as lots of people were coming for a garden party, and I was told to imitate Claude, that's my young cousin, who never does anything wrong except by accident, and then is always apologetic about it. It seems they thought I ate too much raspberry trifle at lunch, and they said Claude never eats too much raspberry trifle. Well, Claude always goes to sleep for half an hour after lunch, because he's told to, and I waited till he was asleep, and tied his hands and started forcible feeding with a whole bucketful of raspberry trifle that they were keeping for the garden party. Lots of it went on to his sailor-suit and some of it on to the bed, but a good deal went down Claude's throat, and they can't say again that he has never been known to eat too much raspberry trifle. That is why I am not allowed to go to the party, and as an additional punishment I must speak French all the afternoon. I've had to tell you all this in English, as there were words like "forcible feeding" that I didn't know the French for; of course I could have invented them, but if I had said *nourriture obligatoire* you wouldn't have had the least idea what I was talking about. *Mais maintenant, nous parlons français.*'

'Oh, very well, *très bien*,' said Mrs Stossen reluctantly; in moments of flurry such French as she knew was not under very good control. '*Là, à l'autre côté de la porte, est un cochon* –'

'*Un cochon? Ah, le petit charmant!*' exclaimed Matilda with enthusiasm.

'*Mais non, pas du tout petit, et pas du tout charmant; un bête féroce* –'

'*Une bête*,' corrected Matilda; 'a pig is masculine as long as you call it a pig, but if you lose your temper with it and call it a ferocious beast it becomes one of us at once. French is a dreadfully unsexing language.'

'For goodness' sake let us talk English then,' said Mrs Stossen. 'Is there any way out of this garden except through the paddock where the pig is?'

'I always go over the wall, by way of the plum tree,' said Matilda.

'Dressed as we are we could hardly do that,' said Mrs Stossen; it was difficult to imagine her doing it in any costume.

'Do you think you could go and get someone who would drive the pig away?' asked Miss Stossen.

'I promised my aunt I would stay here till five o'clock; it's not four yet.'

'I am sure, under the circumstances, your aunt would permit –'

'My conscience would not permit,' said Matilda with cold dignity.

'We can't stay here till five o'clock,' exclaimed Mrs Stossen with growing exasperation.

'Shall I recite to you to make the time pass quicker?' asked Matilda obligingly. '"Belinda, the little Breadwinner" is considered my best piece, or, perhaps, it ought to be something in French. Henri Quatre's address to his soldiers is the only thing I really know in that language.'

'If you will go and fetch someone to drive that animal away I will give you something to buy yourself a nice present,' said Mrs Stossen.

Matilda came several inches lower down the medlar tree.

'That is the most practical suggestion you have made yet for getting out of the garden,' she remarked cheerfully; 'Claude and I are collecting money for the Children's Fresh Air Fund, and we are seeing which of us can collect the biggest sum.'

'I shall be very glad to contribute half a crown, very glad indeed,' said Mrs Stossen, digging that coin out of the depths of a receptacle which formed a detached outwork of her toilet.

'Claude is a long way ahead of me at present,' continued Matilda, taking no notice of the suggested offering; 'you see, he's only eleven, and has golden hair, and those are enormous advantages when you're on the collecting job. Only the other day a Russian lady gave him ten shillings. Russians understand the art of giving far better than we do. I expect Claude will net quite twenty-five shillings this afternoon; he'll have the field to himself, and he'll be able to do the pale, fragile, not-long-for-this-world business to perfection after his raspberry trifle experience. Yes, he'll be *quite* two pounds ahead of me by now.'

With much probing and plucking and many regretful murmurs the beleaguered ladies managed to produce seven-and-sixpence between them.

'I am afraid this is all we've got,' said Mrs Stossen.

Matilda showed no sign of coming down either in the earth or to their figure.

'I could not do violence to my conscience for anything less than ten shillings,' she announced stiffly.

Mother and daughter muttered certain remarks under their breath, in which the word 'beast' was prominent, and probably had no reference to Tarquin.

'I find I *have* got another half-crown,' said Mrs Stossen in a shaking voice; 'here you are. Now please fetch someone quickly.'

Matilda slipped down from the tree, took possession of the donation, and proceeded to pick up a handful of over-ripe medlars from the grass at her feet. Then she climbed over the gate and addressed herself affectionately to the boar-pig.

'Come, Tarquin, dear old boy; you know you can't resist medlars when they're rotten and squashy.'

Tarquin couldn't. By dint of throwing the fruit in front of him at judicious intervals Matilda decoyed him back to his sty, while the delivered captives hurried across the paddock.

'Well, I never! The little minx!' exclaimed Mrs Stossen when she was safely on the high road. 'The animal wasn't savage at all,

and as for the ten shillings, I don't believe the Fresh Air Fund will
see a penny of it!'

There she was unwarrantably harsh in her judgement. If you
examine the books of the fund you will find the acknowledgement: 'Collected by Miss Matilda Cuvering, 2s.6d.'

The Brogue

The hunting season had come to an end, and the Mullets had not
succeeded in selling the Brogue. There had been a kind of
tradition in the family for the past three or four years, a sort of
fatalistic hope, that the Brogue would find a purchaser before the
hunting was over; but seasons came and went without anything
happening to justify such ill-founded optimism. The animal had
been named Berserker in the earlier stages of its career; it had
been rechristened the Brogue later on, in recognition of the fact
that, once acquired, it was extremely difficult to get rid of. The
unkinder wits of the neighbourhood had been known to suggest
that the first letter of its name was superfluous. The Brogue had
been variously described in sale catalogues as a light-weight
hunter, a lady's hack, and, more simply, but still with a touch of
imagination, as a useful brown gelding, standing 15.1. Toby
Mullet had ridden him for four seasons with the West Wessex;
you can ride almost any sort of horse with the West Wessex as
long as it is an animal that knows the country. The Brogue knew
the country intimately, having personally created most of the
gaps that were to be met with in banks and hedges for many
miles round. His manners and characteristics were not ideal in
the hunting field, but he was probably rather safer to ride to
hounds than he was as a hack on country roads. According to
the Mullet family, he was not really road-shy, but there were one
or two objects of dislike that brought on sudden attacks of what
Toby called the swerving sickness. Motors and cycles he treated
with tolerant disregard, but pigs, wheelbarrows, piles of stones by
the roadside, perambulators in a village street, gates painted too
aggressively white, and sometimes, but not always, the newer
kind of beehives, turned him aside from his tracks in vivid
imitation of the zigzag course of forked lightning. If a pheasant
rose noisily from the other side of a hedgerow the Brogue would

spring into the air at the same moment, but this may have been
due to a desire to be companionable. The Mullet family
contradicted the widely prevalent report that the horse was a
confirmed crib-biter.

It was about the third week in May that Mrs Mullet, relict of
the late Sylvester Mullet, and mother of Toby and a bunch of
daughters, assailed Clovis Sangrail on the outskirts of the village
with a breathless catalogue of local happenings.

'You know our new neighbour, Mr Penricarde?' she vocifer-
ated; 'awfully rich, owns tin mines in Cornwall, middle-aged and
rather quiet. He's taken the Red House on a long lease and spent
a lot of money on alterations and improvements. Well, Toby's
sold him the Brogue!'

Clovis spent a moment or two in assimilating the astonishing
news; then he broke out into unstinted congratulation. If he had
belonged to a more emotional race he would probably have
kissed Mrs Mullet.

'How wonderfully lucky to have pulled it off at last! Now you
can buy a decent animal. I've always said that Toby was clever.
Ever so many congratulations.'

'Don't congratulate me. It's the most unfortunate thing that
could have happened!' said Mrs Mullet dramatically.

Clovis stared at her in amazement.

'Mr Penricarde,' said Mrs Mullet, sinking her voice to what she
imagined to be an impressive whisper, though it rather resembled
a hoarse, excited squeak, 'Mr Penricarde has just begun to pay
attentions to Jessie. Slight at first, but now unmistakable. I was a
fool not to have seen it sooner. Yesterday, at the Rectory garden
party, he asked her what her favourite flowers were, and she told
him carnations, and today a whole stack of carnations has
arrived, clove and malmaison and lovely dark red ones, regular
exhibition blooms, and a box of chocolates that he must have got
on purpose from London. And he's asked her to go round the
links with him tomorrow. And now, just at this critical moment,
Toby has sold him that animal. It's a calamity!'

'But you've been trying to get the horse off your hands for
years,' said Clovis.

'I've got a houseful of daughters,' said Mrs Mullet, 'and I've
been trying – well, not to get them off my hands, of course, but a

husband or two wouldn't be amiss among the lot of them; there are six of them, you know.'

'I don't know,' said Clovis, 'I've never counted, but I expect you're right as to the number; mothers generally know these things.'

'And now,' continued Mrs Mullet, in her tragic whisper, 'when there's a rich husband-in-prospect imminent on the horizon Toby goes and sells him that miserable animal. It will probably kill him if he tries to ride it; anyway it will kill any affection he might have felt towards any member of our family. What is to be done? We can't very well ask to have the horse back; you see, we praised it up like anything when we thought there was a chance of his buying it, and said it was just the animal to suit him.'

'Couldn't you steal it out of his stable and send it to grass at some farm miles away?' suggested Clovis; 'write "Votes for Women" on the stable door, and the thing would pass for a Suffragette outrage. No one who knew the horse could possibly suspect you of wanting to get it back again.'

'Every newspaper in the country would ring with the affair,' said Mrs Mullet; 'can't you imagine the headline, "Valuable Hunter Stolen by Suffragettes"? The police would scour the countryside till they found the animal.'

'Well, Jessie must try and get it back from Penricarde on the plea that it's an old favourite. She can say it was only sold because the stable had to be pulled down under the terms of an old repairing lease, and that now it has been arranged that the stable is to stand for a couple of years longer.'

'It sounds a queer proceeding to ask for a horse back when you've just sold him,' said Mrs Mullet, 'but something must be done, and done at once. The man is not used to horses, and I believe I told him it was as quiet as a lamb. After all, lambs go kicking and twisting about as if they were demented, don't they?'

'The lamb has an entirely unmerited character for sedateness,' agreed Clovis.

Jessie came back from the golf links next day in a state of mingled elation and concern.

'It's all right about the proposal,' she announced; 'he came out with it at the sixth hole. I said I must have time to think it over. I accepted him at the seventh.'

'My dear,' said her mother, 'I think a little more maidenly

reserve and hesitation would have been advisable, as you've known him so short a time. You might have waited till the ninth hole.'

'The seventh is a very long hole,' said Jessie; 'besides, the tension was putting us both off our game. By the time we'd got to the ninth hole we'd settled lots of things. The honeymoon is to be spent in Corsica, with perhaps a flying visit to Naples if we feel like it, and a week in London to wind up with. Two of his nieces are to be asked to be bridesmaids, so with our lot there will be seven, which is rather a lucky number. You are to wear your pearl grey, with any amount of Honiton lace jabbed into it. By the way, he's coming over this evening to ask your consent to the whole affair. So far all's well, but about the Brogue it's a different matter. I told him the legend about the stable, and how keen we were about buying the horse back, but he seems equally keen on keeping it. He said he must have horse exercise now that he's living in the country, and he's going to start riding tomorrow. He's ridden a few times in the Row, on an animal that was accustomed to carry octogenarians and people undergoing rest cures, and that's about all his experience in the saddle – oh, and he rode a pony once in Norfolk, when he was fifteen and the pony twenty-four; and tomorrow he's going to ride the Brogue! I shall be a widow before I'm married, and I do so want to see what Corsica's like; it looks so silly on the map.'

Clovis was sent for in haste, and the developments of the situation put before him.

'Nobody can ride that animal with any safety,' said Mrs Mullet 'except Toby, and he knows by long experience what it is going to shy at, and manages to swerve at the same time.'

'I did hint to Mr Penricarde – to Vincent, I should say – that the Brogue didn't like white gates,' said Jessie.

'White gates!' exclaimed Mrs Mullet; 'did you mention what effect a pig has on him? He'll have to go past Lockyer's farm to get to the high road, and there's sure to be a pig or two grunting about in the lane.'

'He's taken rather a dislike to turkeys lately,' said Toby.

'It's obvious that Penricarde mustn't be allowed to go out on that animal,' said Clovis, 'at least not till Jessie has married him, and tired of him. I tell you what: ask him to a picnic tomorrow, starting at an early hour; he's not the sort to go out for a ride before breakfast. The day after I'll get the rector to drive him over to Crowleigh before lunch, to see the new cottage hospital they're building there. The Brogue will be standing idle in the stable and Toby can offer to exercise it; then it can pick up a stone or something of the sort and go conveniently lame. If you hurry on the wedding a bit the lameness fiction can be kept up till the ceremony is safely over.'

Mrs Mullet belonged to an emotional race, and she kissed Clovis.

It was nobody's fault that the rain came down in torrents the next morning, making a picnic a fantastic impossibility. It was also nobody's fault, but sheer ill-luck, that the weather cleared up sufficiently in the afternoon to tempt Mr Penricarde to make his first essay with the Brogue. They did not get as far as the pigs at Lockyer's farm; the rectory gate was painted a dull unobtrusive green, but it had been white a year or two ago, and the Brogue never forgot that he had been in the habit of making a violent curtsey, a back-pedal and a swerve at this particular point of the road. Subsequently, there being apparently no further call on his services, he broke his way into the rectory orchard, where he found a hen turkey in a coop; later visitors to the orchard found the coop almost intact, but very little left of the turkey.

Mr Penricarde, a little stunned and shaken, and suffering from a bruised knee and some minor damages, good-naturedly ascribed the accident to his own inexperience with horses and country roads, and allowed Jessie to nurse him back into complete recovery and golf-fitness within something less than a week.

In the list of wedding presents which the local newspaper published a fortnight or so later appeared the following item:

'Brown saddle-horse, "The Brogue", bridegroom's gift to bride.'

'Which shows,' said Toby Mullet, 'that he knew nothing.'

'Or else,' said Clovis, 'that he has a very pleasing wit.'

Cousin Teresa

Basset Harrowcluff returned to the home of his fathers, after an absence of four years, distinctly well pleased with himself. He was only thirty-one, but he had put in some useful service in an out-of-the-way, though not unimportant, corner of the world. He had quieted a province, kept open a trade route, enforced the tradition of respect which is worth the ransom of many kings in out-of-the-way regions, and done the whole business on rather less expenditure than would be requisite for organizing a charity in the home country. In Whitehall and places where they think, they doubtless thought well of him. It was not inconceivable, his father allowed himself to imagine, that Basset's name might figure in the next list of Honours.

Basset was inclined to be rather contemptuous of his half-brother, Lucas, whom he found feverishly engrossed in the same medley of elaborate futilities that had claimed his whole time and energies, such as they were, four years ago, and almost as far back before that as he could remember. It was the contempt of the man of action for the man of activities, and it was probably reciprocated. Lucas was an over-well nourished individual, some nine years Basset's senior, with a colouring that would have been accepted as a sign of intensive culture in an asparagus, but probably meant in this case mere abstention from exercise. His hair and forehead furnished a recessional note in a personality that was in all other respects obtrusive and assertive. There was certainly no Semitic blood in Lucas's parentage, but his appearance contrived to convey at least a suggestion of Jewish extraction. Clovis Sangrail, who knew most of his associates by sight, said it was undoubtedly a case of protective mimicry.

Two days after Basset's return, Lucas frisked in to lunch in a state of twittering excitement that could not be restrained even for the immediate consideration of soup, but had to be verbally discharged in spluttering competition with mouthfuls of vermicelli.

'I've got hold of an idea for something immense,' he babbled, 'something that is simply It.'

Basset gave a short laugh that would have done equally well as a snort, if one had wanted to make the exchange. His half-brother was in the habit of discovering futilities that were 'simply It' at frequently recurring intervals. The discovery generally meant that he flew up to town, preceded by glowingly-worded telegrams, to see someone connected with the stage or the publishing world, got together one or two momentous luncheon parties, flitted in and out of 'Gambrinus' for one or two evenings, and returned home with an air of subdued importance and the asparagus tint slightly intensified. The great idea was generally forgotten a few weeks later in the excitement of some new discovery.

'The inspiration came to me whilst I was dressing,' announced Lucas; 'it will be *the* thing in the next music-hall *revue*. All London will go mad over it. It's just a couplet; of course there will be other words, but they won't matter. Listen:

> Cousin Teresa takes out Caesar,
> Fido, Jock, and the big borzoi.

'A lilting, catchy sort of refrain, you see, and big-drum business on the two syllables of bor-zoi. It's immense. And I've thought out all the business of it; the singer will sing the first verse alone, then during the second verse Cousin Teresa will walk through, followed by four wooden dogs on wheels; Caesar will be an Irish terrier, Fido a black poodle, Jock a fox-terrier, and the borzoi, of course, will be a borzoi. During the third verse Cousin Teresa will come on alone, and the dogs will be drawn across by themselves from the opposite wing; then Cousin Teresa will catch on to the singer and go off-stage in one direction, while the dogs' procession goes off in the other, crossing en route, which is always very effective. There'll be a lot of applause there, and for the fourth verse Cousin Teresa will come on in sables and the dogs will all have coats on. Then I've got a great idea for the fifth verse; each of the dogs will be led on by a Nut, and Cousin Teresa will come on from the opposite side, crossing en route, always effective, and then she turns round and leads the whole lot of them off on a string, and all the time every one singing like mad:

> Cousin Teresa takes out Caesar,
> Fido, Jock, and the big borzoi.

'Tum-Tum! Drum business on the two last syllables. I'm so excited, I shan't sleep a wink tonight. I'm off tomorrow by the ten-fifteen. I've wired to Hermanova to lunch with me.'

If any of the rest of the family felt any excitement over the creation of Cousin Teresa, they were signally successful in concealing the fact.

'Poor Lucas does take his silly little ideas seriously,' said Colonel Harrowcluff afterwards in the smoking-room.

'Yes,' said his younger son, in a slightly less tolerant tone, 'in a day or two he'll come back and tell us that his sensational masterpiece is above the heads of the public, and in about three weeks' time he'll be wild with enthusiasm over a scheme to dramatize the poems of Herrick or something equally promising.'

And then an extraordinary thing befell. In defiance of all precedent Lucas's glowing anticipations were justified and endorsed by the course of events. If Cousin Teresa was above the heads of the public, the public heroically adapted itself to her altitude. Introduced as an experiment at a dull moment in a new *revue*, the success of the item was unmistakable; the calls were so insistent and uproarious that even Lucas's ample devisings of additional 'business' scarcely sufficed to keep pace with the demand. Packed houses on successive evenings confirmed the verdict of the first night audience, stalls and boxes filled significantly just before the turn came on, and emptied significantly after the last *encore* had been given. The manager tearfully acknowledged that Cousin Teresa was It. Stage hands and supers and programme sellers acknowledged it to one another without the least reservation. The name of the *revue* dwindled to secondary importance, and vast letters of electric blue blazoned the words 'Cousin Teresa' from the front of the great palace of pleasure. And, of course, the magic of the famous refrain laid its spell all over the Metropolis. Restaurant proprietors were obliged to provide the members of their orchestras with painted wooden dogs on wheels, in order that the much-demanded and always conceded melody should be rendered with the necessary spectacular effects, and the crash of bottles and forks on the tables at the mention of the big borzoi usually drowned the sincerest efforts of drum or cymbals. Nowhere and at no time could one get away from the double thump that brought up the rear of the refrain; revellers reeling home at night banged it on doors and hoardings, milkmen clashed their cans to its cadence, messenger boys hit smaller messenger boys resounding double smacks on the same principle. And the more thoughtful circles of the great city were not deaf to the claims and significance of the popular melody. An enterprising and emancipated preacher discoursed from his pulpit on the inner meaning of 'Cousin Teresa', and Lucas Harrowcluff was invited to lecture on the subject of his great achievement to members of the Young Men's Endeavour League, the Nine Arts

Club, and other learned and willing-to-learn bodies. In Society it seemed to be the one thing people really cared to talk about; men and women of middle age and average education might be seen together in corners earnestly discussing, not the question whether Serbia should have an outlet on the Adriatic, or the possibilities of a British success in international polo contests, but the more absorbing topic of the problematic Aztec or Nilotic origin of the Teresa *motiv*.

'Politics and patriotism are so boring and so out of date,' said a revered lady who had some pretensions to oracular utterance; 'we are too cosmopolitan nowadays to be really moved by them. That is why one welcomes an intelligible production like "Cousin Teresa" that has a genuine message for one. One can't under-stand the message all at once, of course, but one felt from the very first that it was there. I've been to see it eighteen times and I'm going again tomorrow and on Thursday. One can't see it often enough.'

'It would be rather a popular move if we gave this Harrowcluff person a knighthood or something of the sort,' said the Minister reflectively.

'Which Harrowcluff?' asked his secretary.

'Which? There is only one, isn't there?' said the Minister; 'the "Cousin Teresa" man, of course. I think everyone would be pleased if we knighted him. Yes, you can put him down on the list of certainties – under the letter L.'

'The letter L,' said the secretary, who was new to his job; 'does that stand for Liberalism or liberality?'

Most of the recipients of Ministerial favour were expected to qualify in both of those subjects.

'Literature,' explained the Minister.

And thus, after a fashion, Colonel Harrowcluff's expectation of seeing his son's name in the list of Honours was gratified.

Dusk

Norman Gortsby sat on a bench in the Park, with his back to a strip of bush-planted sward, fenced by the park railings, and the Row fronting him across a wide stretch of carriage drive. Hyde

Park Corner, with its rattle and hoot of traffic, lay immediately to his right. It was some thirty minutes past six on an early March evening, and dusk had fallen heavily over the scene, dusk, mitigated by some faint moonlight and many street lamps. There was a wide emptiness over road and sidewalk, and yet there were many unconsidered figures moving silently through the half-light or dotted unobtrusively on bench and chair, scarcely to be distinguished from the shadowed gloom in which they sat.

The scene pleased Gortsby and harmonized with his present mood. Dusk, to his mind, was the hour of the defeated. Men and women who had fought and lost, who hid their fallen fortunes and dead hopes as far as possible from the scrutiny of the curious, came forth in this hour of gloaming, when their shabby clothes and bowed shoulders and unhappy eyes might pass unnoticed, or, at any rate, unrecognized.

> A king that is conquered must see strange looks,
> So bitter a thing is the heart of man.

The wanderers in the dusk did not choose to have strange looks fasten on them, therefore they came out in this bat-fashion, taking their pleasure sadly in a pleasure-ground that had emptied of its rightful occupants. Beyond the sheltering screen of bushes and palings came a realm of brilliant lights and noisy, rushing traffic. A blazing, many-tiered stretch of windows shone through the dusk and almost dispersed it, marking the haunts of those other people, who held their own life's struggle, or at any rate had not to admit failure. So Gortsby's imagination pictured things as he sat on his bench in the almost deserted walk. He was in the mood to count himself among the defeated. Money troubles did not press on him; had he so wished he could have strolled into the thoroughfares of light and noise, and taken his place among the jostling ranks of those who enjoyed prosperity or struggled for it. He had failed in a more subtle ambition, and for the moment he was heart sore and disillusionized, and not disinclined to take a certain cynical pleasure in observing and labelling his fellow wanderers as they went their ways in the dark stretches between the lamp-lights.

On the bench by his side sat an elderly gentlemen with a drooping air of defiance that was probably the remaining vestige of self-respect in an individual who had ceased to defy success-fully anybody or anything. His clothes could scarcely be called shabby, at least they passed muster in the half-light, but one's imagination could not have pictured the wearer embarking on the purchase of a half-crown box of chocolates or laying out ninepence on a carnation buttonhole. He belonged unmistakably to that forlorn orchestra to whose piping no one dances; he was one of the world's lamenters who induces no responsive weeping. As he rose to go Gortsby imagined him returning to a home circle where he was snubbed and of no account, or to some bleak lodging where his ability to pay a weekly bill was the beginning and end of the interest he inspired. His retreating figure vanished slowly into the shadows, and his place on the bench was taken almost immediately by a young man, fairly well dressed but scarcely more cheerful of mien than his predecessor. As if to emphasize the fact that the world went badly with him the new-comer unburdened himself of an angry and very audible expletive as he flung himself into the seat.

'You don't seem in a very good temper,' said Gortsby, judging that he was expected to take due notice of the demonstration.

The young man turned to him with a look of disarming frankness which put him instantly on his guard.

'You wouldn't be in a good temper if you were in the fix I'm in,' he said; 'I've done the silliest thing I've ever done in my life.'

'Yes?' said Gortsby dispassionately.

'Came up this afternoon, meaning to stay at the Patagonian Hotel in Berkshire Square,' continued the young man; 'when I got there I found it had been pulled down some weeks ago and a cinema theatre run up on the site. The taxi driver recommended me to another hotel some way off and I went there. I just sent a letter to my people, giving them the address, and then I went out to buy some soap – I'd forgotten to pack any and I hate using hotel soap. Then I strolled about a bit, had a drink at a bar and looked at the shops, and when I came to turn my steps back to the hotel I suddenly realized that I didn't remember its name or even what street it was in. There's a nice predicament for a fellow who hasn't any friends or connections in London! Of course I can wire to my people for the address, but they won't have got my letter till tomorrow; meantime I'm without any money, came out with about a shilling on me, which went buying the soap and getting the drink, and here I am, wandering about with twopence in my pocket and nowhere to go for the night.'

There was an eloquent pause after the story had been told. 'I suppose you think, I've spun you rather an impossible yarn,' said the young man presently, with a suggestion of resentment in his voice.

'Not at all impossible,' said Gortsby judicially; 'I remember doing exactly the same thing once in a foreign capital, and on that occasion there were two of us, which made it more remarkable. Luckily we remembered that the hotel was on a sort of canal, and when we struck the canal we were able to find our way back to the hotel.'

The youth brightened at the reminisence. 'In a foreign city I wouldn't mind so much,' he said; 'one could go to one's Consul and get the requisite help from him. Here in one's own land one is far more derelict if one gets into a fix. Unless I can find some decent chap to swallow my story and lend me some money I seem likely to spend the night on the Embankment. I'm glad, anyhow, that you don't think the story outrageously improbable.'

He threw a good deal of warmth into the last remark, as though perhaps to indicate his hope that Gortsby did not fall far short of the requisite decency.

'Of course,' said Gortsby slowly, 'the weak point of your story is that you can't produce the soap.'

The young man sat forward hurriedly, felt rapidly in the pockets of his overcoat, and then jumped to his feet.

'I must have lost it,' he muttered angrily.

'To lose an hotel and a cake of soap on one afternoon suggests wilful carelessness,' said Gortsby, but the young man scarcely waited to hear the end of the remark. He flitted away down the path, his head held high, with an air of somewhat jaded jauntiness.

'It was a pity,' mused Gortsby; 'the going out to get one's own soap was the one convincing touch in the whole story, and yet it was just that little detail that brought him to grief. If he had had the brilliant forethought to provide himself with a cake of soap, wrapped and sealed with all the solicitude of the chemist's counter, he would have been a genius in his particular line. In his particular line genius certainly consists of an infinite capacity for taking precautions.'

With that reflection Gortsby rose to go; as he did so an exclamation of concern escaped him. Lying on the ground by the side of the bench was a small oval packet, wrapped and sealed with the solicitude of a chemist's counter. It could be nothing else but a cake of soap, and it had evidently fallen out of the youth's overcoat pocket when he flung himself down on the seat. In another moment Gortsby was scudding along the dusk-shrouded path in anxious quest for a youthful figure in a light overcoat. He had nearly given up the search when he caught sight of the object of his pursuit standing irresolutely on the border of the carriage drive, evidently uncertain whether to strike across the Park or make for the bustling pavements of Knightsbridge. He turned round sharply with an air of defensive hostility when he found Gortsby hailing him.

'The important witness to the genuineness of your story has turned up,' said Gortsby, holding out the cake of soap; 'it must have slid out of your overcoat pocket when you sat down on the seat. I saw it on the ground after you left. You must excuse my disbelief, but appearances were really rather against you, and now, as I appealed to the testimony of the soap I think I ought to abide by its verdict. If the loan of a sovereign is any good to you –'

The young man hastily removed all doubt on the subject by pocketing the coin.

'Here is my card with my address,' continued Gortsby; 'any day this week will do for returning the money, and here is the soap – don't lose it again; it's been a good friend to you.'

'Lucky thing your finding it,' said the youth, and then, with a catch in his voice, he blurted out a word or two of thanks and fled headlong in the direction of Knightsbridge.

'Poor boy, he as nearly as possible broke down,' said Gortsby to himself. 'I don't wonder either; the relief from his quandary must have been acute. It's a lesson to me not to be too clever in judging by circumstances.'

As Gortsby retraced his steps past the seat where the little drama had taken place he saw an elderly gentleman poking and peering beneath it and on all sides of it, and recognized his earlier fellow occupant.

'Have you lost anything, sir?' he asked.

'Yes, sir, a cake of soap.'

Fur

'You look worried, dear,' said Eleanor.

'I am worried,' admitted Suzanne; 'not worried exactly, but anxious. You see, my birthday happens *next* week –'

'You lucky person,' interrupted Eleanor; 'my birthday doesn't come till the end of March.'

'Well, old Bertram Kneyght is over in England just now from the Argentine. He's a kind of distant cousin of my mother's, and so enormously rich that we've never let the relationship drop out of sight. Even if we don't see him or hear from him for years he is always Cousin Bertram when he does turn up. I can't say he's ever been of much solid use to us, but yesterday the subject of my birthday cropped up, and he asked me to let him know what I wanted for a present.'

'Now, I understand the anxiety,' observed Eleanor.

'As a rule when one is confronted with a problem like that,' said Suzanne, 'all one's ideas vanish; one doesn't seem to have a desire in the world. Now it so happens that I have been very keen on a little Dresden figure that I saw somewhere in Kensington; about thirty-six shillings, quite beyond my means. I was very nearly describing the figure, and giving Bertram the address of the shop. And then it suddenly struck me that thirty-six shillings was such a ridiculously inadequate sum for a man of his immense wealth to spend on a birthday present. He could give thirty-six pounds as easily as you or I could buy a bunch of violets. I don't want to be greedy, of course, but I don't like being wasteful.'

'The question is,' said Eleanor, 'what are his ideas as to present-giving? Some of the wealthiest people have curiously cramped views on that subject. When people grow gradually rich their requirements and standard of living expand in proportion, while their present-giving instincts often remain in the undeveloped condition of their earlier days. Something showy and not-too-expensive in a shop is their only conception of the ideal gift. That is why even quite good shops have their counters and windows crowded with things worth about four shillings that look as if they might be worth seven-and-six, and are priced at ten shillings and labelled "seasonable gifts".'

'I know,' said Suzanne; 'that is why it is so risky to be vague when one is giving indications of one's wants. Now if I say to him: "I am going out to Davos this winter, so anything in the travelling line would be acceptable," he *might* give me a dressing-bag with gold-mounted fittings, but, on the other hand, he might give me Baedeker's *Switzerland*, or *Ski-ing without Tears*, or something of that sort.'

'He would be more likely to say: "She'll be going to lots of dances, a fan will be sure to be useful".'

'Yes, and I've got tons of fans, so you see where the danger and anxiety lies. Now if there is one thing more than another that I urgently want it is furs. I simply haven't any. I'm told that Davos is full of Russians, and they are sure to wear the most lovely sables and things. To be among people who are smothered in furs when one hasn't any oneself makes one want to break most of the Commandments.'

'If it's furs that you're out for,' said Eleanor, 'you will have to superintend the choice of them in person. You can't be sure that your cousin knows the difference between silver-fox and ordinary squirrel.'

'There are some heavenly silver-fox stoles at Goliath and Mastodon's,' said Suzanne, with a sigh; 'if I could only inveigle Bertram into their building and take him for a stroll through the fur department!'

'He lives somewhere near there, doesn't he?' said Eleanor. 'Do you know what his habits are? Does he take a walk at any particular time of day?'

'He usually walks down at his club about three o'clock, if it's a fine day. That takes him right past Goliath and Mastodon's.'

'Let us two meet him accidentally at the street corner tomorrow,' said Eleanor; 'we can walk a little way with him, and with luck we ought to be able to side-track him into the shop. You can say you want to get a hair-net or something. When we're safely there I can say: "I wish you'd tell me what you want for your birthday." Then you'll have everything ready to hand – the rich cousin, the fur department, and the topic of birthday presents.'

'It's a great idea,' said Suzanne; 'you really are a brick. Come round tomorrow at twenty to three; don't be late, we must carry out our ambush to the minute.'

At a few minutes to three the next afternoon the fur-trappers walked warily towards the selected corner. In the near distance rose the colossal pile of Messrs Goliath and Mastodon's famed establishment. The afternoon was brilliantly fine, exactly the sort of weather to tempt a gentleman of advancing years into the discreet exercise of a leisurely walk.

'I say, dear, I wish you'd do something for me this evening,' said Eleanor to her companion; 'just drop in after dinner on some pretext or other, and stay on to make a fourth at bridge with Adela and the aunts. Otherwise I shall have to play, and Harry Scarisbrooke is going to come in unexpectedly about nine-fifteen, and I particularly wanted to be free to talk to him while the others are playing.'

'Sorry, my dear, no can do,' said Suzanne; 'ordinary bridge at threepence a hundred, with such dreadfully slow players as your aunts, bores me to tears. I nearly go to sleep over it.'

'But I most particularly want an opportunity to talk with Harry,' urged Eleanor, an angry glint coming into her eyes.

'Sorry, anything to oblige, but not that,' said Suzanne cheerfully; the sacrifices of friendship were beautiful in her eyes as long as she was not asked to make them.

Eleanor said nothing further on the subject but the corners of her mouth rearranged themselves.

'There's our man!' exclaimed Suzanne suddenly; 'hurry!'

Mr Bertram Kneyght greeted his cousin and her friend with genuine heartiness, and readily accepted their invitation to explore the crowded mart that stood temptingly at their elbow. The plate-glass doors swung open and the trio plunged bravely into the jostling throng of buyers and loiterers.

'Is it always as full as this?' asked Bertram of Eleanor.

'More or less, and autumn sales are on just now,' she replied.

Suzanne, in her anxiety to pilot her cousin to the desired haven of the fur department, was usually a few paces ahead of the others, coming back to them now and then if they lingered for a moment at some attractive counter, with the nervous solicitude of a parent rook encouraging its young ones on their first flying expedition.

'It's Suzanne's birthday on Wednesday next,' confided Eleanor to Bertram Kneyght at a moment when Suzanne had left them unusually far behind; 'my birthday comes the day before, so we are both on the look-out for something to give each other.'

'Ah,' said Bertram. 'Now, perhaps you can advise me on that very point. I want to give Suzanne something, and I haven't the least idea what she wants.'

'She's rather a problem,' said Eleanor. 'She seems to have everything one can think of, lucky girl. A fan is always useful; she'll be going to a lot of dances at Davos this winter. Yes, I should think a fan would please her more than anything. After our birthdays are over we inspect each other's muster of presents, and I always feel dreadfully humble. She gets such nice things, and I never have anything worth showing. You see, none of my relations or any of the people who give me presents are at all well off, so I can't expect them to do anything more than just remember the day with some little trifle. Two years ago an uncle on my mother's side of the family, who had come into a small legacy, promised me a silver-fox stole for my birthday. I can't tell you how excited I was about it, and I pictured myself showing it off to all my friends and enemies. Then just at that moment his wife died, and, of course, poor man, he could not be expected to think of birthday presents at such a time. He has lived abroad ever since, and I never got my fur. Do you know, to this day I can scarcely look at a silver-fox pelt in a shop window or round anyone's neck without feeling ready to burst into tears. I suppose if I hadn't had the prospect of getting one I shouldn't feel that way. Look, there is the fan counter, on your left; you can easily slip away into the crowd. Get her as nice a one as you can see – she is such a dear, dear girl.'

'Hullo, I thought I had lost you,' said Suzanne, making her way through an obstructive knot of shoppers. 'Where is Bertram?'

'I got separated from him long ago. I thought he was on ahead with you,' said Eleanor. 'We shall never find him in this crush.'

Which turned out to be a true prediction.

'All our trouble and forethought thrown away,' said Suzanne sulkily, when they had pushed their way fruitlessly through half a dozen departments.

'I can't think why you didn't grab him by the arm,' said

Eleanor; 'I would have if I'd known him longer, but I'd only just been introduced. It's nearly four now, we'd better have tea.'

Some days later Suzanne rang Eleanor up on the telephone.

'Thank you very much for the photograph frame. It was just what I wanted. Very good of you. I say, do you know what that Kneyght person has given me? Just what you said he would – a wretched fan. What? Oh, yes, quite a good enough fan in its way, but still . . .'

'You must come and see what he's given me,' came in Eleanor's voice over the 'phone.

'You! Why should he give you anything?'

'Your cousin appears to be one of those rare people of wealth who take a pleasure in giving good presents,' came the reply.

'I wondered why he was so anxious to know where she lived,' snapped Suzanne to herself as she rang off.

A cloud has arisen between the friendships of the two young women; as far as Eleanor is concerned the cloud has a silver-fox lining.

Laura

'You are not really dying, are you?' asked Amanda.

'I have the doctor's permission to live till Tuesday,' said Laura.

'But today is Saturday; this is serious!' gasped Amanda.

'I don't know about it being serious; it is certainly Saturday,' said Laura.

'Death is always serious,' said Amanda.

'I never said I was going ʼɔ die. I am presumably going to leave off being Laura, but I shall go on being something. An animal of some kind, I suppose. You see, when one hasn't been very good in the life one has just lived, one reincarnates in some lower organism. And I haven't been very good, when one comes to think of it. I've been petty and mean and vindictive and all that sort of thing when circumstances have seemed to warrant it.'

'Circumstances never warrant that sort of thing,' said Amanda hastily.

'If you don't mind my saying so,' observed Laura, 'Egbert is a circumstance that would warrant any amount of that sort of thing. You're married to him – that's different; you've sworn to love, honour and endure him: I haven't.'

'I don't see what's wrong with Egbert,' protested Amanda.

'Oh, I dare say the wrongness has been on my part,' admitted Laura dispassionately; 'he has merely been the extenuating circumstance. He made a thin, peevish kind of fuss, for instance, when I took the collie puppies from the farm out for a run the other day.'

'They chased his young broods of speckled Sussex and drove two sitting hens off their nests, besides running all over the flower beds. You know how devoted he is to his poultry and garden.'

'Anyhow, he needn't have gone on about it for the entire evening, and then have said, "Let's say no more about it" just when I was beginning to enjoy the discussion. That's where one of my petty vindictive revenges came in,' added Laura with an unrepentant chuckle. 'I turned the entire family of speckled Sussex into his seedling shed the day after the puppy episode.'

'How could you?' exclaimed Amanda.

'It came quite easy,' said Laura; 'two of the hens pretended to be laying at the time, but I was firm.'

'And we thought it was an accident!'

'You see,' resumed Laura, 'I really *have* some grounds for supposing that my next incarnation will be in a lower organism. I shall be an animal of some kind. On the other hand, I haven't been a bad sort in my way, so I think I may count on being a nice animal, something elegant and lively, with a love of fun. An otter, perhaps.'

'I can't imagine you as an otter,' said Amanda.

'Well, I don't suppose you can imagine me as an angel, if it comes to that,' said Laura.

Amanda was silent. She couldn't.

'Personally I think an otter life would be rather enjoyable,' continued Laura; 'salmon to eat all the year round, and the satisfaction of being able to catch the trout in their own homes without having to wait for hours till they condescend to rise to the fly you've been dangling before them; and an elegant svelte figure –'

'Think of the otter hounds,' interposed Amanda; 'how dreadful to be hunted and harried and finally worried to death!'

'Rather fun with half the neighbourhood looking on, and

anyhow not worse than this Saturday-to-Tuesday business of
dying by inches; and then I should go on into something else. If I
had been a moderately good otter I suppose I should get back into
human shape of some sort; probably something rather primitive –
a little brown, unclothed Nubian boy, I should think.'

'I wish you would be serious,' sighed Amanda; 'you really
ought to be if you're only going to live till Tuesday.'

As a matter of fact Laura died on Monday.

'So dreadfully upsetting,' Amanda complained to her uncle-in-
law, Sir Lulworth Quayne. 'I've asked quite a lot of people down
for golf and fishing, and the rhododendrons are just looking their
best.'

'Laura always was inconsiderate,' said Sir Lulworth; 'she was
born during Goodwood week, with an Ambassador staying in the
house who hated babies.'

'She had the maddest kind of ideas,' said Amanda; 'do you
know if there was any insanity in her family?'

'Insanity? No, I never heard of any. Her father lives in West
Kensington, but I believe he's sane on all other subjects.'

'She had an idea that she was going to be reincarnated as an
otter,' said Amanda.

'One meets with those ideas of reincarnation so frequently
even in the West,' said Sir Lulworth, 'that one can hardly set
them down as being mad. And Laura was such an unaccount-
able person in this life that I should not like to lay down definite
rules as to what she might be doing in an after state.'

'You think she really might have passed into some animal
form?' asked Amanda. She was one of those who shape their
opinions rather readily from the standpoint of those around
them.

Just then Egbert entered the breakfast-room, wearing an air of
bereavement that Laura's demise would have been insufficient, in
itself, to account for.

'Four of my speckled Sussex have been killed,' he exclaimed;
'the very four that were to go to the show on Friday. One of them
was dragged away and eaten right in the middle of that new
carnation bed that I've been to such trouble and expense over.
My best flower bed and my best fowls singled out for destruction;
it almost seems as if the brute that did the deed had special

knowledge how to be as devastating as possible in a short space
of time.'

'Was it a fox, do you think?' asked Amanda.

'Sounds more like a polecat,' said Sir Lulworth.

'No,' said Egbert, 'there were marks of webbed feet all over the
place, and we followed the tracks down to the stream at the
bottom of the garden; evidently an otter.'

Amanda looked quickly and furtively across at Sir Lulworth.

Egbert was too agitated to eat any breakfast, and went out to
superintend the strengthening of the poultry yard defences.

'I think she might at least have waited till the funeral was
over,' said Amanda in a scandalized voice.

'It's her own funeral, you know,' said Sir Lulworth; 'it's a nice
point in etiquette how far one ought to show respect to one's own
mortal remains.'

Disregard for mortuary convention was carried to further
lengths next day; during the absence of the family at the funeral
ceremony the remaining survivors of the speckled Sussex were
massacred. The marauder's line of retreat seemed to have
embraced most of the flower beds on the lawn, but the
strawberry beds in the lower garden had also suffered.

'I shall get the otter hounds to come here at the earliest
possible moment,' said Egbert savagely.

'On no account! You can't dream of such a thing!' exclaimed
Amanda. 'I mean, it wouldn't do, so soon after a funeral in the
house.'

'It's a case of necessity,' said Egbert; 'once an otter takes to that
sort of thing it won't stop.'

'Perhaps it will go elsewhere now that there are no more fowls
left,' suggested Amanda.

'One would think you wanted to shield the beast,' said Egbert.

'There's been so little water in the stream lately,' objected
Amanda; 'it seems hardly sporting to hunt an animal when it has
so little chance of taking refuge anywhere.'

'Good gracious!' fumed Egbert, 'I'm not thinking about sport. I
want to have the animal killed as soon as possible.'

Even Amanda's opposition weakened when, during church
time on the following Sunday, the otter made its way into the
house, raided half a salmon from the larder and worried it into
scaly fragments on the Persian rug in Egbert's studio.

'We shall have it hiding under our beds and biting pieces out of our feet before long,' said Egbert, and from what Amanda knew of this particular otter she felt that the possibility was not a remote one.

On the evening preceding the day fixed for the hunt Amanda spent a solitary hour walking by the banks of the stream, making what she imagined to be hound noises. It was charitably supposed by those who overheard her performance, that she was practising for farmyard imitations at the forthcoming village entertainment.

It was her friend and neighbour, Aurora Burret, who brought her news of the day's sport.

'Pity you weren't out; we had quite a good day. We found it at once, in the pool just below your garden.'

'Did you – kill?' asked Amanda.

'Rather. A fine she-otter. Your husband got rather badly bitten in trying to "tail it". Poor beast, I felt quite sorry for it, it had such a human look in its eyes when it was killed. You'll call me silly, but do you know who the look reminded me of? My dear woman, what is the matter?'

When Amanda had recovered to a certain extent from her attack of nervous prostration Egbert took her to the Nile Valley to recuperate. Change of scene speedily brought about the desired recovery of health and mental balance. The escapades of an adventurous otter in search of a variation of diet were viewed in their proper light. Amanda's normally placid temperament reasserted itself. Even a hurricane of shouted curses, coming from her husband's dressing-room, in her husband's voice, but hardly in his usual vocabulary, failed to disturb her serenity as she made a leisurely toilet one evening in a Cairo hotel.

'What is the matter? What has happened?' she asked in amused curiosity.

'The little beast has thrown all my clean shirts into the bath! Wait till I catch you, you little –'

'What little beast?' asked Amanda, suppressing a desire to laugh; Egbert's language was so hopelessly inadequate to express his outraged feelings.

'A little beast of a naked brown Nubian boy,' spluttered Egbert.

And now Amanda is seriously ill.

The Lull

'I've asked Latimer Springfield to spend Sunday with us and stop the night,' announced Mrs Durmot at the breakfast-table.

'I thought he was in the throes of an election,' remarked her husband.

'Exactly; the poll is on Wednesday, and the poor man will have worked himself to a shadow by that time. Imagine what electioneering must be like in this awful soaking rain, going along slushy country roads and speaking to damp audiences in draughty schoolrooms, day after day for a fortnight. He'll have to put in an appearance at some place of worship on Sunday morning, and he can come to us immediately afterwards and have a thorough respite from everything connected with politics. I won't let him even think of them. I've had the picture of Cromwell dissolving the Long Parliament taken down from the staircase, and even the portrait of Lord Rosebery's "Ladas" removed from the smoking-room. And, Vera,' added Mrs Durmot, turning to her sixteen-year-old niece, 'be careful what colour ribbon you wear in your hair; not blue or yellow on any account; those are the rival party colours, and emerald green or orange would be almost as bad, with this Home Rule business to the fore.'

'On state occasions I always wear a black ribbon in my hair,' said Vera with crushing dignity.

Latimer Springfield was a rather cheerless, oldish young man, who went into politics somewhat in the spirit in which other people might go into half mourning. Without being an enthusiast, however, he was a fairly strenuous plodder, and Mrs Durmot had been reasonably near the mark in asserting that he was working at high pressure over this election. The restful lull which his hostess enforced on him was decidedly welcome, and yet the nervous excitement of the contest had too great a hold on him to be totally banished.

'I know he's going to sit up half the night working up points for his final speeches,' said Mrs Durmot regretfully; 'however, we've kept politics at arm's length all the afternoon and evening. More than that we cannot do.'

'That remains to be seen,' said Vera, but she said it to herself.

Latimer had scarcely shut his bedroom door before he was

immersed in a sheaf of notes and pamphlets, while a fountain-pen and pocket-book were brought into play for the due marshalling of useful facts and discreet fictions. He had been at work for perhaps thirty-five minutes, and the house was seemingly consecrated to the healthy slumber of country life, when a stifled squealing and scuffling in the passage was followed by a loud tap at his door. Before he had time to answer, a much-encumbered Vera burst into the room with the question: 'I say, can I leave these here?'

'These' were a small black pig and a lusty specimen of black-red gamecock.

Latimer was moderately fond of animals, and particularly interested in small livestock rearing from the economic point of view; in fact one of the pamphlets on which he was at that moment engaged warmly advocated the further development of the pig and poultry industry in our rural districts; but he was pardonably unwilling to share even a commodious bedroom with samples of henroost and sty products.

'Wouldn't they be happier somewhere outside?' he asked, tactfully expressing his own preference in the matter in an apparent solicitude for theirs.

'There is no outside,' said Vera impressively, 'nothing but a waste of dark, swirling waters. The reservoir at Brinkley has burst.'

'I didn't know there was a reservoir at Brinkley,' said Latimer.

'Well, there isn't now, it's jolly well all over the place, and as we stand particularly low we're the centre of an inland sea just at present. You see the river has overflowed its banks as well.'

'Good gracious! Have any lives been lost?'

'Heaps, I should say. The second housemaid has already identified three bodies that have floated past the billiard-room window as being the young man she's engaged to. Either she's engaged to a large assortment of the population round here or else she's very careless at identification. Of course it may be the same body coming round again and again in a swirl; I hadn't thought of that.'

'But we ought to go out and do rescue work, oughtn't we?' said Latimer, with the instinct of a Parliament candidate for getting into the local limelight.

'We can't,' said Vera decidedly, 'we haven't any boats and

we're cut off by a raging torrent from any human habitation. My aunt particularly hoped you would keep to your room and not add to the confusion, but she thought it would be so kind of you if you would take in Hartlepool's Wonder, the gamecock, you know, for the night. You see, there are eight other gamecocks, and they fight like furies if they get together, so we're putting one in each bedroom. The fowl-houses are all flooded out, you know. And then I thought perhaps you wouldn't mind taking in this wee piggie; he's rather a little love, but he has a vile temper. He gets that from his mother – not that I like to say things against her when she's lying dead and drowned in her sty, poor thing. What he really wants is a man's firm hand to keep him in order. I'd try and grapple with him myself, only I've got my chow in my room, you know, and he goes for pigs wherever he finds them.'

'Couldn't the pig go in the bathroom?' asked Latimer faintly, wishing that he had taken up as determined a stand on the subject of bedroom swine as the chow had.

'The bathroom?' Vera laughed shrilly. 'It'll be full of Boy Scouts till morning if the hot water holds out.'

'Boy Scouts?'

'Yes, thirty of them came to rescue us while the water was only waist-high; then it rose another three feet or so and we had to rescue them. We're giving them hot baths in batches and drying their clothes in the hot-air cupboard, but, of course, drenched clothes don't dry in a minute, and the corridor and staircase are beginning to look like a bit of coast scenery by Tuke. Two of the boys are wearing your Melton overcoat; I hope you don't mind.'

'It's a new overcoat,' said Latimer, with every indication of minding dreadfully.

'You'll take every care of Hartlepool's Wonder, won't you?' said Vera. 'His mother took three firsts at Birmingham, and he was second in the cockerel class last year at Gloucester. He'll probably roost on the rail at the bottom of your bed. I wonder if he'd feel more at home if some of his wives were up here with him? The hens are all in the pantry, and I think I could pick out Hartlepool Helen; she's his favourite.'

Latimer showed a belated firmness on the subject of Hartlepool Helen, and Vera withdrew without pressing the point, having first settled the gamecock on his extemporized perch and taken an affectionate farewell of the pigling. Latimer undressed and got into bed with all due speed, judging that the pig would abate its inquisitorial restlessness once the light was turned out. As a substitute for a cozy, straw-bedded sty the room offered, at first inspection, few attractions, but the disconsolate animal suddenly discovered an appliance in which the most luxuriously contrived piggeries were notably deficient. The sharp edge of the underneath part of the bed was pitched at exactly the right elevation to permit the pigling to scrape himself ecstatically backwards and forwards, with an artistic humping of the back at the crucial moment and an accompanying gurgle of long-drawn delight. The gamecock, who may have fancied that he was being rocked in the branches of a pine-tree, bore the motion with greater fortitude than Latimer was able to command. A series of slaps directed at the pig's body were accepted more as an additional and pleasing irritant than as a criticism of conduct or a hint to desist; evidently something more than a man's firm hand was needed to deal with the case. Latimer slipped out of bed in search of a weapon of dissuasion. There was sufficient light in the room to enable the pig to detect this manoeuvre, and the vile temper, inherited from the drowned mother, found full play. Latimer bounded back into bed, and his conqueror, after a few threatening snorts and champings of its jaws, resumed its massage operations with renewed zeal. During the long wakeful hours which ensued Latimer tried to distract his mind from his own immediate troubles by dwelling with decent sympathy on the second house-maid's bereavement, but he found himself more often wondering how many Boy Scouts were sharing his Melton overcoat. The role of Saint Martin *malgré lui* was not one which appealed to him.

Towards dawn the pigling fell into a happy slumber, and Latimer might have followed its example, but at about the same time Stupor Hartlepooli gave a rousing crow, clattered down to the floor and forthwith commenced a spirited combat with his reflection in the wardrobe mirror. Remembering that the bird was more or less under his care Latimer performed Hague Tribunal offices by draping a bath-towel over the provocative mirror, but the ensuing peace was local and short-lived. The deflected energies of the gamecock found new outlet in a sudden and sustained attack on the sleeping and temporarily inoffensive pigling, and the duel which followed was desperate and embittered beyond any possibility of effective intervention. The feathered combatant had the advantage of being able, when hard pressed, to take refuge on the bed, and freely availed himself of this circumstance; the pigling never quite succeeded in hurling himself on to the same eminence, but it was not from want of trying.

Neither side could claim any decisive success, and the struggle had been practically fought to a standstill by the time that the maid appeared with the early morning tea.

'Lor, sir,' she exclaimed in undisguised astonishment, 'do you want those animals in your room?'

Want!

The pigling, as though aware that it might have outstayed its welcome, dashed out at the door, and the gamecock followed it at a more dignified pace.

'If Miss Vera's dog sees that pig –!' exclaimed the maid, and hurried off to avert such a catastrophe.

A cold suspicion was stealing over Latimer's mind; he went to the window and drew up the blind. A light, drizzling rain was falling, but there was not the faintest trace of any inundation.

Some half-hour later he met Vera on the way to the breakfast-room.

'I should not like to think of you as a deliberate liar,' he observed coldly, 'but one occasionally has to do things one does not like.'

'At any rate I kept your mind from dwelling on politics all the night,' said Vera.

Which was, of course, perfectly true.

The Lumber-Room

The children were to be driven, as a special treat, to the sands at Jagborough. Nicholas was not to be one of the party; he was in disgrace. Only that morning he had refused to eat his wholesome bread-and-milk on the seemingly frivolous ground that there was a frog in it. Older and wiser and better people had told him that there could not possibly be a frog in his bread-and-milk and that he was not to talk nonsense; he continued, nevertheless, to talk what seemed the veriest nonsense, and described with much detail the colouration and markings of the alleged frog. The dramatic part of the incident was that there really was a frog in Nicholas' basin of bread-and-milk; he had put it there himself, so he felt entitled to know something about it. The sin of taking a frog from the garden and putting in into a bowl of wholesome bread-and-milk was enlarged on at great length, but the fact that stood out clearest in the whole affair, as it presented itself to the mind of Nicholas, was that the older, wiser, and better people had been proved to be profoundly in error in matters about which they had expressed the utmost assurance.

'You said there couldn't possibly be a frog in my bread-and-milk; there *was* a frog in my bread-and-milk,' he repeated, with the insistence of a skilled tactician who does not intend to shift from favourable ground.

So his boy-cousin and girl-cousin and his quite uninteresting younger brother were to be taken to Jagborough sands that afternoon and he was to stay at home. His cousins' aunt, who insisted, by an unwarranted stretch of imagination, in styling herself his aunt also, had hastily invented the Jagborough expedition in order to impress on Nicholas the delights that he had justly forfeited by his disgraceful conduct at the breakfast-table. It was her habit, whenever one of the children fell from grace, to improvise something of a festival nature from which the offender would be rigorously debarred; if all the children sinned collectively they were suddenly informed of a circus in the neighbouring town, a circus of unrivalled merit and uncounted elephants, to which, but for their depravity, they would have been taken that very day.

A few decent tears were looked for on the part of Nicholas when the moment for the departure of the expedition arrived. As a matter of fact, however, all the crying was done by his girl-cousin, who scraped her knee rather painfully against the step of the carriage as she was scrambling in.

'How she did howl,' said Nicholas cheerfully, as the party drove off without any of the elation of high spirits that should have characterized it.

'She'll soon get over that,' said the *soi-disant* aunt; 'it will be a glorious afternoon for racing about over those beautiful sands. How they will enjoy themselves!'

'Bobby won't enjoy himself much, and he won't race much either,' said Nicholas with a grim chuckle; 'his boots are hurting him. They're too tight.'

'Why didn't he tell me they were hurting?' asked the aunt with some asperity.

'He told you twice, but you weren't listening. You often don't listen when we tell you important things.'

'You are not to go into the gooseberry garden,' said the aunt, changing the subject.

'Why not?' demanded Nicholas.

'Because you are in disgrace,' said the aunt loftily.

Nicholas did not admit the flawlessness of the reasoning; he felt perfectly capable of being in disgrace and in a gooseberry garden at the same moment. His face took on an expression of considerable obstinacy. It was clear to his aunt that he was determined to get into the gooseberry garden, 'only,' as she remarked to herself, 'because I have told him he is not to.'

Now the gooseberry garden had two doors by which it might be entered, and once a small person like Nicholas could slip in there he could effectually disappear from view amid the masking growth of artichokes, raspberry canes, and fruit bushes. The aunt had many other things to do that afternoon, but she spent an hour or two in trivial gardening operations among flower beds and shrubberies, whence she could keep a watchful eye on the two doors that led to the forbidden paradise. She was a woman of few ideas, with immense powers of concentration.

Nicholas made one or two sorties into the front garden, wriggling his way with obvious stealth of purpose towards one or other of the doors, but never able for a moment to evade the aunt's watchful eye. As a matter of fact, he had no intention of trying to get into the gooseberry garden, but it was extremely convenient for him that his aunt should believe that he had; it was a belief that would keep her on self-imposed sentry-duty for the greater part of the afternoon. Having thoroughly confirmed and fortified her suspicions, Nicholas slipped back into the house and rapidly put into execution a plan of action that had long germinated in his brain. By standing on a chair in the library one could reach a shelf on which reposed a fat, important-looking key. The key was as important as it looked; it was the instrument which kept the mysteries of the lumber-room secure from

unauthorized intrusion, which opened a way only for aunts and
such-like privileged persons. Nicholas had not had much experience of the art of fitting keys into keyholes and turning locks, but
for some days past he had practised with the key of the school-
room door; he did not believe in trusting too much to luck and
accident. The key turned stiffly in the lock, but it turned. The
door opened, and Nicholas was in an unknown land, compared
with which the gooseberry garden was a stale delight, a mere
material pleasure.

Often and often Nicholas had pictured to himself what the
lumber-room might be like, that region that was so carefully
sealed from youthful eyes and concerning which no questions
were ever answered. It came up to his expectations. In the first
place it was large and dimly lit, one high window opening on to
the forbidden garden being its only source of illumination. In the
second place it was a storehouse of unimagined treasures. The
aunt-by-assertion was one of those people who think that things
spoil by use and consign them to dust and damp by way of
preserving them. Such parts of the house as Nicholas knew best
were rather bare and cheerless, but here there were wonderful
things for the eye to feast on. First and foremost there was a piece
of framed tapestry that was evidently meant to be a fire-screen.
To Nicholas it was a living, breathing story; he sat down on a roll
of Indian hangings, glowing in wonderful colours beneath a layer
of dust, and took in all the details of the tapestry picture. A man,
dressed in the hunting costume of some remote period, had just
transfixed a stag with an arrow; it could not have been a difficult
shot because the stag was only one or two paces away from him;
in the thickly growing vegetation that the picture suggested it
would not have been difficult to creep up to a feeding stag, and
the two spotted dogs that were springing forward to join in the
chase had evidently been trained to keep to heel till the arrow
was discharged. That part of the picture was simple, if interesting,
but did the huntsman see, what Nicholas saw, that four galloping
wolves were coming in his direction through the wood? There
might be more than four of them hidden behind the trees, and in
any case would the man and his dogs be able to cope with the
four wolves if they made an attack? The man had only two
arrows left in his quiver, and he might miss with one or both of
them; all one knew about his skill in shooting was that he could

hit a large stag at a ridiculously short range. Nicholas sat for many golden minutes revolving the possibilities of the scene; he was inclined to think that there were more than four wolves and that the man and his dogs were in a tight corner.

But there were other objects of delight and interest claiming his instant attention; there were quaint twisted candlesticks in the shape of snakes, and a teapot fashioned like a china duck, out of whose open beak the tea was supposed to come. How dull and shapeless the nursery teapot seemed in comparison! And there was a carved sandal-wood box packed tight with aromatic cotton-wool, and between the layers of cotton-wool were little brass figures, hump-necked bulls, and peacocks and goblins, delightful to see and to handle. Less promising in appearance was a large square book with plain black covers; Nicholas peeped into it, and, behold, it was full of coloured pictures of birds. And such birds! In the garden, and in the lanes when he went for a walk, Nicholas came across a few birds, of which the largest were an occasional magpie or wood-pigeon; here were herons and bustards, kites, toucans, tiger-bitterns, brush turkeys, ibises, golden pheasants, a whole portrait gallery of undreamed-of creatures. And as he was admiring the colouring of the mandarin duck and assigning a life-history to it, the voice of his aunt in shrill vociferation of his name came from the gooseberry garden without. She had grown suspicious at his long disappearance, and had leapt to the conclusion that he had climbed over the wall behind the sheltering screen of the lilac bushes; she was now engaged in energetic and rather hopeless search for him among the artichokes and raspberry canes.

'Nicholas, Nicholas!' she screamed, 'you are to come out of this at once. It's no use trying to hide there; I can see you all the time.'

It was probably the first time for twenty years that anyone had smiled in that lumber-room.

Presently the angry repetitions of Nicholas' name gave way to a shriek, and a cry for somebody to come quickly, Nicholas shut the book, restored it carefully to its place in a corner, and shook some dust from a neighbouring pile of newspapers over it. Then he crept from the room, locked the door, and replaced the key exactly where he had found it. His aunt was still calling his name when he sauntered into the front garden.

'Who's calling?' he asked.

'Me,' came the answer from the other side of the wall; 'didn't you hear me? I've been looking for you in the gooseberry garden, and I've slipped into the rain-water tank. Luckily there's no water in it, but the sides are slippery and I can't get out. Fetch the little ladder from under the cherry tree –'

'I was told I wasn't to go into the gooseberry garden,' said Nicholas promptly.

'I told you not to, and now I tell you that you may,' came the voice from the rain-water tank, rather impatiently.

'Your voice doesn't sound like aunt's,' objected Nicholas; 'you may be the Evil One tempting me to be disobedient. Aunt often tells me that the Evil One tempts me and that I always yield. This time I'm not going to yield.'

'Don't talk nonsense,' said the prisoner in the tank; 'go and fetch the ladder.'

'Will there be strawberry jam for tea?' asked Nicholas innocently.

'Certainly there will be,' said the aunt, privately resolving that Nicholas should have none of it.

'Now I know that you are the Evil One and not aunt,' shouted Nicholas gleefully; 'when we asked aunt for strawberry jam yesterday she said there wasn't any. I know there are four jars of it in the store cupboard, because I looked, and of course you know it's there, but *she* doesn't, because she said there wasn't any. Oh, Devil, you *have* sold yourself!'

There was an unusual sense of luxury in being able to talk to an aunt as though one was talking to the Evil One, but Nicholas knew, with childish discernment, that such luxuries were not to be over-indulged in. He walked noisily away, and it was a kitchenmaid, in search of parsley, who eventually rescued the aunt from the rain-water tank.

Tea that evening was partaken of in a fearsome silence. The tide had been at its highest when the children had arrived at Jagborough Cove, so there had been no sands to play on – a circumstance that the aunt had overlooked in the haste of organizing her punitive expedition. The tightness of Bobby's boots had had disastrous effect on his temper the whole of the afternoon, and altogether the children could not have been said to have enjoyed themselves. The aunt maintained the frozen muteness of one who has suffered undignified and unmerited detention in a rain-water tank for thirty-five minutes. As for Nicholas, he, too, was silent, in the absorption of one who has much to think about; it was just possible, he considered, that the huntsman would escape with his hounds while the wolves feasted on the stricken stag.

The Open Window

'My aunt will be down presently, Mr Nuttel,' said a very self-possessed young lady of fifteen; 'in the meantime you must try and put up with me.'

Framton Nuttel endeavoured to say the correct something which should duly flatter the niece of the moment without unduly discounting the aunt that was to come. Privately he doubted more than ever whether these formal visits on a succession of total strangers would do much towards helping the nerve cure which he was supposed to be undergoing.

'I know how it will be,' his sister had said when he was preparing to migrate to this rural retreat; 'you will bury yourself down there and not speak to a living soul, and your nerves will be worse than ever from moping. I shall just give you letters of introduction to all the people I know there. Some of them, as far as I can remember, were quite nice.'

Framton wondered whether Mrs Sappleton, the lady to whom he was presenting one of the letters of introduction, came into the nice division.

'Do you know many of the people round here?' asked the niece, when she judged that they had had sufficient silent communion.

'Hardly a soul,' said Framton. 'My sister was staying here, at the rectory, you know, some four years ago, and she gave me letters of introduction to some of the people here.'

He made the last statement in a tone of distinct regret.

'Then you know practically nothing about my aunt?' pursued the self-possessed young lady.

'Only her name and address,' admitted the caller. He was wondering whether Mrs Sappleton was in the married or widowed state. An undefinable something about the room seemed to suggest masculine habitation.

'Her great tragedy happened just three years ago,' said the child; 'that would be since your sister's time.'

'Her tragedy?' asked Framton; somehow in this restful country spot tragedies seemed out of place.

'You may wonder why we keep that window wide open on an October afternoon,' said the niece, indicating a large french window that opened on to a lawn.

'It is quite warm for the time of the year,' said Framton; 'but has that window got anything to do with the tragedy?'

'Out through that window, three years ago to a day, her husband and her two young brothers went off for their day's shooting. They never came back. In crossing the moor to their favourite snipe-shooting ground they were all three engulfed in a treacherous piece of bog. It had been that dreadful wet summer, you know, and places that were safe in other years gave way suddenly without warning. Their bodies were never recovered. That was the dreadful part of it.' Here the child's voice lost its self-possessed note and became falteringly human. 'Poor aunt always thinks that they will come back some day, they and the little brown spaniel that was lost with them, and walk in at that window just as they used to do. That is why the window is kept open every evening till it is quite dusk. Poor dear aunt, she has often told me how they went out, her husband with his white waterproof coat over his arm, and Ronnie, her youngest brother, singing, "Bertie, why do you bound?" as he always did to tease her, because she said it got on her nerves. Do you know, sometimes on still, quiet evenings like this, I almost get a creepy feeling that they will all walk in through that window –'

She broke off with a little shudder. It was a relief to Framton when the aunt bustled into the room with a whirl of apologies for being late in making her appearance.

'I hope Vera has been amusing you?' she said.

'She has been very interesting,' said Framton.

'I hope you don't mind the open window,' said Mrs Sappleton briskly; 'my husband and brothers will be home directly from shooting, and they always come in this way. They've been out for snipe in the marshes today, so they'll make a fine mess over my poor carpets. So like you men-folk, isn't it?'

She rattled on cheerfully about the shooting and the scarcity of birds, and the prospects for duck in the winter. To Framton it was all purely horrible. He made a desperate but only partially successful effort to turn the talk on to a less ghastly topic; he was conscious that his hostess was giving him only a fragment of her attention, and her eyes were constantly straying past him to the open window and the lawn beyond. It was certainly an unfortunate coincidence that he should have paid his visit on this tragic anniversary.

'The doctors agree in ordering me complete rest, an absence of mental excitement, and avoidance of anything in the nature of violent physical exercise,' announced Framton, who laboured under the tolerably wide-spread delusion that total strangers and chance acquaintances are hungry for the least detail of one's ailments and infirmities, their cause and cure. 'On the matter of diet they are not much in agreement,' he continued.

'No?' said Mrs Sappleton, in a voice which only replaced a yawn at the last moment. Then she suddenly brightened into alert attention – but not to what Framton was saying.

'Here they are at last!' she cried. 'Just in time for tea, and don't they look as if they were muddy up to the eyes!'

Framton shivered slightly and turned towards the niece with a look intended to convey sympathetic comprehension. The child was staring out through the open window with dazed horror in her eyes. In a chill shock of nameless fear Framton swung round in his seat and looked in the same direction.

In the deepening twilight three figures were walking across the lawn towards the window; they all carried guns under their arms, and one of them was additionally burdened with a white coat hung over his shoulders. A tired brown spaniel kept close at their heels. Noiselessly they neared the house, and then a hoarse young voice chanted out of the dusk: 'I said, Bertie, why do you bound?'

Framton grabbed wildly at his stick and hat; the hall-door, the gravel-drive, and the front gate were dimly noted stages in his headlong retreat. A cyclist coming along the road had to run into the hedge to avoid imminent collision.

'Here we are, my dear,' said the bearer of the white mackintosh, coming in through the window; 'fairly muddy, but most of it's dry. Who was that who bolted out as we came up?'

'A most extraordinary man, a Mr Nuttel,' said Mrs Sappleton; 'could only talk about his illnesses, and dashed off without a

word of good-bye or apology when you arrived. One would think
he had seen a ghost.'

'I expect it was the spaniel,' said the niece calmly; 'he told me
he had a horror of dogs. He was once hunted into a cemetery
somewhere on the banks of the Ganges by a pack of pariah dogs,
and had to spend the night in a newly dug grave with the
creatures snarling and grinning and foaming just above him.
Enough to make anyone lose their nerve.'

Romance at short notice was her speciality.

The Quince Tree

'I've just been to see old Betsy Mullen,' announced Vera to her
aunt, Mrs Bebberly Cumble; 'she seems in rather a bad way about
her rent. She owes about fifteen weeks of it, and says she doesn't
know where any of it is to come from.'

'Betsy Mullen always is in difficulties with her rent, and the
more people help her with it the less she troubles about it,' said
the aunt. 'I certainly am not going to assist her any more. The
fact is, she will have to go into a smaller and cheaper cottage;
there are several to be had at the other end of the village for half
the rent that she is paying, or supposed to be paying, now. I told
her a year ago that she ought to move.'

'But she wouldn't get such a nice garden anywhere else,'
protested Vera, 'and there's such a jolly quince tree in the corner.
I don't suppose there's another quince tree in the whole parish.
And she never makes any quince jam; I think to have a quince
tree and not to make quince jam shows such strength of
character. Oh, she can't possibly move away from that garden.'

'When one is sixteen,' said Mrs Bebberly Cumble severely, 'one
talks of things being impossible which are merely uncongenial. It
is not only possible but it is desirable that Betsy Mullen should
move into smaller quarters; she has scarcely enough furniture to
fill that big cottage.'

'As far as value goes,' said Vera after a short pause, 'there is
more in Betsy's cottage than in any other house for miles round.'

'Nonsense,' said the aunt; 'she parted with whatever old china
ware she had long ago.'

'I'm not talking about anything that belongs to Betsy herself,' said Vera darkly; 'but of course, you don't know what I know, and I don't suppose I ought to tell you.'

'You must tell me at once,' exclaimed the aunt, her senses leaping into alertness like those of a terrier suddenly exchanging a bored drowsiness for the lively anticipation of an immediate rat hunt.

'I'm perfectly certain that I oughtn't to tell you anything about it,' said Vera, 'but, then, I often do things that I oughtn't to do.'

'I should be the last person to suggest that you should do anything that you ought not to do –' began Mrs Bebberly Cumble impressively.

'And I am always swayed by the last person who speaks to me,' admitted Vera, 'so I'll do what I ought not to do and tell you.'

Mrs Bebberly Cumble thrust a very pardonable sense of exasperation into the background of her mind and demanded impatiently:

'What is there in Betsy Mullen's cottage that you are making such a fuss about?'

'It's hardly fair to say that *I've* made a fuss about it,' said Vera; 'this is the first time I've mentioned the matter, but there's been no end of trouble and mystery and newspaper speculation about it. It's rather amusing to think of the columns of conjecture in the Press and the police and detectives hunting about everywhere at home and abroad, and all the while that innocent-looking little cottage has held the secret.'

'You don't mean to say it's the Louvre picture, La Something or other, the woman with the smile, that disappeared about two years ago?' exclaimed the aunt with rising excitement.

'Oh, no, not that,' said Vera, 'but something quite as important and just as mysterious – if anything, rather more scandalous.'

'Not the Dublin –?'

Vera nodded.

'The whole jolly lot of them.'

'In Betsy's cottage? Incredible!'

'Of course Betsy hasn't any idea as to what they are,' said Vera; 'she just knows that they are something valuable and that she must keep quiet about them. I found out quite by accident what they were and how they came to be there. You see, the people who had them were at their wits' end to know where to

stow them away for safe keeping, and someone who was
motoring through the village was struck by the snug loneliness of
the cottage and thought it would be just the thing. Mrs Lamper
arranged the matter with Betsy and smuggled the things in.'

'Mrs Lamper?'

'Yes, she does a lot of district visiting, you know.'

'I am quite aware that she takes soup and flannel and
improving literature to the poorer cottages,' said Mrs Bebberly
Cumble, 'but that is hardly the same sort of thing as disposing of
stolen goods, and she must have known something about their
history; anyone who reads the papers, even casually, must have
been aware of the theft, and I should think the things were not
hard to recognize. Mrs Lamper has always had the reputation of
being a very conscentious woman.'

'Of course she was screening someone else,' said Vera. 'A
remarkable feature of the affair is the extraordinary number of
quite respectable people who have involved themselves in its
meshes by trying to shield others. You would be really astonished
if you knew some of the names of the individuals mixed up in it,
and I don't suppose a tithe of them knew who the original
culprits were; and now I've got you entangled in the mess by
letting you into the secret of the cottage.'

'You most certainly have not entangled me,' said Mrs Bebberly
Cumble indignantly. 'I have no intention of shielding anybody.
The police must know about it at once; a theft is a theft, whoever
is involved. If respectable people choose to turn themselves into
receivers and disposers of stolen goods, well, they've ceased to be
respectable, that's all. I shall telephone immediately —'

'Oh, aunt,' said Vera reproachfully, 'it would break the poor
Canon's heart if Cuthbert were to be involved in a scandal of this
sort. You know it would.'

'Cuthbert involved! How can you say such things when you
know how much we all think of him?'

'Of course I know you think a lot of him, and that he's engaged
to marry Beatrice, and that it will be a frightfully good match,
and that he's your ideal of what a son-in-law ought to be. All the
same, it was Cuthbert's idea to stow the things away in the
cottage, and it was his motor that brought them. He was only
doing it to help his friend Pegginson, you know — the Quaker
man, who is always agitating for a smaller Navy. I forget how he

got involved in it. I warned you that there were lots of quite respectable people mixed up in it, didn't I? That's what I meant when I said it would be impossible for old Betsy to leave the cottage; the things take up a good bit of room, and she couldn't go carrying them about with her other goods and chattels without attracting notice. Of course if she were to fall ill and die it would be equally unfortunate. Her mother lived to be over ninety, she tells me, so with due care and an absence of worry she ought to last for another dozen years at least. By that time perhaps some other arrangements will have been made for disposing of the wretched things.'

'I shall speak to Cuthbert about it – after the wedding,' said Mrs Bebberly Cumble.

'The wedding isn't till next year,' said Vera, in recounting the story to her best girl friend, 'and meanwhile old Betsy is living rent free, with soup twice a week and my aunt's doctor to see her whenever she has a finger ache.'

'But how on earth did you get to know about it all?' asked her friend, in admiring wonder.

'It was a mystery –' said Vera.

'Of course it was a mystery, a mystery that baffled everybody. What beats me is how you found out –'

'Oh, about the jewels? I invented that part,' explained Vera; 'I mean the mystery was where old Betsy's arrears of rent were to come from; and she would have hated leaving that jolly quince tree.'

The Romancers

It was autumn in London, that blessed season between the harshness of winter and the insincerities of summer; a trustful season when one buys bulbs and sees in the registration of one's vote, believing perpetually in spring and a change of Government.

Morton Crosby sat on a bench in a secluded corner of Hyde Park, lazily enjoying a cigarette and watching the slow grazing promenade of a pair of snow-geese, the male looking rather like an albino edition of the russet-hued female. Out of the corner of his eye Crosby also noted with some interest the hesitating hoverings of a human figure, which had passed and repassed his seat two or three times at shortening intervals, like a wary crow about to alight near some possibly edible morsel. Inevitably the figure came to an anchorage on the bench, within easy talking distance of its original occupant. The uncared-for clothes, the aggressive, grizzled beard, and the furtive, evasive eye of the newcomer bespoke the professional cadger, the man who would undergo hours of humiliating tale-spinning and rebuff rather than adventure on half a day's decent work.

For a while the newcomer fixed his eyes straight in front of him in a strenuous, unseeing gaze; then his voice broke out with the insinuating inflection of one who has a story to retail well worthy any loiterer's while to listen to.

'It's a strange world,' he said.

As the statement met with no response he altered it to the form of a question.

'I dare say you've found it to be a strange world, mister?'

'As far as I am concerned,' said Crosby, 'the strangeness has worn off in the course of thirty-six years.'

'Ah,' said the greybeard, 'I could tell you things that you'd hardly believe. Marvellous things that have really happened to me.'

'Nowadays there is not demand for marvellous things that have really happened,' said Crosby discouragingly; 'the professional writers of fiction turn these things out so much better. For instance, my neighbours tell me wonderful, incredible things that their Aberdeens and chows and borzois have done; I never listen to them. On the other hand, I have read *The Hound of the Baskervilles* three times.'

The greybeard moved uneasily in his seat; then he opened up new country.

'I take it that you are a professing Christian,' he observed.

'I am a prominent and I think I may say an influential member of the Mussulman community of Eastern Persia,' said Crosby, making an excursion himself into the realms of fiction.

The greybeard was obviously disconcerted at this new check of introductory conversation, but the defeat was only momentary.

'Persia. I should never have taken you for a Persian,' he remarked, with a somewhat aggrieved air.

'I am not,' said Crosby; 'my father was an Afghan.'

'An Afghan!' said the other, smitten into bewildered silence for a moment. Then he recovered himself and renewed his attack.

'Afghanistan. Ah! We've had some wars with that country; now, I dare say, instead of fighting it we might have learned something from it. A very wealthy country, I believe. No real poverty there.'

He raised his voice on the word 'poverty' with a suggestion of intense feeling. Crosby saw the opening and avoided it.

'It possesses, nevertheless, a number of highly talented and ingenious beggars,' he said; 'if I had not spoken so disparagingly of marvellous things that have really happened I would tell you the story of Ibrahim and the eleven camel-loads of blotting-paper. Also I have forgotten exactly how it ended.'

'My own life-story is a curious one,' said the stranger, apparently stifling all desire to hear the history of Ibrahim; 'I was not always as you see me now.'

'We are supposed to undergo complete change in the course of every seven years,' said Crosby, as an explanation of the foregoing announcement.

'I mean I was not always in such distressing circumstances as I am at present,' pursued the stranger doggedly.

'That sounds rather rude,' said Crosby stiffly, 'considering that you are at present talking to a man reputed to be one of the most gifted conversationalists of the Afghan border.'

'I don't mean in that way,' said the greybeard hastily; 'I've been very much interested in your conversation. I was alluding to my unfortunate financial situation. You mayn't hardly believe it, but at the present moment I am absolutely without a farthing. Don't see any prospect of getting any money, either, for the next few days. I don't suppose you've ever found yourself in such a position,' he added.

'In the town of Yom,' said Crosby, 'which is in Southern Afghanistan, and which also happens to be my birthplace, there was a Chinese philosopher who used to say that one of the three chief human blessings was to be absolutely without money. I forget what the other two were.'

'Ah, I dare say,' said the stranger, in a tone that betrayed no enthusiasm for the philosopher's memory, 'and did he practise what he preached? That's the test.'

'He lived happily with very little money or resources,' said Crosby.

'Then I expect he had friends who would help him liberally whenever he was in difficulties, such as I am in at present.'

'In Yom,' said Crosby, 'it is not necessary to have friends in order to obtain help. Any citizen of Yom would help a stranger as a matter of course.'

The greybeard was now genuinely interested. The conversation had at last taken a favourable turn.

'If someone, like me, for instance, who was in undeserved difficulties, asked a citizen of that town you speak of for a small loan to tide over a few days' impecuniosity – five shillings, or perhaps a rather larger sum – would it be given to him as a matter of course?'

'There would be a certain preliminary,' said Crosby; 'one would take him to a wine-shop and treat him to a measure of wine, and then after a little high-flown conversation, one would put the desired sum in his hand and wish him good-day. It is a roundabout way of performing a simple transaction, but in the East all ways are roundabout.'

The listener's eyes were glittering.

'Ah,' he exclaimed, with a thin sneer ringing meaningly through his words, 'I suppose you've given up all those generous customs since you left your town. Don't practise them now, I expect.'

'No one who has lived in Yom,' said Crosby fervently, 'and remembers its green hills covered with apricot and almond trees, and the cold water that rushes down like a caress from the upland snows and dashes under the little wooden bridges, no one who remembers these things and treasures the memory of them would ever give up a single one of its unwritten laws and customs. To me they are as binding as though I still lived in that hallowed home of my youth.'

'Then if I was to ask you for a small loan –' began the greybeard fawningly, edging nearer on the seat and hurriedly wondering how large he might safely make his request, 'if I was to ask you for, say –'

'At any other time, certainly,' said Crosby; 'in the months of November and December, however, it is absolutely forbidden for anyone of our race to give or receive loans or gifts; in fact, one does not willingly speak of them. It is considered unlucky. We will therefore close this discussion.'

'But it is still October!' exclaimed the adventurer with an eager, angry whine, as Crosby rose from his seat; 'wants eight days to the end of the month!'

'The Afghan November began yesterday,' said Crosby severely, and in another moment he was striding across the Park, leaving his recent companion scowling and muttering furiously on the seat.

'I don't believe a word of his story,' he chattered to himself; 'pack of nasty lies from beginning to end. Wish I'd told him so to his face. Calling himself an Afghan.'

The snorts and snarls that escaped from him for the next quarter of an hour went far to support the truth of the old saying that two of a trade never agree.

The Seventh Pullet

'It's not the daily grind that I complain of,' said Blenkinthrope resentfully; 'it's the dull grey sameness of my life outside of office hours. Nothing of interest comes my way, nothing remarkable or out of the common. Even the little things that I do try to find some interest in don't seem to interest other people. Things in my garden, for instance.'

'The potato that weighed just over two pounds,' said his friend Gorworth.

'Did I tell you about that?' said Blenkinthrope; 'I was telling the others in the train this morning. I forgot if I'd told you.'

'To be exact you told me that it weighed just under two pounds, but I took into account the fact that abnormal vegetables and freshwater fish have an after-life, in which growth is not arrested.'

'You're just like the others,' said Blenkinthrope sadly; 'you only make fun of it.'

'The fault is with the potato, not with us,' said Gorworth; 'we are not in the least interested in it because it is not in the least interesting. The men you go up in the train with every day are just in the same case as yourself; their lives are commonplace and not very interesting to themselves, and they certainly are not going to wax enthusiastic over the commonplace events in other men's lives. Tell them something startling, dramatic, piquant, that has happened to yourself or to someone in your family, and you will capture their interest at once. They will talk about you with a certain personal pride to all their acquaintances. "Man I know intimately, fellow called Blenkinthrope, lives down my way, had two of his fingers clawed clean off by a lobster he was carrying home to supper. Doctor says entire hand may have to come off." Now that is conversation of a very high order. But imagine walking into a tennis club with the remark: "I know a man who has grown a potato weighing two and a quarter pounds".'

'But hang it all, my dear fellow,' said Blenkinthrope impatiently, 'haven't I just told you that nothing of a remarkable nature ever happens to me?'

'Invent something,' said Gorworth. Since winning a prize for excellence in Scriptural knowledge at a preparatory school he had felt licensed to be a little more unscrupulous than the circle he moved in. Much might surely be excused to one who in early life could give a list of seventeen trees mentioned in the Old Testament.

'What sort of thing?' asked Blenkinthrope, somewhat snappishly.

'A snake got into your hen-run yesterday morning and killed six out of seven pullets, first mesmerizing them with its eyes and then biting them as they stood helpless. The seventh pullet was one of that French sort, with feathers all over its eyes, so it escaped the mesmeric snare, and just flew at what it could see of the snake and pecked it to pieces.'

'Thank you,' said Blenkinthrope stiffly; 'it's a very clever invention. If such a thing had really happened in my poultry-run I admit I should have been proud and interested to tell people about it. But I'd rather stick to fact, even if it is plain fact.' All the same his mind dwelt wistfully on the story of the Seventh Pullet. He could picture himself telling it in the train amid the absorbed interest of his fellow-passengers. Unconsciously all sorts of little details and improvements began to suggest themselves.

Wistfulness was still his dominant mood when he took his seat in the railway carriage the next morning. Opposite him sat

Stevenham, who had attained to a recognized brevet of importance through the fact of an uncle having dropped dead in the act of voting at a Parliamentary election. That had happened three years ago, but Stevenham was still deferred to on all questions of home and foreign politics.

'Hullo, how's the giant mushroom, or whatever it was?' was all the notice Blenkinthrope got from his fellow travellers.

Young Duckby, whom he mildly disliked, speedily monopolized the general attention by an account of a domestic bereavement.

'Had four young pigeons carried off last night by a whacking big rat. Oh, a monster he must have been; you could tell by the size of the hole he made breaking into the loft.'

No moderate-sized rat ever seemed to carry out any predatory operations in these regions; they were all enormous in their enormity.

'Pretty hard lines that,' continued Duckby, seeing that he had secured the attention and respect of the company; 'four squeakers carried off at one swoop. You'd find it rather hard to match that in the way of unlooked-for bad luck.'

'I had six pullets out of a pen of seven killed by a snake yesterday afternoon,' said Blenkinthrope, in a voice which he hardly recognized at his own.

'By a snake?' came in excited chorus.

'It fascinated them with its deadly, glittering eyes, one after the other, and struck them down while they stood helpless. A bedridden neighbour, who wasn't able to call for assistance, witnessed it all from her bedroom window.'

'Well, I never!' broke in the chorus, with variations.

'The interesting part of it is about the seventh pullet, the one that didn't get killed,' resumed Blenkinthrope, slowly lighting a cigarette. His diffidence had left him, and he was beginning to realize how safe and easy depravity can seem once one has the courage to begin. 'The six dead birds were Minorcas; the seventh was a Houdan with a mop of feathers all over its eyes. It could hardly see the snake at all, so of course it wasn't mesmerized like the others. It just could see something wriggling on the ground, and went for it and pecked it to death.'

'Well, I'm blessed!' exclaimed the chorus.

In the course of the next few days Blenkinthrope discovered how little the loss of one's self-respect affects one when one has gained the esteem of the world. His story found its way into one of the poultry papers, and was copied thence into a daily news-sheet as a matter of general interest. A lady wrote from the North of Scotland recounting a similar episode which she had witnessed as occurring between a stoat and a blind grouse. Somehow a lie seems so much less reprehensible when one can call it a lee.

For a while the adapter of the Seventh Pullet story enjoyed to the full his altered standing as a person of consequence, one who had had some share in the strange events of his times. Then he was thrust once again into the cold grey background by the sudden blossoming into importance of Smith-Paddon, a daily fellow traveller, whose little girl had been knocked down and nearly hurt by a car belonging to a musical-comedy actress. The actress was not in the car at the time, but she was in numerous photographs which appeared in the illustrated papers of Zoto Dobreen inquiring after the well-being of Maisie, daughter of Edmund Smith-Paddon, Esq. With this new human interest to absorb them the travelling companions were almost rude when Blenkinthrope tried to explain his contrivance for keeping vipers and peregrine falcons out of his chicken-run.

Gorworth, to whom he unburdened himself in private, gave him the same counsel as theretofore.

'Invent something.'

'Yes, but what?'

The ready affirmative coupled with the question betrayed a significant shifting of the ethical standpoint.

It was a few days later that Blenkinthrope revealed a chapter of family history to the customary gathering in the railway carriage.

'Curious thing happened to my aunt, the one who lives in Paris,' he began. He had several aunts, but they were all geographically distributed over Greater London.

'She was sitting on a seat in the Bois the other afternoon, after lunching at the Roumanian Legation.'

Whatever the story gained in picturesqueness for the dragging-in of diplomatic 'atmosphere', it ceased from that moment to command any acceptance as a record of current events. Gorworth had warned his neophyte that this would be the case, but the traditional enthusiasm of the neophyte had triumphed over discretion.

'She was feeling rather drowsy, the effect probably of the champagne, which she's not in the habit of taking in the middle of the day.'

A subdued murmur of admiration went round the company. Blenkinthrope's aunts were not used to taking champagne in the middle of the year, regarding it exclusively as a Christmas and New Year accessory.

'Presently a rather portly gentleman passed by her seat and paused an instant to light a cigar. At that moment a youngish man came up behind him, drew the blade from a swordstick, and stabbed him half a dozen times through and through. "Scoundrel," he cried to his victim, "you do not know me. My name is Henri Leturc." The elder man wiped away some of the blood that was spattering his clothes, turned to his assailant, and said: "And since when has an attempted assassination been considered an introduction?" Then he finished lighting his cigar and walked away. My aunt had intended screaming for the police, but seeing the indifference with which the principal in the affair treated the matter she felt that it would be an impertinence on her part to interfere. Of course I need hardly say she put the whole thing down to the effects of a warm, drowsy afternoon and the Legation champagne. Now comes the astonishing part of my story. A fortnight later a bank manager was stabbed to death with a swordstick in that very part of the Bois. His assassin was the son of a charwoman formerly working at the bank, who had been dismissed from his job by the manager on account of chronic intemperance. His name was Henri Leturc.'

From that moment Blenkinthrope was tacitly accepted as the Munchausen of the party. No effort was spared to draw him out from day to day in the exercise of testing their powers of credulity, and Blenkinthrope, in the false security of an assured and receptive audience, waxed industrious and ingenious in supplying the demand for marvels. Duckby's satirical story of a tame otter that had a tank in the garden to swim in, and whined restlessly whenever the water-rate was overdue, was scarcely an unfair parody of some of Blenkinthrope's wilder efforts. And then one day came Nemesis.

Returning to his villa one evening Blenkinthrope found his wife stitting in front of a pack of cards, which she was scrutinizing with unusual concentration.

'The same old patience-game?' he asked carelessly.

'No dear; this is the Death's Head patience, the most difficult of them all. I've never got it to work out, and somehow I should be rather frightened if I did. Mother only got it out once in her life; she was afraid of it, too. Her great-aunt had done it once and fallen dead from excitement the next moment, and mother always had a feeling that she would die if she ever got it out. She died the same night that she did it. She was in bad health at the time, certainly, but it was a strange coincidence.'

'Don't do it if it frightens you,' was Blenkinthrope's practical comment as he left the room. A few minutes later his wife called to him.

'John, it gave me such a turn, I nearly got it out. Only the five of diamonds held me up at the end. I really thought I'd done it.'

'Why, you can do it,' said Blenkinthrope, who had come back to the room; 'if you shift the eight of clubs on to that open nine the five can be moved on to the six.'

His wife made the suggested move with hasty, trembling fingers, and piled the outstanding cards on to their respective packs. Then she followed the example of her mother and great-grand-aunt.

Blenkinthrope had been genuinely fond of his wife, but in the midst of his bereavement one dominant thought obtruded itself. Something sensational and real had at last come into his life; no longer was it a grey, colourless record. The headlines which might appropriately describe his domestic tragedy kept shaping themselves in his brain. 'Inherited presentiment comes true.' 'The Death's Head patience: Card-game that justified its sinister name in three generations.' He wrote out a full story of the fatal occurrence for the *Essex Vedette*, the editor of which was a friend of his, and to another friend he gave a condensed account, to be taken up to the office of one of the halfpenny dailies. But in both cases his reputation as a romancer stood fatally in the way of the fulfilment of his ambitions. 'Not the right thing to be Munchausening in a time of sorrow,' agreed his friends among themselves, and a brief note of regret at the 'sudden death of the wife of our respected neighbour, Mr John Blenkinthrope, from heart failure', appearing in the news column of the local paper was the forlorn outcome of his visions of widespread publicity.

Blenkinthrope shrank from the society of his erstwhile travelling companions and took to travelling townwards by an earlier train. He sometimes tries to enlist the sympathy and attention of a chance acquaintance in details of the whistling prowess of his best canary or the dimensions of his largest beetroot; he scarcely recognizes himself as the man who was once spoken about and pointed out as the owner of the Seventh Pullet.

The She-Wolf

Leonard Bilsiter was one of those people who have failed to find this world attractive or interesting, and who have sought compensation in an 'unseen world' of their own experience or imagination – or invention. Children do that sort of thing successfully, but children are content to convince themselves, and do not vulgarize their beliefs by trying to convince other people. Leonard Bilsiter's beliefs were for 'the few', that is to say, anyone who would listen to him.

His dabblings in the unseen might not have carried him beyond the customary platitudes of the drawing-room visionary if accident had not reinforced his stock-in-trade of mystical lore. In company with a friend, who was interested in a Ural mining concern, he had made a trip across Eastern Europe at a moment when the great Russian railway strike was developing from a threat to a reality; its outbreak caught him on the return journey, somewhere on the further side of Perm, and it was while waiting for a couple of days at a wayside station in a state of suspended locomotion that he made the acquaintance of a dealer in harness and metalware, who profitably whiled away the tedium of the long halt by initiating his English travelling companion in a fragmentary system of folk-lore that he had picked up from Trans-Baikal traders and natives. Leonard returned to his home circle garrulous about his Russian strike experiences, but oppressively reticent about certain dark mysteries, which he alluded to under the resounding title of Siberian Magic. The reticence wore off in a week or two under the influence of an entire lack of general curiosity, and Leonard began to make more detailed allusions to the enormous powers which this new esoteric force, to use his own description of it, conferred on the initiated few who knew how to wield it. His aunt, Cecilia Hoops, who loved sensation perhaps rather better than she loved the truth, gave him as clamorous an advertisement as anyone could wish for by retailing an account of how he had turned a vegetable marrow into a wood-pigeon before her very eyes. As a manifestation of the possession of supernatural powers, the story was discounted in some quarters by the respect accorded to Mrs Hoops' powers of imagination.

However divided opinion might be on the question of Leonard's status as a wonderworker or a charlatan, he certainly arrived at Mary Hampton's house-party with a reputation for pre-eminence in one or other of those professions, and he was not disposed to shun such publicity as might fall to his share. Esoteric forces and unusual powers figured largely in whatever conversation he or his aunt had a share in, and his own performances, past and potential, were the subject of mysterious hints and dark avowals.

'I wish you would turn me into a wolf, Mr Bilsiter,' said his hostess at luncheon the day after his arrival.

'My dear Mary,' said Colonel Hampton, 'I never knew you had a craving in that direction.'

'A she-wolf, of course,' continued Mrs Hampton; 'it would be too confusing to change one's sex as well as one's species at a moment's notice.'

'I don't think one should jest on these subjects,' said Leonard.

'I'm not jesting, I'm quite serious, I assure you. Only don't do it today; we have only eight available bridge players, and it would break up one of our tables. Tomorrow we shall be a larger party. Tomorrow night, after dinner –'

'In our present imperfect understanding of these hidden forces I think one should approach them with humbleness rather than mockery,' observed Leonard, with such severity that the subject was forthwith dropped.

Clovis Sangrail had sat unusually silent during the discussion on the possibilities of Siberian Magic; after lunch he side-tracked Lord Pabham into the comparative seclusion of the billiard-room and delivered himself of a searching question.

'Have you such a thing as a she-wolf in your collection of wild animals? A she-wolf of moderately good temper?'

Lord Pabham considered. 'There is Louisa,' he said, 'a rather fine specimen of the timber-wolf. I got her two years ago in exchange for some Arctic foxes. Most of my animals get to be fairly tame before they've been with me very long; I think I can say Louisa has an angelic temper, as she-wolves go. Why do you ask?'

'I was wondering whether you would lend her to me for tomorrow night,' said Clovis, with the careless solicitude of one who borrows a collar stud or a tennis racquet.

'Tomorrow night?'

'Yes, wolves are nocturnal animals, so the late hours won't hurt her,' said Clovis, with the air of one who has taken everything into consideration; 'one of your men could bring her over from Pabham Park after dusk, and with a little help he ought to be able to smuggle her into the conservatory at the same moment that Mary Hampton makes an unobtrusive exit.'

Lord Pabham stared at Clovis for a moment in pardonable bewilderment; then his face broke into a wrinkled network of laughter.

'Oh, that's your game, is it? You are going to do a little Siberian Magic on your own account. And is Mrs Hampton willing to be a fellow-conspirator?'

'Mary is pledged to see me through with it, if you will guarantee Louisa's temper.'

'I'll answer for Louisa,' said Lord Pabham.

By the following day the house-party had swollen to larger proportions, and Bilsiter's instinct for self-advertisement expanded duly under the stimulant of an increased audience. At dinner that evening he held forth at length on the subject of unseen forces and untested powers, and his flow of impressive eloquence continued unabated while coffee was being served in the drawing-room preparatory to a general migration to the card-room. His aunt ensured a respectful hearing for his utterances, but her sensation-loving soul hankered after something more dramatic than mere vocal demonstration.

'Won't you do something to *convince* them of your powers, Leonard?' she pleaded; 'change something into another shape. He can, you know, if he only chooses to,' she informed the company.

'Oh, do,' said Mavis Pellington earnestly, and her request was echoed by nearly everyone present. Even those who were not open to conviction were perfectly willing to be entertained by an exhibition of amateur conjuring.

Leonard felt that something tangible was expected of him.

'Has anyone present,' he asked, 'got a threepenny bit or some small object of no particular value –'

'You're surely not going to make coins disappear, or something primitive of that sort?' said Clovis contemptuously.

'I think it very unkind of you not to carry out my suggestion of turning me into a wolf,' said Mary Hampton, as she crossed over to the conservatory to give her macaws their usual tribute from the dessert dishes.

'I have already warned you of the danger of treating these powers in a mocking spirit,' said Leonard solemnly.

'I don't believe you can do it,' laughed Mary provocatively from the conservatory; 'I dare you to do it if you can. I defy you to turn me into a wolf.'

As she said this she was lost to view behind a clump of azaleas.

'Mrs Hampton –' began Leonard with increased solemnity, but he got no further. A breath of chill air seemed to rush across the room, and at the same time the macaws broke forth into ear-splitting screams.

'What on earth is the matter with those confounded birds, Mary?' exclaimed Colonel Hampton; at the same moment an even more piercing scream from Mavis Pellington stampeded the entire company from their seats. In various attitudes of helpless horror or instinctive defence they confronted the evil-looking grey beast that was peering at them from amid a setting of fern and azalea.

Mrs Hoops was the first to recover from the general chaos of fright and bewilderment.

'Leonard!' she screamed shrilly at her nephew, 'turn it back into Mrs Hampton at once! It may fly at us at any moment. Turn it back!'

'I – I don't know how to,' faltered Leonard, who looked more scared and horrified than anyone.

'What!' shouted Colonel Hampton, 'you've taken the abominable liberty of turning my wife into a wolf, and now you stand there calmly and say you can't turn her back again!'

To do strict justice to Leonard, calmness was not a distinguishing feature of his attitude at the moment.

'I assure you I didn't turn Mrs Hampton into a wolf; nothing was farther from my intentions,' he protested.

'Then where is she, and how came that animal into the conservatory?' demanded the Colonel.

'Of course we must accept your assurance that you didn't turn Mrs Hampton into a wolf,' said Clovis politely, 'but you will agree that appearances are against you.'

'Are we to have all these recriminations with that beast standing there ready to tear us to pieces?' wailed Mavis indignantly.

'Lord Pabham, you know a good deal about wild beasts –' suggested Colonel Hampton.

'The wild beasts that I have been accustomed to,' said Lord Pabham, 'have come with proper credentials from well-known dealers, or have been bred in my own menagerie. I've never before been confronted with an animal that walks unconcernedly out of an azalea bush, leaving a charming and popular hostess unaccounted for. As far as one can judge from *outward* characteristics,' he continued, 'it has the appearance of a well-grown female of the North American timber-wolf, a variety of the common species *canis lupus*.'

'Oh, never mind its Latin name,' screamed Mavis, as the beast came a step or two further into the room; 'can't you entice it away with food, and shut it up where it can't do any harm?'

'If it is really Mrs Hampton, who has just had a very good dinner, I don't suppose food will appeal to it very strongly,' said Clovis.

'Leonard,' beseeched Mrs Hoops tearfully, 'even if this *is* none of your doing can't you use your great powers to turn this dreadful beast into something harmless before it bites us all – a rabbit or something?'

'I don't suppose Colonel Hampton would care to have his wife turned into a succession of fancy animals as though we were playing a round game with her,' interposed Clovis.

'I absolutely forbid it,' thundered the Colonel.

'Most wolves that I've had anything to do with have been inordinately fond of sugar,' said Lord Pabham; 'if you like I'll try the effect on this one.'

He took a piece of sugar from the saucer of his coffee cup and flung it to the expectant Louisa, who snapped it in mid-air. There was a sigh of relief from the company; a wolf that ate sugar when it might at the least have been employed in tearing macaws to pieces had already shed some of its terrors. The sigh deepened to a gasp of thanksgiving when Lord Pabham decoyed the animal out of the room by a pretended largesse of further sugar. There was an instant rush to the vacated conservatory. There was no trace of Mrs Hampton except the plate containing the macaws' supper.

'The door is locked on the inside!' exclaimed Clovis, who had deftly turned the key as he affected to test it.

Everyone turned towards Bilsiter.

'If you haven't turned my wife into a wolf,' said Colonel Hampton, 'will you kindly explain where she has disappeared to, since she obviously could not have gone through a locked door? I will not press you for an explanation of how a North American timber-wolf suddenly appeared in the conservatory, but I think I have some right to inquire what has become of Mrs Hampton.

Bilsiter's reiterated disclaimer was met with a general murmur of impatient disbelief.

'I refuse to stay another hour under this roof,' declared Mavis Pellington.

'If our hostess has really vanished out of human form,' said Mrs Hoops, 'none of the ladies of the party can very well remain. I absolutely decline to be chaperoned by a wolf!'

'It's a she-wolf,' said Clovis soothingly.

The correct etiquette to be observed under the unusual circumstances received no further elucidation. The sudden entry of Mary Hampton deprived the discussion of its immediate interest.

'Someone has mesmerized me,' she exclaimed crossly; 'I found myself in the game larder, of all places, being fed with sugar by Lord Pabham. I hate being mesmerized, and the doctor has forbidden me to touch sugar.'

The situation was explained to her, as far as it permitted of anything that could be called explanation.

'Then you *really* did turn me into a wolf, Mr Bilsiter?' she exclaimed excitedly.

But Leonard had burned the boat in which he might now have embarked on a sea of glory. He could only shake his head feebly.

'It was I who took that liberty,' said Clovis; 'you see, I happen to have lived for a couple of years in North-Eastern Russia, and I have more than a tourist's acquaintance with the magic craft of that region. One does not care to speak about these strange powers, but once in a way, when one hears a lot of nonsense being talked about them, one is tempted to show what Siberian magic can accomplish in the hands of someone who really understands it. I yielded to that temptation. May I have some brandy? The effort has left me rather faint.'

If Leonard Bilsiter could at that moment have transformed Clovis into a cockroach and then have stepped on him he would gladly have performed both operations.

The Schartz-Metterklume Method

Lady Carlotta stepped out on to the platform of the small wayside station and took a turn or two up and down its uninteresting length, to kill time till the train should be pleased to proceed on its way. Then, in the roadway beyond, she saw a horse struggling with a more than ample load, and a carter of the sort that seems to bear a sullen hatred against the animal that helps him to earn a living. Lady Carlotta promptly betook her to the roadway, and put rather a different complexion on the struggle. Certain of her acquaintances were wont to give her plentiful admonition as to the undesirability of interfering on behalf of a distressed animal, such interference being 'none of her business'. Only once had she put the doctrine of non-interference into practice, when one of its most eloquent exponents had been besieged for nearly three hours in a small and extremely uncomfortable may-tree by an angry boar-pig, while Lady Carlotta, on the other side of the fence, had proceeded with the watercolour sketch she was engaged on, and refused to interfere between the boar and his prisoner. It is to be feared that she lost the friendship of the ultimately rescued lady. On this occasion she merely lost the train, which gave way to the first sign of impatience it had shown throughout the journey, and steamed off without her. She bore the desertion with philosophical indifference; her friends and relations were thoroughly well used to the fact of her luggage arriving without her. She wired a vague non-committal message to her destination to say that she was coming on 'by another train'. Before she had time to think what her next move might be, she was confronted by an imposingly attired lady, who seemed to be taking a prolonged mental inventory of her clothes and looks.

'You must be Miss Hope, the governess I've come to meet,' said the apparition, in a tone that admitted of very little argument.

'Very well, if I must I must,' said Lady Carlotta to herself with dangerous meekness.

'I am Mrs Quabarl,' continued the lady; 'and where, pray, is your luggage?'

'It's gone astray,' said the alleged governess; falling in with the excellent rule of life that the absent are always to blame; the luggage had, in point of fact, behaved with perfect correctitude. 'I've just telegraphed about it,' she added, with a nearer approach to truth.

'How provoking,' said Mrs Quabarl; 'these railway companies are so careless. However, my maid can lend you things for the night,' and she led the way to her car.

During the drive to the Quabarl mansion Lady Carlotta was impressively introduced to the nature of the charge that had been thrust upon her; she learned that Claude and Wilfrid were delicate, sensitive young people, that Irene had the artistic temperament highly developed, and that Viola was something or other else of a mould equally commonplace among children of that class and type in the twentieth century.

'I wish them not only to be *taught*,' said Mrs Quabarl, 'but *interested* in what they learn. In their history lessons, for instance, you must try to make them feel that they are being introduced to the life-stories of men and women who really lived, not merely committing a mass of names and dates to memory. French, of course, I shall expect you to talk at meal-times several days in the week.'

'I shall talk French four days of the week and Russian in the remaining three.'

'Russian? My dear Miss Hope, no one in the house speaks or understands Russian.'

'That will not embarrass me in the least,' said Lady Carlotta coldly.

Mrs Quabarl, to use a colloquial expression, was knocked off her perch. She was one of those imperfectly self-assured individuals who are magnificent and autocratic as long as they are not seriously opposed. The least show of unexpected resistance goes a long way towards rendering them cowed and apologetic. When the new governess failed to express wondering admiration of the large newly purchased and expensive car, and lightly alluded to the superior advantages of one or two makes which had just been put on the market, the discomfiture of her patroness became almost abject. Her feelings were those which might have animated a general of ancient warfaring days, on beholding his heaviest battle-elephant ignominiously driven off the field by slingers and javelin throwers.

At dinner that evening, although reinforced by her husband, who usually duplicated her opinions and lent her moral support generally, Mrs Quabarl regained none of her lost ground. The governess not only helped herself well and truly to wine, but held forth with considerable show of critical knowledge on various vintage matters, concerning which the Quabarls were in no wise able to pose as authorities. Previous governesses had limited their conversation in the wine topic to a respectful and doubtless sincere expression of a preference for water. When this one went as far as to recommend a wine firm in whose hands you could not go very far wrong Mrs Quabarl thought it time to turn the conversation into more usual channels.

'We got very satisfactory references about you from Canon Teep,' she observed; 'a very estimable man, I should think.'

'Drinks like a fish and beats his wife, otherwise a very lovable character,' said the governess imperturbably.

'My *dear* Miss Hope! I trust you are exaggerating,' exclaimed the Quabarls in unison.

'One must in justice admit that there is some provocation,' continued the romancer. 'Mrs Teep is quite the most irritating bridge-player that I have ever sat down with; her leads and declarations would condone a certain amount of brutality in her partner, but to souse her with the contents of the only soda-water syphon in the house on a Sunday afternoon, when one couldn't get another, argues an indifference to the comfort of others which I cannot altogether overlook. You may think me hasty in my judgments, but it was practically on account of the syphon incident that I left.'

'We will talk of this some other time,' said Mrs Quabarl hastily.

'I shall never allude to it again,' said the governess with decision.

Mr Quabarl made a welcome diversion by asking what studies the new instructress proposed to inaugurate on the morrow.

'History to begin with,' she informed him.

'Ah, history,' he observed sagely; 'now in teaching them history you must take care to interest them in what they learn. You must make them feel they are being introduced to the life-stories of men and women who really lived –'

'I've told her all that,' interposed Mrs Quabarl.

'I teach history on the Schartz-Metterklume method,' said the governess loftily.

'Ah, yes,' said her listeners, thinking it expedient to assume an acquaintance at least with the name.

'What are you children doing out here?' demanded Mrs Quabarl the next morning, on finding Irene sitting rather glumly at the head of the stairs, while her sister was perched in an attitude of depressed discomfort on the window-seat behind her, with a wolf-skin rug almost covering her.

'We are having a history lesson,' came the unexpected reply. 'I am supposed to be Rome, and Viola up there is the she-wolf; not a real wolf, but the figure of one that the Romans used to set store by – I forget why. Claude and Wilfrid had gone to fetch the shabby women.'

'The shabby women?'

'Yes, they've got to carry them off. They didn't want to, but Miss Hope got one of father's fives-bats and said she'd give them a number nine spanking if they didn't, so they've gone to do it.'

A loud, angry screaming from the direction of the lawn drew Mrs Quabarl thither in hot haste, fearful lest the threatened castigation might even now be in process of infliction. The outcry, however, came principally from the two small daughters of the lodge-keeper, who were being hauled and pushed towards the house by the panting and dishevelled Claude and Wilfrid, whose task was rendered even more arduous by the incessant, if not very effectual, attacks of the captured maidens' small brother. The governess, fives-bat in hand, sat negligently on the stone balustrade, presiding over the scene with the cold impartiality of a Goddess of Battles. A furious and repeated chorus of 'I'll tell muvver' rose from the lodge children, but the lodge-mother, who was hard of hearing, was for the moment immersed in the preoccupation of her washtub. After an apprehensive glance in the direction of the lodge (the good woman was gifted with the highly militant temper which is sometimes the privilege of deafness) Mrs Quabarl flew indignantly to the rescue of the struggling captives.

'Wilfrid! Claude! Let those children go at once. Miss Hope, what on earth is the meaning of this scene?'

'Early Roman history; the Sabine women, don't you know? It's the Schartz-Metterklume method to make children understand history by acting it themselves; fixes it in their memory, you know. Of course, if, thanks to your interference, your boys go through life thinking that the Sabine women ultimately escaped I really cannot be held responsible.'

'You may be very clever and modern, Miss Hope,' said Mrs Quabarl firmly, 'but I should like you to leave here by the next train. Your luggage will be sent after you as soon as it arrives.'

'I'm not certain exactly where I shall be for the next few days,' said the dismissed instructress of youth; 'you might keep my luggage till I wire my address. There are only a couple of trunks and some golf-clubs and a leopard cub.'

'A leopard cub!' gasped Mrs Quabarl. Even in her departure this extraordinary person seemed destined to leave a trail of embarrassment behind her.

'Well, it's rather left off being a cub; it's more than half-grown, you know. A fowl every day and a rabbit on Sundays is what it usually gets. Raw beef makes it too excitable. Don't trouble about getting the car for me, I'm rather inclined for a walk.'

And Lady Carlotta strode out of the Quabarl horizon.

The advent of the genuine Miss Hope, who had made a mistake as to the day on which she was due to arrive, caused a turmoil which that good lady was quite unused to inspiring. Obviously the Quabarl family had been woefully befooled, but a certain amount of relief came with the knowledge.

'How tiresome for you, dear Carlotta,' said her hostess, when the overdue guest ultimately arrived; 'how very tiresome losing your train and having to stop overnight in a strange place.'

'Oh, dear, no,' said Lady Carlotta; 'not at all tiresome — for me.'

The Stalled Ox

Theophil Eshley was an artist by profession, a cattle painter by force of environment. It is not to be supposed that he lived on a ranch or a dairy farm, in an atmosphere pervaded with horn and hoof, milking-stool, and branding-iron. His home was in a park-like, villa-dotted district that only just escaped the reproach of being suburban. On one side of his garden there abutted a small, picturesque meadow, in which an enterprising neighbour pastured some small picturesque cows of the Channel Island persuasion. At noonday in summertime the cows stood knee-deep in tall meadow-grass under the shade of a group of walnut trees, with the sunlight falling in dappled patches on their mouse-sleek coats. Eshley had conceived and executed a dainty picture of two reposeful milch-cows in a setting of walnut tree and meadow-grass and filtered sunbeam, and the Royal Academy encourages orderly, methodical habits in its children. Eshley had painted a successful and acceptable picture of cattle drowsing picturesquely under walnut trees, and as he had begun, so, of necessity, he went on. His 'Noontide Peace', a study of two dun cows under a walnut tree was followed by 'A Mid-day Sanctuary', a study of a walnut tree, with two dun cows under it. In due succession there came 'Where the Gad-Flies Cease from Troubling', 'The Haven of the Herd', 'A Dream in Dairyland', studies of walnut trees and dun cows. His two attempts to break away from his own tradition were signal failures: 'Turtle Doves Alarmed by Sparrowhawk' and 'Wolves on the Roman Campagna' came back to his studio in the guise of abominable heresies, and Eshley climbed back into grace and the public gaze with 'A Shaded Nook Where Drowsy Milkers Dream'.

On a fine afternoon in late autumn he was putting some finishing touches to a study of meadow weeds when his neighbour, Adela Pingsford, assailed the outer door of his studio with loud peremptory knockings.

'There is an ox in my garden,' she announced, in explanation of the tempestuous intrusion.

'An ox,' said Eshley blankly, and rather fatuously; 'what kind of ox?'

'Oh, I don't know what kind,' snapped the lady. 'A common or garden ox, to use the slang expression. It is the garden part of it that I object to. My garden has just been put straight for the winter, and an ox roaming about in it won't improve matters. Besides, there are the chrysanthemums just coming into flower.'

'How did it get into the garden?' asked Eshley.

'I imagine it came in by the gate,' said the lady impatiently; 'it couldn't have climbed the walls, and I don't suppose anyone dropped it from an aeroplane as a Bovril advertisement. The immediately important question is not how it got in, but how to get it out.'

'Won't it go?' said Eshley.

'If it was anxious to go,' said Adela Pingsford rather angrily, 'I should not have come here to chat with you about it. I'm practically all alone; the housemaid is having her afternoon out and the cook is lying down with an attack of neuralgia. Anything that I may have learned at school or in after life about how to remove a large ox from a small garden seems to have escaped from my memory now. All I could think of was that you were a near neighbour and a cattle painter, presumably more or less familiar with the subjects that you painted, and that you might be of some slight assistance. Possibly I was mistaken.'

'I paint dairy cows, certainly,' admitted Eshley, 'but I cannot claim to have had any experience in rounding up stray oxen. I've seen it done on a cinema film, of course, but there were always horses and lots of other accessories; besides, one never knows how much of those pictures are faked.'

Adela Pingsford said nothing, but led the way to her garden. It was normally a fair-sized garden, but it looked small in comparison with the ox, a huge mottled brute, dull red about the head and shoulders, passing to dirty white on the flanks and hind-quarters, with shaggy ears and large blood-shot eyes. It bore about as much resemblance to the dainty paddock heifers that Eshley was accustomed to paint as the chief of a Kurdish nomad clan would to a Japanese tea-shop girl. Eshley stood very near the gate while he studied the animal's appearance and demeanour. Adela Pingsford continued to say nothing.

'It's eating a chrysanthemum,' said Eshley at last, when the silence had become unbearable.

'How observant you are,' said Adela bitterly. 'You seem to notice everything. As a matter of fact, it has got six chrysanthemums in its mouth at the present moment.'

The necessity for doing something was becoming imperative. Eshley took a step or two in the direction of the animal, clapped hands, and made noises of the 'Hish' and 'Shoo' variety. If the ox heard them it gave no outward indication of the fact.

'If any hens should ever stray into my garden,' said Adela, 'I should certainly send for you to frighten them out. You "shoo" beautifully. Meanwhile, do you mind trying to drive that ox away? That is a *Mademoiselle Louise Bichot* that he's begun on now,' she added in icy calm, as a glowing orange head was crushed into the huge munching mouth.

'Since you have been so frank about the variety of the chrysanthemum,' said Eshley, 'I don't mind telling you that this is an Ayrshire ox.'

The icy calm broke down; Adela Pingsford used language that sent the artist instinctively a few feet nearer to the ox. He picked up a pea-stick and flung it with some determination against the animal's mottled flanks. The operation of mashing *Mademoiselle Louise Bichot* into a petal salad was suspended for a long moment, while the ox gazed with concentrated inquiry at the stick-thrower. Adela gazed with equal concentration and more obvious hostility at the same focus. As the beast neither lowered its head nor stamped its feet Eshley ventured on another javelin exercise with another pea-stick. The ox seemed to realize at once that it was to go; it gave a hurried final pluck at the bed where the chrysanthemums had been, and strode swiftly up the garden. Eshley ran to head it towards the gate, but only succeeded in quickening its pace from a walk to a lumbering trot. With an air of inquiry, but with no real hesitation, it crossed the tiny strip of turf that the charitable called the croquet lawn, and pushed its way through the open French window into the morning-room. Some chrysanthemums and other autumn herbage stood about the room in vases, and the animal resumed its browsing operations; all the same, Eshley fancied that the beginnings of a hunted look had come into its eyes, a look that counselled respect. He discontinued his attempt to interfere with its choice of surroundings.

'Mr Eshley,' said Adela in a shaking voice, 'I asked you to drive that beast out of my garden, but I did not ask you to drive it into my house. If I must have it anywhere on the premises, I prefer the garden to the morning-room.'

'Cattle drives are not in my line,' said Eshley; 'if I remember, I told you so at the outset.'

'I quite agree,' retorted the lady, 'painting pretty pictures of pretty little cows in what you're suited for. Perhaps you'd like to do a nice sketch of that ox making itself at home in my morning-room?'

This time it seemed as if the worm had turned; Eshley began striding away.

'Where are you going?' screamed Adela.

'To fetch implements,' was the answer.

'Implements? I won't have you use a lasso. The room will be wrecked if there's a struggle.'

But the artist marched out of the garden. In a couple of minutes he returned, laden with easel, sketching-stool, and painting materials.

'Do you mean to say that you're going to sit quietly down and paint that brute while it's destroying my morning-room?' gasped Adela.

'It was your suggestion,' said Eshley, setting his canvas in position.

'I forbid it; I absolutely forbid it!' stormed Adela.

'I don't see what standing you have in the matter,' said the artist; 'you can hardly pretend that it's your ox, even by adoption.'

'You seem to forget that it's in my morning-room, eating my flowers,' came the raging retort.

'You seem to forget that the cook has neuralgia,' said Eshley; 'she may be just dozing off into a merciful sleep and your outcry will waken her. Consideration for others should be the guiding principle of people in our station of life.'

'The man is mad!' exclaimed Adela tragically. A moment later it was Adela herself who appeared to go mad. The ox had finished the vase-flowers and the cover of *Israel Kalisch*, and appeared to be thinking of leaving its rather restricted quarters. Eshley noticed its restlessness and promptly flung it some bunches of Virginia leaves as an inducement to continue the sitting.

'I forget how the proverb runs,' he observed; 'something about "better a dinner of herbs than a stalled ox where hate is". We seem to have all the ingredients for the proverb ready to hand.'

'I shall go to the Public Library and get them to telephone for the police,' announced Adela, and, raging audibly, she departed.

Some minutes later the ox, awakening probably to the suspicion that oil cake and chopped mangold was waiting for it in some appointed byre, stepped with much precaution out of the morning-room, stared with grave inquiry at the no longer obtrusive and pea-stick-throwing human, and then lumbered heavily but swiftly out of the garden. Eshley packed up his tools and followed the animal's example and 'Larkdene' was left to neuralgia and the cook.

The episode was the turning-point in Eshley's artistic career. His remarkable picture, 'Ox in a Morning-room, Late Autumn', was one of the sensations and successes of the next Paris Salon, and when it was subsequently exhibited at Munich it was bought by the Bavarian Government, in the teeth of the spirited bidding of three meat-extract firms. From that moment his success was continuous and assured, and the Royal Academy was thankful, two years later, to give a conspicuous position on its walls to his large canvas 'Barbary Apes Wrecking a Boudoir'.

Ashley presented Adela Pingsford with a new copy of *Israel Kalisch*, and a couple of finely flowering plants of *Madame André Blusset*, but nothing in the nature of real reconciliation has taken place between them.

The Story-Teller

It was a hot afternoon, and the railway carriage was correspondingly sultry and the next stop was at Templecombe, nearly an hour ahead. The occupants of the carriage were a small girl, and a smaller girl, and a small boy. An aunt belonging to the children occupied one corner seat, and the further corner seat on the opposite side was occupied by a bachelor who was a stranger to their party, but the small girls and the small boy emphatically occupied the compartment. Both the aunt and the children were conversational in a limited, persistent way, reminding one of the attentions of a housefly that refused to be discouraged. Most of the aunt's remarks seemed to begin with 'Don't', and nearly all of the children's remarks began with 'Why?' The bachelor said nothing out loud.

'Don't, Cyril, don't,' exclaimed the aunt, as the small boy began smacking the cushions of the seat, producing a cloud of dust at each blow.

'Come and look out of the window,' she added.

The child moved reluctantly to the window. 'Why are those sheep being driven out of that field?' he asked.

'I expect they are being driven to another field where there is more grass,' said the aunt weakly.

'But there is lots of grass in that field,' protested the boy; 'there's nothing else but grass there. Aunt, there's lots of grass in that field.'

'Perhaps the grass in the other field is better,' suggested the aunt fatuously.

'Why is it better?' came the swift, inevitable question.

'Oh, look at those cows!' exclaimed the aunt. Nearly every field along the line had contained cows or bullocks, but she spoke as though she were drawing attention to a rarity.

'Why is the grass in the other field better?' persisted Cyril.

The frown on the bachelor's face was deepening to a scowl. He was a hard, unsympathetic man, the aunt decided in her mind. She was utterly unable to come to any satisfactory decision about the grass in the other field.

The smaller girl created a diversion by beginning to recite 'On the Road to Mandalay'. She only knew the first line, but she put her limited knowledge to the fullest possible use. She repeated the line over and over again in a dreamy but resolute and very audible voice; it seemed to the bachelor as though someone had had a bet with her that she could not repeat the line aloud two thousand times without stopping. Whoever it was who had made the wager was likely to lose his bet.

'Come over here and listen to a story,' said the aunt, when the bachelor had looked twice at her and once at the communication cord.

The children moved listlessly towards the aunt's end of the carriage. Evidently her reputation as a story-teller did not rank high in their estimation.

In a low, confidential voice, interrupted at frequent intervals by loud, petulant questions from her listeners, she began an unenterprising, and deplorably uninteresting story about a little girl who was good, and made friends with everyone on account of her goodness, and was finally saved from a mad bull by a number of rescuers who admired her moral character.

'Wouldn't they have saved her if she hadn't been good?' demanded the bigger of the small girls. It was exactly the question that the bachelor had wanted to ask.

'Well, yes,' admitted the aunt lamely, 'but I don't think they would have run quite so fast to her help if they had not liked her so much.'

'It's the stupidest story I've ever heard,' said the bigger of the small girls, with immense conviction.

'I didn't listen after the first bit, it was so stupid,' said Cyril.

The smaller girl made no actual comment on the story, but she had long ago recommenced a murmured repetition of her favourite line.

'You don't seem to be a success as a story-teller,' said the bachelor suddenly from his corner.

The aunt bristled in instant defence at this unexpected attack.

'It's a very difficult thing to tell stories that children can both understand and appreciate,' she said stiffly.

'I don't agree with you,' said the bachelor.

'Perhaps you would like to tell them a story,' was the aunt's retort.

'Tell us a story,' demanded the bigger of the small girls.

'Once upon a time,' began the bachelor, 'there was a little girl called Bertha, who was extraordinarily good.'

The children's momentarily-aroused interest began at once to flicker; all stories seemed dreadfully alike, no matter who told them.

'She did all that she was told, she was always truthful, she kept her clothes clean, ate milk puddings as though they were jam tarts, learned her lessons perfectly, and was polite in her manners.'

'Was she pretty?' asked the bigger of the small girls.

'Not as pretty as any of you,' said the bachelor, 'but she was horribly good.'

There was a wave of reaction in favour of the story; the word horrible in connection with goodness was a novelty that commended itself. It seemed to introduce a ring of truth that was absent from the aunt's tales of infant life.

'She was so good,' continued the bachelor, 'that she won

several medals for goodness, which she always wore, pinned on to her dress. There was a medal for obedience, another medal for punctuality, and a third for good behaviour. They were large metal medals and they clicked against one another as she walked. No other child in the town where she lived had as many as three medals, so everybody knew that she must be an extra good child.'

'Horribly good,' quoted Cyril.

'Everybody talked about her goodness, and the Prince of the country got to hear about it, and he said that as she was so very good she might be allowed once a week to walk in his park, which was just outside the town. It was a beautiful park, and no children were ever allowed in it, so it was a great honour for Bertha to be allowed to go there.'

'Were there any sheep in the park?' demanded Cyril.

'No,' said the bachelor, 'there were no sheep.'

'Why weren't there any sheep?' came the inevitable question arising out of that answer.

The aunt permitted herself a smile, which might almost have been described as a grin.

'There were no sheep in the park,' said the bachelor, 'because the Prince's mother had once had a dream that her son would either be killed by a sheep or else by a clock falling on him. For that reason the Prince never kept a sheep in his park or a clock in his palace.'

The aunt suppressed a gasp of admiration.

'Was the Prince killed by a sheep or by a clock?' asked Cyril.

'He is still alive, so we can't tell whether the dream will come true,' said the bachelor unconcernedly; 'anyway, there were no sheep in the park, but there were lots of little pigs running all over the place.'

'What colour were they?'

'Black with white faces, white with black spots, black all over, grey with white patches, and some were white all over.'

The story-teller paused to let a full idea of the park's treasures sink into the children's imagination; then he resumed:

'Bertha was rather sorry to find that there were no flowers in the park. She had promised her aunts, with tears in her eyes, that she would not pick any of the kind Prince's flowers, and she had meant to keep her promise, so of course it made her feel silly to find that there were no flowers to pick.'

'Why weren't there any flowers?'

'Because the pigs had eaten them all,' said the bachelor promptly. 'The gardeners had told the Prince that you couldn't have pigs and flowers, so he decided to have pigs and no flowers.'

There was a murmur of approval at the excellence of the Prince's decision; so many people would have decided the other way.

'There were lots of other delightful things in the park. There were ponds with gold and blue and green fish in them, and trees with beautiful parrots that said clever things at a moment's notice, and humming birds that hummed all the popular tunes of the day. Bertha walked up and down and enjoyed herself immensely, and thought to herself: "If I were not so extraordinarily good I should not have been allowed to come into this beautiful park and enjoy all that there is to be seen in it," and her three medals clinked against one another as she walked and helped to remind her how very good she really was. Just then an enormous wolf came prowling into the park to see if it could catch a fat little pig for its supper.'

'What colour was it?' asked the children, amid an immediate quickening of interest.

'Mud-colour all over, with a black tongue and pale grey eyes that gleamed with unspeakable ferocity. The first thing that it saw in the park was Bertha; her pinafore was so spotlessly white and clean that it could be seen from a great distance. Bertha saw the wolf and saw that it was stealing towards her, and she began to wish that she had never been allowed to come into the park. She ran as hard as she could, and the wolf came after her with huge leaps and bounds. She managed to reach a shrubbery of myrtle bushes and she hid herself in one of the thickest of the bushes. The wolf came sniffing among the branches, its black tongue lolling out of its mouth and its pale grey eyes glaring with rage. Bertha was terribly frightened, and thought to herself: "If I had not been so extraordinarily good I should have been safe in the town at this moment." However, the scent of the myrtle was so strong that the wolf could not sniff out where Bertha was hiding, and the bushes were so thick that he might have hunted about in them for a long time without catching sight of her, so he thought he might as well go off and catch a little pig instead. Bertha was trembling very much at having the wolf prowling and sniffing so near her, and as she trembled a medal for obedience clinked against the medals for good conduct and punctuality. The wolf was just moving away when he heard the sound of the medals clinking and stopped to listen; they clinked again in a bush quite near him. He dashed into the bush, his pale grey eyes gleaming with ferocity and triumph and dragged Bertha out and devoured her to the last morsel. All that was left of her were her shoes, bits of clothing, and the three medals for goodness.'

'Were any of the little pigs killed?'

'No, they all escaped.'

'The story began badly,' said the smaller of the small girls, 'but it had a beautiful ending.'

'It is the most beautiful story that I ever heard,' said the bigger of the small girls, with immense decision.

'It is the *only* beautiful story I have ever heard,' said Cyril.

A dissentient opinion came from the aunt.

'A most improper story to tell to young children! You have undermined the effect of years of careful teaching.'

'At any rate,' said the bachelor, collecting his belongings preparatory to leaving the carriage, 'I kept them quiet for ten minutes, which was more than you were able to do.'

'Unhappy woman!' he observed to himself as he walked down the platform of Templecombe station; 'for the next six months or so those children will assail her in public with demands for an improper story!'

A Touch of Realism

'I hope you've come full of suggestions for Christmas,' said Lady Blonze to her latest arrived guest; 'the old-fashioned Christmas and the up-to-date Christmas are both so played out. I want to have something really original this year.'

'I was staying with the Mathesons last month,' said Blanche Boveal eagerly, 'and we had such a good idea. Everyone in the house-party had to be a character and behave consistently all the time, and at the end of the visit one had to guess what everyone's character was. The one who was voted to have acted his or her character best got a prize.'

'It sounds amusing,' said Lady Blonze.

'I was St Francis of Assisi,' continued Blanche; 'we hadn't got to keep to our right sexes. I kept getting up in the middle of a meal and throwing out food to the birds; you see, the chief thing that one remembers of St Francis is that he was fond of the birds. Everyone was so stupid about it, and thought that I was the old man who feeds the sparrows in the Tuileries Gardens. Then Colonel Pentley was the Jolly Miller on the banks of Dee.'

'How on earth did he do that?' asked Bertie van Tahn.

'"He laughed and sang from morn till night,"' explained Blanche.

'How dreadful for the rest of you,' said Bertie; 'and anyway he wasn't on the banks of Dee.'

'One had to imagine that,' said Blanche.

'If you could imagine all that you might as well imagine cattle on the further bank and keep on calling them home, Mary-fashion, across the sands of Dee. Or you might change the river to the Yarrow and imagine it was on the top of you, and say you were Willie, or whoever it was, drowned in Yarrow.'

'Of course it's easy to make fun of it,' said Blanche sharply, 'but it was extremely interesting and amusing. The prize was rather a fiasco, though. You see, Millie Matheson said her character was Lady Bountiful, and as she was our hostess of course we all had to vote that she had carried out her character better than anyone. Otherwise I ought to have got the prize.'

'It's quite an idea for a Christmas party,' said Lady Blonze; 'we must certainly do it here.'

Sir Nicholas was not so enthusiastic. 'Are you quite sure, my dear, that you're wise in doing this thing?' he said to his wife when they were alone together. 'It might do very well at the Mathesons, where they had rather a staid, elderly house-party, but here it will be a different matter. There is the Durmot flapper, for instance, who simply stops at nothing, and you know what Van Tahn is like. Then there is Cyril Skatterly; he has madness on one side of his family and a Hungarian grandmother on the other.'

'I don't see what they could do that would matter,' said Lady Blonze.

'It's the unknown that is to be dreaded,' said Sir Nicholas. 'If Skatterly took it into his head to represent a Bull of Bashan, well, I'd rather not be here.'

'Of course we shan't allow any Bible characters. Besides, I don't know what the Bulls of Bashan really did that was so very dreadful; they just came round and gaped, as far as I remember.'

'My dear, you don't know what Skatterly's Hungarian imagination mightn't read into the part; it would be small satisfaction to say to him afterwards: "You've behaved as no Bull of Bashan would have behaved."'

'Oh, you're an alarmist,' said Lady Blonze; 'I particularly want to have this idea carried out. It will be sure to be talked about a lot.'

'That is quite possible,' said Sir Nicholas.

Dinner that evening was not a particularly lively affair; the strain of trying to impersonate a self-imposed character or to glean hints of identity from other people's conduct acted as a check on the natural festivity of such a gathering. There was a general feeling of gratitude and acquiescence when good-natured Rachel Klammerstein suggested that there should be an hour or two's respite from 'the game' while they all listened to a little piano-playing after dinner. Rachel's love of piano music was not indiscriminate, and concentrated itself chiefly on selections rendered by her idolized offspring, Moritz and Augusta, who, to do them justice, played remarkably well.

The Klammersteins were deservedly popular as Christmas guests; they gave expensive gifts lavishly on Christmas Day and New Year, and Mrs Klammerstein had already dropped hints of her intention to present the prize for the best enacted character in the game competition. Everyone had brightened at this prospect; if it had fallen to Lady Blonze, as hostess, to provide the prize, she would have considered that a little souvenir of some twenty or twenty-five shillings' value would meet the case, whereas coming from a Klammerstein source it would certainly run to several guineas.

The close time for impersonation efforts came to an end with the final withdrawal of Moritz and Augusta from the piano. Blanche Boveal retired early, leaving the room in a series of laboured leaps that she hoped might be recognized as a tolerable imitation of Pavlova. Vera Durmot, the sixteen-year-old flapper, expressed her confident opinion that the performance was intended to typify Mark Twain's famous jumping frog, and her diagnosis of the case found general acceptance. Another guest to set an example of early bed-going was Waldo Plubley, who conducted his life on a minutely regulated system of time-tables and hygienic routine. Waldo was a plump, indolent young man of seven-and-twenty, whose mother had early in his life decided for him that he was unusually delicate, and by dint of much coddling and home-keeping had succeeded in making him physically soft and mentally peevish. Nine hours' unbroken sleep, preceded by elaborate breathing exercises and other hygienic ritual, was among the indispensable regulations which Waldo imposed on himself, and there were innumerable small observances which he exacted from those who were in any way obliged to minister to his requirements; a special teapot for the decoction of his early tea was always solemnly handed over to the bedroom staff of any house in which he happened to be staying. No one had ever quite mastered the mechanism of this precious vessel, but Bertie van Tahn was responsible for the legend that its spout had to be kept facing north during the process of infusion.

On this particular night the irreducible nine hours were severely mutilated by the sudden and by no means noiseless incursion of a pyjama-clad figure into Waldo's room at an hour midway between midnight and dawn.

'What is the matter? What are you looking for?' asked the awakened and astonished Waldo, slowly recognizing Van Tahn, who appeared to be searching hastily for something he had lost.

'Looking for sheep,' was the reply.

'Sheep?' exclaimed Waldo.

'Yes, sheep. You don't suppose I'm looking for giraffes, do you?'

'I don't see why you should expect to find either in my room,' retorted Waldo furiously.

'I can't argue the matter at this hour of the night,' said Bertie, and began hastily rummaging in the chest of drawers. Shirts and underwear went flying on to the floor.

'There are no sheep here, I tell you,' screamed Waldo.

'I've only got your word for it,' said Bertie, whisking most of the bedclothes on to the floor; 'if you weren't concealing something you wouldn't be so agitated.'

Waldo was by this time convinced that Van Tahn was raving mad, and made an anxious effort to humour him.

'Go back to bed like a dear fellow,' he pleaded, 'and your sheep will turn up all right in the morning.'

'I daresay,' said Bertie gloomily, 'without their tails. Nice fool I shall look with a lot of Manx sheep.'

And by way of emphasizing his annoyance at the prospect he sent Waldo's pillows flying to the top of the wardrobe.

'But *why* no tails?' asked Waldo, whose teeth were chattering with fear and rage and lowered temperature.

'My dear boy, have you never heard the ballad of Little Bo-Peep?' said Bertie with a chuckle. 'It's my character in the Game, you know. If I didn't go hunting about for my lost sheep no one would be able to guess who I was; and now go to sleepy weeps like a good child or I shall be cross with you.'

'I leave you to imagine,' wrote Waldo in the course of a long letter to his mother, 'how much sleep I was able to recover that night, and you know how essential nine uninterrupted hours of slumber are to my health.'

On the other hand he was able to devote some wakeful hours to exercises in breathing wrath and fury against Bertie van Tahn.

Breakfast at Blonzecourt was a scattered meal, on the 'come when you please' principle, but the house-party was supposed to gather in full strength at lunch. On the day after the 'Game' had been started there were, however, some notable absentees. Waldo Plubley, for instance, was reported to be nursing a headache. A large breakfast and an 'A.B.C.' had been taken up to his room, but he had made no appearance in the flesh.

'I expect he's playing up to some character,' said Vera Durmot; 'isn't there a thing of Molière's, *'Le Malade Imaginaire'*? I expect he's that.'

Eight or nine lists came out, and were duly pencilled with the suggestion.

'And where are the Klammersteins?' asked Lady Blonze; 'they're usually so punctual.'

'Another character pose, perhaps,' said Bertie van Tahn; '"the Lost Ten Tribes".'

'But there are only three of them. Besides, they'll want their lunch. Hasn't anyone seen anything of them?'

'Didn't you take them out in your car?' asked Blanche Boveal, addressing herself to Cyril Skatterly.

'Yes, took them out to Slogberry Moor immediately after breakfast. Miss Durmot came too.'

'I saw you and Vera come back,' said Lady Blonze, 'but I didn't see the Klammersteins. Did you put them down in the village?'

'No,' said Skatterly shortly.

'But where are they? Where did you leave them?'

'We left them on Slogberry Moor,' said Vera calmly.

'On Slogberry Moor? Why, it's more than thirty miles away! How are they going to get back?'

'We didn't stop to consider that,' said Skatterly; 'we asked them to get out for a moment, on the pretence that the car had stuck, and then we dashed off full speed and left them there.'

'But how dare you do such a thing? It's most inhuman! Why, it's been snowing for the last hour.'

'I expect there'll be a cottage or farmhouse somewhere if they walk a mile or two.'

'But why on earth have you done it?'

The question came in a chorus of indignant bewilderment.

'*That* would be telling what our characters are meant to be,' said Vera.

'Didn't I warn you?' said Sir Nicholas tragically to his wife.

'It's something to do with Spanish history; we don't mind giving you that clue,' said Skatterly, helping himself cheerfully to salad, and then Bertie van Tahn broke forth into peals of joyous laughter.

'I've got it! Ferdinand and Isabella deporting the Jews! Oh, lovely! Those two have certainly won the prize; we shan't get anything to beat that for thoroughness.'

Lady Blonze's Christmas party was talked about and written about to an extent that she had not anticipated in her most ambitious moments. The letters from Waldo's mother would alone have made it memorable.

Bertie's Christmas Eve

It was Christmas Eve, and the family circle of Luke Steffink, Esq., was aglow with the amiability and random mirth which the occasion demanded. A long and lavish dinner had been partaken of, waits had been round and sung carols, the house-party had regaled itself with more caroling on its own account, and there had been romping which, even in a pulpit reference, could not have been condemned as ragging. In the midst of the general glow, however, there was one black unkindled cinder.

Bertie Steffink, nephew of the aforementioned Luke, had early in life adopted the profession of ne'er-do-weel; his father had been something of the kind before him. At the age of eighteen Bertie had commenced that round of visits to our Colonial possessions, so seemly and desirable in the case of a Prince of the Blood, so suggestive of insincerity in a young man of the middle-class. He had gone to grow tea in Ceylon and fruit in British Columbia, and to help sheep to grow wool in Australia. At the age of twenty he had just returned from some similar errand in Canada, from which it may be gathered that the trial he gave to these various experiments was of the summary drum-head nature. Luke Steffink, who fulfilled the troubled rôle of guardian and deputy-parent to Bertie, deplored the persistent manifestation of the homing instinct on his nephew's part, and his solemn thanks earlier in the day for the blessing of reporting a united family had no reference to Bertie's return.

Arrangements had been promptly made for packing the youth off to a distant corner of Rhodesia, whence return would be a difficult matter; the journey to this uninviting destination was imminent, in fact a more careful and willing traveller would have already begun to think about his packing. Hence Bertie was in no mood to share in the festive spirit which displayed itself around him, and resentment smouldered within him at the eager, self-absorbed discussion of social plans for the coming months which he heard on all sides. Beyond depressing his uncle and the family circle generally by singing 'Say au revoir, and not good-bye,' he had taken no part in the evening's conviviality.

Eleven o'clock had struck some half-hour ago, and the elder Steffinks began to throw out suggestions leading up to that process which they called retiring for the night.

'Come, Teddie, it's time you were in your little bed, you know,' said Luke Steffink to his thirteen-year-old son.

'That's where we all ought to be,' said Mrs Steffink.

'There wouldn't be room,' said Bertie.

The remark was considered to border on the scandalous;

everybody ate raisins and almonds with the nervous industry of
sheep feeding during threatening weather.

'In Russia,' said Horace Bordenby, who was staying in the
house as a Christmas guest, 'I've read that the peasants believe
that if you go into a cow-house or stable at midnight on
Christmas Eve you will hear the animals talk. They're supposed
to have the gift of speech at that one moment of the year.'

'Oh, *do* let's *all* go down to the cow-house and listen to what
they've got to say!' exclaimed Beryl, to whom anything was
thrilling and amusing if you did it in a troop.

Mrs Steffink made a laughing protest, but gave a virtual
consent by saying, 'We must all wrap up well, then.' The idea
seemed a scatterbrained one to her, and almost heathenish, but it
afforded an opportunity for 'throwing the young people together',
and as such she welcomed it. Mr Horace Bordenby was a young
man with quite substantial prospects, and he had danced with
Beryl at a local subscription ball a sufficient number of times to
warrant the authorized inquiry on the part of the neighbours
whether 'there was anything in it'. Though Mrs Steffink would
not have put it in so many words, she shared the idea of the
Russian peasantry that on this night the beasts might speak.

The cow-house stood at the junction of the garden with a small
paddock, an isolated survival, in a suburban neighbourhood, of
what had once been a small farm. Luke Steffink was complacently proud of his cow-house and his two cows; he felt that they
gave him a stamp of solidity which no number of Wyandottes or
Orpingtons could impart. They even seemed to link him in a sort
of inconsequent way with those patriarchs who derived importance from their floating capital of flocks and herds, he-asses and
she-asses. It had been an anxious and momentous occasion when
he had had to decide definitely between 'the Byre' and 'the
Ranch' for the naming of his villa residence. A December
midnight was hardly the moment he would have chosen for
showing his farm-building to visitors, but since it was a fine
night, and the young people were anxious for an excuse for a
mild frolic, Luke consented to chaperon the expedition. The
servants had long since gone to bed, so the house was left in
charge of Bertie, who scornfully declined to stir out on the pretext
of listening to bovine conversation.

'We must go quietly,' said Luke, as he headed the procession of giggling young folk, brought up in the rear by the shawled and hooded figure of Mrs Steffink; 'I've always laid stress on keeping this a quiet and orderly neighbourhood.'

It was a few minutes to midnight when the party reached the cow-house and made its way in by the light of Luke's stable lantern. For a moment everyone stood in silence, almost with a feeling of being in church.

'Daisy – the one lying down – is by a shorthorn bull out of a Guernsey cow,' announced Luke in a hushed voice, which was in keeping with the foregoing impression.

'Is she?' said Bordenby, rather as if he had expected her to be by Rembrandt.

'Myrtle is –'

Myrtle's family history was cut short by a little scream from the women of the party.

The cow-house door had closed noiselessly behind them and the key had turned gratingly in the lock; then they heard Bertie's voice pleasantly wishing them good-night and his footsteps retreating along the garden path.

Luke Steffink strode to the window; it was a small square opening of the old-fashioned sort, with iron bars let into the stonework.

'Unlock the door this instant,' he shouted, with as much air of menacing authority as a hen might assume when screaming through the bars of a coop at a marauding hawk. In reply to his summons the hall-door closed with a defiant bang.

A neighbouring clock struck the hour of midnight. If the cows had received the gift of human speech at that moment they would not have been able to make themselves heard. Seven or eight other voices were engaged in describing Bertie's present conduct and his general character at a high pressure of excitement and indignation.

In the course of half an hour or so everything that it was permissible to say about Bertie had been said some dozens of times, and other topics began to come to the front – the extreme mustiness of the cow-house, the possibility of it catching fire, and the probability of it being a Rowton House for the vagrant rats of the neighbourhood. And still no sign of deliverance came to the unwilling vigil-keepers.

Towards one o'clock the sound of rather boisterous and

undisciplined carol-singing approached rapidly, and came to a
sudden anchorage, apparently just outside the garden-gate. A
motor-load of youthful 'bloods', in a high state of conviviality,
had made a temporary halt for repairs; the stoppage, however,
did not extend to the vocal efforts of the party, and the watchers
in the cow-shed were treated to a highly unauthorized rendering
of 'Good King Wenceslas', in which the adjective 'good' appeared
to be very carelessly applied.

The noise had the effect of bringing Bertie out into the garden,
but he utterly ignored the pale, angry faces peering out at the
cow-house window, and concentrated his attention on the
revellers outside the gate.

'Wassail, you chaps!' he shouted.

'Wassail, old sport!' they shouted back; 'we'd jolly well drink
y'r health, only we've nothing to drink it in.'

'Come and wassail inside,' said Bertie hospitably; 'I'm all alone,
and there's heaps of "wet".'

They were total strangers, but his touch of kindness made
them instantly his kin. In another moment the unauthorized
version of King Wenceslas, which, like many other scandals,
grew worse on repetition, went echoing up the garden path; two
of the revellers gave an impromptu performance on the way by
executing the staircase waltz up the terraces of what Luke
Steffink, hitherto with some justification, called his rock-garden.
The rock part of it was still there when the waltz had been
accorded its third encore. Luke, more than ever like a cooped hen
behind the cow-house bars, was in a position to realize the
feelings of concert-goers unable to countermand the call for an
encore which they neither desire nor deserve.

The hall door closed with a bang on Bertie's guests, and the
sounds of merriment became faint and muffled to the weary
watchers at the other end of the garden. Presently two ominous
pops, in quick succession, made themselves distinctly heard.

'They've got at the champagne!' exclaimed Mrs Steffink.

'Perhaps it's the sparkling Moselle,' said Luke hopefully.

Three or four more pops were heard.

'The champagne *and* the sparkling Moselle,' said Mrs Steffink.

Luke uncorked an expletive which, like brandy in a temper-
ance household, was only used on rare emergencies. Mr Horace
Bordenby had been making use of similar expressions under his

breath for a considerable time past. The experiment of 'throwing the young people together' had been prolonged beyond a point when it was likely to produce any romantic result.

Some forty minutes later the hall door opened and disgorged a crowd that had thrown off any restraint of shyness that might have influenced its earlier actions. Its vocal efforts in the direction of carol-singing were now supplemented by instrumental music; a Christmas-tree that had been prepared for the children of the gardener and other household retainers had yielded a rich spoil of tin trumpets, rattles, and drums. The life-story of King Wenceslas had been dropped, Luke was thankful to notice, but it was intensely irritating for the chilled prisoners in the cow-house to be told that it was a hot time in the old town tonight, together with some accurate but entirely superfluous information as to the imminence of Christmas morning. Judging by the protests which began to be shouted from the upper windows of neighbouring houses the sentiments prevailing in the cow-house were heartily echoed in other quarters.

The revellers found their car, and, what was more remarkable, managed to drive off in it, with a parting fanfare of tin trumpets. The lively beat of a drum disclosed the fact that the master of the revels remained on the scene.

'Bertie!' came in an angry, imploring chorus of shouts and screams from the cow-house window.

'Hullo,' cried the owner of the name, turning his rather errant steps in the direction of the summons; 'are you people still there? Must have heard everything cows got to say by this time. If you haven't, no use waiting. After all, it's a Russian legend, and Russian Chrismush Eve not due for 'nother fortnight. Better come out.'

After one or two ineffectual attempts he managed to pitch the key of the cow-house door in through the window. Then, lifting his voice in the strains of 'I'm afraid to go home in the dark', with a lusty drum accompaniment, he led the way back to the house. The hurried procession of the released that followed in his steps came in for a good deal of the adverse comment that his exuberant display had evoked.

It was the happiest Christmas Eve he had ever spent. To quote his own words, he had a rotten Christmas.

Excepting Mrs Pentherby

It was Reggie Bruttle's own idea for converting what had threatened to be an albino elephant into a beast of burden that should help him along the stony road of his finances. 'The Limes', which had come to him by inheritance without any accompanying provision for its upkeep, was one of those pretentious, unaccommodating mansions which none but a man of wealth could afford to live in, and which not one wealthy man in a hundred would choose on its merits. It might easily languish in the estate market for years, set round with notice-boards proclaiming it, in the eyes of a sceptical world, to be an eminently desirable residence.

Reggie's scheme was to turn it into the headquarters of a prolonged country-house party, in session during the months from October till the end of March – a party consisting of young or youngish people of both sexes, too poor to be able to do much hunting or shooting on a serious scale, but keen on getting their fill of golf, bridge, dancing, and occasional theatre-going. No one was to be on the footing of a paying guest, but everyone was to rank as a paying host; a committee would look after the catering and expenditure, and an informal sub-committee would make itself useful in helping forward the amusement side of the scheme.

As it was only an experiment, there was to be a general agreement on the part of those involved in it to be as lenient and mutually helpful to one another as possible. Already a promising nucleus, including one or two young married couples, had been got together, and the thing seemed to be fairly launched.

'With good management and a little unobtrusive hard work, I think the thing ought to be a success,' said Reggie, and Reggie was one of those people who are painstaking first and optimistic afterwards.

'There is one rock on which you will unfailingly come to grief, manage you never so wisely,' said Major Dagberry cheerfully; 'the women will quarrel. Mind you,' continued this prophet of disaster, 'I don't say that some of the men won't quarrel too, probably they will; but the women are bound to. You can't prevent it; it's in the nature of the sex. The hand that rocks the cradle rocks the world, in a volcanic sense. A woman will endure discomforts, and make sacrifices, and go without things to an heroic extent, but the one luxury she will not go without is her quarrels. No matter where she may be, or how transient her appearance on a scene, she will install her feminine feuds as assuredly as a Frenchman would concoct soup in the waste of the Arctic regions. At the commencement of a sea voyage, before the male traveller knows half a dozen of his fellow-passengers by sight, the average woman will have started a couple of enmities, and laid in material for one or two more – provided, of course, that there are sufficient women aboard to permit quarrelling in the plural. If there's no one else she will quarrel with the stewardess. This experiment of yours is to run for six months; in less than five weeks there will be war to the knife declaring itself in half a dozen different directions.'

'Oh, come, there are only eight women in the party; they won't all pick quarrels quite as soon as that,' protested Reggie.

'They won't all originate quarrels, perhaps,' conceded the Major, 'but they will all take sides, and just as Christmas is upon you, with its conventions of peace and good will, you will find yourself in for a glacial epoch of cold, unforgiving hostility, with an occasional Etna flare of open warfare. You can't help it, old boy; but, at any rate, you can't say you were not warned.'

The first five weeks of the venture falsified Major Dagberry's prediction and justified Reggie's optimism. There were, of course, occasional small bickerings, and the existence of certain jealousies might be detected below the surface of everyday intercourse; but, on the whole, the womenfolk got on remarkably well together. There was, however, a notable exception. It had not taken five weeks for Mrs Pentherby to get herself cordially disliked by the members of her own sex; five days had been amply sufficient. Most of the women declared that they had detested her the moment they set eyes on her; but that was probably an afterthought.

With the menfolk she got on well enough, without being of the type of woman who can only bask in male society; neither was she lacking in the general qualities which make an individual useful and desirable as a member of a co-operative community. She did not try to 'get the better of' her fellow-hosts by snatching little advantages or cleverly evading her just contributions; she was not inclined to be boring or snobbish in the way of personal reminiscence. She played a fair game of bridge, and her card-room manners were irreproachable. But wherever she came in contact with her own sex the light of battle kindled at once; her talent for arousing animosity seemed to border on positive genius.

Whether the object of her attentions was thick-skinned or sensitive, quick-tempered or good-natured, Mrs Pentherby managed to achieve the same effect. She exposed little weaknesses, she prodded sore places, she snubbed enthusiasms, she was generally right in a matter of argument, or, if wrong, she somehow contrived to make her adversary appear foolish and opinionated. She did, and said, horrible things in a matter-of-fact innocent way, and she did, and said, matter-of-fact innocent things in a horrible way. In short, the unanimous feminine verdict on her was that she was objectionable.

There was no question of taking sides, as the Major had anticipated; in fact, dislike of Mrs Pentherby was almost a bond of union between the other women, and more than one threatening disagreement had been rapidly dissipated by her obvious and malicious attempts to inflame and extend it; and the most irritating thing about her was her successful assumption of unruffled composure at moments when the tempers of her adversaries were with difficulty kept under control. She made her most scathing remarks in the tone of a tube conductor announcing that the next station is Brompton Road – the measured, listless tone of one who knows he is right, but is utterly indifferent to the fact that he proclaims.

On one occasion Mrs Val Gwepton, who was not blessed with the most reposeful of temperaments, fairly let herself go, and gave Mrs Pentherby a vivid and truthful *résumé* of her opinion of her. The object of this unpent storm of accumulated animosity waited patiently for a lull, and then remarked quietly to the angry little woman –

'And now, my dear Mrs Gwepton, let me tell you something that I've been wanting to say for the last two or three minutes, only you wouldn't give me a chance; you've got a hairpin dropping out on the left side. You thin-haired women always find it difficult to keep your hairpins in.'

'What can one do with a woman like that?' Mrs Val demanded afterwards of a sympathizing audience.

Of course, Reggie received numerous hints as to the unpopularity of this jarring personality. His sister-in-law openly tackled him on the subject of her many enormities. Reggie listened with the attenuated regret that one bestows on an earthquake disaster in Bolivia or a crop failure in Eastern Turkestan, events which seem so distant that one can almost persuade oneself they haven't happened.

'That woman has got some hold over him,' opined his sister-in-law darkly; 'either she is helping him to finance the show, and presumes on the fact, or else, which Heaven forbid, he's got some queer infatuation for her. Men do take the most extraordinary fancies.'

Matters never came exactly to a crisis. Mrs Pentherby, as a source of personal offence, spread herself over so wide an area that no one woman of the party felt impelled to rise up and declare that she absolutely refused to stay another week in the same house with her. What is everybody's tragedy is nobody's tragedy. There was even a certain consolation in comparing notes as to specific acts of offence. Reggie's sister-in-law had the added interest of trying to discover the secret bond which blunted his condemnation of Mrs Pentherby's long catalogue of misdeeds. There was little to go on from his manner towards her in public, but he remained obstinately unimpressed by anything that was said against her in private.

With the one exception of Mrs Pentherby's unpopularity, the house-party scheme was a success on its first trial, and there was no difficulty about reconstructing it on the same lines for another winter session. It so happened that most of the women of the party, and two or three of the men, would not be available on this occasion, but Reggie had laid his plans well ahead and booked plenty of 'fresh blood' for the new departure. It would be, if anything, rather a larger party than before.

'I'm so sorry I can't join this winter,' said Reggie's sister-in-law, 'but we must go to our cousins in Ireland; we've put them off so often. What a shame! You'll have none of the same women this time.'

'Excepting Mrs Pentherby,' said Reggie demurely.

'Mrs Pentherby! *Surely*, Reggie, you're not going to be so idiotic as to have that woman again! She'll set all the women's backs up just as she did this time. What *is* this mysterious hold she's got over you?'

'She's invaluable,' said Reggie; 'she's my official quarreller.'

'Your – what did you say?' gasped his sister-in-law.

'I introduced her into the house-party for the express purpose of concentrating the feuds and quarrelling that would otherwise have broken out in all directions among the women-kind. I didn't need the advice and warning of sundry friends to foresee that we shouldn't get through six months of close companionship without a certain amount of pecking and sparring, so I thought the best thing was to localize and sterilize it in one process. Of course, I made it well worth the lady's while, and she didn't know any of you from Adam, and as you don't even know her real name, she didn't mind getting herself disliked in a useful cause.'

'You mean to say she was in the know all the time?'

'Of course she was, and so were one or two of the men, so she was able to have a good laugh with us behind the scenes when she'd done anything particularly outrageous. And she really enjoyed herself. You see, she's in the position of poor relation in a rather pugnacious family, and her life has been largely spent in smoothing over other people's quarrels. You can imagine the welcome relief of being able to go about saying and doing perfectly exasperating things to a whole houseful of women – and all in the cause of peace.'

'I think you are the most odious person in the whole world,' said Reggie's sister-in-law. Which was not strictly true; more than anybody, more than ever she disliked Mrs Pentherby. It was impossible to calculate how many quarrels that woman had done her out of.

For the Duration of the War

The Rev. Wilfrid Gaspilton, in one of those clerical migrations inconsequent-seeming to the lay mind, had removed from the moderately fashionable parish of St Luke's, Kensingate, to the immoderately rural parish of St Chuddocks, somewhere in Yondershire. There were doubtless substantial advantages connected with the move, but there were certainly some very

obvious drawbacks. Neither the migratory clergyman nor his
wife were able to adapt themselves naturally and comfortably to
the conditions of country life. Beryl, Mrs Gaspilton, had always
looked indulgently on the country as a place where people of
irreproachable income and hospitable instincts cultivated tennis-
lawns and rose-gardens and Jacobean pleasaunces, wherein
selected gatherings of interested week-end guests might disport
themselves. Mrs Gaspilton considered herself as distinctly an
interesting personality, and from a limited standpoint she was
doubtless right. She had indolent dark eyes and a comfortable
chin, which belied the slightly plaintive inflection which she
threw into her voice at suitable intervals. She was tolerably well
satisfied with the smaller advantages of life, but she regretted that
Fate had not seen its way to reserve for her some of the ampler
successes for which she felt herself well qualified. She would have
liked to be the centre of a literary, slightly political salon, where
discerning satellites might have recognized the breadth of her
outlook on human affairs and the undoubted smallness of her
feet. As it was, Destiny had chosen for her that she should be the
wife of a rector, and had now further decreed that a country
rectory should be the background to her existence. She rapidly
made up her mind that her surroundings did not call for
exploration: Noah had predicted the Flood, but no one expected
him to swim about in it. Digging in a wet garden or trudging
through muddy lanes were exertions which she did not propose
to undertake. As long as the garden produced asparagus and
carnations at pleasingly frequent intervals Mrs Gaspilton was
content to approve of its expense and otherwise ignore its
existence. She would fold herself up, so to speak, in an elegant,
indolent little world of her own, enjoying the minor recreations of
being gently rude to the doctor's wife and continuing the
leisurely production of her one literary effort, *The Forbidden
Horsepond*, a translation of Baptiste Lepoy's *L'Abreuvoir interdit*. It
was a labour which had already been so long drawn-out that it
seemed probable that Baptiste Lepoy would drop out of vogue
before her translation of his temporarily famous novel was
finished. However, the languid prosecution of the work had
invested Mrs Gaspilton with a certain literary dignity, even in
Kensingate circles, and would place her on a pinnacle in St

Chuddocks, where hardly anyone read French, and assuredly no one had heard of *L'Abreuvoir interdit*.

The Rector's wife might be content to turn her back complacently on the country; it was the Rector's tragedy that the country turned its back on him. With the best intention in the world and the immortal example of Gilbert White before him, the Rev. Wilfrid found himself as bored and ill at ease in his new surroundings as Charles II would have been at a modern Wesleyan Conference. The birds that hopped across his lawn hopped across it as though it were their lawn, and not his, and gave him plainly to understand that in their eyes he was infinitely less interesting than a garden worm or the rectory cat. The hedgeside and meadow flowers were equally uninspiring; the lesser celandine seemed particularly unworthy of the attention that English poets had bestowed on it, and the Rector knew that he would be utterly miserable if left alone for a quarter of an hour in its company. With the human inhabitants of his parish he was no better off; to know them was merely to know their ailments, and the ailments were almost invariably rheumatism. Some, of course, had other bodily infirmities, but they always had rheumatism as well. The Rector had not yet grasped the fact that in rural cottage life not to have rheumatism is as glaring an omission as not to have been presented at Court would be in more ambitious circles. And with all this dearth of local interest there was Beryl shutting herself off with her ridiculous labours on *The Forbidden Horsepond*.

'I don't see why you should suppose that anyone wants to read Baptiste Lepoy in English,' the Reverend Wilfrid remarked to his wife one morning, finding her surrounded with her usual elegant litter of dictionaries, fountain pens, and scribbling paper; 'hardly anyone bothers to read him now in France.'

'My dear,' said Beryl, with an intonation of gentle weariness, 'haven't two or three leading London publishers told me they wondered no one had ever translated *L'Abreuvoir interdit*, and begged me –'

'Publishers always clamour for the books that no one has ever written, and turn a cold shoulder on them as soon as they're written. If St Paul were living now they would pester him to write an Epistle to the Esquimaux, but no London publisher would dream of reading his Epistle to the Ephesians.'

'Is there any asparagus anywhere in the garden?' asked Beryl; 'because I've told cook —'

'Not anywhere in the garden,' snapped the Rector, 'but there's no doubt plenty in the asparagus-bed, which is the usual place for it.'

And he walked away into the region of fruit trees and vegetable beds to exchange irritation for boredom. It was there, among the gooseberry bushes and beneath the medlar trees, that the temptation to the perpetration of a great literary fraud came to him.

Some weeks later the *Bi-Monthly Review* gave to the world, under the guarantee of the Rev. Wilfrid Gaspilton, some fragments of Persian verse, alleged to have been unearthed and translated by a nephew who was at present campaigning somewhere in the Tigris valley. The Rev. Wilfrid possessed a host of nephews; and it was, of course, quite possible that one or more of them might be in military employ in Mesopotamia, though no one could call to mind any particular nephew who could have been suspected of being a Persian scholar.

The verses were attributed to one Ghurab, a hunter, or, according to other accounts, warden of the royal fishponds, who lived, in some unspecified century, in the neighbourhood of Karmanshah. They breathed a spirit of comfortable, even-tempered satire and philosophy, disclosing a mockery that did not trouble to be bitter, a joy in life that was not passionate to the verge of being troublesome.

> A Mouse that prayed for Allah's aid
>   Blasphemed when no such aid befell:
> A Cat, who feasted on that mouse,
>   Thought Allah managed vastly well.
>
> Pray not for aid to One who made
>   A set of never-changing Laws,
> But in your need remember well
>   He gave you speed, or guile — or claws.
>
> Some laud a life of mild content:
>   Content may fall, as well as Pride.
> The Frog who hugged his lowly Ditch
>   Was much disgruntled when it dried.

'You are not on the Road to Hell,'
  You tell me with fanatic glee:
Vain boaster, what shall that avail
  If Hell is on the road to thee?

A Poet praised the Evening Star,
  Another praised the Parrot's hue:
A Merchant praised his merchandise,
  And he, at least, praised what he knew.

It was this verse which gave the critics and commentators some
clue as to the probable date of the composition; the parrot, they
reminded the public, was in high vogue as a type of elegance in
the days of Hafiz of Shiraz; in the quatrains of Omar it makes no
appearance.

The next verse, it was pointed out, would apply to the political
conditions of the present day as strikingly as to the region and
era for which it was written –

A Sultan dreamed day-long of Peace,
  The while his Rivals' armies grew:
They changed his Day-dreams into sleep
  – The Peace, methinks, he never knew.

Woman appeared little, and wine not at all in the verse of the
hunter-poet, but there was at least one contribution to the love-
philosophy of the East –

O Moon-faced Charmer, with Star-drownèd Eyes,
  And cheeks of soft delight, exhaling musk,
They tell me that thy charm will fade; ah well,
  The Rose itself grows hue-less in the Dusk.

Finally, there was a recognition of the Inevitable, a chill breath
blowing across the poet's comfortable estimate of life –

There is a sadness in each Dawn,
  A sadness that you cannot rede:
The joyous Day brings in its train
  The Feast, the Loved One, and the Steed.

Ah, there shall come a Dawn at last
  That brings no life-stir to your ken,

> A long, cold Dawn without a Day,
> And ye shall rede its sadness then.

The verses of Ghurab came on the public at a moment when a comfortable, slightly quizzical philosophy was certain to be welcome, and their reception was enthusiastic. Elderly colonels, who had outlived the love of truth, wrote to the papers to say that they had been familiar with the works of Ghurab in Afghanistan, and Aden, and other suitable localities a quarter of a century ago. A Ghurab-of-Karmanshah Club sprang into existence, the members of which alluded to each other as Brother Ghurabians on the slightest provocation. And to the flood of inquiries, criticisms, and requests for information, which naturally poured in on the discoverer, or rather the discloser, of this long-hidden poet, the Rev. Wilfrid made one effectual reply: Military considerations forbade any disclosures which might throw unnecessary light on his nephew's movements.

After the war the Rector's position will be one of unthinkable embarrassment, but for the moment, at any rate, he has driven *The Forbidden Horsepond* out of the field.

The Interlopers

In a forest of mixed growth somewhere on the eastern spurs of the Carpathians, a man stood one winter night watching and listening, as though he waited for some beast of the woods to come within the range of his vision, and, later, of his rifle. But the game for whose presence he kept so keen an outlook was none that figured in the sportsman's calendar as lawful and proper for the chase; Ulrich von Gradwitz patrolled the dark forest in quest of a human enemy.

The forest lands of Gradwitz were of wide extent and well stocked with game; the narrow strip of precipitous woodland that lay on its outskirts was not remarkable for the game it harboured or the shooting it afforded, but it was the most jealously guarded of all its owner's territorial possessions. A famous lawsuit, in the days of his grandfather, had wrested it from the illegal possession of a neighbouring family of petty landowners; the dispossessed party had never acquiesced in the judgment of the Courts, and a long series of poaching affrays and similar scandals had embittered the relationship between the families for three generations. The neighbour feud had grown into a personal one since Ulrich had come to be head of his family; if there was a man in the world whom he detested and wished ill to it was Georg Znaeym, the inheritor of the quarrel and the tireless game-snatcher and raider of the disputed border-forest. The feud might, perhaps, have died down or been compromised if the personal ill-will of the two men had not stood in the way; as boys they had thirsted for one another's blood, as men each prayed that misfortune might fall on the other, and this wind-scourged winter night Ulrich had banded together his foresters to watch the dark forest, not in quest of four-footed quarry, but to keep a look-out for the prowling thieves whom he suspected of being afoot from across the land boundary. The roebuck, which usually kept in the sheltered hollows during a storm-wind, were running like driven things tonight, and there was movement and unrest among the creatures that were wont to sleep through the dark hours. Assuredly there was a disturbing element in the forest, and Ulrich could guess the quarter from whence it came.

He strayed away by himself from the watchers whom he had placed in ambush on the crest of the hill, and wandered far down the steep slopes amid the wild tangle of undergrowth, peering through the tree-trunks and listening through the whistling and skirling of the wind and the restless beating of the branches for sight or sound of the marauders. If only on this wild night, in this dark, lone spot, he might come across Georg Znaeym, man to man, with none to witness – that was the wish that was uppermost in his thoughts. And as he stepped round the trunk of a huge beech he came face to face with the man he sought.

The two enemies stood glaring at one another for a long silent moment. Each had a rifle in his hand, each had hate in his heart and murder uppermost in his mind. The chance had come to give full play to the passions of a lifetime. But a man who has been brought up under the code of a restraining civilization cannot easily nerve himself to shoot down his neighbour in cold blood and without word spoken, except for an offence against his heart and honour. And before the moment of hesitation had given way to action a deed of Nature's own violence overwhelmed them both. A fierce shriek of the storm had been answered by a splitting crash over their heads, and ere they could leap aside a mass of falling beech tree had thundered down on them. Ulrich von Gradwitz found himself stretched on the ground, one arm numb beneath him and the other held almost as helplessly in a tight tangle of forked branches, while both legs were pinned beneath the fallen mass. His heavy shooting-boots had saved his feet from being crushed to pieces, but if his fractures were not as serious as they might have been, at least it was evident that he could not move from his present position till someone came to release him. The descending twigs had slashed the skin of his face, and he had to wink away some drops of blood from his eyelashes before he could take in a general view of the disaster. At his side, so near that under ordinary circumstances he could almost have touched him, lay Georg Znaeym, alive and struggling, but obviously as helplessly pinned down as himself. All round them lay a thick-strewn wreckage of splintered branches and broken twigs.

Relief at being alive and exasperation at his captive plight brought a strange medley of pious thank-offerings and sharp curses to Ulrich's lips. Georg, who was nearly blinded with the blood which trickled across his eyes, stopped his struggling for a moment to listen, and then gave a short, snarling laugh.

'So you're not killed, as you ought to be, but you're caught anyway,' he said; 'caught fast. Ho, what a jest, Ulrich von Gradwitz snarled in his stolen forest. There's real justice for you!'

And he laughed again, mockingly and savagely.

'I'm caught in my own forest-land,' retorted Ulrich. 'When my men come to release us you will wish, perhaps, that you were in a better plight than caught poaching on a neighbour's land, shame on you.'

Georg was silent for a moment; then he answered quietly.

'Are you sure that your men will find much to release? I have men, too, in the forest tonight, close behind me, and *they* will be here first and do the releasing. When they drag me out from under these damned branches it won't need much clumsiness on their part to roll this mass of trunk right over on the top of you. Your men will find you dead under a fallen beech tree. For form's sake I shall send my condolences to your family.'

'It is a useful hint,' said Ulrich fiercely. 'My men had orders to follow in ten minutes' time, seven of which must have gone by already, and when they get me out – I will remember the hint. Only as you will have met your death poaching on my lands, I don't think I can decently send any message of condolence to your family.'

'Good,' snarled Georg, 'good. We fight this quarrel out to the death, you and I and our foresters, with no cursed interlopers to come between us. Death and damnation to you, Ulrich von Gradwitz.'

'The same to you, Georg Znaeym, forest-thief, game-snatcher.'

Both men spoke with the bitterness of possible defeat before them, for each knew that it might be long before his men would seek him out or find him; it was a bare matter of chance which party would arrive first on the scene.

Both had now given up the useless struggle to free themselves from the mass of wood that held them down. Ulrich limited his endeavours to an effort to bring his one partially free arm near enough to his outer coat pocket to draw out his wine-flask. Even when he had accomplished that operation it was long before he could manage the unscrewing of the stopper or get any of the liquid down his throat. But what a Heaven-sent draught it seemed! It was an open winter, and little snow had fallen as yet, hence the captives suffered less from the cold than might have been the case at that season of the year; nevertheless, the wine was warming and reviving to the wounded man, and he looked across with something like a throb of pity to where his enemy lay, just keeping the groans of pain and weariness from crossing his lips.

'Could you reach this flask if I threw it over to you?' asked Ulrich suddenly; 'there is good wine in it, and one may as well be as comfortable as one can. Let us drink, even if tonight one of us dies.'

'No, I can scarcely see anything; there is so much blood caked round my eyes,' said Georg, 'and in any case I don't drink wine with an enemy.'

Ulrich was silent for a few minutes, and lay listening to the weary screeching of the wind. An idea was slowly forming and growing in his brain, an idea that gained strength every time that he looked across at the man who was fighting so grimly against pain and exhaustion. In the pain and languor that Ulrich himself was feeling the old fierce hatred seemed to be dying down.

'Neighbour,' he said presently, 'do as you please if your men come first. It was a fair compact. But as for me, I've changed my mind. If my men are the first to come you shall be the first to be helped, as though you were my guest. We have quarrelled like devils all our lives over this stupid strip of forest, where the trees can't even stand upright in a breath of wind. Lying here tonight, thinking, I've come to think we've been rather fools; there are better things in life than getting the better of a boundary dispute. Neighbour, if you will help me to bury the old quarrel I – I will ask you to be my friend.'

Georg Znaeym was silent for so long that Ulrich thought, perhaps, he had fainted with the pain of his injuries. Then he spoke slowly and in jerks.

'How the whole region would stare and gabble if we rode into the market-square together. No one living can remember seeing a Znaeym and a von Gradwitz talking to one another in friendship. And what peace there would be among the forester folk if we ended our feud tonight. And if we choose to make peace among our people there is none other to interfere, no interlopers from outside . . . You would come and keep the Sylvester night beneath my roof, and I would come and feast on some high day at your castle . . . I would never fire a shot on your land, save when you invited me as a guest; and you should come and shoot with me down in the marshes where the wildfowl are. In all the country-side there are none that could hinder if we willed to make peace. I never thought to have wanted to do other than hate you all my life, but I think I have changed my mind about things too, this last half-hour. And you offered me your wine-flask . . . Ulrich von Gradwitz, I will be your friend.'

For a space both men were silent, turning over in their minds the wonderful changes that this dramatic reconciliation would bring about. In the cold, gloomy forest, with the wind tearing in fitful gusts through the naked branches and whistling round the tree-trunks, they lay and waited for the help that would now bring release and succour to both parties. And each prayed a private prayer that his men might be the first to arrive, so that he might be the first to show honourable attention to the enemy that had become a friend.

Presently, as the wind dropped for a moment, Ulrich broke silence.

'Let's shout for help,' he said; 'in this lull our voices may carry a little way.'

'They won't carry far through the trees and undergrowth,' said Georg, 'but we can try. Together, then.'

The two raised their voices in a prolonged hunting call.

'Together again,' said Ulrich a few minutes later, after listening in vain for an answering halloo.

'I heard something that time, I think,' said Ulrich.

'I heard nothing but the pestilential wind,' said Georg hoarsely.

There was silence again for some minutes, and then Ulrich gave a joyful cry.

'I can see figures coming through the wood. They are following in the way I came down the hillside.'

Both men raised their voices in as loud a shout as they could muster.

'They hear us! They've stopped. Now they see us. They're running down the hill towards us,' cried Ulrich.

'How many of them are there?' asked Georg.

'I can't see distinctly,' said Ulrich; 'nine or ten.'

'Then they are yours,' said Georg; 'I had only seven out with me.'

'They are making all the speed they can, brave lads,' said Ulrich gladly.

'Are they your men?' asked Georg. 'Are they your men?' he repeated impatiently as Ulrich did not answer.

'No,' said Ulrich with a laugh, the idiotic chattering laugh of a man unstrung with hideous fear.

'Who are they?' asked Georg quickly, straining his eyes to see what the other would gladly not have seen.

'Wolves.'

Louise

'The tea will be quite cold, you'd better ring for some more,' said the Dowager Lady Beanford.

Susan Lady Beanford was a vigorous old woman who had coquetted with imaginary ill-health for the greater part of a lifetime; Clovis Sangrail irreverently declared that she had caught a chill at the Coronation of Queen Victoria and had never let it go again. Her sister, Jane Thropplestance, who was some years her junior, was chiefly remarkable for being the most absent-minded woman in Middlesex.

'I've really been unusually clever this afternoon,' she remarked gaily, as she rang for the tea. 'I've called on all the people I meant to call on, and I've done all the shopping that I set out to do. I even remembered to try and match that silk for you at Harrod's but I'd forgotten to bring the pattern with me, so it was no use. I really think that was the only important thing I forgot during the whole afternoon. Quite wonderful for me, isn't it?'

'What have you done with Louise?' asked her sister. 'Didn't you take her out with you? You said you were going to.'

'Good gracious,' exclaimed Jane, 'what *have* I done with Louise? I must have left her somewhere.'

'But where?'

'That's just it. Where have I left her? I can't remember if the Carrywoods were at home or if I just left cards. If they were at home I may have left Louise there to play bridge. I'll go and telephone to Lord Carrywood and find out.'

'Is that you, Lord Carrywood?' she queried over the telephone; 'it's me, Jane Thropplestance. I want to know, have you seen Louise?'

'"Louise",' came the answer, 'it's been my fate to see it three times. At first, I must admit, I wasn't impressed by it, but the music grows on one after a bit. Still, I don't think I want to see it again just at present. Were you going to offer me a seat in your box?'

'Not the opera "Louise" – my niece, Louise Thropplestance. I thought I might have left her at your house.'

'You left cards on us this afternoon, I understand, but I don't think you left a niece. The footman would have been sure to have mentioned it if you had. Is it going to be a fashion to leave nieces on people as well as cards? I hope not; some of these houses in Berkeley Square have practically no accommodation for that sort of thing.'

'She's not at the Carrywoods,' announced Jane, returning to her tea; 'now I come to think of it, perhaps I left her at the silk counter at Selfridge's. I may have told her to wait there a moment while I went to look at the silks in a better light, and I may easily have forgotten about her when I found I hadn't your pattern with me. In that case she's still sitting there. She wouldn't move unless she was told to; Louise has no initiative.'

'You said you tried to match the silk at Harrod's,' interjected the dowager.

'Did I? Perhaps it was Harrod's. I really don't remember. It was one of those places where every one is so kind and sympathetic and devoted that one almost hates to take even a reel of cotton away from such pleasant surroundings.'

'I think you might have taken Louise away. I don't like the idea of her being there among a lot of strangers. Supposing some unprincipled person was to get into conversation with her.'

'Impossible. Louise has no conversation. I've never discovered a single topic on which she'd anything to say beyond "Do you think so? I dare say you're right." I really thought her reticence about the fall of the Ribot Ministry was ridiculous, considering how much her dear mother used to visit Paris. This bread and butter is cut far too thin; it crumbles away long before you can get it to your mouth. One feels so absurd, snapping at one's food in mid-air, like a trout leaping at may-fly.'

'I am rather surprised,' said the dowager, 'that you can sit there making a hearty tea when you've just lost a favourite niece.'

'You talk as if I'd lost her in a churchyard sense, instead of having temporarily mislaid her. I'm sure to remember presently where I left her.'

'You didn't visit any place of devotion, did you? If you've left her mooning about Westminster Abbey or St Peter's, Eaton Square, without being able to give any satisfactory reason why she's there, she'll be seized under the Cat and Mouse Act and sent to Reginald McKenna.'

'That would be extremely awkward,' said Jane, meeting an irresolute piece of bread and butter halfway; 'we hardly know the McKennas, and it would be very tiresome having to telephone to some unsympathetic private secretary, describing Louise to him and asking to have her sent back in time for dinner. Fortunately, I didn't go to any place of devotion, though I did get mixed up with a Salvation Army procession. It was quite interesting to be at close quarters with them, they're so absolutely different to what they used to be when I first remember them in the 'eighties. They used to go about then unkempt and dishevelled, in a sort of smiling rage with the world, and now they're spruce and jaunty and flamboyantly decorative, like a geranium bed with religious convictions. Laura Kettleway was going on about them in the lift of the Dover Street Tube the other day, saying what a lot of good work they did, and what a loss it would have been if they'd never existed. "If they had never existed," I said, "Granville Barker would have been certain to have invented something that looked exactly like them." If you say things like that, quite loud, in a Tube lift, they always sound like epigrams.'

'I think you ought to do something about Louise,' said the dowager.

'I'm trying to think whether she was with me when I called on Ada Spelvexit. I rather enjoyed myself there. Ada was trying, as usual, to ram that odious Koriatoffski woman down my throat, knowing perfectly well that I detest her, and in an unguarded moment she said: "She's leaving her present house and going to Lower Seymour Street." "I dare say she will, if she stays there long enough," I said. Ada didn't see it for about three minutes, and then she was positively uncivil. No, I am certain I didn't leave Louise there.'

'If you could manage to remember where you *did* leave her, it would be more to the point than these negative assurances,' said Lady Beanford; 'so far, all that we know is that she is not at the Carrywoods', or Ada Spelvexit's, or Westminster Abbey.'

'That narrows the search down a bit,' said Jane hopefully; 'I rather fancy she must have been with me when I went to Mornay's. I know I went to Mornay's, because I remember meeting that delightful Malcolm What's-his-name there – you know whom I mean. That's the great advantage of people having unusual first names, you needn't try and remember what their other name is. Of course I know one or two other Malcolms, but none that could possibly be described as delightful. He gave me two tickets for the Happy Sunday Evenings in Sloane Square. I've probably left them at Mornay's, but still it was awfully kind of him to give them to me.'

'Do you think you left Louise there?'

'I might telephone and ask. Oh, Robert, before you clear the tea-things away I wish you'd ring up Mornay's, in Regent Street, and ask if I left two theatre tickets and one niece in their shop this afternoon.'

'A niece, ma'am?' asked the footman.

'Yes, Miss Louise didn't come home with me, and I'm not sure where I left her.'

'Miss Louise has been upstairs all the afternoon, ma'am, reading to the second kitchenmaid, who has the neuralgia. I took up tea to Miss Louise at a quarter to five o'clock, ma'am.'

'Of course, how silly of me. I remember now, I asked her to read the *Faërie Queene* to poor Emma, to try to send her to sleep. I always get someone to read the *Faërie Queene* to me when I have neuralgia, and it usually sends me to sleep. Louise doesn't seem to have been successful, but one can't say she hasn't tried. I expect after the first hour or so the kitchenmaid would rather have been left alone with her neuralgia, but of course Louise wouldn't leave off till someone told her to. Anyhow, you can ring up Mornay's, Robert, and ask whether I left two theatre tickets there. Except for your silk, Susan, those seem to be the only things I've forgotten this afternoon. Quite wonderful for me.'

Morlvera

The Olympic Toy Emporium occupied a conspicuous frontage in an important West End street. It was happily named Toy Emporium, because one would never have dreamed of according it the familiar and yet pulse-quickening name of toyshop. There was an air of cold splendour and elaborate failure about the wares that were set out in its ample windows; they were the sort of toys that a tired shop-assistant displays and explains at Christmastime to exclamatory parents and bored, silent children. The animal toys looked more like natural history models than the comfortable, sympathetic companions that one would wish, at a certain age, to take to bed with one, and to smuggle into the bathroom. The mechanical toys incessantly did things that no one could want a toy to do more than half a dozen times in its lifetime; it was a merciful reflection that in any right-minded nursery the lifetime would certainly be short.

Prominent among the elegantly dressed dolls that filled an entire section of the window frontage was a large hobble-skirted lady in a confection of peach-coloured velvet, elaborately set off with leopard skin accessories, if one may use such a conveniently comprehensive word in describing an intricate feminine toilette. She lacked nothing that is to be found in a carefully detailed fashion-plate – in fact, she might be said to have something more than the average fashion-plate female possesses; in place of a vacant, expressionless stare she had character in her face. It must be admitted that it was bad character, cold, hostile, inquisitorial, with a sinister lowering of one eyebrow and a merciless hardness about the corners of the mouth. One might have imagined histories about her by the hour, histories in which unworthy ambition, the desire for money, and an entire absence of all decent feeling would play a conspicuous part.

As a matter of fact, she was not without her judges and biographers, even in this shop-window stage of her career. Emmeline, aged ten, and Bert, aged seven, had halted on the way from their obscure back street to the minnow-stocked water of St James's Park, and were critically examining the hobble-skirted doll, and dissecting her character in no very tolerant spirit. There is probably a latent enmity between the necessarily under-clad and the unnecessarily over-dressed, but a little kindness and good-fellowship on the part of the latter will often change the sentiment to admiring devotion; if the lady in peach-coloured velvet and leopard skin had worn a pleasant expression in addition to her other elaborate furnishings, Emmeline at least might have respected and even loved her. As it was, she gave her a horrible reputation, based chiefly on a second-hand knowledge of gilded depravity derived from the conversation of those who were skilled in the art of novelette reading. Bert filled in a few damaging details from his own limited imagination.

'She is a bad lot, that one is,' declared Emmeline, after a long unfriendly stare; ''er 'usband 'ates 'er.'

''E knocks 'er abart,' said Bert with enthusiasm.

'No, 'e don't, cos 'e's dead; she poisoned 'im slow and gradual, so that nobody didn't know. Now she wants to marry a lord, with 'eaps and 'eaps of money. 'E's got a wife already, but she's going to poison 'er, too.'

'She's a bad lot,' said Bert with growing hostility.

''Er mother 'ates 'er, and she's afraid of 'er, too, cos she's got a serkestic tongue; always talking serkesms, she is. She's greedy too; if there's fish going, she eats 'er own share and 'er little girl's as well, though the little girl is dellikit.'

'She 'ad a little boy once,' said Bert, 'but she pushed 'im into the water when nobody wasn't looking.'

'No, she didn't,' said Emmeline, 'she sent 'im away to be kep' by poor people, so 'er husbind wouldn't know where 'e was. They ill-treat 'im somethink cruel.'

'Wot's 'er nime?' asked Bert, thinking that it was time that so interesting a personality should be labelled.

''Er nime?' said Emmeline, thinking hard, ''er nime's Morlvera.' It was as near as she could get to the name of an adventuress who figured prominently in a cinema drama. There was silence for a moment while the possibilities of the name were turned over in the children's minds.

'Those clothes she's got on ain't paid for, and never won't be,' said Emmeline; 'she thinks she'll get the rich lord to pay for 'em, but 'e wont. 'E's given 'er jools, 'underds of pounds' worth.'

''E won't pay for the clothes,' said Bert with conviction. Evidently there was some limit to the weak good nature of wealthy lords.

At that moment a motor carriage with liveried servants drew up at the emporium entrance; a large lady, with a penetrating and rather hurried manner of talking, stepped out, followed slowly and sulkily by a small boy, who had a very black scowl on his face and a very white sailor suit over the rest of him. The lady was continuing an argument which had probably commenced in Portman Square.

'Now, Victor, you are to come in and buy a nice doll for your cousin Bertha. She gave you a beautiful box of soldiers on your birthday, and you must give her a present on hers.'

'Bertha is a fat little fool,' said Victor, in a voice that was as loud as his mother's and had more assurance in it.

'Victor, you are not to say such things. Bertha is not a fool, and she is not in the least fat. You are to come in and choose a doll for her.'

The couple passed into the shop, out of view and hearing of the two back-street children.

'My, he is in a wicked temper,' exclaimed Emmeline, but both she and Bert were inclined to side with him against the absent Bertha, who was doubtless as fat and foolish as he had described her to be.

'I want to see some dolls,' said the mother of Victor to the nearest assistant; 'it's for a little girl of eleven.'

'A fat little girl of eleven,' added Victor by way of supplementary information.

'Victor, if you say such rude things about your cousin, you shall go to bed the moment we get home, without any tea.'

'This is one of the newest things we have in dolls,' said the assistant, removing a hobble-skirted figure in peach-coloured velvet from the window; 'leopard-skin toque and stole, the latest fashion. You won't get anything newer than that anywhere. It's an exclusive design.'

'Look!' whispered Emmeline outside; 'they've bin and took Morlvera.'

There was a mingling of excitement and a certain sense of bereavement in her mind; she would have liked to gaze at that embodiment of overdressed depravity for just a little longer.

'I 'spect she's going away in a kerridge to marry the rich lord,' hazarded Bert.

'She's up to no good,' said Emmeline vaguely.

Inside the shop the purchase of the doll had been decided on.

'It's a beautiful doll, and Bertha will be delighted with it,' asserted the mother of Victor loudly.

'Oh, very well,' said Victor sulkily; 'you needn't have it stuck into a box and wait an hour while it's being done up into a parcel. I'll take it as it is, and we can go round to Manchester Square and give it to Bertha, and get the thing done with. That will save me the trouble of writing, "For dear Bertha, with Victor's love', on a bit of paper.'

'Very well,' said his mother, 'we can go to Manchester Square on our way home. You must wish her many happy returns of tomorrow, and give her the doll.'

'I won't let the little beast kiss me,' stipulated Victor.

His mother said nothing; Victor had not been half as troublesome as she had anticipated. When he chose he could really be dreadfully naughty.

Emmeline and Bert were just moving away from the window when Morlvera made her exit from the shop, very carefully held in Victor's arms. A look of sinister triumph seemed to glow in her hard, inquisitorial face. As for Victor, a certain scornful serenity

had replaced the earlier scowls; he had evidently accepted defeat
with a contemptuous good grace.

The tall lady gave a direction to the footman and settled herself
in the carriage. The little figure in the white sailor suit clambered
in beside her, still carefully holding the elegantly garbed doll.

The car had to be backed a few yards in the process of turning.
Very stealthily, very gently, very mercilessly Victor sent Morlvera
flying over his shoulder, so that she fell into the road just behind
the retrogressing wheel. With a soft, pleasant-sounding scrunch
the car went over the prostrate form, then it moved forward
again with another scrunch. The carriage moved off and left Bert
and Emmeline gazing in scared delight at a sorry mess of petrol-
smeared velvet, sawdust, and leopard skin, which was all that
remained of the hateful Morlvera. They gave a shrill cheer, and
then raced away shuddering from the scene of so much rapidly
enacted tragedy.

Later that afternoon, when they were engaged in the pursuit of
minnows by the waterside in St James's Park, Emmeline said in a
solemn undertone to Bert –

'I've been finking. Do you know oo 'e was? 'E was 'er little boy
wot she'd sent away to live wiv poor folks. 'E come back and
done that.'

The Occasional Garden

'Don't talk to me about town gardens,' said Elinor Rapsley;
'which means, of course, that I want you to listen to me for an
hour or so while I talk about nothing else. "What a nice-sized
garden you've got," people said to us when we first moved here.
What I suppose they meant to say was what a nice-sized site for a
garden we'd got. As a matter of fact, the size is all against it; it's
too large to be ignored altogether and treated as a yard, and it's
too small to keep giraffes in. You see, if we could keep giraffes or
reindeer or some other species of browsing animal there we could
explain the general absence of vegetation by a reference to the
fauna of the garden: "You can't have wapiti *and* Darwin tulips,
you know, so we didn't put down any bulbs last year." As it is,
we haven't got the wapiti, and the Darwin tulips haven't
survived the fact that most of the cats of the neighbourhood hold

a parliament in the centre of the tulip bed; that rather forlorn-looking strip that we intended to be a border of alternating geranium and spiraea has been utilized by the cat-parliament as a division lobby. Snap divisions seem to have been rather frequent of late, far more frequent than the geranium blooms are likely to be. I shouldn't object so much to ordinary cats, but I do complain of having a congress of vegetarian cats in my garden; they must be vegetarians, my dear, because, whatever ravages they may commit among the sweet-pea seedlings, they never seem to touch the sparrows; there are always just as many adult sparrows in the garden on Saturday as there were on Monday, not to mention newly fledged additions. There seems to have been an irreconcilable difference of opinions between sparrows and Providence since the beginning of time as to whether a crocus looks best standing upright with its roots in the earth or in a recumbent posture with its stem neatly severed; the sparrows always have the last word in the matter, at least in our garden they do. I fancy that Providence must have originally intended to bring in an amending Act, or whatever it's called, providing either for a less destructive sparrow or a more indestructible crocus. The one consoling point about our garden is that it's not visible from the drawing-room or the smoking-room, so unless people are dining or lunching with us they can't spy out the nakedness of the land. That is why I am so furious with Gwenda Pottingdon, who has practically forced herself on me for lunch on Wednesday next; she heard me offer the Paulcote girl lunch if she was up shopping on that day, and, of course, she asked if she might come too. She is only coming to gloat over my bedraggled and flowerless borders and to sing the praises of her own detestably over-cultivated garden. I'm sick of being told that it's the envy of the neighbourhood; it's like everything else that belongs to her – her car, her dinner-parties, even her headaches, they are all superlative; no one else ever had anything like them. When her eldest child was confirmed it was such a sensational event, according to her account of it, that one almost expected questions to be asked about it in the House of Commons and now she's coming on purpose to stare at my few miserable pansies and the gaps in my sweet-pea border, and to give me a glowing full-length description of the rare and sumptuous blooms in her rose-garden.'

'My dear Elinor,' said the Baroness, 'you would save yourself all this heart-burning and a lot of gardener's bills, not to mention sparrow anxieties, simply by paying an annual subscription to the O.O.S.A.'

'Never heard of it,' said Elinor; 'what is it?'

'The Occasional-Oasis Supply Association,' said the Baroness; 'it exists to meet cases exactly like yours, cases of backyards that are of no practical use for gardening purposes, but are required to blossom into decorative scenic backgrounds at stated intervals, when a luncheon or dinner-party is contemplated. Supposing, for instance, you have people coming to lunch at one-thirty; you just ring up the Association at about ten o'clock the same morning, and say, "Lunch garden". That is all the trouble you have to take. By twelve forty-five your yard is carpeted with a strip of velvety turf, with a hedge of lilac or red may, or whatever happens to be in season, as a background, one or two cherry trees in blossom, and clumps of heavily flowered rhododendrons filling in the odd corners; in the foreground you have a blaze of carnations or Shirley poppies, or tiger lilies in full bloom. As soon as the lunch is over and your guests have departed the garden departs also, and all the cats in Christendom can sit in council in your yard without causing you a moment's anxiety. If you have a bishop or an antiquary or something of that sort coming to lunch you just mention the fact when you are ordering the garden, and you get an old-world pleasaunce, with clipped yew hedges and a sun-dial and hollyhocks, and perhaps a mulberry tree, and borders of sweet-williams and Canterbury bells, and an old-fashioned beehive or two tucked away in a corner. Those are the ordinary lines of supply that the Oasis Association undertakes, but by paying a few guineas a year extra you are entitled to its emergency E.O.N. service.'

'What on earth is an E.O.N. service?'

'It's just like a conventional signal to indicate special cases like the incursion of Gwenda Pottingdon. It means you've got someone coming to lunch or dinner whose garden is alleged to be "the envy of the neighbourhood".'

'Yes,' exclaimed Elinor, with some excitement, 'and what happens then?'

'Something that sounds like a miracle out of the Arabian Nights. Your backyard becomes voluptuous with pomegranate and almond trees, lemon groves, and hedges of flowering cactus, dazzling banks of azaleas, marble-basined fountains, in which chestnut-and-white pond-herons step daintily amid exotic water-lilies, while golden pheasants strut about on alabaster terraces. The whole effect rather suggests the idea that Providence and Norman Wilkinson have dropped mutual jealousies and collaborated to produce a background for an open-air Russian Ballet; in point of fact, it is merely the background to your luncheon party. If there is any kick left in Gwenda Pottingdon, or whoever your E.O.N. guest of the moment may be, just mention carelessly that your climbing putella is the only one in England, since the one at Chatsworth died last winter. There isn't such a thing as a climbing putella, but Gwenda Pottingdon and her kind don't usually know one flower from another without prompting.'

'Quick,' said Elinor, 'the address of the Association.'

Gwenda Pottingdon did not enjoy her lunch. It was a simple yet elegant meal, excellently cooked and daintily served, but the piquant sauce of her own conversation was notably lacking. She had prepared a long succession of eulogistic comments on the wonders of her town garden, with its unrivalled effects of horticultural magnificence, and, behold, her theme was shut in on every side by the luxuriant hedge of Siberian berberis that formed a glowing background to Elinor's bewildering fragment of fairyland. The pomegranate and lemon trees, the terraced fountain, where golden carp slithered and wriggled amid the roots of gorgeous-hued irises, the banked masses of exotic blooms, the pagoda-like enclosure, where Japanese sand-badgers disported themselves, all these contributed to take away Gwenda's appetite and moderate her desire to talk about gardening matters.

'I can't say I admire the climbing putella,' she observed shortly, 'and anyway it's not the only one of its kind in England; I happen to know of one in Hampshire. How gardening is going out of fashion, I suppose people haven't the time for it nowadays.'

Altogether it was quite one of Elinor's most successful luncheon parties.

It was distinctly an unforeseen catastrophe that Gwenda should have burst in on the household four days later at lunchtime and made her way unbidden into the dining-room.

'I thought I must tell you that my Elaine has had a watercolour sketch accepted by the Latent Talent Art Guild; it's to be exhibited at their summer exhibition at the Hackney Gallery. It will be the sensation of the moment in the art world – Hallo, what on earth has happened to your garden? It's not there!'

'Suffragettes,' said Elinor promptly; 'didn't you hear about it? They broke in and made hay of the whole thing in about ten minutes. I was so heartbroken at the havoc that I had the whole place cleared out; I shall have it laid out again on rather more elaborate lines.

'That,' she said to the Baroness afterwards, 'is what I call having an emergency brain.'

The Penance

Octavian Ruttle was one of those lively cheerful individuals on whom amiability had set its unmistakable stamp, and, like most of his kind, his soul's peace depended in large measure on the unstinted approval of his fellows. In hunting to death a small tabby cat he had done a thing of which he scarcely approved himself, and he was glad when the gardener had hidden the body in its hastily dug grave under a lone oak-tree in the meadow, the same tree that the hunted quarry had climbed as a last effort towards safety. It had been a distasteful and seemingly ruthless deed, but circumstances had demanded the doing of it. Octavian kept chickens; at least he kept some of them; others vanished from his keeping, leaving only a few bloodstained feathers to mark the manner of their going. The tabby cat from the large grey house that stood with its back to the meadow had been detected in many furtive visits to the hen-coops, and after due negotiation with those in authority at the grey house a sentence of death had been agreed on. 'The children will mind, but they need not know,' had been the last word on the matter.

The children in question were a standing puzzle to Octavian; in the course of a few months he considered that he should have known their names, ages, the dates of their birthdays, and have been introduced to their favourite toys. They remained, however, as non-commital as the long blank wall that shut them off from the meadow, a wall over which their three heads sometimes appeared at odd moments. They had parents in India – that much Octavian had learned in the neighbourhood; the children, beyond grouping themselves garment-wise into sexes, a girl and two boys, carried their life-story no further on his behoof. And now it seemed he was engaged in something which touched them closely, but must be hidden from their knowledge.

The poor helpless chickens had gone one by one to their doom, so it was meet that their destroyer should come to a violent end, yet Octavian felt some qualms when his share of the violence was ended. The little cat, headed off from its wonted tracks of safety, had raced unfriended from shelter to shelter, and its end had been rather piteous. Octavian walked through the long grass of the meadow with a step less jaunty than usual. And as he passed beneath the shadow of the high blank wall he glanced up and became aware that his hunting had had undesired witnesses. Three white set faces were looking down at him, and if ever an artist wanted a threefold study of cold human hate, impotent yet unyielding, raging yet masked in stillness, he would have found it in the triple gaze that met Octavian's eye.

'I'm sorry, but it had to be done,' said Octavian, with genuine apology in his voice.

'Beast!'

The answer came from three throats with startling intensity.

Octavian felt that the blank wall would not be more impervious to his explanations than the bunch of human hostility that peered over its coping; he wisely decided to withhold his peace overtures till a more hopeful occasion.

Two days later he ransacked the best sweet shop in the neighbouring market town for a box of chocolates that by its size and contents should fitly atone for the dismal deed done under the oak tree in the meadow. The first two specimens that were shown him he hastily rejected; one had a group of chickens pictured on its lid, the other bore the portrait of a tabby kitten. A third sample was more simply bedecked with a spray of painted poppies, and Octavian hailed the flowers of forgetfulness as a happy omen. He felt distinctly more at ease with his surroundings when the imposing package had been sent across to the grey house, and a message returned to say that it had been duly given to the children. The next morning he sauntered with purposeful steps past the long blank wall on his way to the chicken-run and piggery that stood at the bottom of the meadow. The three children were perched at their accustomed look-out, and their range of sight did not seem to concern itself with Octavian's presence. As he became depressingly aware of the aloofness of their gaze he also noted a strange variegation in the herbage at his feet; the greensward for a considerable space around was strewn and speckled with chocolate-coloured hail, enlivened here and there with gay tinsel-like wrappings or the glistening mauve of crystallized violets. It was as though the fairy paradise of a greedy-minded child had taken shape and substance in the vegetation of the meadow. Octavian's blood-money had been flung back at him in scorn.

To increase his discomfiture the march of events tended to shift the blame of ravaged chicken-coops from the supposed culprit who had already paid full forfeit; the young chicks were still carried off, and it seemed highly probable that the cat had only haunted the chicken-run to prey on the rats which harboured there. Through the flowing channels of servant talk the children learned of this belated revision of verdict, and Octavian one day picked up a sheet of copy-book paper on which was painstakingly written: 'Beast. Rats eated your chickens.' More ardently than ever did he wish for an opportunity for sloughing off the disgrace that enwrapped him, and earning some happier nickname from his three unsparing judges.

And one day a chance inspiration came to him. Olivia, his two-year old daughter, was accustomed to spend the hour from high noon till one o'clock with her father while the nursemaid gobbled and digested her dinner and novelette. About the same time the blank wall was usually enlivened by the presence of its three small wardens. Octavian, with seeming carelessness of purpose, brought Olivia well within hail of the watchers and noted with hidden delight the growing interest that dawned in that hitherto sternly hostile quarter. His little Olivia, with her sleepy placid ways, was going to succeed where he, with his anxious well-meant overtures, had so signally failed. He brought her a large yellow dahlia, which she grasped tightly in one hand and regarded with a stare of benevolent boredom, such as one might bestow on amateur classical dancing performed in aid of a deserving charity. Then he turned shyly to the group perched on the wall and asked with affected carelessness, 'Do you like flowers?' Three solemn nods rewarded his venture.

'Which sorts do you like best?' he asked, this time with a distinct betrayal of eagerness in his voice.

'Those with all the colours, over there.' Three chubby arms pointed to a distant tangle of sweet-pea. Child-like, they had asked for what lay farthest from hand, but Octavian trotted off gleefully to obey their welcome behest. He pulled and plucked with unsparing hand, and brought every variety of tint that he could see into his bunch that was rapidly becoming a bundle. Then he turned to retrace his steps, and found the blank wall blanker and more deserted than ever, while the foreground was void of all trace of Olivia. Far down the meadow three children were pushing a go-cart at the utmost speed they could muster in the direction of the piggeries; it was Olivia's go-cart and Olivia sat in it, somewhat bumped and shaken by the pace at which she was being driven, but apparently retaining her wonted composure of mind. Octavian stared for a moment at the rapidly moving group, and then started in hot pursuit, shedding as he ran sprays of blossom from the mass of sweet-pea that he still clutched in his hands. Fast as he ran the children had reached the piggery before he could overtake them, and he arrived just in time to see Olivia, wondering but unprotesting, hauled and pushed up to the roof of the nearest sty. They were old buildings in some need of repair, and the rickety roof would certainly not have borne Octavian's weight if he had attempted to follow his daughter and her captors on their new vantage ground.

'What are you going to do with her?' he panted. There was no mistaking the grim trend of mischief in those flushed but sternly composed young faces.

'Hang her in chains over a slow fire,' said one of the boys. Evidently they had been reading English history.

'Frow her down and the pigs will d'vour her, every bit 'cept the palms of her hands,' said the other boy. It was also evident that they had studied Biblical history.

The last proposal was the one which most alarmed Octavian, since it might be carried into effect at a moment's notice; there had been cases, he remembered, of pigs eating babies.

'You surely wouldn't treat my poor little Olivia in that way?' he pleaded.

'You killed our little cat,' came in stern reminder from three throats.

'I'm very sorry I did,' said Octavian, and if there is a standard of measurement in truths Octavian's statement was assuredly a large nine.

'We shall be very sorry when we've killed Olivia,' said the girl, 'but we can't be sorry till we've done it.'

The inexorable child-logic rose like an unyielding rampart before Octavian's scared pleadings. Before he could think of any fresh line of appeal his energies were called out in another direction. Olivia had slid off the roof and fallen with a soft, unctuous splash into a morass of muck and decaying straw. Octavian scrambled hastily over the pigsty wall to her rescue, and at once found himself in a quagmire that engulfed his feet. Olivia, after the first shock of surprise at her sudden drop through the air, had been mildly pleased at finding herself in close and unstinted contact with the sticky element that oozed around her, but as she began to sink gently into the bed of slime a feeling dawned on her that she was not after all very happy, and she began to cry in the tentative fashion of the normally good child. Octavian, battling with the quagmire, which seemed to have learned the rare art of giving way at all points without yielding an inch, saw his daughter slowly disappearing in the engulfing slush, her smeared face further distorted with the contortions of whimpering wonder, while from their perch on the pigsty roof the three children looked down with the cold unpitying detachment of the Parcae Sisters.

'I can't reach her in time,' gasped Octavian, 'she'll be choked in the muck. Won't you help her?'

'No one helped our cat,' came the inevitable reminder.

'I'll do anything to show you how sorry I am about that,' cried Octavian, with a further desperate flounder, which carried him scarcely two inches forward.

'Will you stand in a white sheet by the grave?'

'Yes,' screamed Octavian.

'Holding a candle?'

'An' saying "I'm a miserable Beast"?'

Octavian agreed to both suggestions.

'For a long, long time?'

'For half an hour,' said Octavian. There was an anxious ring in his voice as he named the time-limit; was there not the precedent of a German king who did open-air penance for several days and nights at Christmas-time clad only in his shirt? Fortunately the children did not appear to have read German history, and half an hour seemed long and goodly in their eyes.

'All right,' came with threefold solemnity from the roof, and a moment later a short ladder had been laboriously pushed across to Octavian, who lost no time in propping it against the low pigsty wall. Scrambling gingerly along its rungs he was able to lean across the morass that separated him from his slowly foundering offspring and extract her like an unwilling cork from its slushy embrace. A few minutes later he was listening to the shrill and repeated assurances of the nursemaid that her previous experience of filthy spectacles had been on a notably smaller scale.

That same evening when twilight was deepening into darkness Octavian took up his position as penitent under the lone oak-tree, having first carefully undressed the part. Clad in a zephyr shirt, which on this occasion thoroughly merited its name, he held in one hand a lighted candle and in the other a watch, into which the soul of a dead plumber seemed to have passed. A box of matches lay at his feet and was resorted to on the fairly frequent occasions when the candle succumbed to the night breezes. The house loomed inscrutable in the middle distance, but as Octavian conscientiously repeated the formula of his penance he felt certain that three pairs of solemn eyes were watching his moth-shared vigil.

And the next morning his eyes were gladdened by a sheet of copy-book paper lying beside the blank wall, on which was written the message 'Un-Beast'.

Quail Seed

'The outlook is not encouraging for us smaller businesses,' said Mr Scarrick to the artist and his sister, who had taken rooms over his suburban grocery store. 'These big concerns are offering all sorts of attractions to the shopping public which we couldn't afford to imitate, even on a small scale – reading-rooms and playrooms and gramophones and Heaven knows what. People don't care to buy half a pound of sugar nowadays unless they can listen to Harry Lauder and have the latest Australian cricket scores ticked off before their eyes. With the big Christmas stock we've got in we ought to keep half a dozen assistants hard at work, but as it is my nephew Jimmy and myself can pretty well attend to it ourselves. It's a nice stock of goods, too, if I could only run it off in a few weeks' time, but there's no chance of that – not unless the London line was to get snowed up for a fortnight before Christmas. I did have a sort of idea of engaging Miss Luffcombe to give recitations during afternoons; she made a great hit at the Post Office entertainments with her rendering of "Little Beatrice's Resolve".'

'Anything less likely to make your shop a fashionable shopping centre I can't imagine,' said the artist, with a very genuine shudder; 'if I were trying to decide between the merits of Carlsbad plums and confected figs as a winter dessert it would infuriate me to have my train of thought entangled with little Beatrice's resolve to be an Angel of Light or a girl scout. No,' he continued, 'the desire to get something thrown in for nothing is a ruling passion with the feminine shopper, but you can't afford to pander effectively to it. Why not appeal to another instinct, which dominates not only the woman shopper but the male shopper – in fact, the entire human race?'

'What is that instinct, sir?' said the grocer.

Mrs Greyes and Miss Fritten had missed the 2.18 to Town, and as there was not another train till 3.12 they thought that they might as well make their grocery purchases at Scarrick's. It would not be sensational, they agreed, but it would still be shopping.

For some minutes they had the shop almost to themselves, as far as customers were concerned, but while they were debating the respective virtues and blemishes of two competing brands of anchovy paste they were startled by an order, given across the counter, for six pomegranates and a packet of quail seed. Neither commodity was in general demand in that neighbourhood. Equally unusual was the style and appearance of the customer; about sixteen years old, with dark olive skin, large dusky eyes, and thick, low-growing, blue-black hair, he might have made his living as an artist's model. As a matter of fact he did. The bowl of beaten brass that he produced for the reception of his purchases was distinctly the most astonishing variation on the string bag or marketing basket of suburban civilization that his fellow-shoppers had ever seen. He threw a gold piece, apparently of some exotic currency, across the counter, and did not seem disposed to wait for any change that might be forthcoming.

'The wine and figs were not paid for yesterday,' he said; 'keep what is over of the money for our future purchases.'

'A very strange-looking boy?' said Mrs Greyes interrogatively to the grocer as soon as his customer had left.

'A foreigner, I believe,' said Mr Scarrick, with a shortness that was entirely out of keeping with his usually communicative manner.

'I wish for a pound and a half of the best coffee you have,' said an authoritative voice a moment or two later. The speaker was a tall, authoritative-looking man of rather outlandish aspect, remarkable among other things for a full black beard, worn in a style more in vogue in early Assyria than in a London suburb of the present day.

'Has a dark-faced boy been here buying pomegranates?' he asked suddenly, as the coffee was being weighed out to him.

The two ladies almost jumped on hearing the grocer reply with an unblushing negative.

'We have a few pomegranates in stock,' he continued, 'but there has been no demand for them.'

'My servant will fetch the coffee as usual,' said the purchaser, producing a coin from a wonderful metal-work purse. As an apparent afterthought he fired out the question: 'Have you, perhaps any quail seed?'

'No,' said the grocer, without hesitation, 'we don't stock it.'

'What will he deny next?' said Mrs Greyes under her breath. What made it seem so much worse was the fact that Mr Scarrick had quite recently presided at a lecture on Savonarola.

Turning up the deep astrachan collar of his long coat, the stranger swept out of the shop, with the air, as Miss Fritten afterwards described it, of a Satrap proroguing a Sanhedrim. Whether such a pleasant function ever fell to a Satrap's lot she was not quite certain, but the smile faithfully conveyed her meaning to a large circle of acquaintances.

'Don't let's bother about the 3.12,' said Mrs Greyes; 'let's go and talk this over at Laura Lipping's. It's her day.'

When the dark-faced boy arrived at the shop next day with his brass marketing bowl there was quite a fair gathering of customers, most of whom seemed to be spinning out their purchasing operations with the air of people who had very little to do with their time. In a voice that was heard all over the shop, perhaps because everbody was intently listening, he asked for a pound of honey and a packet of quail seed.

'More quail seed!' said Miss Fritten. 'Those quails must be voracious, or else it isn't quail seed at all.'

'I believe it's opium, and the bearded man is a detective,' said Mrs Greyes brilliantly.

'I don't,' said Laura Lipping; 'I'm sure it's something to do with the Portuguese Throne.'

'More likely to be a Persian intrigue on behalf of the ex-Shah,' said Miss Fritten; 'the bearded man belongs to the Government Party. The quail seed is a countersign, of course; Persia is almost next door to Palestine, and quails come into the Old Testament, you know.'

'Only as a miracle,' said her well-informed younger sister; 'I've thought all along it was part of a love intrigue.'

The boy who had so much interest and speculation centred on him was on the point of departing with his purchases when he was waylaid by Jimmy, the nephew-apprentice, who, from his post at the cheese and bacon counter, commanded a good view of the street.

'We have some very fine Jaffa oranges,' he said hurriedly, pointing to a corner where they were stored, behind a high rampart of biscuit tins. There was evidently more in the remark than met the ear. The boy flew at the oranges with the enthusiasm of a ferret finding a rabbit family at home after a long day of fruitless subterranean research. Almost at the same moment the bearded stranger stalked into the shop, and flung an order for a pound of dates and a tin of the best Smyrna halva across the counter. The most adventurous housewife in the locality had never heard of halva, but Mr Scarrick was apparently able to produce the best Smyrna variety of it without a moment's hesitation.

'We might be living in the Arabian Nights,' said Miss Fritten excitedly.

'Hush! Listen,' beseeched Mrs Greyes.

'Has the dark-faced boy, of whom I spoke yesterday, been here today?' asked the stranger.

'We've had rather more people than usual in the shop today,' said Mr Scarrick, 'but I can't recall a boy such as you describe.'

Mrs Greyes and Miss Fritten looked round triumphantly at their friends. It was, of course, deplorable that anyone should treat the truth as an article temporarily and excusably out of stock, but they felt gratified that the vivid accounts they had given of Mr Scarrick's traffic in falsehoods should receive confirmation at first hand.

'I shall never again be able to believe what he tells me about the absence of colouring matter in the jam,' whispered an aunt of Mrs Greyes tragically.

The mysterious stranger took his departure; Laura Lipping distinctly saw a snarl of baffled rage reveal itself behind his heavy moustache and upturned astrachan collar. After a cautious interval the seeker after oranges emerged from behind the biscuit tins, having apparently failed to find any individual orange that satisfied his requirements. He, too, took his departure, and the shop was slowly emptied of its parcel- and gossip-laden customers. It was Emily Yorling's 'day', and most of the shoppers made their way to her drawing-room. To go direct from a shopping expedition to a tea-party was what was known locally as 'living in a whirl'.

Two extra assistants had been engaged for the following afternoon, and their services were in brisk demand; the shop was crowded. People bought and bought, and never seemed to get to the end of their lists. Mr Scarrick had never had so little difficulty in persuading customers to embark on new experiences in grocery wares. Even those women whose purchases were of modest proportions dawdled over them as though they had brutal drunken husbands to go home to. The afternoon had dragged uneventfully on, and there was a distinct buzz of unpent excitement when a dark-eyed boy carrying a brass bowl entered the shop. The excitement seemed to have communicated itself to Mr Scarrick; abruptly, deserting a lady who was making insincere inquiries about the home life of the Bombay duck, he intercepted the newcomer on his way to the accustomed counter and informed him, amid a death-like hush, that he had run out of quail seed.

The boy looked nervously round the shop, and turned hesitatingly to go. He was again intercepted, this time by the nephew, who darted out from behind his counter and said something about a better line of oranges. The boy's hesitation vanished; he almost scuttled into the obscurity of the orange corner. There was an expectant turn of public attention towards the door, and the tall bearded stranger made a really effective entrance. The aunt of Mrs Greyes declared afterwards that she found herself subconsciously repeating 'The Assyrian came down like a wolf on the fold' under her breath, and she was generally believed.

The newcomer, too, was stopped before he reached the counter, but not by Mr Scarrick or his assistant. A heavily veiled lady, whom no one had hitherto noticed, rose languidly from a seat and greeted him in a clear, penetrating voice.

'Your Excellency does his shopping himself?' she said.

'I order the things myself,' he explained; 'I find it difficult to make my servants understand.'

In a lower, but still perfectly audible, voice the veiled lady gave him a piece of casual information.

'They have some excellent Jaffa oranges here.' Then with a tinkling laugh she passed out of the shop.

The man glared all round the shop, and then, fixing his eyes instinctively on the barrier of biscuit tins, demanded loudly of the grocer: 'You have, perhaps, some good Jaffa oranges?'

Everyone expected an instant denial on the part of Mr Scarrick of any such possession. Before he could answer, however, the boy had broken forth from the sanctuary. Holding his empty brass bowl before him he passed out into the street. His face was variously described afterwards as masked with studied indifference, overspread with ghastly pallor, and blazing with defiance. Some said that his teeth chattered, others that he went out whistling the Persian National Hymn. There was no mistaking, however, the effect produced by the encounter on the man who had seemed to force it. If a rabid dog or a rattlesnake had suddenly thrust its companionship on him he could scarcely have displayed a greater access of terror. His air of authority and assertiveness had gone, his masterful stride had given way to a furtive pacing to and fro, as of an animal seeking an outlet for escape. In a dazed perfunctory manner, always with his eyes turning to watch the shop entrance, he gave a few random orders, which the grocer made a show of entering in his book. Now and then he walked out into the street, looked anxiously in all directions, and hurried back to keep up his pretence of shopping. From one of these sorties he did not return; he had dashed away into the dusk, and neither he nor the dark-faced boy nor the veiled lady were seen again by the expectant crowds that continued to throng the Scarrick establishment for days to come.

'I can never thank you and your sister sufficiently,' said the grocer.

'We enjoyed the fun of it,' said the artist modestly, 'and as for the model, it was a welcome variation on posing for hours for "The Lost Hylas".'

'At any rate,' said the grocer, 'I insist on paying for the hire of the black beard.'

The Seven Cream Jugs

'I suppose we shall never see Wilfrid Pigeoncote here now that he has become heir to the baronetcy and to a lot of money,' observed Mrs Peter Pigeoncote regretfully to her husband.

'Well, we can hardly expect to,' he replied, 'seeing that we always choked him off from coming to see us when he was a prospective nobody. I don't think I've set eyes on him since he was a boy of twelve.'

'There was a reason for not wanting to encourage his acquaintanceship,' said Mrs Peter. 'With that notorious failing of his he was not the sort of person one wanted in one's house.'

'Well, the failing still exists, doesn't it?' said her husband; 'or do you suppose a reform of character is entailed along with the estate?'

'Oh, of course, there is still that drawback,' admitted the wife, 'but one would like to make the acquaintance of the future head of the family, if only out of mere curiosity. Besides, cynicism apart, his being rich *will* make a difference in the way people will look at his failing. When a man is absolutely wealthy, not merely well-to-do, all suspicion of sordid motive naturally disappears; the thing becomes merely a tiresome malady.'

Wilfrid Pigeoncote had suddenly become heir to his uncle, Sir Wilfrid Pigeoncote, on the death of his cousin, Major Wilfrid Pigeoncote, who had succumbed to the after-effects of a polo accident. (A Wilfrid Pigeoncote had covered himself with honours in the course of Marlborough's campaigns, and the name Wilfrid had been a baptismal weakness in the family ever since.) The new heir to the family dignity and estates was a young man of about five-and-twenty, who was known more by reputation than by person to a wide circle of cousins and kinsfolk. And the reputation was an unpleasant one. The numerous other Wilfrids in the family were distinguished one from another chiefly by the names of their residences or professions, as Wilfrid of Hubbledown, and young Wilfrid the Gunner, but this particular scion was known by the ignominious and expressive label of Wilfrid the Snatcher. From his late schooldays onward he had been possessed by an acute and obstinate form of kleptomania; he had the acquisitive instinct of the collector without any of the collector's discrimination. Anything that was smaller and more portable than a sideboard and above the value of ninepence, had an irresistible attraction for him, provided that it fulfilled the necessary condition of belonging to someone else. On the rare occasions when he was included in a country-house party, it was usual and almost necessary for his host, or some member of the family, to make a friendly inquisition through his baggage on the eve of his departure, to see if he had packed up 'by mistake' anyone else's property. The search usually produced a large and varied yield.

'This is funny,' said Peter Pigeoncote to his wife, some half-hour after their conversation; 'here's a telegram from Wilfrid saying he's passing through here in his motor, and would like to stop and pay us his respects. Can stay for the night if it doesn't inconvenience us. Signed "Wilfrid Pigeoncote". Must be the Snatcher; none of the others have a motor. I suppose he's bringing us a present for the silver wedding.'

'Good gracious!' said Mrs Peter, as a thought struck her; 'this is rather an awkward time to have a person with his failing in the house. All those silver presents set out in the drawing-room, and others coming by every post; I hardly know what we've got and what are still to come. We can't lock them all up; he's sure to want to see them.'

'We must keep a sharp look-out, that's all,' said Peter reassuringly.

'But these practised kleptomaniacs are so clever,' said his wife apprehensively, 'and it will be so awkward if he suspects that we are watching him.'

Awkwardness was indeed the prevailing note that evening when the passing traveller was being entertained. The talk flitted nervously and hurriedly from one impersonal topic to another. The guest had none of the furtive, half-apologetic air that his cousins had rather expected to find; he was polite, well-assured, and, perhaps, just a little inclined to 'put on side'. His hosts, on the other hand, wore an uneasy manner that might have been the hallmark of conscious depravity. In the drawing-room, after dinner, their nervousness and awkwardness increased.

'Oh, we haven't shown you the silver-wedding presents,' said Mrs Peter suddenly, as though struck by a brilliant idea for entertaining the guest; 'here they all are. Such nice, useful gifts. A few duplicates, of course.'

'Seven cream jugs,' put in Peter.

'Yes, isn't it annoying,' went on Mrs Peter; 'seven of them. We feel that we must live on cream for the rest of our lives. Of course, some of them can be changed.'

Wilfrid occupied himself chiefly with such of the gifts as were of antique interest, carrying one or two of them over to the lamp to examine their marks. The anxiety of his hosts at these moments resembled the solicitude of a cat whose newly-born kittens are being handed round for inspection.

'Let me see; did you give me back the mustard-pot? This is its place here,' piped Mrs Peter.

'Sorry. I put it down by the claret-jug,' said Wilfrid, busy with another object.

'Oh, just let me have that sugar-sifter again,' asked Mrs Peter, dogged determination showing through her nervousness. 'I must label who it comes from before I forget.'

Vigilance was not completely crowned with a sense of victory. After they had said 'Good night' to their visitor, Mrs Peter expressed her conviction that he had taken something.

'I fancy, by his manner, that there was something up,' corroborated her husband. 'Do you miss anything?'

'I can only make it thirty-four, and I think it should be thirty-five,' she announced. 'I can't remember if thirty-five includes the Archdeacon's cruet-stand that hasn't arrived yet.'

'How on earth are we to know?' said Peter. 'The mean pig hasn't brought us a present, and I'm hanged if he shall carry one off.'

'Tomorrow, when he's having his bath,' said Mrs Peter excitedly, 'he's sure to leave his keys somewhere, and we can go through his portmanteau. It's the only thing to do.'

On the morrow an alert watch was kept by the conspirators behind half-closed doors, and when Wilfrid, clad in a gorgeous bath-robe, had made his way to the bathroom, there was a swift and furtive rush by two excited individuals towards the principal guest-chamber. Mrs Peter kept guard outside, while her husband first made a hurried and successful search for the keys, and then plunged at the portmanteau with the air of a disagreeably conscientious Customs official. The quest was a brief one; a silver cream jug lay embedded in the folds of some zephyr shirts.

'The cunning brute,' said Mrs Peter; 'he took a cream jug because there were so many; he thought one wouldn't be missed. Quick, fly down with it and put it back among the others.'

Wilfrid was late in coming down to breakfast, and his manner showed plainly that something was amiss.

'It's an unpleasant thing to have to say,' he blurted out presently, 'but I'm afraid you must have a thief among your servants. Something's been taken out of my portmanteau. It was a little present from my mother and myself for your silver wedding. I should have given it to you last night after dinner, only it happened to be a cream jug, and you seemed annoyed at having so many duplicates, so I felt rather awkward about giving you another. I thought I'd get it changed for something else, and now it's gone.'

'Did you say it was from your *mother* and yourself?' asked Mr and Mrs Peter almost in unison. The Snatcher had been an orphan these many years.

'Yes, my mother's at Cairo just now, and she wrote to me at Dresden to try and get you something quaint and pretty in the old silver line, and I pitched on this cream jug.'

Both the Pigeoncotes had turned deadly pale. The mention of Dresden had thrown a sudden light on the situation. It was Wilfrid the Attaché, a very superior young man, who rarely came within their social horizon, whom they had been entertaining unawares in the supposed character of Wilfrid the Snatcher. Lady Ernestine Pigeoncote, his mother, moved in circles which were entirely beyond their compass of ambitions, and the son would probably one day be an Ambassador. And they had rifled and despoiled his portmanteau! Husband and wife looked blankly and desperately at one another. It was Mrs Peter who arrived first at an inspiration.

'How dreadful to think there are thieves in the house! We keep the drawing-room locked up at night, of course, but anything might be carried off while we are at breakfast.'

She rose and went out hurriedly, as though to assure herself that the drawing-room was not being stripped of its silverware, and returned a moment later, bearing a cream jug in her hands.

'There are eight cream jugs now, instead of seven,' she cried; 'this one wasn't there before. What a curious trick of memory, Mr Wilfrid! You must have slipped downstairs with it last night and put it there before we locked up, and forgotten all about having done it in the morning.'

'One's mind often plays one little tricks like that,' said Mr Peter, with desperate heartiness. 'Only the other day I went into the town to pay a bill, and went in again next day, having clean forgotten that I'd –'

'It is certainly the jug that I brought for you,' said Wilfrid, looking closely at it; 'it was in my portmanteau when I got my bath-robe out this morning, before going to my bath, and it was not there when I unlocked the portmanteau on my return. Someone had taken it while I was away from the room.'

The Pigeoncotes had turned paler than ever. Mrs Peter had a final inspiration.

'Get me my smelling-salts, dear,' she said to her husband; 'I think they're in the dressing-room.'

Peter dashed out of the room with glad relief; he had lived so long during the last few minutes that a golden wedding seemed within measurable distance.

Mrs Peter turned to her guest with confidential coyness.

'A diplomat like you will know how to treat this as if it hadn't happened. Peter's little weakness; it runs in the family.'

'Good Lord! Do you mean to say he's a kleptomaniac, like Cousin Snatcher?'

'Oh, not exactly,' said Mrs Peter, anxious to whitewash her husband a little greyer than she was painting him. 'He would never touch anything he found lying about, but he can't resist making a raid on things that are locked up. The doctors have a special name for it. He must have pounced on your portmanteau the moment you went to your bath, and taken the first thing he came across. Of course, he had no motive for taking a cream jug; we've already got *seven*, as you know – not, of course, that we don't value the kind gift you and your mother – Hush, here's Peter coming.'

Mrs Peter broke off in some confusion, and tripped out to meet her husband in the hall.

'It's all right,' she whispered to him; 'I've explained everything. Don't say anything more about it.'

'Brave little woman,' said Peter, with a gasp of relief; 'I could never have done it.'

Diplomatic reticence does not necessarily extend to family affairs. Peter Pigeoncote was never able to understand why Mrs Consuelo van Bullyon, who stayed with them in the spring, always carried two very obvious jewel-cases with her to the bathroom, explaining them to anyone she chanced to meet in the corridor as her manicure and face-massage set.

The Sheep

The enemy had declared 'no trumps'. Rupert played out his ace and king of clubs and cleared the adversary of that suit; then the Sheep, whom the Fates had inflicted on him for a partner, took the third round with the queen of clubs, and, having no other club to lead back, opened another suit. The enemy won the remainder of the tricks – and the rubber.

'I had four more clubs to play; we only wanted the odd trick to win the rubber,' said Rupert.

'But I hadn't another club to lead you,' exclaimed the Sheep, with his ready, defensive smile.

'It didn't occur to you to throw your queen away on my king and leave me with the command of the suit,' said Rupert, with polite bitterness.

'I suppose I ought to have – I wasn't certain what to do. I'm awfully sorry,' said the Sheep.

Being awfully and uselessly sorry formed a large part of his occupation in life. If a similar situation had arisen in a subsequent hand he would have blundered just as certainly, and he would have been just as irritatingly apologetic.

Rupert stared gloomily across at him as he sat smiling and fumbling with his cards. Many men who have good brains for business do not possess the rudiments of a card-brain, and Rupert would not have judged and condemned his prospective brother-in-law on the evidence of his bridge play alone. The tragic part of it was that he smiled and fumbled through life just as fatuously and apologetically as he did at the card-table. And behind the defensive smile and the well-worn expressions of regret there shone a scarcely believable but quite obvious self-satisfaction. Every sheep of the pasture probably imagines that in an emergency it could become terrible as an army with banners – one has only to watch how they stamp their feet and stiffen their necks when a minor object of suspicion comes into view and behaves meekly. And probably the majority of human sheep see themselves in imagination taking great parts in the world's more impressive dramas, forming swift, unerring decisions in moments of crisis, cowing mutinies, allaying panics, brave, strong, simple, but, in spite of their natural modesty, always slightly spectacular.

'Why in the name of all that is unnecessary and perverse should Kathleen choose this man for her future husband?' was the question that Rupert asked himself ruefully. There was young Malcolm Athling, as nice-looking, decent, level-headed a fellow as anyone could wish to meet, obviously her very devoted admirer, and yet she must throw herself away on this pale-eyed, weak-mouthed embodiment of self-approving ineptitude. If it had been merely Kathleen's own affair Rupert would have shrugged his shoulders and philosophically hoped that she might make the best of an undeniably bad bargain. But Rupert had no heir; his own boy lay underground somewhere on the Indian frontier, in goodly company. And the property would pass in due course to Kathleen and Kathleen's husband. The Sheep would live there in the beloved old home, rearing up other little Sheep, fatuous and rabbit-faced and self-satisfied like himself, to dwell in the land and possess it. It was not a soothing prospect.

Towards dusk on the afternoon following the bridge experience Rupert and the Sheep made their way homeward after a day's mixed shooting. The Sheep's cartridge bag was nearly empty, but his game bag showed no signs of over-crowding. The birds he had shot at had seemed for the most part as impervious to death or damage as the hero of a melodrama. And for each failure to drop his bird he had some explanation or apology ready on his lips. Now he was striding along in front of his host, chattering happily over his shoulder, but obviously on the look-out for some belated rabbit or wood-pigeon that might haply be secured as an eleventh-hour addition to his bag. As they passed the edge of a small copse a large bird rose from the ground and flew slowly towards the trees, offering an easy shot to the oncoming sportsmen. The Sheep banged forth with both barrels, and gave an exultant cry.

'Hooray! I've shot a thundering big hawk.'

'To be exact, you've shot a honey-buzzard. That is the hen bird of one of the few pairs of honey-buzzards breeding in the United Kingdom. We've kept them under the strictest preservation for the last four years; every game-keeper and village gun loafer for twenty miles round has been warned and bribed and threatened to respect their sanctity, and egg-snatching agents have been carefully guarded against during the breeding season. Hundreds of lovers of rare birds have delighted in seeing their snap-shotted portraits in *Country Life*, and now you've reduced the hen bird to a lump of broken feathers.'

Rupert spoke quietly and evenly, but for a moment or two a gleam of positive hatred shone in his eyes.

'I say, I'm so sorry,' said the Sheep, with his apologetic smile. 'Of course I remember hearing about the buzzards, but somehow I didn't connect this bird with them. And it was such an easy shot –'

'Yes,' said Rupert; 'that was the trouble.'

Kathleen found him in the gun-room smoothing out the

feathers of the dead bird. She had already been told of the catastrophe.

'What a horrid misfortune,' she said sympathetically.

'It was my dear Robbie who first discovered them, the last time he was home on leave. Don't you remember how excited he was about them? Let's go and have some tea.'

Both bridge and shooting were given a rest for the next two or three weeks. Death, who enters into no compacts with party whips, had forced a Parliamentary vacancy on the neighbourhood at the least convenient season, and the local partisans on either side found themselves immersed in the discomforts of a mid-winter election. Rupert took his politics seriously and keenly. He belonged to that type of strangely but rather happily constituted individuals which these islands seem to produce in a fair plenty; men and women who for no personal profit or gain go forth from their comfortable firesides or club card-rooms to hunt to and fro in the mud and rain and wind for the capture or tracking of a stray vote here and there on their party's behalf – not because they think they ought to, but because they want to. And his energies were welcome enough on this occasion, for the seat was a closely disputed possession, and its loss or retention would count for much in the present position of the Parliamentary game. With Kathleen to help him, he had worked his corner of the constituency with tireless, well-directed zeal, taking his share of the dull routine work as well as of the livelier episodes. The talking part of the campaign wound up on the eve of the poll with a meeting in a centre where more undecided votes were supposed to be concentrated than anywhere else in the division. A good final meeting here would mean everything. And the speakers, local and imported, left nothing undone to improve the occasion. Rupert was down for the unimportant task of moving the complimentary vote to the chairman which should close the proceedings.

'I'm so hoarse,' he protested, when the moment arrived; 'I don't believe I can make my voice heard beyond the platform.'

'Let me do it,' said the Sheep; 'I'm rather good at that sort of thing.'

The chairman was popular with all parties, and the Sheep's opening words of complimentary recognition received a round of applause. The orator smiled expansively on his listeners and seized the opportunity to add a few words of political wisdom on his own account. People looked at the clock or began to grope for umbrellas and discarded neck-wraps. Then, in the midst of a string of meaningless platitudes, the Sheep delivered himself of one of those blundering remarks which travel from one end of a constituency to the other in half an hour, and are seized on by the other side as being more potent on their behalf than a ton of election literature. There was a general shuffling and muttering across the length and breadth of the hall, and a few hisses made themselves heard. The Sheep tried to whittle down his remark, and the chairman unhesitatingly threw him over in his speech of thanks, but the damage was done.

'I'm afraid I lost touch with the audience rather over that remark,' said the Sheep afterwards, with his apologetic smile abnormally developed.

'You lost us the election,' said the chairman, and he proved a true prophet.

A month or so of winter sport seemed a desirable pick-me-up after the strenuous work and crowning discomfiture of the election. Rupert and Kathleen hied them away to a small Alpine resort that was just coming into prominence, and thither the Sheep followed them in due course, in his rôle of husband-elect. The wedding had been fixed for the end of March.

It was a winter of early and unseasonable thaws, and the far end of the local lake, at a spot where swift currents flowed into it, was decorated with notices, written in three languages, warning skaters not to venture over certain unsafe patches. The folly of approaching too near these danger spots seemed to have a natural fascination for the Sheep.

'I don't see what possible danger there can be,' he protested, with his inevitable smile, when Rupert beckoned him away from the proscribed area; 'the milk that I put out on my window-sill last night was frozen an inch deep.'

'It hadn't got a strong current flowing through it,' said Rupert; 'in any case, there is not much sense in hovering round a doubtful piece of ice when there are acres of good ice to skate over. The secretary of the ice-committee has warned you once already.'

A few minutes later Rupert heard a loud squeal of fear, and saw a dark spot blotting the smoothness of the lake's frozen surface. The Sheep was struggling helplessly in an ice-hole of his own making. Rupert gave one loud curse, and then dashed full tilt for the shore; outside a low stable building on the lake's edge he remembered having seen a ladder. If he could slide it across the ice-hole before the Sheep went under the rescue would be comparatively simple work. Other skaters were dashing up from a distance, and, with the ladder's help, they could get him out of his death-trap without having to trust themselves on the margin of rotten ice. Rupert sprang on to the surface of lumpy, frozen snow, and staggered to where the ladder lay. He had already lifted it when the rattle of a chain and a furious outburst of growls burst on his hearing, and he was dashed to the ground by a mass of white and tawny fur. A sturdy young yard-dog, frantic with the pleasure of performing his first piece of active guardian service, was ramping and snarling over him, rendering the task of regaining his feet or securing the ladder a matter of considerable difficulty. When he had at last succeeded in both efforts he was just by a hair's-breadth too late to be of any use. The Sheep had definitely disappeared under the ice-rift.

Kathleen Athling and her husband stay the greater part of the year with Rupert, and a small Robbie stands in some danger of being idolized by a devoted uncle. But for twelve months of the year Rupert's most inseparable and valued companion is a sturdy tawny and white yard-dog.

Shock Tactics

On a late spring afternoon Ella McCarthy sat on a green-painted chair in Kensington Gardens, staring listlessly at an uninteresting stretch of park landscape, that blossomed suddenly into tropical radiance as an expected figure appeared in the middle distance.

'Hullo, Bertie!' she exclaimed sedately, when the figure arrived at the painted chair that was the nearest neighbour to her own, and dropped into it eagerly, yet with a certain due regard for the set of his trousers; 'hasn't it been a perfect spring afternoon?'

The statement was a distinct untruth as far as Ella's own feelings were concerned; until the arrival of Bertie the afternoon had been anything but perfect.

Bertie made a suitable reply, in which a questioning note seemed to hover.

'Thank you ever so much for those lovely handkerchiefs,' said Ella, answering the unspoken question; 'they were just what I've been wanting. There's only one thing spoilt my pleasure in your gift,' she added, with a pout.

'What was that?' asked Bertie anxiously, fearful that perhaps he had chosen a size of handkerchief that was not within the correct feminine limit.

'I should have liked to have written and thanked you for them as soon as I got them,' said Ella, and Bertie's sky clouded at once.

'You know what mother is,' he protested; 'she opens all my letters, and if she found I'd been giving presents to anyone there'd have been something to talk about for the next fortnight.'

'Surely, at the age of twenty –' began Ella.

'I'm not twenty till September,' interrupted Bertie.

'At the age of nineteen years and eight months,' persisted Ella, 'you might be allowed to keep your correspondence private to yourself.'

'I ought to be, but things aren't always what they ought to be. Mother opens every letter that comes into the house, whoever it's for. My sisters and I have made rows about it time and again, but she goes on doing it.'

'I'd find some way to stop her if I were in your place,' said Ella valiantly, and Bertie felt that the glamour of his anxiously deliberated present had faded away in the disagreeable restriction that hedged round its acknowledgement.

'Is anything the matter?' asked Bertie's friend Clovis when they met that evening at the swimming-bath.

'Why do you ask?' said Bertie.

'When you wear a look of tragic gloom in a swimming-bath,' said Clovis, 'it's especially noticeable from the fact that you're wearing very little else. Didn't she like the handkerchiefs?'

Bertie explained the situation.

'It is rather galling, you know,' he added, 'when a girl has a lot of things she wants to write to you and can't send a letter except by some roundabout, underhand way.'

'One never realizes one's blessings while one enjoys them,' said Clovis; 'now I have to spend a considerable amount of ingenuity inventing excuses for not having written to people.'

'It's not a joking matter,' said Bertie resentfully: 'you wouldn't find it funny if your mother opened all your letters.'

'The funny thing to me is that you should let her do it.'

'I can't stop it. I've argued about it –'

'You haven't used the right kind of argument, I expect. Now, if every time one of your letters was opened you lay on your back on the dining-table during dinner and had a fit, or roused the entire family in the middle of the night to hear you recite one of Blake's "Poems of Innocence", you would get a far more respectful hearing for future protests. People yield more consideration to a mutilated mealtime or a broken night's rest, than ever they would to a broken heart.'

'Oh, dry up,' said Bertie crossly, inconsistently splashing Clovis from head to foot as he plunged into the water.

It was a day or two after the conversation in the swimming-bath that a letter addressed to Bertie Heasant slid into the letter-box at his home, and thence into the hands of his mother. Mrs Heasant was one of those empty-minded individuals to whom other people's affairs are perpetually interesting. The more private they are intended to be the more acute is the interest they arouse. She would have opened this particular letter in any case; the fact that it was marked 'private', and diffused a delicate but penetrating aroma merely caused her to open it with headlong haste rather than matter-of-course deliberation. The harvest of sensation that rewarded her was beyond all expectations.

> 'Bertie, carissimo,' it began, 'I wonder if you will have the nerve to do it: it will take some nerve, too. Don't forget the jewels. They are a detail, but details interest me.
>
> >   'Yours as ever,
> >   'CLOTILDE.
>
> 'Your mother must not know of my existence. If questioned swear you never heard of me.'

For years Mrs Heasant had searched Bertie's correspondence diligently for traces of possible dissipation or youthful entanglements, and at last the suspicions that had stimulated her inquisitorial zeal were justified by this one splendid haul. That anyone wearing the exotic name 'Clotilde' should write to Bertie under the incriminating announcement 'as ever' was sufficiently electrifying, without the astounding allusion to the jewels. Mrs Heasant could recall novels and dramas wherein jewels played an exciting and commanding rôle, and here, under her own roof, before her very eyes as it were, her own son was carrying on an intrigue in which jewels were merely an interesting detail. Bertie was not due home for another hour, but his sisters were available for the immediate unburdening of a scandal-laden mind.

'Bertie is in the toils of an adventuress,' she screamed; 'her name is Clotilde,' she added, as if she thought they had better know the worst at once. There are occasions when more harm than good is done by shielding young girls from a knowledge of the more deplorable realities of life.

By the time Bertie arrived his mother had discussed every possible and improbable conjecture as to his guilty secret; the girls limited themselves to the opinion that their brother had been weak rather than wicked.

'Who is Clotilde?' was the question that confronted Bertie almost before he had got into the hall. His denial of any knowledge of such a person was met with an outburst of bitter laughter.

'How well you have learned your lesson!' exclaimed Mrs Heasant. But satire gave way to furious indignation when she realized that Bertie did not intend to throw any further light on her discovery.

'You shan't have any dinner till you've confessed everything,' she stormed.

Bertie's reply took the form of hastily collecting material for an impromptu banquet from the larder and locking himself into his bedroom. His mother made frequent visits to the locked door and shouted a succession of interrogations with the persistence of one who thinks that if you ask a question often enough an answer will eventually result. Bertie did nothing to encourage the supposition. An hour had passed in fruitless one-sided palaver when another letter addressed to Bertie and marked 'private' made its appearance in the letter-box. Mrs Heasant pounced on it with the enthusiasm of a cat that has missed its mouse and to whom a second has been unexpectedly vouchsafed. If she hoped for further disclosures assuredly she was not disappointed.

'So you have really done it!' the letter abruptly commenced; 'Poor

Dagmar. Now she is done for I almost pity her. You did it very well, you wicked boy, the servants all think it was suicide, and there will be no fuss. Better not touch the jewels till after the inquest.

'CLOTILDE.'

Anything that Mrs Heasant had previously done, in the way of outcry was easily surpassed as she raced upstairs and beat frantically on her son's door.

'Miserable boy, what have you done to Dagmar?'

'It's Dagmar now, is it?' he snapped; 'it will be Geraldine next.'

'That it should come to this, after all my efforts to keep you at home of an evening,' sobbed Mrs Heasant; 'it's no use you trying to hide things from me; Clotilde's letter betrays everything.'

'Does it betray who she is?' asked Bertie, 'I've heard so much about her, I should like to know something about her home-life. Seriously, if you go on like this I shall fetch a doctor; I've often enough been preached at about nothing, but I've never had an imaginary harem dragged into the discussion.'

'Are these letters imaginary?' screamed Mrs Heasant; 'what about the jewels, and Dagmar, and the theory of suicide?'

No solution of these problems was forthcoming through the bedroom door, but the last post of the evening produced another letter for Bertie, and its contents brought Mrs Heasant that enlightenment which had already dawned on her son.

'Dear Bertie,' it ran; 'I hope I haven't distracted your brain with the spoof letters I've been sending in the name of a fictitious Clotilde. You told me the other day that the servants, or somebody at your home, tampered with your letters, so I thought I would give anyone that opened them something exciting to read. The shock might do them good.

'Yours,
'CLOVIS SANGRAIL.'

Mrs Heasant knew Clovis slightly, and was rather afraid of him. It was not difficult to read between the lines of his successful hoax. In a chastened mood she rapped once more at Bertie's door.

'A letter from Mr Sangrail. It's all been a stupid hoax. He wrote those other letters. Why, where are you going?'

Bertie had opened the door; he had on his hat and overcoat.

'I'm going for a doctor to come and see if anything's the matter with you. Of course it was all a hoax, but no person in his right mind could have believed all that rubbish about murder and suicide and jewels. You've been making enough noise to bring the house down for the last hour or two.'

'But what was I to think of those letters?' whimpered Mrs Heasant.

'I should have known what to think of them,' said Bertie; 'if you choose to excite yourself over other people's correspondence it's your own fault. Anyhow, I'm going for a doctor.'

It was Bertie's great opportunity, and he knew it. His mother was conscious of the fact that she would look rather ridiculous if the story got about. She was willing to pay hush-money.

'I'll never open your letters again,' she promised.

And Clovis has no more devoted slave than Bertie Heasant.

Tea

James Cushat-Prinkly was a young man who had always had a settled conviction that one of these days he would marry; up to the age of thirty-four he had done nothing to justify that conviction. He liked and admired a great many women collectively and dispassionately without singling out one for especial matrimonial consideration, just as one might admire the Alps without feeling that one wanted any particular peak as one's own private property.

His lack of initiative in this matter aroused a certain amount of impatience among the sentimentally minded women-folk of his home circle; his mother, his sisters, an aunt-in-residence, and two or three intimate matronly friends, regarded his dilatory approach to the married state with a disapproval that was far from being inarticulate. His most innocent flirtations were watched with the straining eagerness which a group of unexercised terriers concentrates on the slightest movements of a human being who may be reasonably considered likely to take them for a walk. No decent-souled mortal can long resist the pleading of several pairs of walk-beseeching dog-eyes; James Cushat-Prinkly was not sufficiently obstinate or indifferent to home influences to disregard the obviously expressed wish of his family that he should become enamoured of some nice marriageable girl, and when his Uncle Jules departed this life and bequeathed him a comfortable little legacy it really seemed the correct thing to do to set about discovering someone to share it with him. The process of discovery was carried on more by the force of suggestion and the weight of public opinion than by any initiative of his own; a clear working majority of his female relatives and the aforesaid matronly friends had pitched on Joan Sebastable as the most suitable young woman in his range of acquaintance to whom he might propose marriage, and James became gradually accustomed to the idea that he and Joan would go together through the prescribed stages of congratulations, present-receiving, Norwegian or Mediterranean hotels, and eventual domesticity. It was necessary, however, to ask the lady what she thought about the matter; the family had so far conducted and directed the flirtation with ability and discretion, but the actual proposal would have to be an individual effort.

Cushat-Prinkly walked across the Park towards the Sebastable residence in a frame of mind that was moderately complacent. As the thing was going to be done he was glad to feel that he was going to get it settled and off his mind that afternoon. Proposing marriage, even to a nice girl like Joan, was a rather irksome business, but one could not have a honeymoon in Minorca and a subsequent life of married happiness without such preliminary. He wondered what Minorca was really like as a place to stop in; in his mind's eye it was an island in perpetual half-mourning, with black or white Minorca hens running all over it. Probably it would not be a bit like that when one came to examine it. People who had been in Russia had told him that they did not remember having seen any Muscovy ducks there, so it was possible that there there would be no Minorca fowls on the island.

His Mediterranean musings were interrupted by the sound of a clock striking the half-hour. Half-past four. A frown of dissatisfaction settled on his face. He would arrive at the Sebastable mansion just at the hour of afternoon tea. Joan would be seated at a low table, spread with an array of silver kettles and cream jugs and delicate porcelain teacups, behind which her voice would tinkle pleasantly in a series of little friendly questions about weak or strong tea, how much, if any, sugar, milk, cream, and so forth. 'Is it one lump? I forgot. You do take milk, don't you? Would you like some more hot water, if it's too strong?'

Cushat-Prinkly had read of such things in scores of novels, and hundreds of actual experiences had told him that they were true to life. Thousands of women, at this solemn afternoon hour, were sitting behind dainty porcelain and silver fittings, with their voices tinkling pleasantly in a cascade of solicitous little questions. Cushat-Prinkly detested the whole system of afternoon tea. According to his theory of life a woman should lie on a divan or couch, talking with incomparable charm or looking unutterable thoughts, or merely silent as a thing to be looked on, and from behind a silken curtain a small Nubian page should, silently, bring in a tray with cups and dainties, to be accepted, silently, as a matter of course, without drawn-out chatter about cream and sugar and hot water. If one's soul was really enslaved at one's mistress's feet, how could one talk coherently about weakened tea? Cushat-Prinkly had never expounded his views on the subject to his mother; all her life she had been accustomed to tinkle pleasantly at tea-time behind dainty porcelain and silver, and if he had spoken to her about divans and Nubian pages she would have urged him to take a week's holiday at the seaside. Now, as he passed through a tangle of small streets that led indirectly to the elegant Mayfair terrace for which he was bound, a horror at the idea of confronting Joan Sebastable at her tea-table seized on him. A momentary deliverance presented itself; on one floor of a narrow little house at the noisier end of Esquimault Street lived Rhoda Ellam, a sort of remote cousin, who made a living by creating hats out of costly materials. The hats really looked as if they had come from Paris; the cheques she got for them unfortunately never looked as if they were going to Paris. However, Rhoda appeared to find life amusing and to have a fairly good time in spite of her straitened circumstances. Cushat-Prinkly decided to climb up to her floor and defer by half-an-hour or so the important business which lay before him; by spinning out his visit he could contrive to reach the Sebastable mansion after the last vestiges of dainty porcelain had been cleared away.

Rhoda welcomed him into a room that seemed to do duty as workshop, sitting-room, and kitchen combined, and to be wonderfully clean and comfortable at the same time.

'I'm having a picnic meal,' she announced. 'There's caviare in

that jar at your elbow. Begin on that brown bread-and-butter
while I cut some more. Find yourself a cup; the teapot is behind
you. Now tell me about hundreds of things.'

She made no other allusion to food, but talked amusingly and
made her visitor talk amusingly too. At the same time she cut the
bread-and-butter with a masterly skill and produced red pepper
and sliced lemon, where so many women would merely have
produced reasons and regrets for not having any. Cushat-Prinkly
found that he was enjoying an excellent tea without having to
answer as many questions about it as a Minister for Agriculture
might be called on to reply to during an outbreak of cattle plague.

'And now tell me why you have come to see me,' said Rhoda
suddenly. 'You arouse not merely my curiosity but my business
instincts. I hope you've come about hats. I heard that you had
come into a legacy the other day, and, of course, it struck me that
it would be a beautiful and desirable thing for you to celebrate
the event by buying brilliantly expensive hats for all your sisters.
They may not have said anything about it, but I feel sure the
same idea has occurred to them. Of course, with Goodwood on
us, I am rather rushed just now, but in my business we're
accustomed to that; we live in a series of rushes – like the infant
Moses.'

'I didn't come about hats,' said her visitor. 'In fact I don't think
I really came about anything. I was passing and I just thought I'd
look in and see you. Since I've been sitting talking to you,
however, a rather important idea has occurred to me. If you'll
forget Goodwood for a moment and listen to me, I'll tell you what
it is.'

Some forty minutes later James Cushat-Prinkly returned to the
bosom of his family, bearing an important piece of news.

'I'm engaged to be married,' he announced.

A rapturous outbreak of congratulation and self-applause
broke out.

'Ah, we knew! We saw it coming! We foretold it weeks ago!'

'I'll bet you didn't,' said Cushat-Prinkly. 'If anyone had told me
at lunch-time today that I was going to ask Rhoda Ellam to
marry me and that she was going to accept me, I would have
laughed at the idea.'

The romantic suddenness of the affair in some measure
compensated James's women-folk for the ruthless negation of all

their patient effort and skilled diplomacy. It was rather trying to have to deflect their enthusiasm at a moment's notice from Joan Sebastable to Rhoda Ellam; but, after all, it was James's wife who was in question, and his tastes had some claim to be considered.

On a September afternoon of the same year, after the honeymoon in Minorca had ended, Cushat-Prinkly came into the drawing-room of his new house in Granchester Square. Rhoda was seated at a low table, behind a service of dainty porcelain and gleaming silver. There was a pleasant tinkling note in her voice as she handed him a cup.

'You like it weaker than that, don't you? Shall I put some more hot water to it? No?'

The Toys of Peace

'Harvey,' said Eleanor Bope, handing her brother a cutting from a London morning paper* of the 19th of March, 'just read this about children's toys, please; it exactly carries out some of our ideas about influence and upbringing.'

'In the view of the National Peace Council,' ran the extract, 'there are grave objections to presenting our boys with regiments of fighting men, batteries of guns, and squadrons of "Dreadnoughts". Boys, the Council admits, naturally love fighting and all the panoply of war . . . but that is no reason for encouraging, and perhaps giving permanent form to, their primitive instincts. At the Children's Welfare Exhibition, which opens at Olympia in three weeks' time, the Peace Council will make an alternative suggestion to parents in the shape of an exhibition of "peace toys". In front of a specially-painted representation of the Peace Palace at The Hague will be grouped, not miniature soldiers but miniature civilians, not guns but ploughs and the tools of industry . . . It is hoped that manufacturers may take a hint from the exhibit, which will bear fruit in the toy shops.'

'The idea is certainly an interesting and very well-meaning one,' said Harvey; 'whether it would succeed well in practice –'

'We must try,' interrupted his sister; 'you are coming down to us at Easter, and you always bring the boys some toys, so that

---

* An actual extract from a London paper of March 1914.

will be an excellent opportunity for you to inaugurate the new experiment. Go about in the shops and buy any little toys and models that have special bearing on civilian life in its more peaceful aspects. Of course you must explain the toys to the children and interest them in the new idea. I regret to say that the "Siege of Adrianople" toy, that their Aunt Susan sent them, didn't need any explanation; they knew all the uniforms and flags, and even the names of the respective commanders, and when I heard them one day using what seemed to be the most objectionable language they said it was Bulgarian words of command; of course it *may* have been, but at any rate I took the toy away from them. Now I shall expect your Easter gifts to give quite a new impulse and direction to the children's minds; Eric is not eleven yet, and Bertie is only nine-and-a-half, so they are really at a most impressionable age.'

'There is primitive instinct to be taken into consideration, you know,' said Harvey doubtfully, 'and hereditary tendencies as well. One of their great-uncles fought in the most intolerant fashion at Inkerman – he was specially mentioned in dispatches, I believe – and their great-grandfather smashed all his Whig neighbours' hothouses when the great Reform Bill was passed. Still, as you say, they are at an impressionable age. I will do my best.'

On Easter Saturday Harvey Bope unpacked a large, promising-looking red cardboard box under the expectant eyes of his nephews. 'Your uncle has brought you the newest things in toys,' Eleanor had said impressively, and youthful anticipation had been anxiously divided between Albanian soldiery and a Somali camel-corps. Eric was hotly in favour of the latter contingency. 'There would be Arabs on horseback,' he whispered; 'the Albanians have got jolly uniforms, and they fight all day long, and all night, too, when there's a moon, but the country's rocky, so they've got no cavalry.'

A quantity of crinkly paper shavings was the first thing that met the view when the lid was removed; the most exciting toys always began like that. Harvey pushed back the top layer and drew forth a square, rather featureless building.

'It's a fort!' exclaimed Bertie.

'It isn't, it's the palace of the Mpret of Albania,' said Eric, immensely proud of his knowledge of the exotic title; 'it's got no windows, you see, so that passers-by can't fire in at the Royal Family.'

'It's a municipal dust-bin,' said Harvey hurriedly; 'you see all the refuse and litter of a town is collected there, instead of lying about and injuring the health of the citizens.'

In an awful silence he disinterred a little lead figure of a man in black clothes.

'That,' he said, 'is a distinguished civilian, John Stuart Mill. He was an authority on political economy.'

'Why?' asked Bertie.

'Well, he wanted to be; he thought it was a useful thing to be.'

Bertie gave an expressive grunt, which conveyed his opinion that there was no accounting for tastes.

Another square building came out, this time with windows and chimneys.

'A model of the Manchester branch of the Young Women's Christian Association,' said Harvey.

'Are there any lions?' asked Eric hopefully. He had been reading Roman history and thought that where you found Christians you might reasonably expect to find a few lions.

'There are no lions,' said Harvey. 'Here is another civilian, Robert Raikes, the founder of Sunday schools, and here is a model of a municipal wash-house. These little round things are loaves baked in a sanitary bakehouse. That lead figure is a sanitary inspector, this one is a district councillor, and this one is an official of the Local Government Board.'

'What does he do?' asked Eric wearily.

'He sees to things connected with his Department,' said Harvey. 'This box with a slit in it is a ballot-box. Votes are put into it at election times.'

'What is put into it at other times?' asked Bertie.

'Nothing. And here are some tools of industry, a wheelbarrow and a hoe, and I think these are meant for hop-poles. This is a model beehive, and that is a ventilator, for ventilating sewers. This seems to be another municipal dust-bin – no, it is a model of a school of art and a public library. This little lead figure is Mrs Hemans, a poetess, and this is Rowland Hill, who introduced the system of penny postage. This is Sir John Herschel, the eminent astrologer.'

'Are we to play with these civilian figures?' asked Eric.

'Of course,' said Harvey, 'these are toys; they are meant to be played with.'

'But how?'

It was rather a poser. 'You might make two of them contest a seat in Parliament,' said Harvey, 'and have an election –'

'With rotten eggs, and free fights, and ever so many broken heads!' exclaimed Eric.

'And noses all bleeding and everybody drunk as can be,' echoed Bertie, who had carefully studied one of Hogarth's pictures.

'Nothing of the kind,' said Harvey, 'nothing in the least like that. Votes will be put in the ballot-box, and the Mayor will count them – the district councillor will do for the Mayor – and he will say which has received the most votes, and then the two candidates will thank him for presiding, and each will say that the contest has been conducted throughout in the pleasantest and most straightforward fashion, and they part with expressions of mutual esteem. There's a jolly game for you boys to play. I never had such toys when I was young.'

'I don't think we'll play with them just now,' said Eric, with an entire absence of the enthusiasm that his uncle had shown; 'I think perhaps we ought to do a little of our holiday task. It's history this time; we've got to learn up something about the Bourbon period in France.'

'The Bourbon period,' said Harvey, with some disapproval in his voice.

'We've got to know something about Louis the Fourteenth,' continued Eric; 'I've learnt the names of all the principal battles already.'

This would never do. 'There were, of course, some battles fought during his reign,' said Harvey, 'but I fancy the accounts of them were much exaggerated; news was very unreliable in those days, and there were practically no war correspondents, so generals and commanders could magnify every little skirmish they engaged in till they reached the proportions of decisive battles. Louis was really famous, now, as a landscape gardener; the way he laid out Versailles was so much admired that it was copied all over Europe.'

'Do you know anything about Madame Du Barry?' asked Eric; 'didn't she have her head chopped off?'

'She was another great lover of gardening,' said Harvey, evasively; 'in fact, I believe the well-known rose Du Barry was named after her, and now I think you had better play for a little and leave your lessons till later.'

Harvey retreated to the library and spent some thirty or forty minutes in wondering whether it would be possible to compile a history, for use in elementary schools, in which there should be no prominent mention of battles, massacres, murderous intrigues, and violent deaths. The York and Lancaster period and the Napoleonic era would, he admitted to himself, present considerable difficulties, and the Thirty Years' War would entail something of a gap if you left it out altogether. Still, it would be something gained if, at a highly impressionable age, children could be got to fix their attention on the invention of calico printing instead of the Spanish Armada or the Battle of Waterloo.

It was time, he thought, to go back to the boys' room, and see how they were getting on with their peace toys. As he stood outside the door he could hear Eric's voice raised in command; Bertie chimed in now and again with a helpful suggestion.

'That is Louis the Fourteenth,' Eric was saying, 'that one in knee-breeches, that Uncle said invented Sunday schools. It isn't a bit like him, but it'll have to do.'

'We'll give him a purple coat from my paint-box by and by,' said Bertie.

'Yes, an' red heels. That is Madame de Maintenon, that one he called Mrs Hemans. She begs Louis not to go on this expedition, but he turns a deaf ear. He takes Marshal Saxe with him, and we must pretend that they have thousands of men with them. The watchword is *Qui vive?* and the answer is *L'état c'est moi* – that was one of his favourite remarks, you know. They land at Manchester in the dead of night, and a Jacobite conspirator gives them the keys of the fortress.'

Peeping in through the doorway Harvey observed that the municipal dustbin had been pierced with holes to accommodate the muzzles of imaginary cannon, and now represented the principal fortified position in Manchester; John Stuart Mill had been dipped in red ink, and apparently stood for Marshal Saxe.

'Louis orders his troops to surround the Young Women's Christian Association and seize the lot of them. "Once back at the Louvre and the girls are mine," he exclaims. We must use Mrs

Hemans again for one of the girls; she says "Never," and stabs Marshal Saxe to the heart.'

'He bleeds dreadfully,' exclaimed Bertie, splashing red ink liberally over the façade of the Association building.

'The soldiers rush in and avenge his death with the utmost savagery. A hundred girls are killed' – here Bertie emptied the remainder of the red ink over the devoted building – 'and the surviving five hundred are dragged off to the French ships. "I have lost a Marshal," says Louis, "but I do not go back empty-handed."'

Harvey stole away from the room, and sought out his sister.

'Eleanor,' he said, 'the experiment –'

'Yes?'

'Has failed. We have begun too late.'

The Wolves of Cernogratz

'Are there any old legends attached to the castle?' asked Conrad of his sister. Conrad was a prosperous Hamburg merchant, but he was the one poetically-dispositioned member of an eminently practical family.

The Baroness Gruebel shrugged her plump shoulders.

'There are always legends hanging about these old places. They are not difficult to invent and they cost nothing. In this case there is a story that when anyone dies in the castle all the dogs in the village and the wild beasts in the forest howl the night long. It would not be pleasant to listen to, would it?'

'It would be weird and romantic,' said the Hamburg merchant.

'Anyhow, it isn't true,' said the Baroness complacently; 'since we bought the place we have had proof that nothing of the sort happens. When the old mother-in-law died last springtime we all listened, but there was no howling. It is just a story that lends dignity to the place without costing anything.'

'The story is not as you have told it,' said Amalie, the grey old governess. Everyone turned and looked at her in astonishment. She was wont to sit silent and prim and faded in her place at table, never speaking unless someone spoke to her, and there were few who troubled themselves to make conversation with her. Today a sudden volubility had descended on her; she continued to talk, rapidly and nervously, looking straight in front of her and seeming to address no one in particular.

'It is not when *any one* dies in the castle that the howling is heard. It was when one of the Cernogratz family died here that the wolves came from far and near and howled at the edge of the forest just before the death hour. There were only a few couple of wolves that had their lairs in this part of the forest, but at such a time the keepers say there would be scores of them, gliding about in the shadows and howling in chorus, and the dogs of the castle and the village and all the farms round would bay and howl in fear and anger at the wolf chorus, and as the soul of the dying one left its body a tree would crash down in the park. That is what happened when a Cernogratz died in his family castle. But for a stranger dying here, of course no wolf would howl and no tree would fall. Oh, no.'

There was a note of defiance, almost of contempt, in her voice as she said the last words. The well-fed, much-too-well dressed Baroness stared angrily at the dowdy old woman who had come forth from her usual and seemly position of effacement to speak so disrespectfully.

'You seem to know quite a lot about the von Cernogratz legends, Fräulein Schmidt,' she said sharply; 'I did not know that family histories were among the subjects you are supposed to be proficient in.'

The answer to her taunt was even more unexpected and astonishing than the conversational outbreak which had provoked it.

'I am a von Cernogratz myself,' said the old woman, 'that is why I know the family history.'

'You a von Cernogratz? You!' came in an incredulous chorus.

'When we became very poor,' she explained, 'and I had to go out and give teaching lessons, I took another name; I thought it would be more in keeping. But my grandfather spent much of his time as a boy in this castle, and my father used to tell me many stories about it, and, of course, I knew all the family legends and stories. When one has nothing left to one but memories, one guards and dusts them with especial care. I little thought when I took service with you that I should one day come with you to the old home of my family. I could wish it had been anywhere else.'

There was silence when she finished speaking, and then the

Baroness turned the conversation to a less embarrassing topic than family histories. But afterwards, when the old governess had slipped away quietly to her duties, there arose a clamour of derision and disbelief.

'It was an impertinence,' snapped out the Baron, his protruding eyes taking on a scandalized expression; 'fancy the woman talking like that at our table. She almost told us we were nobodies, and I don't believe a word of it. She is just Schmidt and nothing more. She has been talking to some of the peasants about the old Cernogratz family, and raked up their history and their stories.'

'She wants to make herself out of some consequence,' said the Baroness; 'she knows she will soon be past work and she wants to appeal to our sympathies. Her grandfather, indeed!'

The Baroness had the usual number of grandfathers, but she never, never boasted about them.

'I dare say her grandfather was a pantry boy or something of the sort in the castle,' sniggered the Baron; 'that part of the story may be true.'

The merchant from Hamburg said nothing; he had seen tears in the old woman's eyes when she spoke of guarding her memories – or, being of an imaginative disposition, he thought he had.

'I shall give her notice to go as soon as the New Year festivities are over,' said the Baroness; 'till then I shall be too busy to manage without her.'

But she had to manage without her all the same, for in the cold biting weather after Christmas, the old governess fell ill and kept to her room.

'It is most provoking,' said the Baroness, as her guests sat round the fire on one of the last evenings of the dying year; 'all the time that she has been with us I cannot remember that she was ever seriously ill, too ill to go about and do her work, I mean. And now, when I have the house full, and she could be useful in so many ways, she goes and breaks down. One is sorry for her, of course, she looks so withered and shrunken, but it is intensely annoying all the same.'

'Most annoying,' agreed the banker's wife, sympathetically; 'it is the intense cold, I expect, it breaks the old people up. It has been unusually cold this year.'

'The frost is the sharpest that has been known in December for many years,' said the Baron.

'And, of course, she is quite old,' said the Baroness; 'I wish I had given her notice some weeks ago, then she would have left before this happened to her. Why, Wappi, what is the matter with you?'

The small, woolly lapdog had leapt suddenly down from its cushion and crept shivering under the sofa. At the same moment an outburst of angry barking came from the dogs in the castleyard, and other dogs could be heard yapping and barking in the distance.

'What is disturbing the animals?' asked the Baron.

And then the humans, listening intently, heard the sound that had roused the dogs to their demonstrations of fear and rage; heard a long-drawn whining howl, rising and falling, seeming at one moment leagues away, at others sweeping across the snow until it appeared to come from the foot of the castle walls. All the starved, cold misery of a frozen world, all the relentless hunger-fury of the wild, blended with other forlorn and haunting melodies to which one could give no name, seemed concentrated in the wailing cry.

'Wolves!' cried the Baron.

Their music broke forth in one raging burst, seeming to come from everywhere.

'Hundreds of wolves,' said the Hamburg merchant, who was a man of strong imagination.

Moved by some impulse which she could not have explained, the Baroness left her guests and made her way to the narrow, cheerless room where the old governess lay watching the hours of the dying year slip by. In spite of the biting cold of the winter night, the window stood open. With a scandalized exclamation on her lips, the Baroness rushed forward to close it.

'Leave it open,' said the old woman in a voice that for all its weakness carried an air of command such as the Baroness had never heard before from her lips.

'But you will die of cold!' she expostulated.

'I am dying in any case,' said the voice, 'and I want to hear their music. They have come from far and wide to sing the death-music of my family. It is beautiful that they have come; I am the last von Cernogratz that will die in our old castle, and they have come to sing to me. Hark, how loud they are calling!'

The cry of the wolves rose on the still winter air and floated round the castle walls in long-drawn piercing wails; the old woman lay back on her couch with a look of long-delayed happiness on her face.

'Go away,' she said to the Baroness; 'I am not lonely any more. I am one of a great old family . . .'

'I think she is dying,' said the Baroness when she had rejoined her guests; 'I suppose we must send for a doctor. And that terrible howling! Not for much money would I have such death-music.'

'That music is not to be bought for any amount of money,' said Conrad.

'Hark! What is that other sound?' asked the Baron, as a noise of splitting and crashing was heard.

It was a tree falling in the park.

There was a moment of constrained silence, and then the banker's wife spoke.

'It is the intense cold that is splitting the trees. It is also the cold that has brought the wolves out in such numbers. It is many years since we have had such a cold winter.'

The Baroness eagerly agreed that the cold was responsible for these things. It was the cold of the open window, too, which caused the heart failure that made the doctor's ministrations unnecessary for the old Fräulein. But the notice in the newspapers looked very well –

On December 29th, at Schloss Cernogratz, Amalie von Cernogratz, for many years the valued friend of Baron and Baroness Gruebel.

The Gala Programme

An unrecorded episode in Roman history

It was an auspicious day in the Roman Calendar, the birthday of the popular and gifted young Emperor Placidus Superbus. Everyone in Rome was bent on keeping high festival, the weather was at its best, and naturally the Imperial Circus was crowded to its fullest capacity. A few minutes before the hour fixed for the commencement of the spectacle a loud fanfare of trumpets proclaimed the arrival of Caesar, and amid the vociferous acclamations of the multitude the Emperor took his seat in the Imperial Box. As the shouting of the crowd died away an even more thrilling salutation could be heard in the near distance, the angry, impatient roaring and howling of the beasts caged in the Imperial menagerie.

'Explain the programme to me,' commanded the Emperor, having beckoned the Master of the Ceremonies to his side.

That eminent official wore a troubled look.

'Gracious Caesar,' he announced, 'a most promising and entertaining programme has been devised and prepared for your august approval. In the first place there is to be a chariot contest of unusual brilliancy and interest; three teams that have never hitherto suffered defeat are to contend for the Herculaneum Trophy, together with the purse which your Imperial generosity has been pleased to add. The chances of the competing teams are accounted to be as nearly as possible equal, and there is much wagering among the populace. The black Thracians are perhaps the favourites –'

'I know, I know,' interrupted Caesar, who had listened to exhaustive talk on the same subject all the morning; 'what else is there on the programme?'

'The second part of the programme,' said the Imperial Official, 'consists of a grand combat of wild beasts, specially selected for their strength, ferocity, and fighting qualities. There will appear simultaneously in the arena fourteen Nubian lions and lionesses, five tigers, six Syrian bears, eight Persian panthers, and three North African ditto, a number of wolves and lynxes from the Teutonic forests, and seven gigantic wild bulls from the same region. There will also be wild swine of unexampled savageness, a rhinoceros from the Barbary coast, some ferocious man-apes, and a hyena, reputed to be mad.'

'It promises well,' said the Emperor.

'It *promised* well, O Caesar,' said the official dolorously, 'it promised marvellously well; but between the promise and the performance a cloud has arisen.'

'A cloud? What cloud?' queried Caesar, with a frown.

'The Suffragettes,' explained the official; 'they threaten to interfere with the chariot race.'

'I'd like to see them do it!' exclaimed the Emperor indignantly.

'I fear your Imperial wish may be unpleasantly gratified,' said the Master of the Ceremonies; 'we are taking, of course, every possible precaution, and guarding all the entrances to the arena and the stables with a triple guard; but it is rumoured that at the signal for the entry of the chariots five hundred women will let themselves down with ropes from the public seats and swarm all over the course. Naturally no race could be run under such circumstances; the programme will be ruined.'

'On my birthday,' said Placidus Superbus, 'they would not dare to do such an outrageous thing.'

'The more august the occasion, the more desirous they will be to advertise themselves and their cause,' said the harassed official; 'they do not scruple to make riotous interference even with the ceremonies in the temples.'

'Who *are* these Suffragettes?' asked the Emperor. 'Since I came back from the Pannonian expedition I have heard of nothing else but their excesses and demonstrations.'

'They are a political sect of very recent origin, and their aim seems to be to get a big share of political authority into their hands. The means they are taking to convince us of their fitness to help in making and administering the laws consist of wild indulgence in tumult, destruction, and defiance of all authority. They have already damaged some of the most historically valuable of our public treasures, which can never be replaced.'

'Is it possible that the sex which we hold in such honour and for which we feel such admiration can produce such hordes of Furies?' asked the Emperor.

'It takes all sorts to make a sex,' observed the Master of the Ceremonies, who possessed a certain amount of worldly wisdom; 'also,' he continued anxiously, 'it takes very little to upset a gala programme.'

'Perhaps the disturbance that you anticipate will turn out to be an idle threat,' said the Emperor consolingly.

'But if they should carry out their intention,' said the official, 'the programme will be utterly ruined.'

The Emperor said nothing.

Five minutes later the trumpets rang out for the commencement of the entertainment. A hum of excited anticipation ran through the ranks of the spectators, and final bets on the issue of the great race were hurriedly shouted. The gates leading from the stables were slowly swung open, and a troop of mounted attendants rode round the track to ascertain that everything was clear for the momentous contest. Again the trumpets rang out, and then, before the foremost chariot had appeared, there arose a wild tumult of shouting, laughing, angry protests, and shrill screams of defiance. Hundreds of women were being lowered by their accomplices into the area. A moment later they were running and dancing in frenzied troops across the track where the chariots were supposed to compete. No team of arena-trained horses would have faced such a frantic mob; the race was clearly an impossibility. Howls of disappointment and rage rose from the spectators, howls of triumph echoed back from the women in possession. The vain efforts of the circus attendants to drive out the invading horde merely added to the uproar and confusion; as fast as the Suffragettes were thrust away from one portion of the track they swarmed on to another.

The Master of the Ceremonies was nearly delirious from rage and mortification. Placidus Superbus, who remained calm and unruffled as ever, beckoned to him and spoke a word or two in his ear. For the first time that afternoon the sorely tried official was seen to smile.

A trumpet rang out from the Imperial Box; an instant hush fell over the excited throng. Perhaps the Emperor, as a last resort, was going to announce some concession to the Suffragettes.

'Close the stable gates,' commanded the Master of the Ceremonies, 'and open all the menagerie dens. It is the Imperial pleasure that the second portion of the programme be taken first.'

It turned out that the Master of the Ceremonies had in no wise exaggerated the probable brilliancy of this portion of the spectacle. The wild bulls were really wild, and the hyena reputed to be mad thoroughly lived up to its reputation.